CONTENT.

CW01460671

CHAPTER ONE:
A PRIMER ON FINISHING TRIANGLES

TRADITIONAL TRIANGLE

ARM ON THE MAT TRIANGLE

SANKAKU

CHAPTER TWO:
BODY POSITION AND 45 DEGREE INTRODUCTION

DOUBLE WRIST CONTROL

CROSS GRIP

DOUBLE BICEPS RIDE

COLLAR TIE

CORNER LOCK

CHAPTER THREE: O DEGREE INTRODUCTION

IRISH COLLAR

OVERHOOK CONTROL

SHOULDER PIN

UNDERHOOK SHOULDER PIN

RUBBER GUARD

THE CUFF

MASTERING TRIANGLE CHOKES

NEIL MELANSON

with MARSHAL D. CARPER
and LANCE FREIMUTH

VB

VICTORY BELT PUBLISHING INC
LAS VEGAS

First Published in 2011 by Victory Belt Publishing Inc.

ISBN 13: 978-1-936608-09-6

This book is for educational purposes. The publisher and authors of this instructional book are not responsible in any manner whatsoever for any adverse effects arising directly or indirectly as a result of the information provided in this book. If not practiced safely and with caution, martial arts can be dangerous to you and to others. It is important to consult with a professional martial arts instructor before beginning training. It is also very important to consult with a physician prior to training due to the intense and strenuous nature of the techniques in this book.

Printed in The United States

CHAPTER FOUR: 90 DEGREES INTRODUCTION

CHAPTER FIVE: THE FORWARD LEAN INTRO

CHAPTER SIX: HIPS FORWARD INTRODUCTION

K-CONTROL / MIRROR GRIP

K-CONTROL / HEAD CONTROL

K-CONTROL / CROSS GRIP

CHAPTER SEVEN: HALF GUARD AND BUTTERFLY GUARD

HALF GUARD

BUTTERFLY GUARD

CHAPTER EIGHT: COUNTERING ESCAPES

ESCAPE COUNTERS

FOREWORD
by RANDY COUTURE

When I set out to found Xtreme Couture, I knew that bringing in the right coaches was the key to ultimate success. I wanted a coach for each major discipline in mixed martial arts. I needed a boxing coach, a kickboxing coach, a wrestling coach, and a grappling coach. Each coach had to be an expert in his field, but that wasn't enough. I needed them to be open minded, able to see beyond their particular specialty to the bigger picture of MMA. I have been fortunate enough to be able to surround myself with coaches that meet these criteria. They are masters at teaching their individual disciplines, and how those disciplines fit into an MMA context. Since they can work easily together, the slew of talented fighters at Xtreme Couture (as well as myself) receive high-quality, well-rounded MMA training.

Neil Melanson, the head grappling coach at Xtreme Couture and my personal head coach, is an essential part of the coaching team. His specialty is grappling, but he sees how striking and wrestling connect to the ground game, and he knows the importance of proper strength training and conditioning. Neil's strength is using his immense knowledge of grappling to develop a well-rounded fighter. As my head coach, he coordinates my entire training camp. He helps me develop my game plan, and then he works with other coaches so that every member of the team is working together to achieve the same goal. I have put a great deal of faith in Neil, and he has not let me down.

In terms of grappling, Neil is a one-of-a-kind source of knowledge. I initially met Neil through Karo Parisyan, whom Neil had trained with for some time, and I knew that Neil had also trained under a number of guys that I had known for a long time and respected (Gene LeBell, for example). When I worked with him for the first time during preparation for my fight against Antonio Rodrigo Nogueira, his ability to explain techniques and the strategies that made them work astounded me. He was able to explain what Nogueira was likely to do, and then show me how to systemically defend and counter those moves.

What Neil was teaching me was not traditional Brazilian jiu-jitsu. It was catch wrestling. For much of my professional career, I was trying to catch up to Brazilian jiu-jitsu black belts, trying to match their jiu-jitsu technique. Neil taught me how to tap into my thirty years of wrestling experience and apply it to MMA. Rather than try to force myself to think like a jiu-jitsu guy, he got me seeing through the eyes of a wrestler again, tweaking my technique and my strategy so that the techniques I had spent a lifetime mastering could plug into my MMA ground game. And again, everything he taught me was explained clearly and in such detail that I knew exactly when to use a particular technique. That perspective, the way he sees everything a system, is what makes him such a good coach.

Though Neil is physically a large and long individual, his coaching ability allows him to teach techniques to all fighters, regardless of their size, strength, or ability. As a coach at Xtreme Couture, Neil works with amateur and professional fighters. He teaches first-time grapplers and Brazilian jiu-jitsu black belts. He works with lightweights and heavyweights. He is the ideal coach. I have learned a ton from him, and I believe that has been reflected in my recent fights. The other fighters at Xtreme Couture have benefited as well. For example, my son Ryan won four of his amateur fights by submission in the first round, and he won his professional debut by triangle choke in the first round as well. Those submissions, I believe, are a direct result of Neil's coaching.

As a reader of Neil's first book, you are in a unique position to incorporate Neil's one-of-a-kind knowledge into your arsenal from anywhere in the world. The teaching ability that has made him a valuable member of Xtreme Couture is captured in this book. Anyone that has done any kind of grappling knows the triangle choke, but if you flip ahead, even a few pages, you will see that Neil takes the triangle to a new level. The details and the strategy behind each technique and each of his guard systems will allow you to take the techniques from this book directly to the mat and into the cage. Your ground game will never be the same.

Neil and I have been on an amazing journey for the last few years. Working together has been a blast, and we have had a lot of fun. By learning from Neil through his book, you get to share in that journey too. Enjoy it.

INTRODUCTION

I owe my triangle obsession to Karo Parisyan. I had moved from Ohio to California to train under Gokor Chivichyan at the Hayastan MMA Academy. Gokor is an Armenian-born grappler who spent much of his career training under the legendary Gene LeBell. Gokor dominated judo, sambo, and wrestling tournaments for years on an international level and even competed in no-holds-barred tournaments in the early years of mixed martial arts. At the time, I was fascinated by leg locks (and still am), and I knew that training under a leg lock wizard like Gokor would radically change the way I grappled.

After a few months of training under Gokor, another Armenian grappler took me under his wing, Karo. He took a personal interest in me and gave my training direction. One of the first things he did was look at my body type.

"With those long legs, you should be a guard player," Karo said. "Play guard, and look for the triangle."

I started to work the guard more, but I still latched on to other submissions if I had the chance. One training session, I was working for a toehold when Karo came up behind me and slapped the back of my head.

"What? Did you think I was joking?" he asked. "Only the guard and only the triangle."

For the next nine months, I played guard, and the only move I looked for was the triangle, which was difficult in a leg-lock gym. On my back, my legs dangled in the air like a leg-lock buffet. I got hurt a few times, but I persevered, trusting in Karo's wisdom. And he was right. My guard game improved rapidly, as did my triangle choke. The challenge of only looking for one submission was that everyone in the gym knew exactly what I intended to do every time we rolled. Since they knew I wanted the triangle choke and only the triangle choke, I had to develop an elaborate funnel of setups, tricks, and baits to get the submission. I eventually learned that different setups and controls worked more effectively if my opponent was positioned a certain way, and that awareness led to the formation of a system based solely on the triangle that addressed the range of positioning possibilities in the guard.

Even after Karo told me that I could explore other positions and submissions, I continued honing my triangle game, and the result of that work, those thousands of hours on the mat, is contained in this book. I teach my triangle system to professional fighters every day at Xtreme Couture in Las Vegas, Nevada, as a part of my overall system of grappling. What works for top-level fighters can work for you. If you apply the concepts and strategies outlined in this book, your finish rate for the triangle will quadruple. And the best part is that you get to skip my years of trial and error and immediately begin practicing a system of techniques that works.

CHAPTER ONE

A PRIMER ON FINISHING TRIANGLES

THREE TYPES OF TRIANGLES

Starting with finishing options may seem odd, but I feel that I can safely assume that if you are reading this book you are familiar with the triangle choke on the most basic level. Whether you learned it at your gym, from an instructional, or even from watching mixed martial arts on television, you likely understand that to get the triangle choke, you need to clear one of your opponent's arms and trap his head and his other arm between your legs. From there, you exert pressure with your legs to pinch the carotid arteries and shut off blood flow to the brain. If your opponent does not tap out, he will go to sleep.

By covering finishing options first, I can help you improve the triangles that you are already landing in training, and that way we can focus entirely on setups for the bulk of the book. Think of these finishes as the inside of a house, and each door into the house is a different setup. Some doors are fancy. Some doors are simple. Some are out front where they can easily be seen. Some are hidden around back where you might not think to look. But all of the doors—no matter where they are positioned or how they are constructed—lead to the same common area inside of the house, the fundamental core.

I have broken this core into three sections: the traditional triangle, the arm-on-the-mat triangle, and the sankaku. The traditional triangle is the classic triangle that most Brazilian jiu-jitsu fighters strive to achieve, where the trapped arm is passed to the opposite side of your body. The arm on the mat triangle may not look that much different from the traditional triangle, but to efficiently finish the triangle from this position you need to modify the way you squeeze your legs. Despite popular belief, you do not need to pass the arm to the opposite side to get the finish, and I will give you the tools to eliminate that step.

The sankaku is a variation of the triangle that you may have never seen before. It is based on an old-school judo technique where the triangle is applied from the top and finishing pressure is applied by pulling on the arm rather than the head. Sankaku does translate to "triangle," but I emphasize the term sankaku so that my students understand that there are key differences between the sankaku and what most grapplers consider a triangle. The positioning of the sankaku may seem unusual, and it does require a great deal of hip movement and coordination to achieve the sankaku position, but the power of the choke is immense. It's like screwing on a top. If the sankaku is not a part of your arsenal yet, don't worry, this book will introduce you to the submission and show you how it complements the traditional triangle.

ANATOMY OF THE PREFERRED TRIANGLE

Although I will cover a variety of finishes for the triangle choke in this chapter, the traditional triangle choke is the foundation. Most grapplers learn the triangle in their first week of classes, but conveying every nuance of leverage and positioning to a new student in an introductory class is difficult, if not impossible. A well-executed triangle requires a level of finesse and technique that a new student may not be able to grasp, so some key details are left unaddressed in favor of the student understanding the submission on the most basic level. There is nothing wrong with this approach to instruction, and it's normal. Unfortunately, due to class rotations and the business of the gym, that student may never learn the perfect triangle choke. For you to get the most out of my triangle system, your fundamental triangle needs to be strong, and we need to clean up your details.

When I see fighters applying the triangle, I see them making three common mistakes, and you might be making those mistakes too:

1) Many grapplers lose the triangle when they attempt to adjust their legs to finish the choke. They fail to follow what I call the "Order of Control Principle" and give their opponent an opening to rip out. When you adjust for the triangle, first clear the arm that is blocking your hip. Grab his head. Hook his leg. And then open your legs. If you open your legs before you have established control, your opponent will explode out of your triangle and escape.

2) Simply squeezing your opponent's head downward is incorrect and will not consistently apply enough pressure to render him unconscious. Squeezing your knees together after creating an angle with your hips eliminates more space, thus making the choke more powerful when you do pull the head down. When you do pull on the head to finish the triangle, pull it down and then toward the leg that is flush against your opponent's neck to increase the choking power of your hamstring.

3) Failing to curl your top foot toward your shin weakens the power of your legs and can even injure your ankle. Flexing your foot creates a strong hook for your other leg to dig into, making your choke secure and stable, while also reducing space.

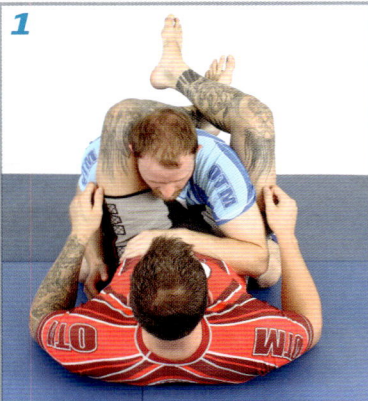

1

I am in position to apply the triangle choke. My left leg has cleared Lance's right arm and my right ankle is crossed over my left ankle, trapping his head and his left arm between my legs. His left forearm is pressing against my stomach, blocking the choke.

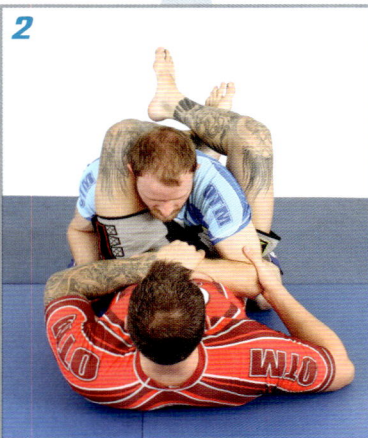

2

I grip Lance's left wrist with my left hand and his left elbow with my right hand. I pull his left elbow away from my hip as much as I can with my arm strength alone.

3

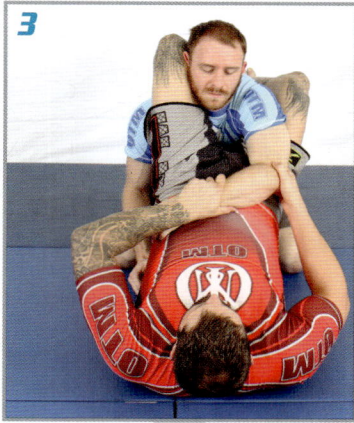

I bridge my hips and straighten my back to begin passing Lance's left arm across my body, the first step of the Order of Control Principle.

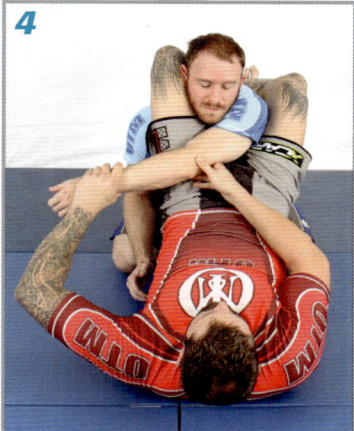

4

Lance's left arm is now completely across my body, freeing my hips and positioning his left shoulder under his neck.

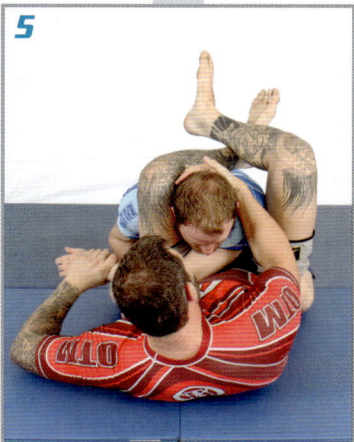

5

I pull my knees to my chest to lock Lance's left arm in place. I let go of his left elbow and control his head with my right hand, completing the second step of the Order of Control Principle.

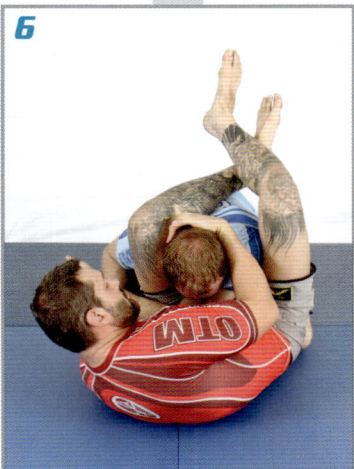

6

With Lance's left arm passed to the opposite side and my right hand controlling his head, I reach to hook his right leg with my left hand.

7

With all of the other steps of the Order of Control Principle complete, I can adjust my legs to finish the triangle. I fold my left leg across the back of Lance's neck. At the same time, my left foot flexes as I pinch my left heel to my butt and squeeze my right knee against the front of his left shoulder to lock him in place. Pinching my right knee in front of his shoulder is an essential part of this technique, and it is a movement that I use constantly when tightening the triangle.

8

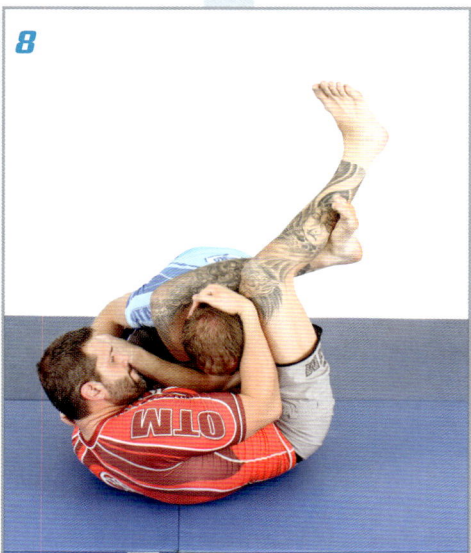

I continue to squeeze my legs together as I extend my right leg to the ceiling. I then curl my right leg over my left shin to lock in the triangle, flexing my foot to strengthen the position. To finish the submission, I twist my hips, aiming my left shoulder toward Lance's right hip as I squeeze my knees together. In this position, my right knee is actually against my left shin, and both of my knees are pointing in the same direction to maximize the angle and pressure of the choke by driving my left hamstring into his carotid artery. With my right hand, I pull his head down and to my left, driving his neck into my left hamstring.

DETAIL

1

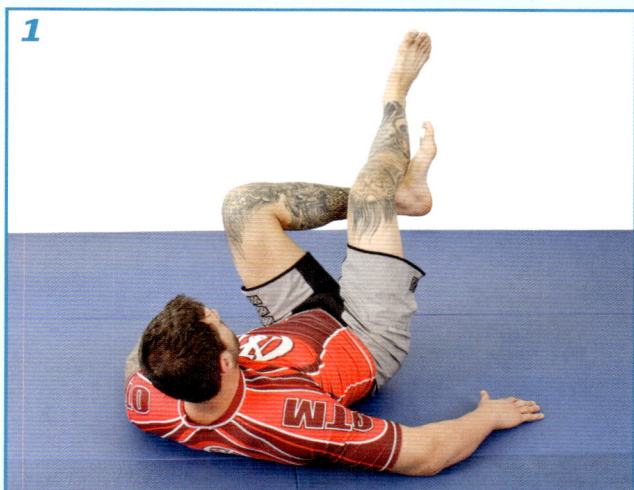

In this photo, I am near the triangle position, but I have not yet set my legs properly, leaving a great deal of space between my legs. If an opponent was between my legs in this photo, he could breathe and work to escape my attack.

2

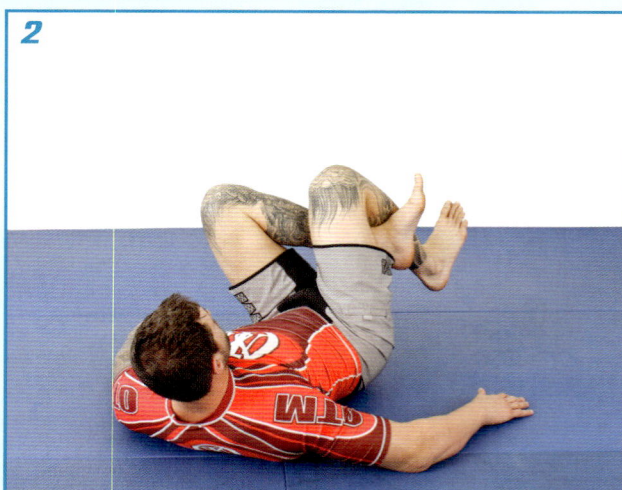

I fold my right leg over my left shin, flexing my left foot to create a hook. I pinch my knees together, angling them in the same direction. The space between my legs is drastically lessened by this movement. If I reach this point against an opponent, the pressure against his neck is immense, forcing him to submit or go to sleep.

METHODS FOR FINISHING THE TRIANGLE: *VARIATION 1*

An opponent will never simply allow you to choke him. He will attempt to protect his neck, create space, and escape. Fortunately, his options are limited, so you can anticipate his counters and pull him deeper into the choke. The most basic defense you will encounter is your opponent posting his trapped arm on the mat to alleviate the pressure on his neck. In that situation, your opponent's position is exceptionally strong, and he is on the verge of neutralizing the triangle. In some situations, you may still be able to finish the choke, but many grapplers prefer to remove that post before finishing the triangle. Bridging your hips into the posted arm will lift it off of the mat, giving you the opportunity to pass the arm to the opposite side and finish the choke in the traditional position. As I said before, you will encounter this defense regularly, so I will cover more options for finishing the triangle with an arm on the mat later in this chapter.

1. I have successfully cleared Lance's right arm, setting my left leg on his right shoulder and trapping his head and left arm between my legs. Since his left hand is posted on the mat next to my left hip, I cannot transition to the traditional choke, so I cross my ankles to stabilize the position.

2. I raise my hips toward the ceiling, driving my heels toward the mat to increase the height and power of my bridge.

3. While maintaining the elevation of my hips, I cup Lance's left elbow with my left hand and control his left forearm with my right hand.

4. I drag Lance's left arm across my body, maneuvering his left elbow to the outside of my left hip.

5. I uncross my ankles and grip my left shin with my right hand as I set my right foot on his left hip, lowering my hips at the same time. I push off of Lance's hip with my right foot to angle my hips, aiming my left shoulder toward his right hip as my left hand continues to control his left arm. This helps me adjust my leg position over the back of Lance's neck to secure a tight triangle position.

6. I lock my right leg over my left ankle and finish the choke by squeezing my knees together, curling my legs down, and pulling Lance's head toward my hips and into my hamstring.

METHODS FOR FINISHING THE TRIANGLE: *VARIATION 2*

If your opponent posts his arm to defend the choke and you bridge your hips to pass that arm to the other side of your body, there is a chance that he could transition to a gable grip defense to protect his neck. In this scenario, your opponent creates a wedge with his inside arm and fights the pressure of the choke by driving your hips away with his arms. You may feel like you can still lock your legs in the triangle position, but pulling on his head actually drives his arms deeper into your hips, making the position uncomfortable for you. Since his arm is on your stomach, you are closer to the traditional triangle than if his hand were on the mat, but you still need to move his arm across your body to get the submission. By creating a more extreme angle than would normally be necessary, you can put yourself in position to finish the choke even if your opponent tries to defend the choke by locking his hands. When you make this transition, you can do it in two ways: you can grab your own shin, or you can control his head. If your hips are already in a good position for the triangle, and you are concerned about your opponent escaping, grabbing your shin is your best option. If you need to adjust your hips, controlling the head will give you more mobility, especially if you are countering the stack in the process.

1

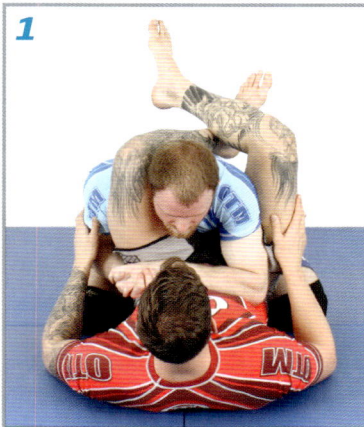

With Lance's head and left arm trapped between my legs, I am in position to potentially finish the triangle. He defends my submission attempt by locking his hands together, wedging his left forearm across my belt line to apply pressure to my hips. I cross my ankles to maintain control of the position.

2

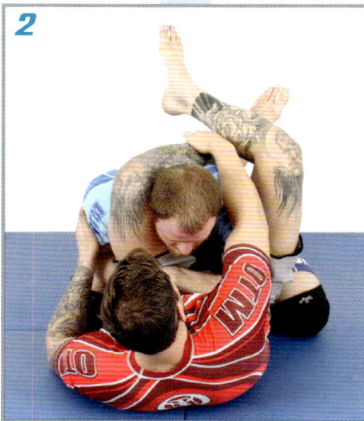

Without uncrossing my legs, I reach over Lance's left shoulder and grab my left shin.

3

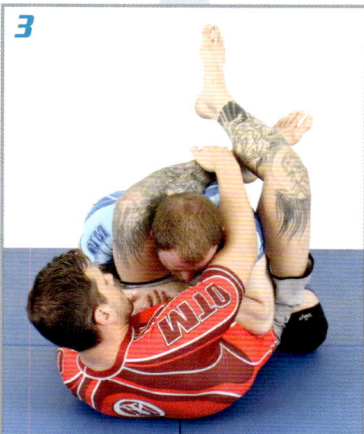

I slide my left arm under Lance's right leg and hook the inside of his left knee.

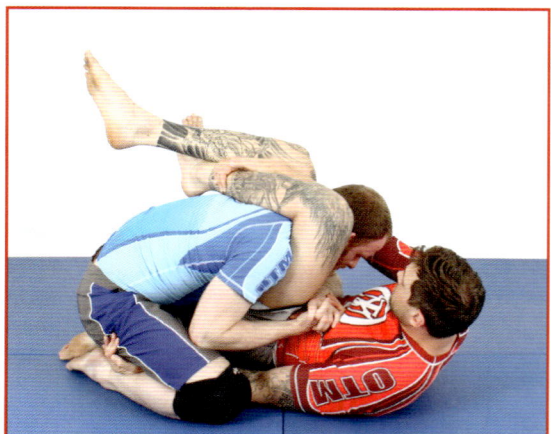

4

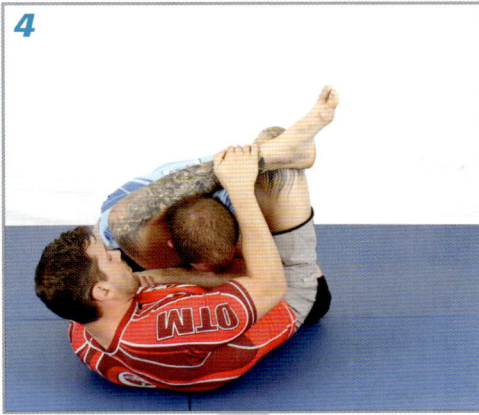

I post my right foot on Lance's left hip and angle my hips by pulling my head toward his right knee, pulling on his knee with my left arm, and pushing off of his hip with my right foot. This angle sets my left calf across the back of his neck.

5

I remove my right foot from Lance's hip and fold my right leg over my left shin, closing the triangle. Notice that my body is now perpendicular to his body so that I am looking into his ear rather than at the top of his head. To finish this variation of the triangle choke, I continue controlling Lance's right leg with my left arm because I can use that control to sweep him if he attempts to stand. My right hand grips the back of his hand, pulling it into my hips as I squeeze my knees together to finish the choke.

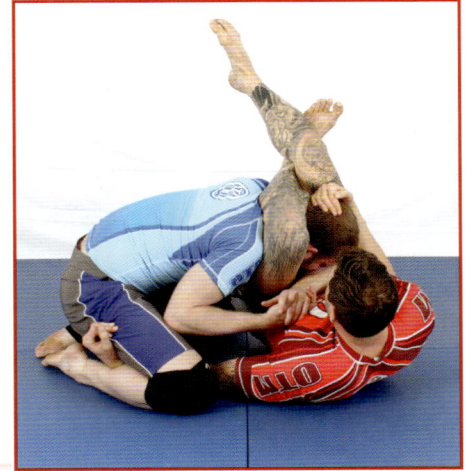

PREFERRED VARIATION: HEAD CONTROL

1

2

If I feel that my hips are too far under Lance because he is driving in, I control his head with my right hand.

If I am controlling Lance's head, my hip shift needs to be more dramatic to put me in position for the triangle. When I open my guard, I pull my left shoulder to his right knee and pinch my RIGHT knee in front of his left shoulder, giving me the angle to set my left calf across the back of his neck. I can now figure-four my legs and skip to the final step to finish the triangle.

METHODS FOR FINISHING THE TRIANGLE: VARIATION 3

When your opponent uses his forearm to drive your hips away from a tight triangle, hooking the leg and swiveling your hips is a great option for creating an angle strong enough to finish the choke, especially if he is stalling the position and maintaining a strong grip. If your opponent is more mobile, you can still move the arm across using the previous technique, but instead I utilize a transition that threatens both an armbar and a triangle if I can. By using this technique, your opponent will naturally protect his arm by attempting to back out, which actually sinks him deeper into the triangle choke. Should my opponent lock his hands again, I can return to Option 2, but, until he does that, I will pursue this option until he taps.

Lance's head and left arm are trapped between my legs. He senses that he is danger of being submitted, so he presses away with his left forearm.

Since Lance is not locking his hands together, I control his left wrist with my right hand, setting my right forearm across his left forearm to pin it to my chest. By keeping as much of my forearm in contact with his as possible, I maximize my control over his arm.

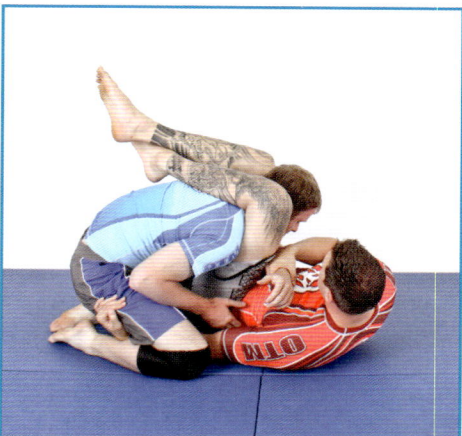

I snake my left arm under Lance's right leg and hook my arm in the crook of his right knee.

4

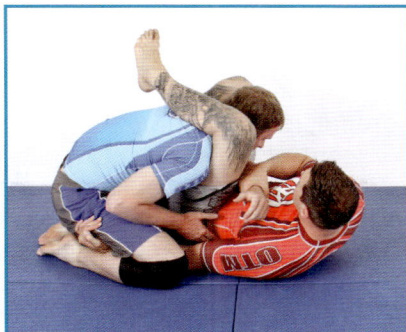

While maintaining control of Lance's right leg and left arm, I plant my right foot on his left hip. I squeeze my right knee into his left shoulder to reduce space and to limit his ability to move.

5

To swivel my hips perpendicular to Lance's hips, I push off of his left hip with my right foot and pull my head toward his right knee with my left arm. As I angle my hips, I pull his left arm toward my left shoulder with my right hand. Since I do not have a free hand to control my shin and dominate his posture, it is very important that I set my shin across the back of his neck and clamp my heel toward my butt.

6

I extend my right leg and maneuver the crook of my right knee in front of my left shin.

7

To finish the submission, I squeeze my knees together. I choose to continue controlling Lance's right arm instead of his head because the angle of this choke makes it extremely powerful. As long as I have his arm isolated, I can prevent him from using that arm to escape, and I can transition to the armbar if I happen to lose the triangle.

METHODS FOR FINISHING THE TRIANGLE: VARIATION 4

In the previous two techniques, I countered the wedge defense by using variations of a technique that hinged on an extreme hip swivel. Experienced grapplers understand the importance of hip placement and angles, so they often defend attacks and establish control by limiting hip movement. If your hips are caged, you can still finish the triangle, but your positioning will not be completely ideal. Since you do not hook the leg in this move, you have no control over your opponent's balance, which could give him the ability to counter if your choke is not strong. Even though this technique has minor shortcomings, you should not disregard it. Antonio Rodrigo Nogueira has used this variation of the triangle successfully in mixed martial arts, proving that the quality of the choke is still there. If you need to use this finishing technique, just be aware that your opponent has more options to escape in this position than in the previous techniques.

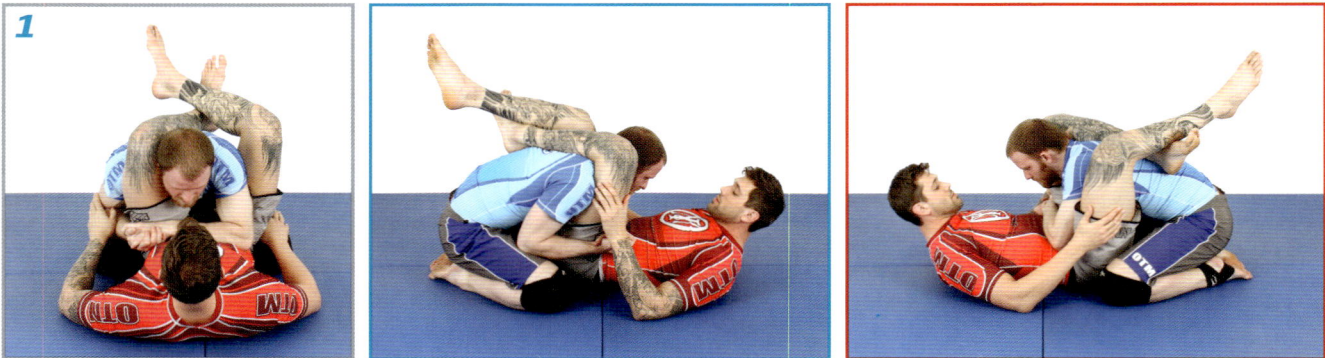

Lance is defending my triangle attempt by locking his hands together and driving his left forearm into my stomach. I have tried to drag his arm across using option two and option three, but he is preventing me from swiveling my hips.

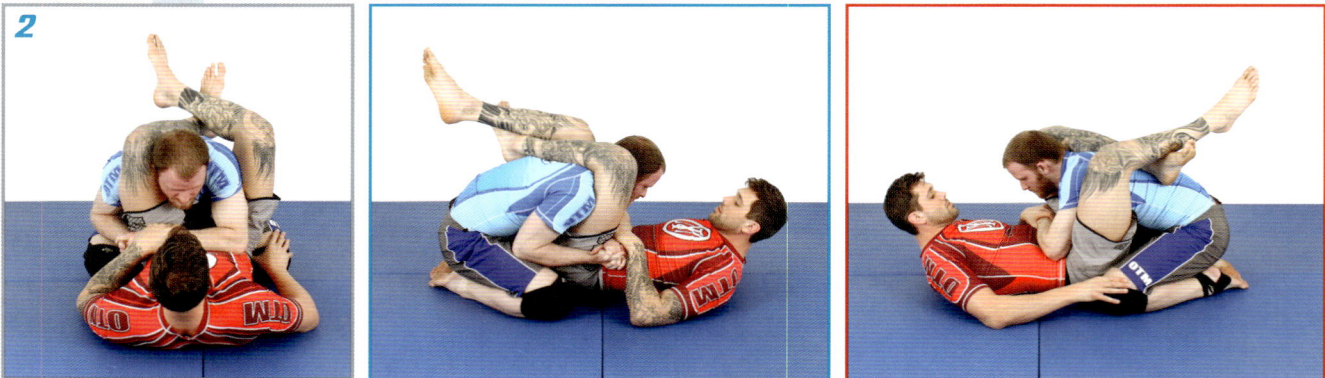

I latch on to Lance's left wrist with my left hand, establishing a cross grip. At the same time, I control his left knee with my right hand. I may not be able to swivel my hips in this position, but by placing my hand on his left knee, I can prevent him from circling to his left, which is an excellent escape option for him.

I bridge my hips into the air as I pull Lance's left arm across my body with my left hand, clearing his elbow from my stomach and bringing it to the outside of my left hip.

4

I pull my knees toward my chest as I lower my hips to the mat to collapse Lance's posture. I feel that he still wants to circle to his left, so I maintain control of his left knee with my right hand.

5

Not wanting to give Lance the opportunity to circle to his left, I push off of his left knee with my right hand to create a slight angle with my hips, aiming my left shoulder toward his right knee. As my hips move into position, my left leg slides up his back, setting my calf across the back of his neck, parallel with his shoulder line. As I always do in this step of the triangle, I curl my left heel toward my butt to help control his posture.

6

My right knee pinches into Lance's head as I maneuver my right foot into the air, setting the inside of my right knee over my left shin. My left hand is still controlling his left wrist, and my right hand is still controlling his left knee.

7

I put both hands on the back of Lance's head and pull down, pinching my knees together and bridging my hips into his neck to finish the triangle. It's important to note the positioning of my left elbow in this step. Even though my left hand is no longer controlling his left wrist, I place my left elbow on his left wrist so that I can still somewhat control his arm and stifle his ability to move and defend.

METHODS FOR FINISHING THE TRIANGLE: VARIATION 5

As basic as the traditional triangle may be, you can apply finishing pressure in a number of different ways. Typically, squeezing your knees and pulling the head, which I demonstrated in the previous techniques, will be enough to force your opponent to tap. However, a difference in body types or a shift in position can make finishing the traditional triangle difficult, even if your positioning appears to be correct. In this technique, rather than using both hands on the back of the head, you pull on the arm and the head to set and finish the choke. The advantage to this approach is that pulling on the arm sucks your opponent's shoulder into his neck, pinching the carotid artery on that side, while pulling his head into your hamstring pinches the carotid artery on the other side. The disadvantage to this technique is that you are somewhat vulnerable to the slam because you are not hooking the leg. This technique is very effective, which Antonio Rodrigo Nogueira has proved repeatedly, and I use it sometimes, but be wary of your opponent's intentions if he begins to stand.

1

I am close to finishing the triangle. Lance's head and left arm are trapped between my legs, and he is pressing his left forearm into my stomach to defend the triangle. I cross my ankles to stabilize the position.

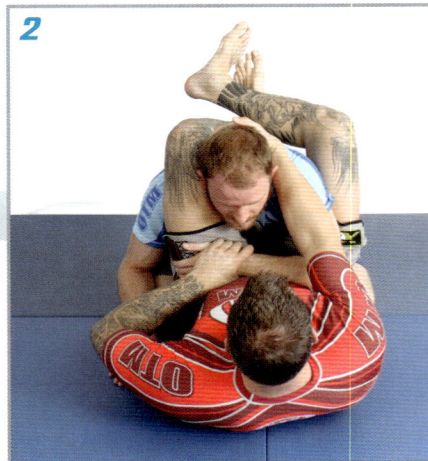

2

I grip the back of Lance's head with my right hand and grab his left wrist with my left hand, establishing a cross grip.

3

To pass Lance's arm, I pop my hips forward and yank his left wrist across my body with my left hand. I maintain control of his head to prevent him from posturing out of the triangle.

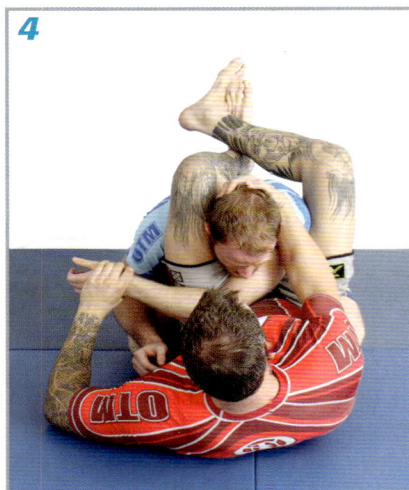

4

I curl my legs and pull on Lance's head to bring him down, locking his left arm across my body. I continue to extend his left arm to my left using my cross grip as though I were trying to drive his biceps into his neck.

5

As I open my guard to set the triangle, I pinch my right knee against Lance's left shoulder and shift my hips to my right, giving me the angle to set my left calf across the back of his neck. My left leg pinches his back throughout this step to give me additional control over his posture.

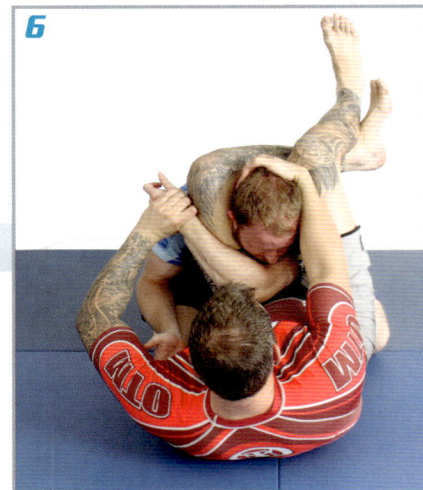

6

I fold my right leg over my left ankle and curl my legs down to lock the triangle, squeezing my knees to begin applying choking pressure. To finish the choke, I pull Lance's right arm out and up to drive his shoulder into the side of his neck. My right hand pulls his head down and to the left, into my hamstring, finishing the choke.

METHODS FOR FINISHING THE TRIANGLE: *VARIATION 6*

Clearing an arm to reach the triangle position can take a great deal of effort and puts you very close to a fight-winning submission. If your opponent shuts down one finishing attempt, do not give up. Keep attacking with triangle variations until you break through his defenses and put him to sleep. Passing the inside arm is an excellent way to finish the triangle, and because of that fact, your opponent is likely to resist any manipulation of that inside arm. If that resistance is combined with an effort to cage your hips, using the previous options may be futile. With so much focus on your hips and his inside arm, however, your opponent is likely to forget that his outside arm is vulnerable. In this technique, you attack that outside arm, creating enough leverage for you to angle your hips and set a proper triangle choke.

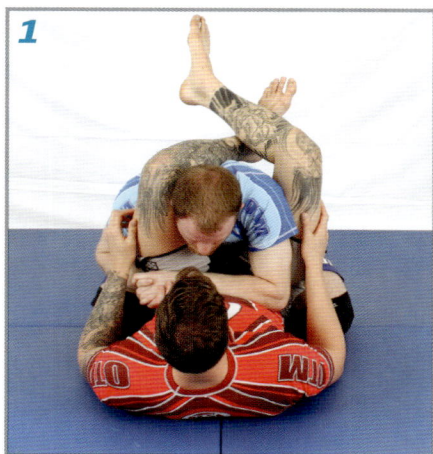

1

Lance is defending my triangle attempt by wedging his left arm against my belt line. He has resisted my attempts to underhook his leg and to pass his left arm across my stomach to my left hip. I decide that I need to change my approach if I want to finish the triangle.

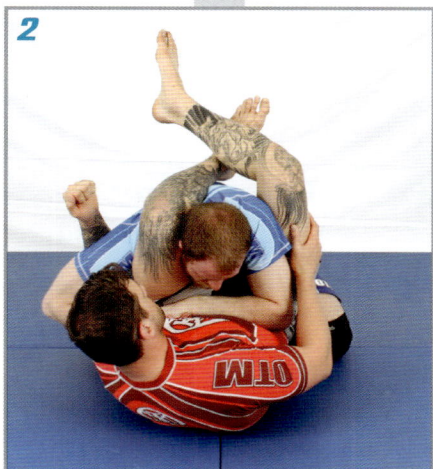

2

I shoot my left arm under Lance's right armpit. My left shoulder follows my left arm so that I can reach my left arm as deep as possible. I perform this movement with speed to lower the likelihood of his blocking my underhook.

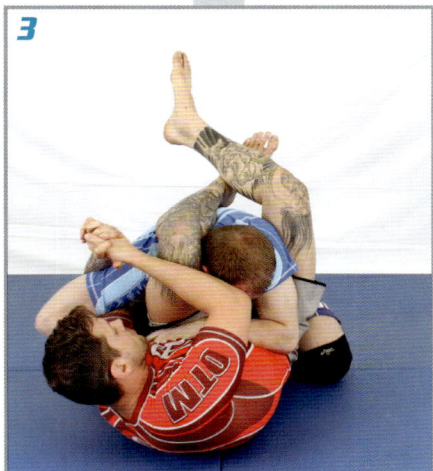

3

I clasp my hands together, setting my right elbow on the right side of Lance's head.

4

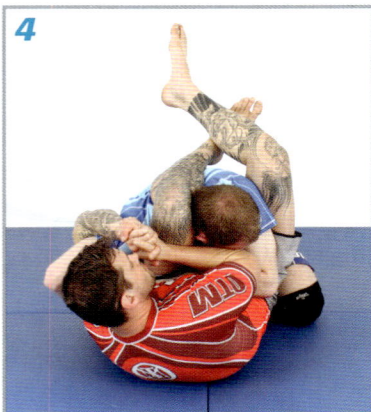

With my hands locked together, I shift my left shoulder toward Lance's right knee by pulling on his right arm with my arms. When I do this, his right arm slides onto my chest. In this position, he is not only in danger of being submitted with the triangle choke, but I could potentially apply an armbar on his left arm or an inverted armbar on his right.

5

Now that my hips are perpendicular to Lance's hips, I post my right foot on his left hip and slide my left leg up his back, setting my calf across the back of his neck.

6

I maneuver my right leg into the air, pinching my right knee against Lance's head as I fold my right leg over my left shin. I maintain control of his right arm with both of my arms throughout this step.

7

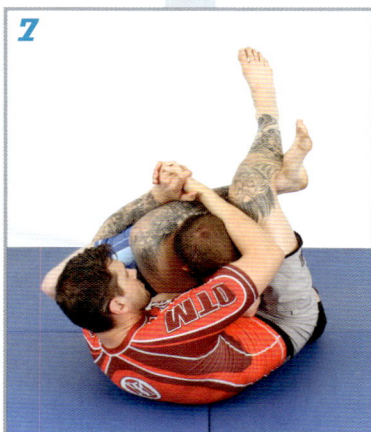

To apply finishing pressure, I set my right forearm on the left side of Lance's head and pull down on my shin with my left arm as I squeeze my knees together. When I perform this step, I do not unclasp my hands when I move them into the finish position. By keeping them locked together, I continue to dominate his right arm and his posture, allowing me to finish the choke.

ANATOMY OF ARM ON THE MAT

When I attack with the triangle when my opponent's hand is posted on the mat, I need to be aware that my approach to the triangle must change for the choke to be effective. That does not mean that the choke is less effective with the arm on the mat. The choke is just different, so I typically do not bother fighting to pass the arm. If I pull on his head as I would normally do in other situations, his jaw will slip underneath his shoulder, which hides his carotid artery and actually protects it from being choked. This is because his shoulder is exposed, changing the angle of my pressure. To finish the triangle in this situation, I focus on squeezing my knees. If I have trouble finishing the choke and feel as though I have adequate control over my opponent, I will try the second squeezing option. It's important to note that once I initiate the squeeze, I flex my hamstring, making the muscle solid, and putting more pressure on the carotid artery. This is a vital step to finishing the arm on the mat triangle. Without flexing the hamstring and making it solid you will have a tough time finishing with the arm on the mat.

I have Lance in the triangle position with his head and left arm trapped between my legs, and my left foot is locked in the crook of my right knee. Since his left hand is on the mat, I can't use a traditional triangle finish.

To apply finishing pressure, I squeeze my knees together, driving my left thigh into the left side of his neck and his right shoulder into the other side of his neck. If he was tucking his chin to hide from the choke, this pressure would expose his neck.

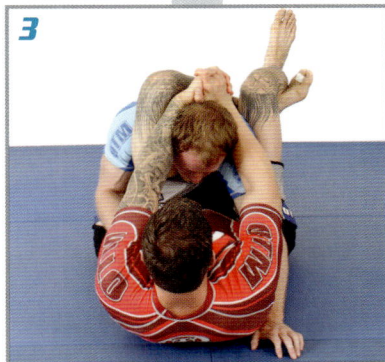

Once my legs are curled, I statically flex my left hamstring, locking my hands together behind Lance's head, I pull the neck into my thigh to finish the choke.

SQUEEZING OPTION 2

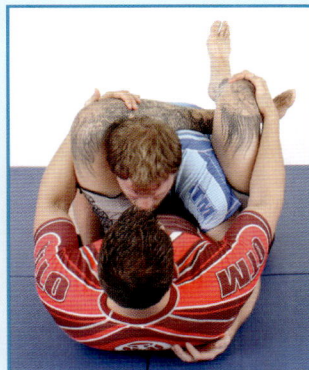

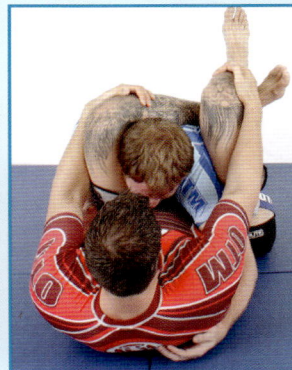

In this variation, I grip my knees with my hands and use my arm strength to increase the squeezing power of my legs. The drawback of this variation is that I do not have control of Lance's head, so if he begins to rip out I need to go back to the first option and control his posture.

OVERHOOK TRIANGLE FINISH

I see many grapplers transition to overhook triangle setups when their opponent posts an arm on the mat, but then they struggle to adjust their legs and resort to yanking down on their opponent's head, trying to finish the triangle through sheer force rather than technique. If you are not finishing the triangle by squeeze alone, your opponent is likely using his post to protect his neck by creating space. If you overhook the arm, you are one step closer to minimizing his ability to defend with that arm, but you need to hook one of his legs with your other arm and create an angle to make your position truly effective. As you may note from the photos, this finish puts you in a position very similar to that of the traditional choke, and the choking power is equal if you position yourself properly.

1

I have Lance's head and left arm trapped between my legs. He has defended my attempts to pass his arm to the opposite side, so I lock his left arm in place by overhooking it with my right arm.

2

I slide my left arm under his right leg and hook it.

3

I post my right foot on Lance's left hip and pull my left shoulder toward his right knee as I swing my left leg up his back and across the back of his neck.

4

To finish the triangle, I lock my left shin in the crook of my right knee and squeeze my knees together without unhooking his right leg or abandoning my overhook on his left arm.

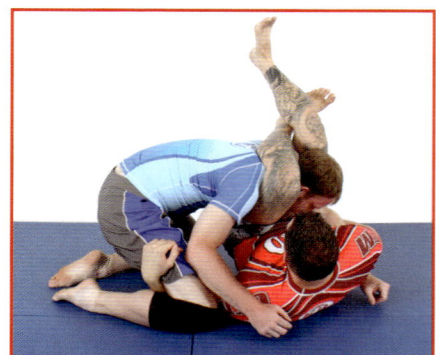

ARMBAR TRIANGLE WITH THE ARM ON THE MAT

For most grapplers, using an overhook against an opponent who posts an arm on the mat is instinctual. The overhook feels strong and provides a sense of security, but it is not always the best option. The overhook is useful for when your opponent is attempting to duck out or is not moving much at all. If he is pulling up and back to evade the triangle, he will likely slip out of the overhook and escape your guard, especially if either of you are sweaty. When your opponent posts on the mat and attempts to duck out of your triangle by moving away from you, he will actually begin to straighten his arm for you. He may feel like his post increases the power of his escape, but he is actually giving you the armbar triangle. The key to making the most of this opportunity is to control his elbow with your hand instead of an overhook. As you will see in the photographs below, gripping with your hand allows you to pinch his wrist in your armpit, while aligning his joint for the armbar. If you used the overhook, you would not have enough control over his joint to properly set the submission.

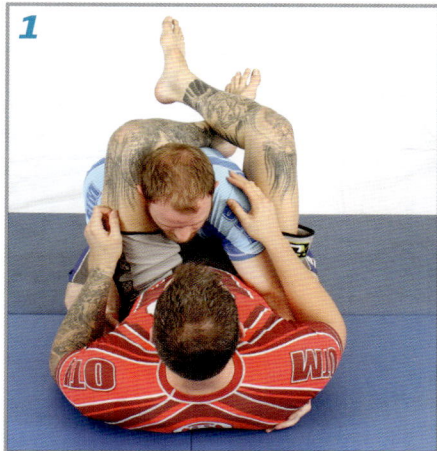

Lance's head and left arm, which is on the mat, are trapped between my legs.

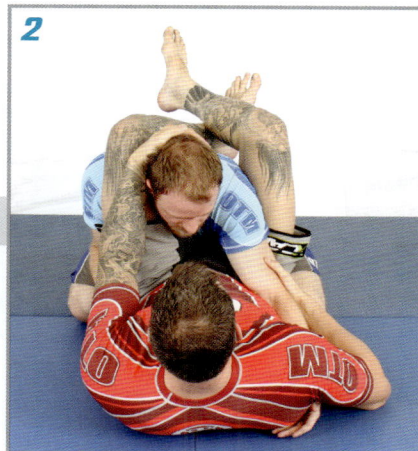

As Lance pulls away from me, I control the back of his head with my left hand and grip his left elbow with my right hand.

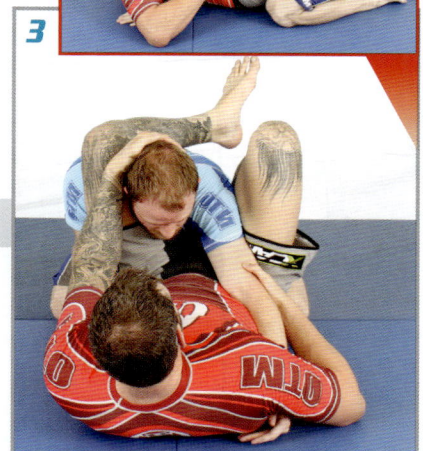

I pull on Lance's elbow with my right hand, bringing it away from my hip so that I can open my guard and post my right foot on his left hip.

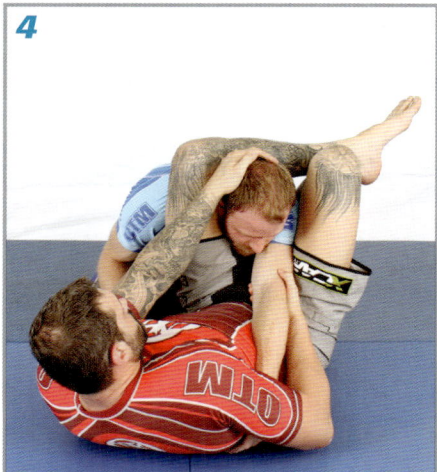

As I hip out and swing my left leg over the back of Lance's neck, I press my right foot into his left hip, pulling on his arm with my right hand. I keep his left wrist pinched in my armpit throughout this movement.

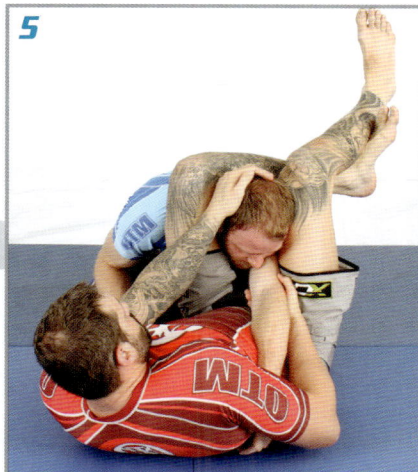

I fold my right leg over my left ankle to lock the triangle, maintaining control of Lance's head to limit his ability to posture.

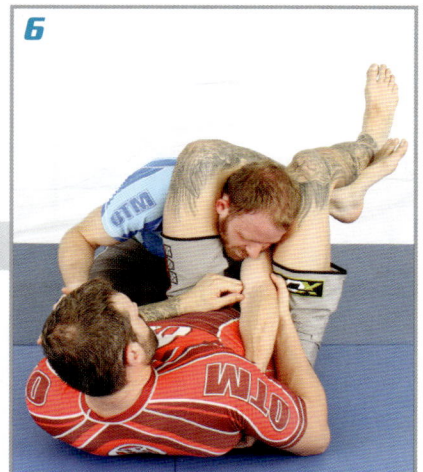

To finish the triangle, I curl down with my legs, while performing a crunch to hyperextend Lance's left arm. For the armbar to be effective, I need to keep my hand on his elbow and keep his arm tucked in my armpit.

NICKSICK FINISH

In general, triangles are a challenge for fighters with shorter legs because they have to rely more on creating angles to properly set a triangle than a long-legged fighter might. One of my students, Eric Nicksick, is a short but very muscular fighter. He loves to work for triangles, but his physique forces him to be more creative with how he finishes chokes. I showed him how to adjust his squeeze for the arm on the mat triangle, and a few weeks later I saw him doing something unusual. To finish the arm on the mat triangle, he locked his foot in the middle of the calf, almost as though he were trying to lock a full triangle but could not, and hugged his knees to strengthen his squeeze. At first I was puzzled, but when I talked to Eric about it he said that he was having a lot of success with that finish. I started playing with it, and I found that the positioning of the ankle at the midpoint of the calf actually created a stronger squeeze than if my ankles were crossed or even if I had locked a full on triangle. The Nicksick finish is now one of my favorite ways to finish the arm on the mat triangle, and I prefer to use it instead of techniques like the teepee (which you will learn later in this section) because I feel that I have more control with the Nicksick.

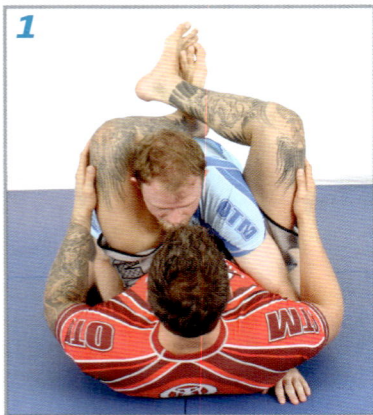

I am in position to finish Lance with a triangle, but his left arm is on the mat, and I do not have the mobility to lock a figure-four.

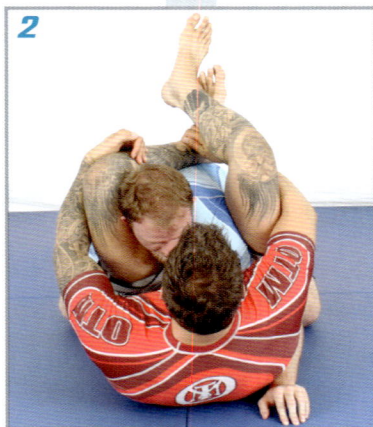

I hug my left leg with my left hand and curl my knees to my chest, making myself heavy to slow Lance's movement. My right hand reaches around my right leg and snakes under my right calf, grabbing my left shin. For this technique, going around my leg rather than between my legs is important because I can adjust my legs without releasing control of my shin, making it difficult for him to move.

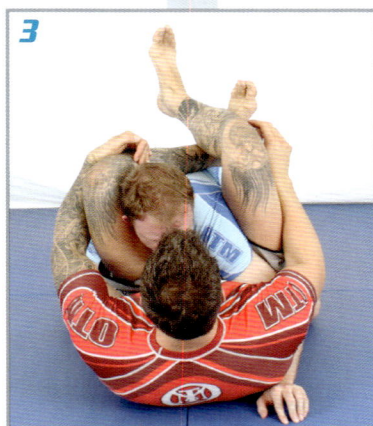

I pull my left shin with my right hand, setting my left ankle in the middle of my right calf, the optimal squeezing position.

4

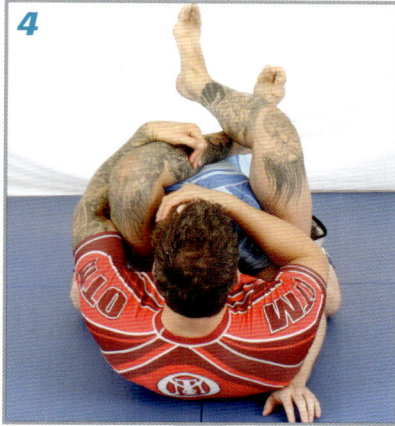

Before I apply the finishing squeeze, I pull down on Lance's head with my right hand to set his neck between my thighs. If I allow his head to drift up, I will have less mass with which to finish the choke.

5

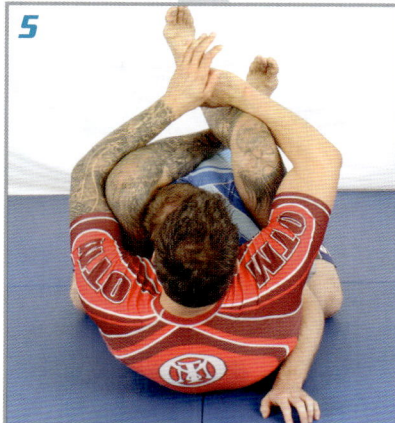

I hug both of my knees and lock my hands together.

6

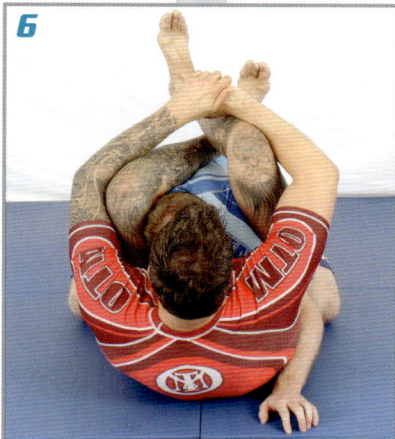

I squeeze my knees together to begin applying the choke. I curl my heels into his back and pull my knees toward my chest to sink the choke as deep as possible.

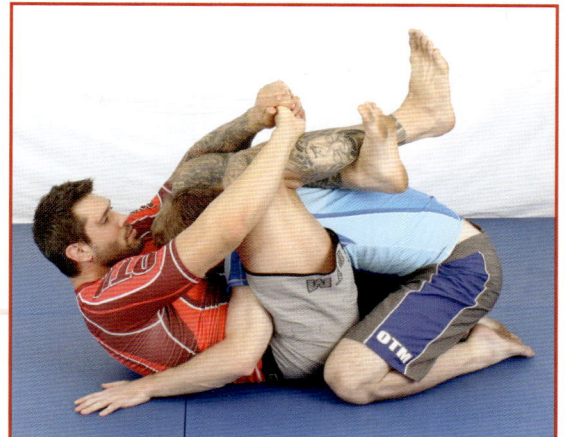

7

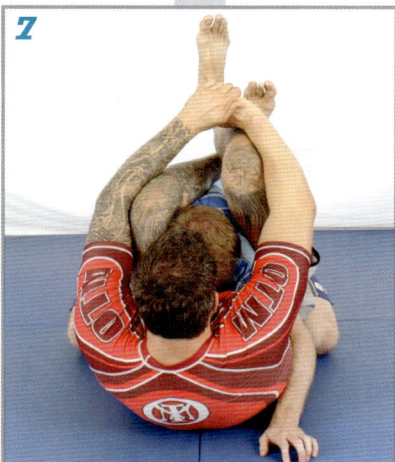

While keeping my hands locked together, I extend my arms to increase the choking power of my legs to finish the choke.

SHORT-LEG FINISH

This option is similar to the Nicksick finish but aims to achieve a more orthodox triangle position. While I prefer the power of the Nicksick finish to the short-leg finish, your build may not give you the squeezing power necessary to finish the Nicksick, so forcing a figure-four could be the better option. If an opponent is exceptionally large or if he angles himself away, your legs could feel as if they are too short to achieve the triangle, and in some cases your legs may be too short to use a more traditional triangle finish. If you grab your own shin, you can use the extra power of your arm to pull your leg into position and rotate your hamstring into your opponent's carotid artery. If you can't finish from here, your opponent's struggle could set you up for the options that we discussed previously.

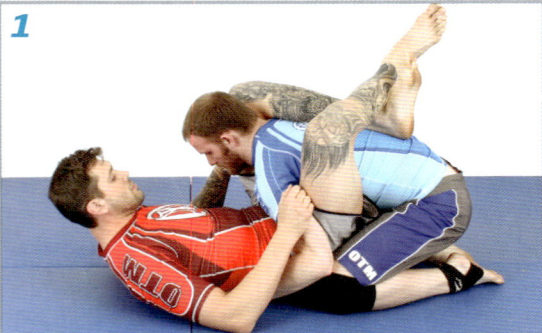

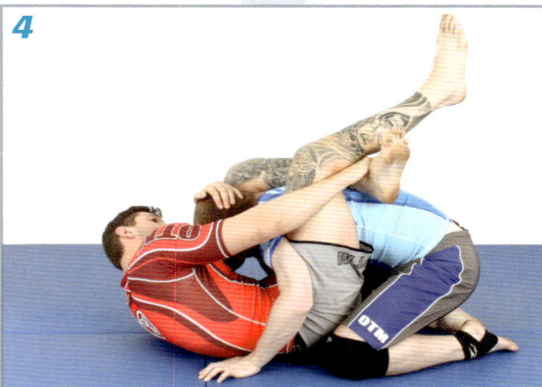

1

Lance is in my guard, and I am in position to finish the triangle. I tried locking my legs into a figure-four, but he is rotating to his right, away from his trapped arm.

2

Without uncrossing my legs, I reach my right hand under my right leg.

3

I grab my left shin with my right hand and pull as though I were trying to lock my left ankle under my right knee for the triangle choke, which naturally rotates my shoulders to the left.

4

As I continue to pull my right ankle toward Lance's left shoulder, I pull his head down to my hips with my left hand. I squeeze my knees together for additional pressure to get the submission.

TEEPEE FINISH

This technique is an arm-assisted head-and-arm leg scissor, but you may know it as "the teepee" because of the popularity of Eddie Bravo's rubber guard. Bravo's approach to the teepee is sound, but when I first attempted the teepee I was consistently getting a neck crank rather than a choke. When I analyzed my approach, I found that I was trying to use my knees to pinch the carotid arteries, which simply was not efficient or effective. In the ideal triangle position, my hamstring is performing the choke because of the angle I achieve for the finish, but with the teepee, the best tools I have for the choke are my thighs. If I let his neck slip up to my knees, I will lose the choke, so before I start to squeeze and extend my legs, I use the teepee grip to set my opponent's neck between my thighs. Once I made that adjustment I began tapping opponents consistently with the teepee. The teepee is now a reliable part of my arsenal, and I typically use it if my opponent prevents me from setting a figure-four position either through technique or sheer size, leaving me parallel with my opponent and unable to reach my ankles for the Nicksick or the short-leg finish. If the teepee fails, I may be able to figure-four my legs because the pinching power of my legs makes my opponent's body narrower, eliminating the space that originally prevented my transition to the triangle. That option is included here as well.

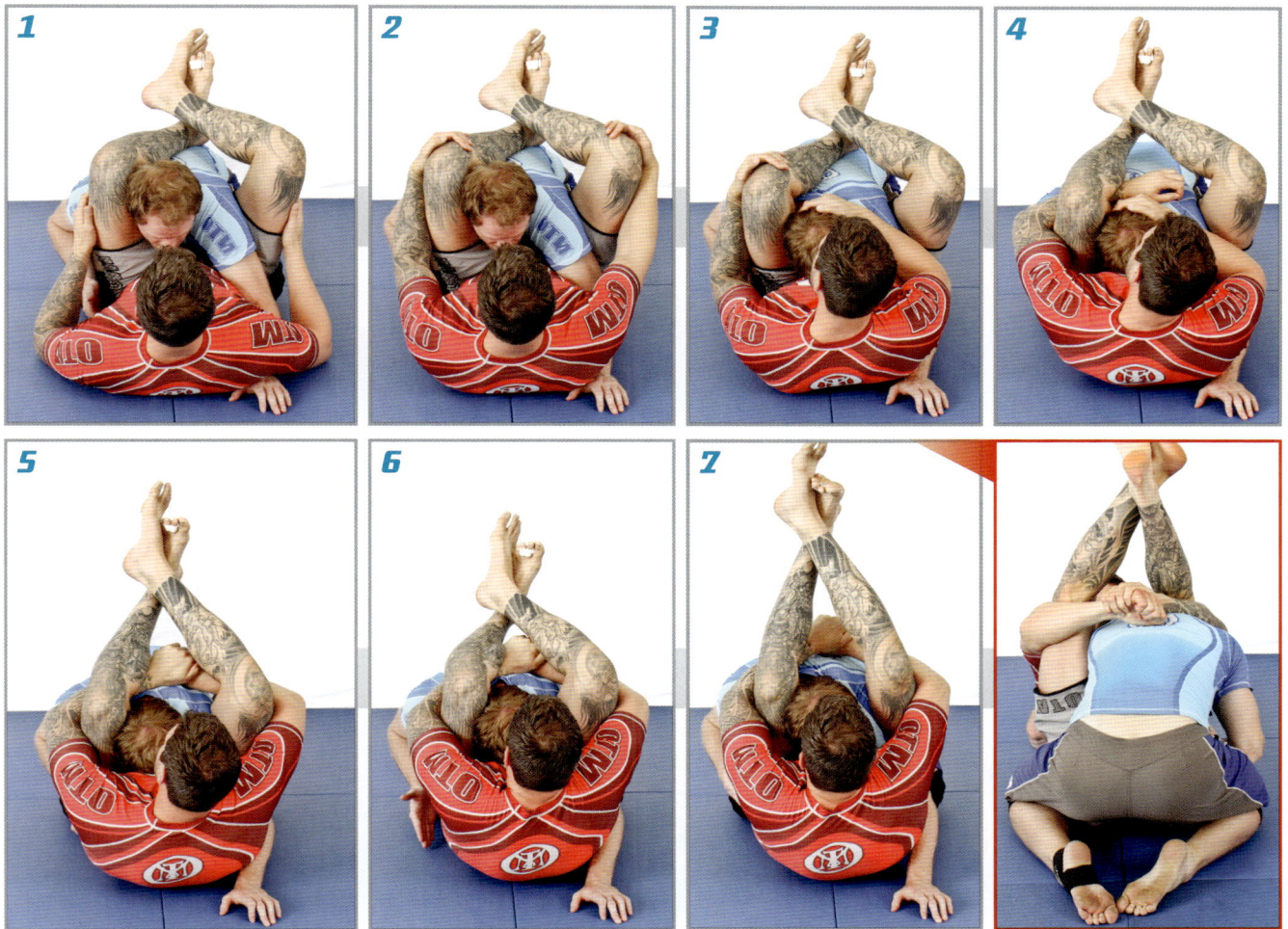

1) I am trapping Lance's head and left arm between my legs, crossing my ankles on his back to control him. His left arm is on the mat, and he has blocked my previous finishing attempts. 2) I curl my legs to bring Lance toward me as I sit up to meet him in the middle, and I reach around my own legs to strengthen my curl. 3) Continuing to suck my legs to my chest, I set my right hand on the back of Lance's head and pull it down to prevent him from posturing out and to set his neck between the meat of my thighs. 4) I hook my left hand under my left knee and control Lance's head with my right hand to delay his ability to posture. 5) I slide my right arm under my right knee and clasp my hands together over Lance's back with an s-grip. I use my grip to pull his body into me to trap his neck between my thighs, which is essential for achieving a choke instead of a crank. 6) To begin applying my finish, I squeeze my knees together and continue using my s-grip to pull Lance's body toward my hips. As you will see on the detail photos on the next page, I have not yet begun extending my legs. Instead, I am focusing entirely on bringing my knees together in this step. 7) Still using my arms to position Lance's neck between my thighs, I scissor my legs together to maximize the choking power of my legs. If my legs are positioned properly, he will go to sleep.

TEEPEE DETAIL

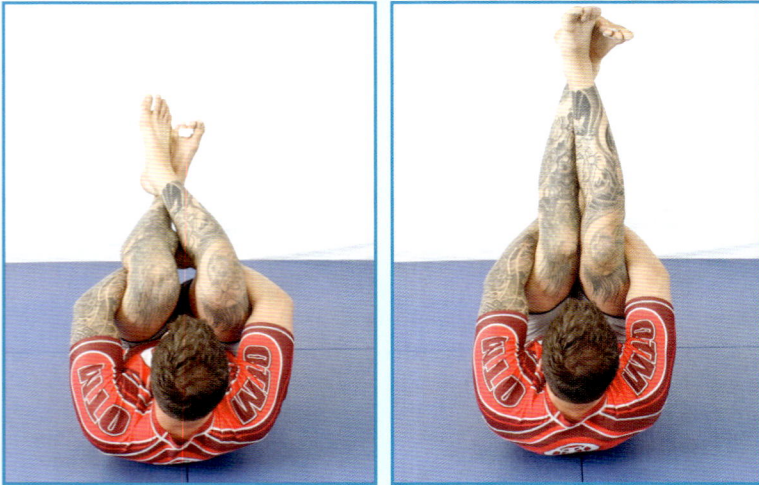

In these two photographs, you can better see how I am positioning my arms and straightening my legs to finish the teepee choke.

TEEPEE TO TRIANGLE CHOKE

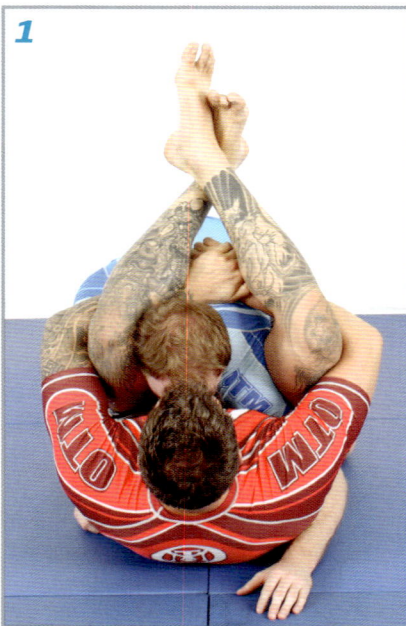

1 If my teepee does not force Lance to tap, I curl my knees back into my chest and continue to squeeze them together to compress his neck into his shoulder.

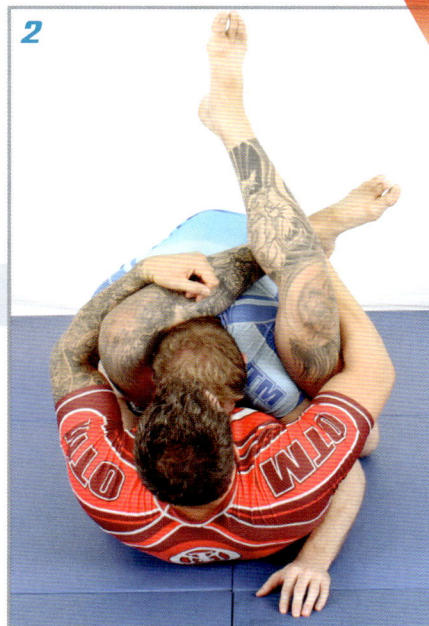

2 I grab my left shin with my right hand. As I pull my left shin into the crook of my right knee, I hug my left knee with my left arm to control Lance's posture and keep my left leg in position for the triangle.

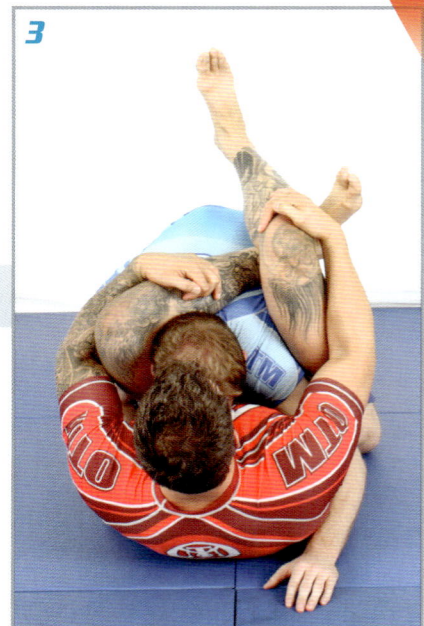

3 I fold my right leg over my left shin to lock the triangle. I hug my knees and squeeze them together to get the finish.

SWITCHING FROM ARM ON THE MAT TO TRADITIONAL FINISH

Sometimes, the arm on the mat finish can be difficult. Grapplers with shorter legs will have a hard time applying the necessary pressure to finish the choke. Typically, I prefer to immediately finish the choke if the arm is on the mat, a concept that I discussed in previous techniques, but I also need to be prepared to transition back to the traditional triangle if my opponent uses his posted arm to shut down my choke. When my opponent digs in and commits to surviving the triangle, I like to apply a new threat, allowing me to adjust and eventually go back in and finish my choke. In this technique, I use the combination of a shoulder lock and an inverted armbar to transition to the triangle because my opponent has successfully pinned my hips and blocked my attempts to hook his leg. The combination of joint lock and choke threats funnels my opponent into giving up the triangle, and the entire transition is painful, making it even more effective.

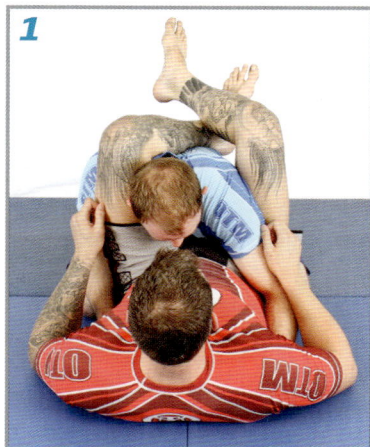

Lance is posting his arm on the mat and has defended my attempts to finish the triangle from this position.

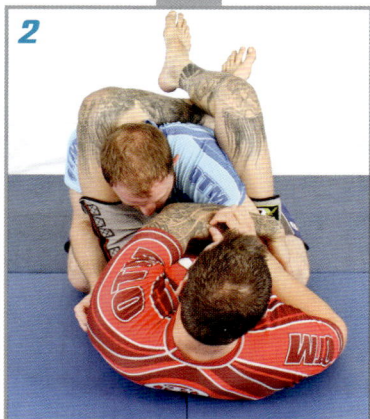

I reach my left hand across my body and cup Lance's left elbow.

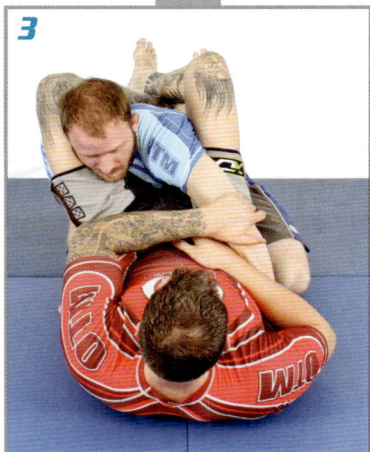

I drive my legs away and straighten my back as I pull Lance's elbow with my left hand, forcing it to bend, relieving the pressure he is applying to my hips.

4

I shoot my right arm under Lance's left arm, establishing an underhook. It's important to note that my legs are still locked together, allowing me to continue controlling his upper body.

5

I establish a three-finger grip (my left thumb between the pointer and middle finger on my right hand, a grip that I will cover in depth later in this book) and pull Lance to my chest, pressing my left forearm into the top of his left shoulder, squeezing as hard as I can to delay him from driving his head into me to protect his arm.

6

To apply the first submission, I drive Lance away with my legs to create Kimura-like pressure, pulling his arm out of its socket. To increase this pressure even more, I rotate my body to the left slightly.

7

Lance slips his left hand up to my neck to protect his shoulder.

8

I immediately transition to the inverted armbar by gripping Lance's left elbow with both of my hands, and twist it toward the sky, while applying downward pressure on the joint. Since his thumb is pointing down in this position, the armbar is even stronger.

9

I feel that Lance is beginning to rotate his left arm out of the inverted armbar as he drives into me to relieve the pressure of the inverted armbar. I begin transitioning to the triangle by posting my right foot on his left hip and sliding my left leg toward the back of his neck.

10

I set my left leg across the back of Lance's neck and curl downward to control his posture. I pinch my right knee against his left shoulder to tighten the position and to block his left elbow from sliding to the outside of my hip. As my legs move into position, I grip his left wrist with my right hand, locking his left arm to my chest.

11

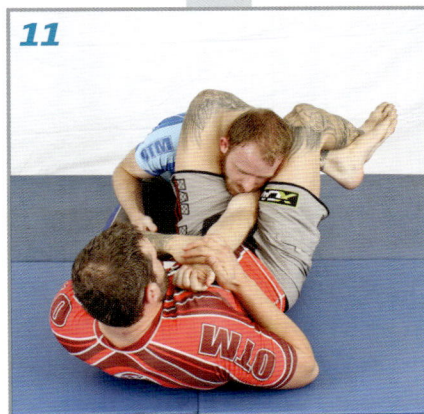

I remove my right foot from Lance's left hip, throwing it over my left shin with my left ankle directly under my right knee. I roll my opponent's arm, pointing his left palm towards the ceiling to ensure pressure is applied to his elbow. To finish, I squeeze my knees together, curl my legs down, and extend my hips towards the ceiling, forcing Lance to tap from the triangle armbar combo.

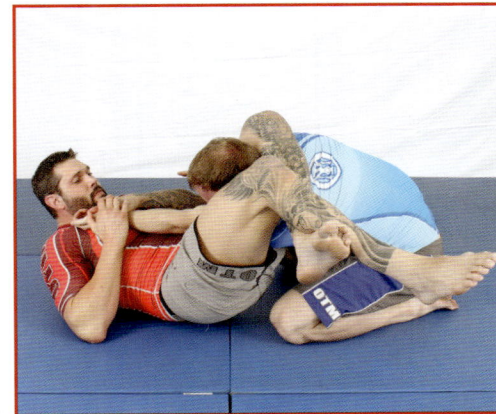

REVERSE TRIANGLE BOTTI FIST FINISH

When you are working to finish an arm on the mat triangle, your opponent will panic when he feels that you can potentially finish the choke. At that point, many grapplers will wrap their trapped arm around your thigh, establishing an overhook, which is an effective way to stall a triangle that can also be used to set up escapes. I have seen grapplers advocate switching to the reverse triangle (locking your figure-four on his opposite shoulder) to counter this defense, but I do not consider the reverse triangle a strong choking position. From the reverse triangle you cannot drive your hamstring into your opponent's neck, and, while you can get the meat of your thigh to close off one carotid artery, you have very little leverage to press your opponent's shoulder into the other carotid. I almost gave up on the reverse triangle until I trained with Rodrigo Botti, a Brazilian jiu-jitsu black belt. He showed me how to use my fist to finish the choke, while maintaining control of my opponent's arm. I had seen the fist choke before, but Botti's approach was more technical than what I had learned and much more effective.

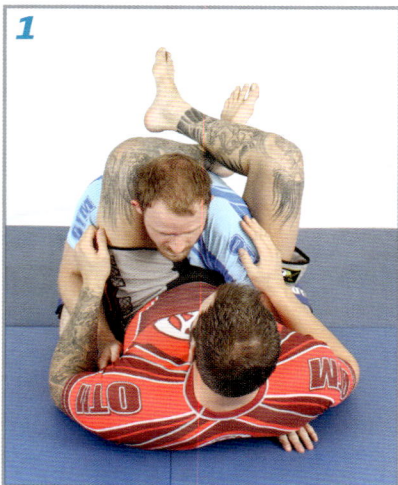

1 Lance's head and left arm are trapped between my legs. His arm is on the mat, but I can't finish the choke.

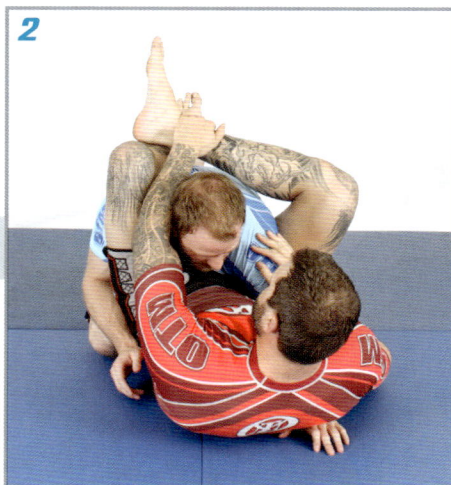

2 My left hand snakes around Lance's head and grabs my right shin as my right arm hugs his left arm to lock it in place.

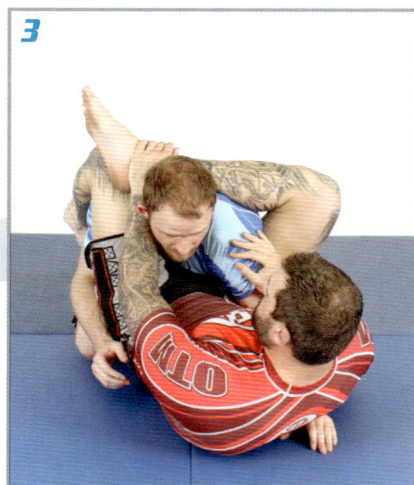

3 I cinch my right leg across the back of Lance's neck by pulling it into place with my left hand.

4 I drape my left leg over my right ankle, locking the figure-four over Lance's right shoulder, while still controlling his left arm with my right arm.

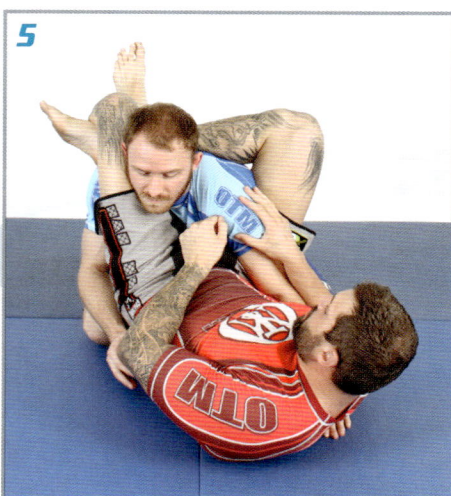

5 I bridge my hips slightly to drive Lance away.

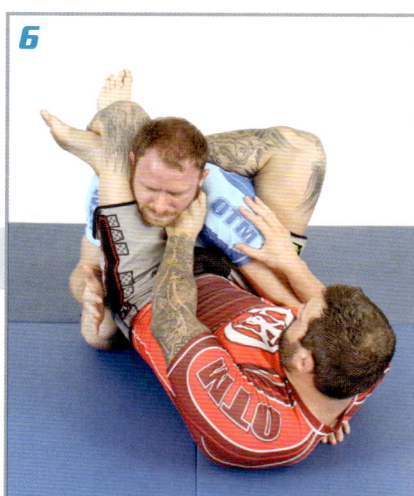

6 I dig my left fist into the left side of Lance's neck, aiming for his carotid artery. To finish the submission, I lock my left elbow straight and curl my legs to my chest as I squeeze my thighs.

SANKAKU TRIANGLE FINISH (WITH SWEEP OPTION)

In the introduction to this chapter I mentioned that you may not be familiar with the sankaku, and that it requires a high level of hip movement and coordination to execute properly. I want to emphasize that if you struggle initially to apply the sankaku you should not get frustrated, and you should not give up on it. As you integrate my triangle system into your game, and as you continue to practice the sankaku, your hip movement and coordination will develop. It won't be long before your training partners are asking you to teach them the sankaku. Even though the process of achieving the sankaku is dynamic, the payoff is huge. The position is difficult to escape because your leg positioning makes you extremely heavy, and the angle that you finish from makes for an incredibly powerful choke with alternate sweeping and finishing options available as well. The key to setting the sankaku is understanding the basic positioning. You want to set your opponent's neck into the crook of your knee. If you think of his chin as a "V" and the bend of your leg as a "V," his head and your leg should fit together perfectly. When in doubt, however, rotate even more, almost as though you are trying to put your head between his legs. Technically, the variation of the sankaku that I show in this technique is a reverse sankaku, but that is not important. The most important details to remember are that you want to lock the "V's" together and that you finish a sankaku by pulling on the arm, not on the head. Later in this book, there are more entries for the sankaku and when to best apply it.

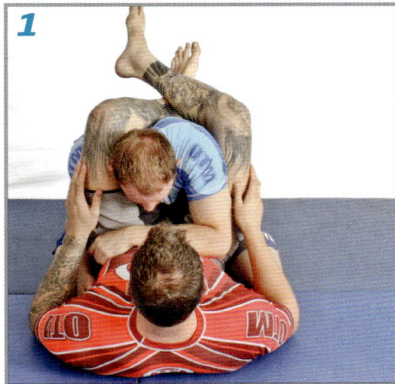

I have cleared Lance's right arm, and I am looking to transition to the sankaku.

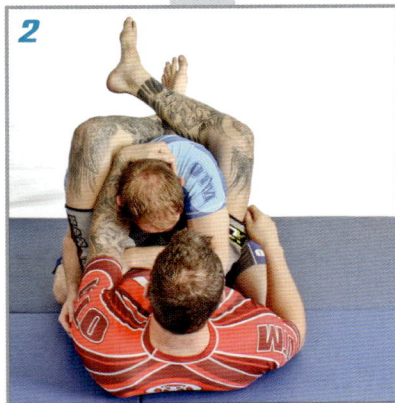

My left hand cups the back of Lance's head.

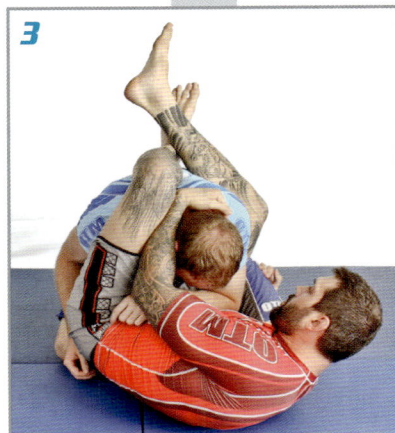

I hook Lance's left leg with my right hand and shift on to my right hip. At the same time, I elevate my hips, shift them out to my left, and push his head toward his left knee. This combination of movements allows me to create the angle that I need to lock the sankaku, while giving me the space to rotate around and behind him. It's important to note that, in this step, my grips are allowing me to control his balance. I do not want to let him fall to his side.

4

I pull on Lance's right leg and push on his head as I pop my hips out and around his head. I lean on to my right shoulder to increase my rotation, turning myself upside down, almost as though I were trying to put myself in a north/south position. This movement lines his chin up with the back of my right knee (locking the two "V's" together) and sets my left leg on the back of his neck, making me feel heavy and breaking his posture.

5

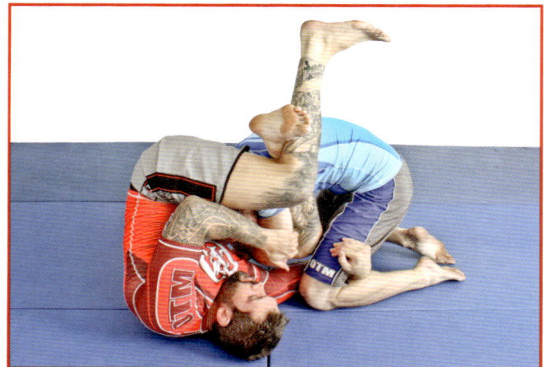

I lock my right foot in the crook of my left knee and grip his triceps with my left hand. From here, I can finish the choke by curling my legs toward my chest, squeezing my legs, and pulling his left arm into his neck.

6

If I cannot finish the choke from my back, I swing my legs to my left to sweep Lance, keeping my legs locked and his leg hooked throughout the sweep.

7

When Lance lands on his side, my left knee is touching my right shin and my left foot is flailed out, not touching the mat. If I let my left foot touch the mat, he could twist out. I maintain my leg hook and pull on his triceps with my left hand to finish the choke. Notice that my legs and his triceps are almost in a straight line. This maximizes the power of the choke by resting his head on the top of my left thigh.

SANKAKU JUDO STYLE: *VARIATION 1*

As I mentioned, the sankaku is a popular judo technique that is most often used to attack the turtle position. In this technique, I am positioned as though I started it against the turtle position, but that may not always be the case. Later in this book, you will see multiple options from setting up this variation of the sankaku. Unfortunately, finishing the sankaku in this situation can be difficult because you cannot reach his inside arm to pull it, leaving you with only the squeezing power of your legs. If your legs cannot finish the choke, you can still use the position to end the fight, but you may need to use a sweep and a spine lock to finish the choke. It's aggressive, powerful, and much more satisfying than using the sankaku as a judo-style pin.

1

Lance is turtled, and I am attacking with the sankaku. My hands are pressing against his left hip, preventing him from stepping over my body and escaping.

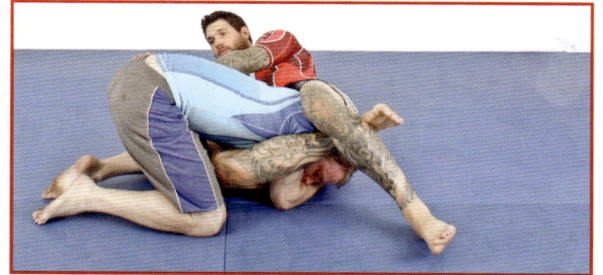

2

I sit up on to my right elbow and slam my chest into Lance's left hip as I reach my left arm over his back and hug his lower torso.

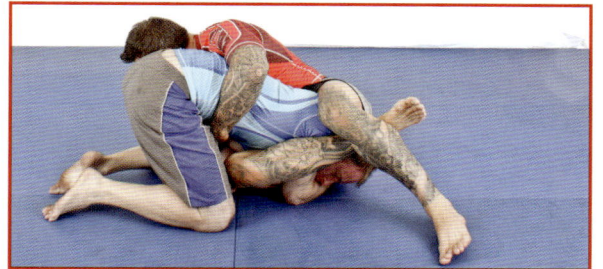

3

I roll Lance by pushing and extending his left leg with my right hand as I sit back, keeping his hip against my chest by continuing to hug with my left arm. If I create space between my chest and his body, the sweep will fail.

4

When Lance lands on his back, I can finish the sankaku. As I squeeze my legs, I grip his right elbow with my right hand and pull his triceps down into his neck. While continuing to hug his waist, I thrust my hips to increase the power of the choke and to apply spine lock pressure.

SANKAKU JUDO STYLE: *VARIATION 2*

If your opponent's base is strong, you may not be able to sweep him with the previous technique. The classic sankaku still requires you to sweep your opponent, but rather than pulling him over, you throw your body over his back to generate momentum, creating a much more powerful sweep. I prefer to use the first variation because it requires less movement to execute, lessening the likelihood of my opponent escaping, but this technique is still useful and effective and should be your second option. When you do use this technique, be aware of your positioning. Maintain the squeeze of your legs and keep everything tight. If you have locked the sankaku, you are very close to finishing the fight. Don't lose the submission by executing a sloppy sweep.

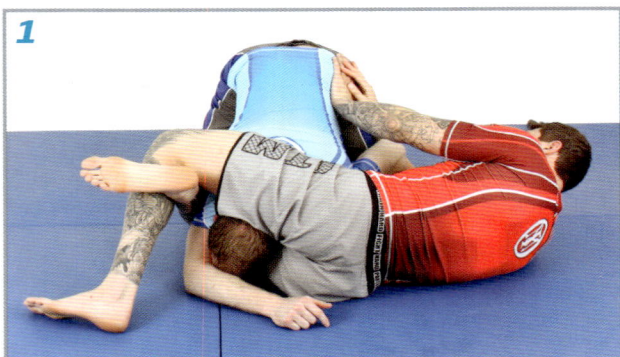

I have Lance locked in the traditional sankaku position. Both of my hands press against his left hip to prevent him from stepping over my body and escaping.

I sit up on to my right elbow, pressing my chest against Lance's left side.

My left arm wraps around Lance's midsection as I come up to my knees.

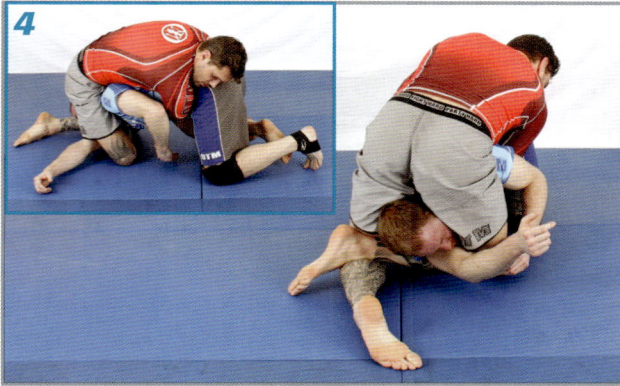

With the sankaku still locked, I snake my right arm between Lance's legs and cup his right ankle with my palm facing upward. At the same time, I shoot my left arm to the outside of his right leg and latch on to the upper portion of his right shin with my left hand.

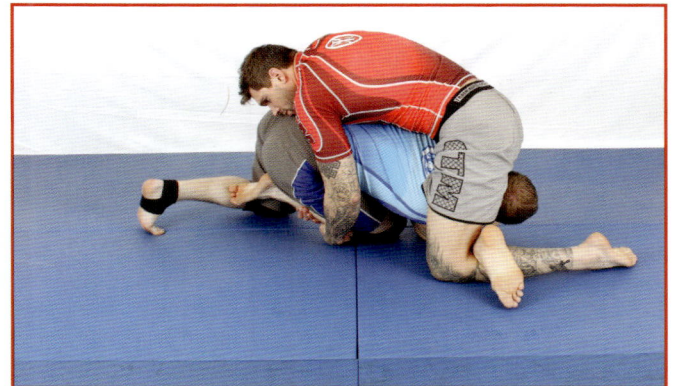

To execute the sweep, I yank Lance's right ankle toward his groin as I shove his left leg under his stomach with my left hand. I then begin to fall to my left as his base on that side weakens.

Lance lands on his back.

I swim my right arm back, trapping Lance's left arm in my right armpit as I grip his right triceps. At the same time, I hug his right hip with my left arm. To finish the choke, I squeeze my legs, thrust my hips forward, and pull on his right arm, applying a sankaku choke with spine-lock pressure.

SANKAKU JUDO STYLE: VARIATION 3

In the previous techniques, I rolled my opponent out of the turtle position to finish the sankaku, but I do not necessarily have to execute a roll to force my opponent to tap. I can finish my opponent from the turtle position with a combination of a choke and spine lock. If you are struggling to force the roll, transitioning to this finishing option will either win you the fight or put your opponent in such immense pain that he will want you to roll him. When he fights to escape the turtle position, you can easily transition to the classic sankaku finish. I recommend looking for a sweep first because the traditional sankaku is more powerful when you are on your side and your opponent is on his back. From the turtle position, your opponent can move to relieve the pressure and hide his arm from the finish, so I tend to go for the sweep (but only if I can get to my knees because I do not want to waste my energy attacking with a low percentage submission). However, if your opponent is forcing you to use it, crank away.

I am in the traditional sankaku position and am pressing against Lance's left hip with both of my hands to prevent him from step-ping over my chest to escape.

I sit up onto my right elbow and drape my left arm over Lance's back, hugging my chest to his back.

I post on my right hand and come up to my knees, immediately locking my hands together against Lance's stomach to bring my chest in line with his spine.

Since my previous attempts to sweep Lance have failed, I stay on my knees. My right hand reaches around his left hip and grabs his left ankle. I push his left ankle toward his groin as I thread my left hand between his legs.

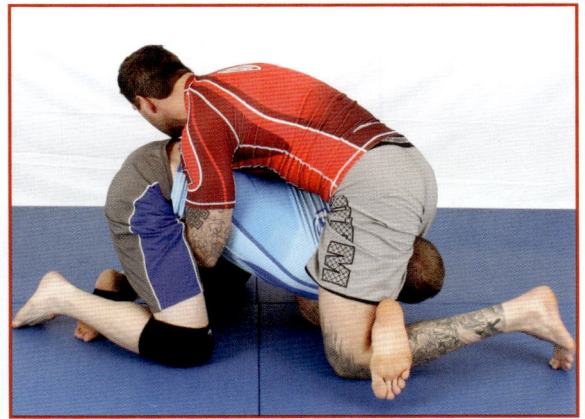

I grab Lance's left ankle with my left hand and reach behind me to grip his left wrist with my right hand.

To finish the sankaku, I pull on Lance's right wrist as though I were starting a lawn mower as I squeeze my legs and thrust my hips into his upper back. He will tap from the pain and the choke.

SANKAKU JUDO STYLE: *VARIATION 4*

The previous techniques assume that your legs are locked in a tight figure-four, putting you in an excellent position to get the choke. If you are having trouble locking the figure-four, whether your opponent is too large or he is defending the choke, you need to transition to an effective spine lock if you want to finish the fight. Since you have lost the strangle, you will use your leg position to control your opponent's movement as you isolate one of his legs and roll. After the roll, you pull on the leg and thrust your hips to hyperextend your opponent's back. This spine lock is actually easier to apply than the previous spine locks because you have two hands on your opponent's leg, but the drawback is that you have lost the choke. If you miss the spine lock here, you are out of attack opportunities, so only transition to this spine lock if you are sure that you are not going to get the choke.

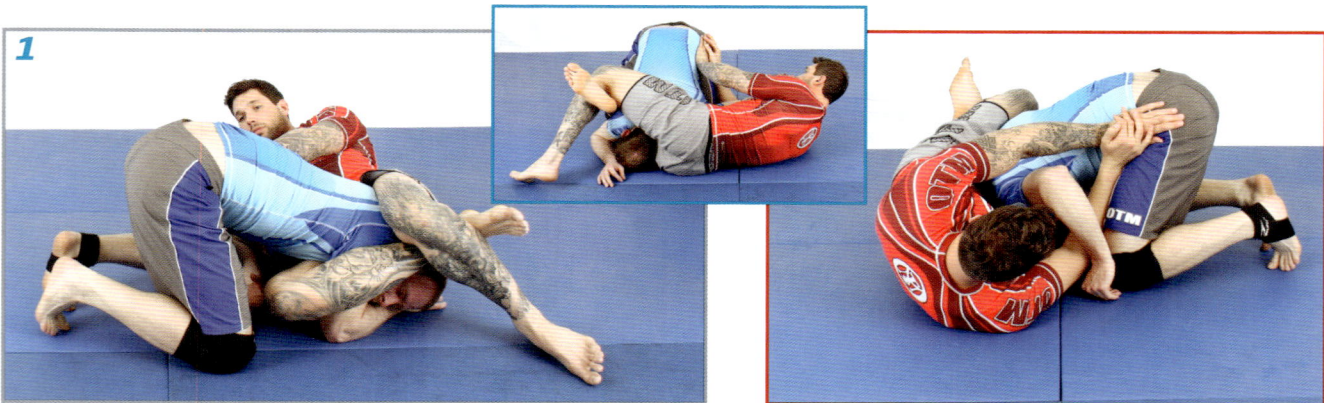

I have Lance locked in the traditional sankaku position. I press on his hips to prevent him from swinging his legs over my body to escape.

I sit up on my right elbow and place my left hand on his lower back to give me some control over his hips.

I hug Lance's waist with my left arm and come up to my knees.

4

I press my chest into Lance's lower back and latch on to his right ankle with both of my hands. It's important that I grab the same side ankle as my opponent's trapped arm.

5

With my two-on-one grip, I pull Lance's right ankle toward my chest.

6

Keeping a tight grip on Lance's ankle and pressing my chest to his back, I fall to my right. It's important to note that I am falling toward the leg that I am not controlling. I do not want to fall on top of the leg that I am controlling because I will not have enough leverage to finish the spine lock.

7

Lance lands on his left side, and I continue to control his right ankle with both hands.

8

While still locking my legs, I pull Lance's right ankle toward my chest and begin to thrust my hips to bring his right knee closer to my body.

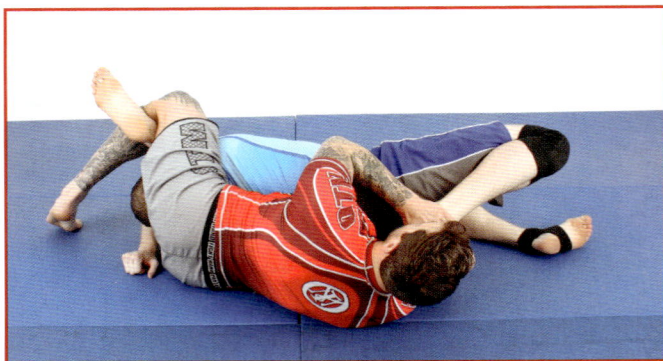

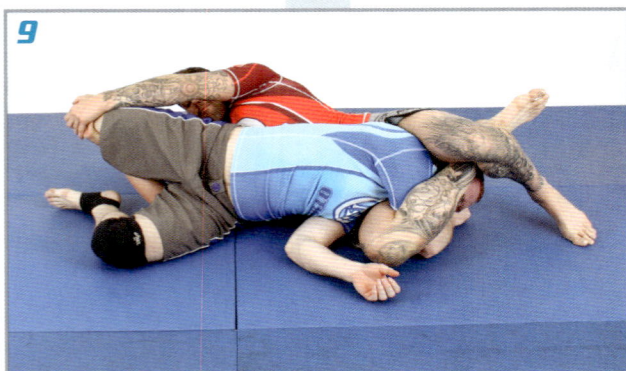

9

Moving one hand at a time, I transfer my two-on-one grip from Lance's right ankle to his right knee.

10

To finish the spine lock, I thrust my hips, straighten my back, and pull Lance's right leg into my chest. He will tap from the excruciating pain.

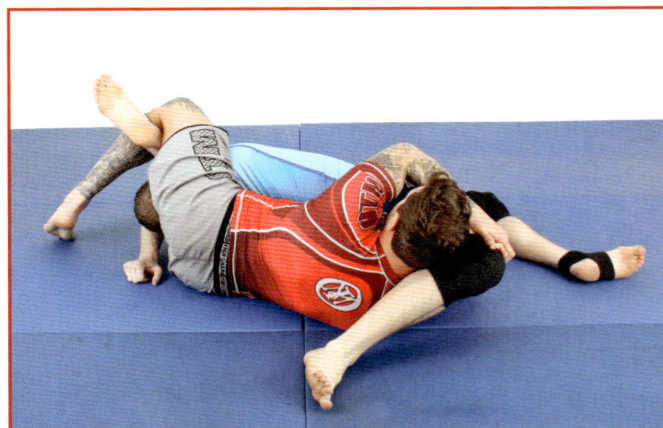

CHAPTER TWO

BODY POSITION AND 45 DEGREE INTRODUCTION

Grappling is a perpetual problem-solving process. You are always trying to determine the best response for your opponent's defenses, taking into account his positioning, his movement, and his intentions. Every position can be beaten, but every position cannot be beaten in the same way. One triangle setup may work flawlessly if your opponent is chest to chest with you, pinning your shoulders to the mat, but that same setup may get your guard passed if you try it when he is sitting back on his heels. Different tools are designed for different situations. The strongest hammer in the world will not solve a problem that requires a screwdriver.

My system addresses the range of positions you are likely to encounter when working from your back and teaches you the fundamental strengths and weaknesses of each position. I then teach you the best methods for controlling your opponent from each position and how to achieve the triangle using each control. I have designed my system in such a way that you will always choose the

best tool for the job, increasing the efficiency of your game and improving your finish percentage.

This book is organized as though it were capturing one seamless match so that you can see how each position connects to the next and you can understand how you may need to flow from option to option as your opponent defends. Your opponent could, of course, skip from one position to another without using the position in between. That is the nature of grappling. As long as you can recognize your opponent's position you can immediately apply the best method of control and begin looking for a submission, no matter how he got there. As you begin to use this system, you are likely to see opportunities for other submissions as you familiarize yourself with each control system. Those submissions are just as viable as the triangle, and I plan to cover the wide range of possibilities for each control position in later books, but feel free to begin exploring and experimenting.

MELANSON'S LAW

Before we delve into each position in great detail, familiarize yourself with the general qualities of each body position and what controls I advocate using for each of those positions. This is also a great quick-reference tool for identifying the positions that may be giving you the most problems at the gym, making it easy to for you to address the issue with the most effective techniques. The following are the five most common positions your opponent will assume while inside of your guard:

MELANSON'S LAW: OPPONENT'S BODY POSITION

45 Degrees:
double-wrist control, cross grip, double biceps ride, corner lock, collar tie

0 Degrees:
irish collar, overhook, shoulder pin, under-hook shoulder pin, rubber guard, the cuff

90 degrees (Sitting on Heels):
sit-up guard (with double wrist-lock grip, headlock grip, or octopus guard)

Forward Lean:
side scissor

Hips Forward:
k-control (with mirror grip, head control, or cross grip)

Those are the main positions you will be working against when fighting from your back. Though I will cover the butterfly guard and half guard later in the book, the positions listed above make up the bulk of the system, so we will spend the majority of the book mastering the attacks from those positions. I will walk you through the details of each control position and each setup, so even if what I am teaching is completely new to you, incorporating my system into your game will be painless.

THREE DIRECTIONS OF MOVEMENT AND LEG AND FOOT CONTROL

When defending against a triangle attack, your opponent can move in any one of three directions to stifle your offense. First, your opponent can move forward, stacking his head towards your head. This increases the distance between your hips and his neck. Without an extreme amount of flexibility, it's very difficult to raise your legs high enough to triangle a stacked opponent. Second, if your opponent postures up, he does the same thing. By elevating his head, he increases distance between your hips and his neck. Also by moving it up, he uses gravity against you, making it very difficult to raise your hips high enough to secure his head and arm in your leg triangle. Finally, your opponent can back out of your guard as you attack with triangle chokes. Although he may be within range of your triangle attacks, by backing out he puts himself in a position that makes it difficult to lock your hamstring around his neck and apply pressure to his carotid arteries.

    The solution to controlling all three of these directions of movement is proper leg and foot control. When you're not wearing a gi, leg and foot control is vital when using the open guard for controlling his three directions of movement and stifling his common defensive measures. Standard leg and foot control consists of placing one foot on your opponent's hip to stop his forward movement, the other leg curled over his back to stop him from backing out, and a secure collar tie on his head to prevent him from posturing up.

    Although there's no sure way to stop your opponent from either stacking, posturing, or backing out of your guard, leg and foot control is a great tool to slow down your opponent's departure long enough to allow you to clear one of his arms and slap on a triangle choke. Strong leg and foot control is critical to the success of my guard system.

Proper Leg and Foot Control

Stack Prevented

I'm utilizing proper leg and foot control by placing my right hand on the back of my opponent's head, my right foot on his left hip, and my left leg curled down on his back. As my opponent tries to stack, my right foot prevents him from driving forward.

No Leg and Foot Control

Opponent Stacking

With no leg and foot control, my opponent drives his head towards my head the moment he feels me pin his wrist to attempt a triangle. This increases the distance between his neck and my hips, making it impossible to secure a triangle choke.

Proper Leg and Foot Control

Back Out Prevented

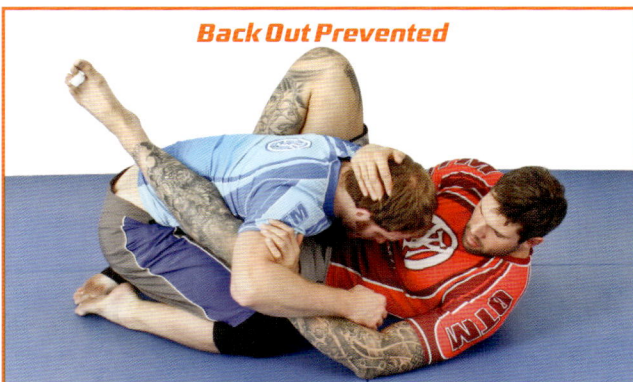

I'm utilizing proper leg and foot control by placing my right hand on the back of my opponent's head, my right foot on his left hip, and my left leg curled down on his back. As my opponent attempts to back out, my left leg will prevent him from ducking out of my guard.

No Leg and Foot Control

Opponent Backing Out

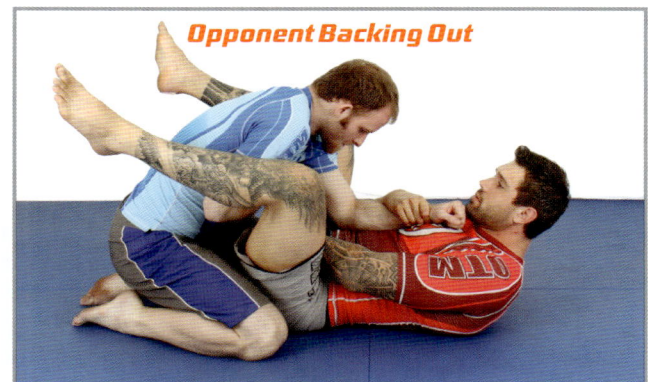

With no leg and foot control, my opponent backs out the moment I attempt to feed his wrist through for a triangle choke. As he ducks out, his neck disappears, making it very difficult for me to lock on a clean triangle choke.

Proper Leg and Foot Control

Posture Prevented

I'm utilizing proper leg and foot control by placing my right hand on the back of my opponent's head, my right foot on his left hip, and my left leg curled down on his back. As my opponent attempts to posture out, my right hand gripped firmly on the crown of his skull keeps his head down, preventing him from elevating his torso.

No Leg and Foot Control

Opponent Posturing

With no collar grip, my opponent immediately rips his head upwards as I try to pin his wrist for a triangle, sufficiently increasing his elevation to the point where I can no longer reach his neck with my legs.

OFFLINE CONCEPT

Leg and foot control is necessary to controlling your opponent's movement without a gi. By placing your foot on his hip and curling your other leg tightly around his back, you can control his movement long enough to isolate a limb and attack with triangle chokes. However, leg and foot control can be difficult to secure. Although the concept is simple, in a real fight, your opponent will be fighting to stay centered inside of your guard. Any attempt to place your feet on his hips will be encountered with serious resistance. Without the proper positioning, securing and retaining leg and foot control is exceedingly difficult.

By shifting offline from your opponent you can give yourself the space you need to plant your foot firmly on his hip, while curling your opposite leg into his back. This is the offline concept. By angling your body to the side of your opponent, and shifting onto your hip, you give yourself the best control options and puts your opponent in a mechanically weak position. To have the best chance of succeeding with your leg and foot control, you need to understand how to move offline from your opponent and how that lets you control his body more efficiently.

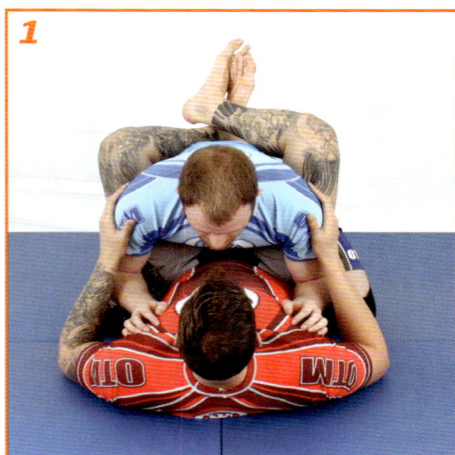

1) I have Lance trapped in my full guard. I'm flat on my back, and I'm eye to eye with my opponent. Because my opponent and I are in a neutral position, it will be difficult for me to secure leg and foot control. 2) I plant my right foot and shift onto my left hip. I'm now on my hip instead of my back, and I'm off-line with my opponent. Instead of being eye to eye with Lance, he's now looking at the mat instead. This gives me the space I need to throw my right foot onto his hip and curl my left leg over his back.

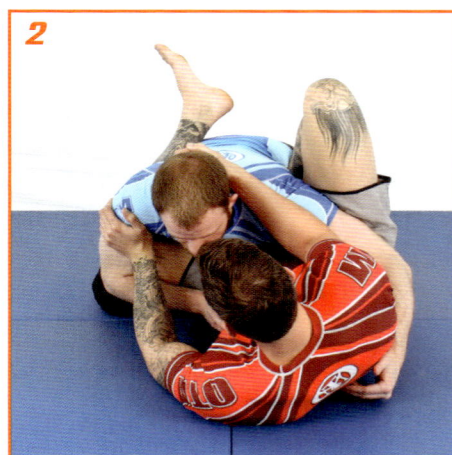

Eye to Eye

Offline

THE 45 DEGREES POSITION OR THE OPTIMAL SUBMISSION ZONE

The easiest position to submit your opponent from is the 45 degrees position. He is hovering over you, not so close that he is stifling your movement and not so far that he is difficult to reach with your arms and legs. Many fighters linger in this position to throw strikes and consequently get caught with a quick submission from the bottom. If you are in the guard, you should never allow yourself to be in this position. If you are playing guard, be thankful that your opponent has made such a huge mistake and get to work nailing him with submissions. The 45 degrees position is optimal for submissions from the guard.

Though I cover a variety of control positions for the 45 degrees position, my favorite method is the collar tie. Control options like double-wrist control, the cross grip, and the double biceps ride are great if you are dominating the hand fight, but they probably will not be your best option if your opponent is aggressive and has a similar skill level to you. Learning those options is important to rounding out your game and expanding your arsenal, but mastering the collar tie will give you more control and your guard more versatility.

The collar tie allows you to control your opponent's posture; create and kill space; and isolate an arm. All this done by gripping the back of his head with one hand and driving that same-side forearm into his collar bone. The push-and-pull strength that the collar tie provides is powerful and great to have if you are on the bottom because you can use it to keep your opponent lower in your guard. This is ideal for triangles because your legs have less distance to travel when his upper body is closer to your hips. Having multiple options and that much control is disruptive for your opponent's thinking process. If you can achieve the collar tie at the 45 degrees position, your opponent should be in trouble.

cross-grip control

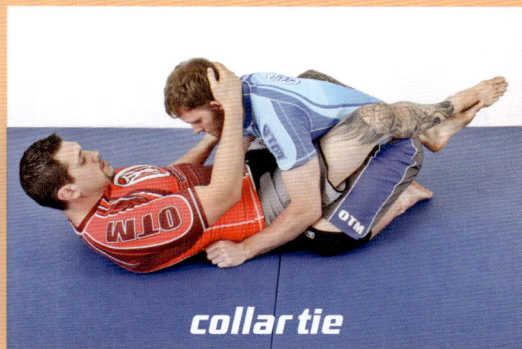

collar tie

double-wrist control

45 degrees position

corner lock

double-biceps ride

STRAIGHT SHOT

The double-wrist straight shot is the classic judo or Brazilian jiu-jitsu setup for the triangle. If you are in the gi and can control your opponent's sleeve, your level of control may be strong enough that you can move his arms into position and force this technique. In submission grappling, you must be dominating the hand fight entirely for this technique to work. As you will notice in the photographs below, I control one of my opponent's wrists with a downward grip (holding the wrist with my pinky finger positioned closest to my opponent's hand) and his other wrist with an upward grip (holding the wrist with my thumb positioned closest to my opponent's hand). In this case, using two different grips optimizes my control. While out-gripping someone to this degree may be somewhat unrealistic if the opponent is ripping or exploding free, the straight shot is an effective attack if the opponent is lingering in the 45 degrees position or moving through the 45 degrees position, driving into you. When applied correctly, the result is a clean, tight finish, but as I said in the introduction, the real trick to making a technique effective is not knowing how to apply it correctly, but knowing when and why to apply it. If you have the opportunity to apply this triangle, take it right away, but if you feel like you do not have enough control to safely execute the technique without losing your position, transition to the leg walk up, which is the next technique.

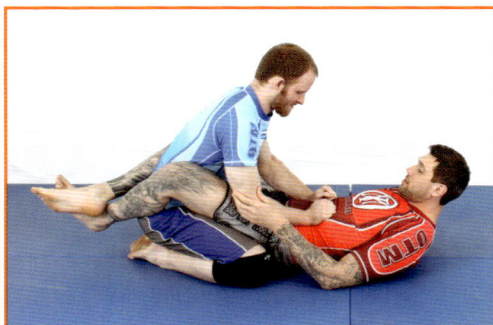

Lance is hovering over me, lingering in the 45 degrees position.

I latch on to Lance's left hand with an upward grip (my thumb closest to his hand, not my pinky) and begin to pummel my left hand under his right arm.

As my left hand circles outward, pushing Lance's right biceps away from his body, I slip my left leg inside, posting my left foot on his right hip as I position my left knee against the right side of his chest. As my left leg moves into place, I begin to create tension on his right arm by driving my left shin into his biceps as I pull his left arm toward my chest.

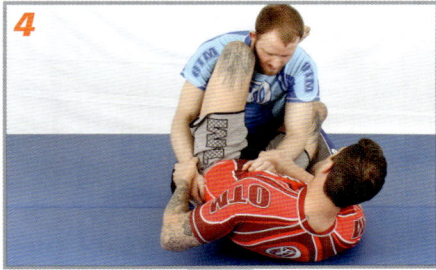

I move off line by shifting onto my right hip. As my hips move, my left hand slides down Lance's right arm and latches on to his right wrist with a downward grip (my pinky closest to his hand, not my thumb), pinning his wrist against my hip. To delay his backward movement, I curl my right leg into his back and use my right hand to pin his left hand to my chest.

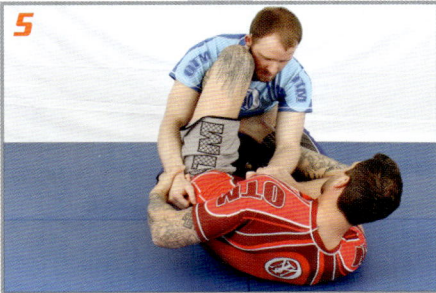

I maneuver my right foot on to Lance's left hip to begin setting up the triangle. I am still dominating the hand fight with double-wrist control. If I need to create more space, I can use this position to scoot my hips my way.

To clear Lance's arm, I use my downward grip to twist his right wrist counterclockwise, forcing his right elbow to flair out. When his right arm nears a 90 degree angle, I maneuver my left foot to the front of his shoulder and begin to press away. At the same time, my right foot pushes into Lance's left hip to help control his posture by keeping him bent over.

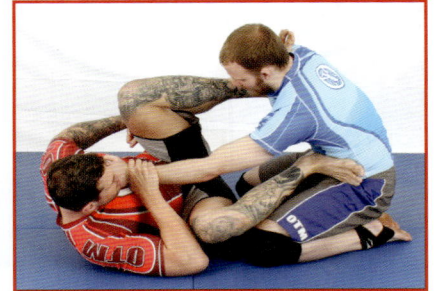

Lance reacts to the pressure against his shoulder by driving into me. When he does that, I spring my hips into the air, kicking my left leg across the back of his neck. To bring him into me, I pull both of his wrists to my left as my left heel drives into the mat to further collapse his posture. It's important to notice that his left arm is now across my body, the ideal position for the traditional triangle, and my right foot is still on his hip, reducing his ability to explode out as my left leg transitions.

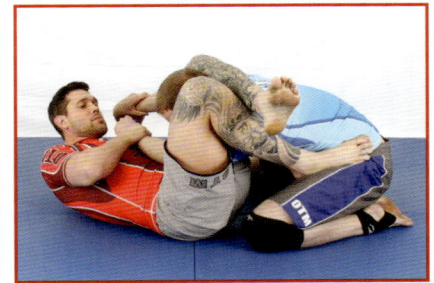

I lock my left ankle in the crook of my right knee and finish the traditional triangle.

HORSE KICK

In the straight shot and the leg walk-up, you attack under the assumption that your opponent is more or less maintaining the 45 degrees position. For the horse kick to work, your opponent needs to be driving into you as though he were trying to transition out of the 45 degrees position into the 0 degrees position. If he is not making that transition on his own, you can generate that forward motion by pushing him back to encourage him to resist and drive back into you, but I do not recommend that because you risk losing the 45 degrees position, which, as I said before, is optimal for submissions. When your opponent does drive into you, the horse kick will land you a clean tight triangle. It's powerful, effective, and violent. When I saw Baret Yoshida using a triangle setup similar to this, his hamstring made a distinct slapping noise when he slammed it against his opponent's neck because he elevated his hips and tricked his opponent into committing to a stronger drive. Once I figured out the mechanics of the move, it became one of my favorite attacks and a regular part of my arsenal. There's something about the sound of a triangle slapping on an opponent that is deeply satisfying.

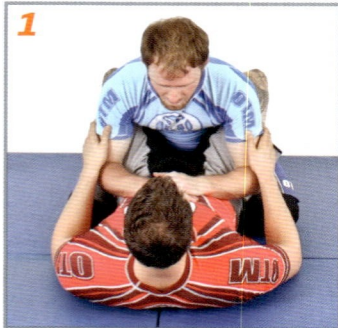

Lance is in my guard and is maintaining the 45 degrees position.

I pummel both of my arms inside of Lance's arms and control his biceps.

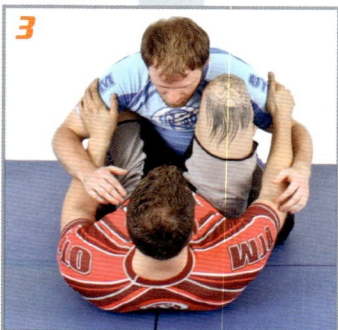

I press on Lance's left biceps with my right hand, circling it to the outside, and slide my right knee inside, posting my right foot on his left hip.

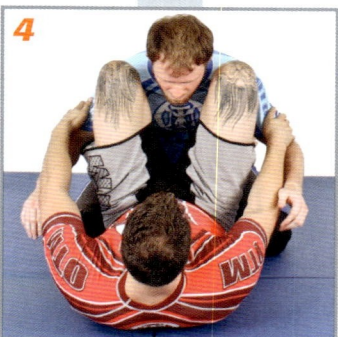

I repeat the previous step on my left side, forcing Lance's right arm to the outside with my left hand, creating enough space to slide my left knee in between us as I post my left foot on his right hip.

5

I slide my hands down Lance's arms and latch on to his wrists. I use upward grips and pin his wrists to my thighs.

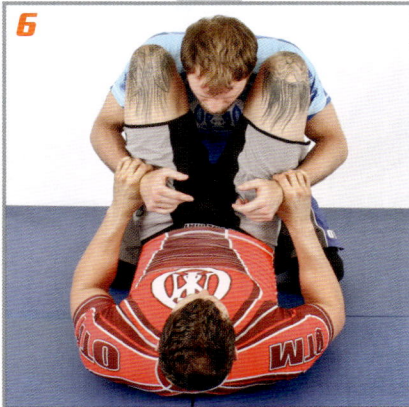

6

Lance suspects that I am setting up an attack, so he begins to drive into me in an attempt to eliminate space.

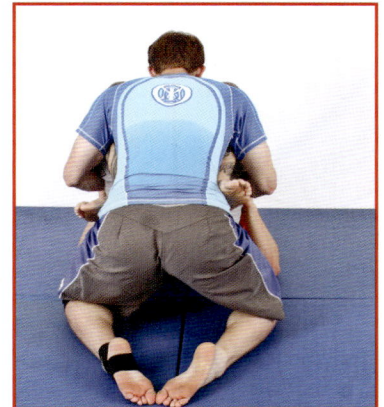

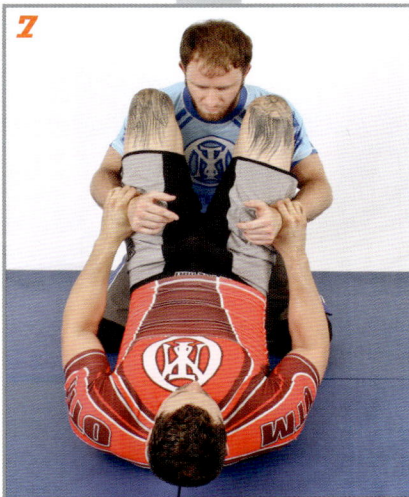

7

I bridge my hips to push Lance away, which encourages him to drive into me even harder.

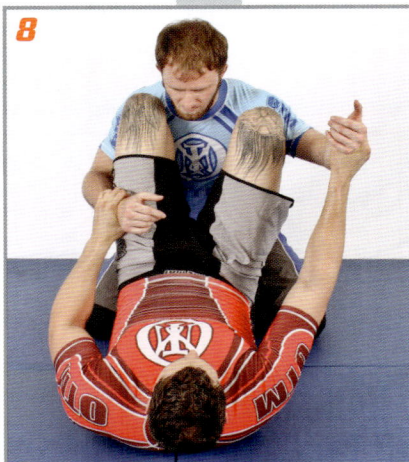

8

I twist Lance's left wrist with my right hand and press it up and to my right, forcing it away from his body.

9

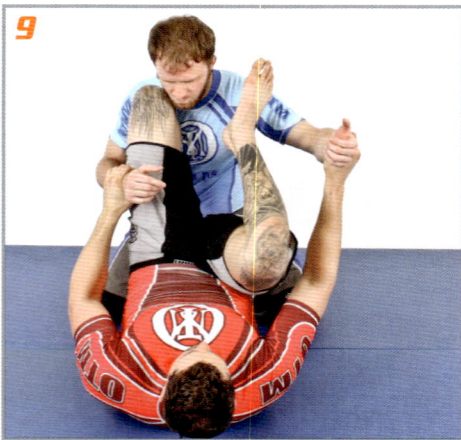

I quickly feed my right foot underneath Lance's left arm.

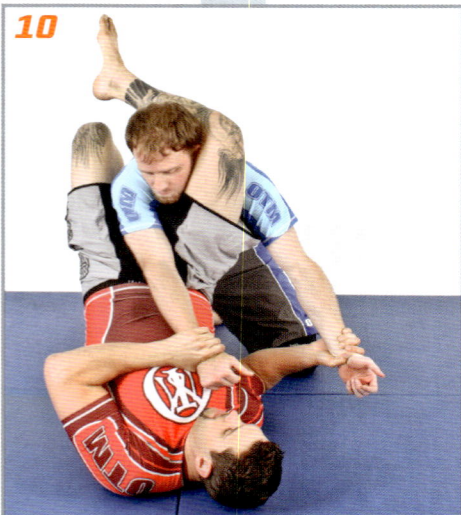

10

While keeping my left foot posted on Lance's hip, I slip my left knee to the outside of his right arm and pull his right arm across my body with my left hand. When my left knee moves to the outside, the tension holding him back disappears, and he falls forward. As he falls, I press off of his hip with my left foot, elevating my hips toward his neck as my right foot kicks across the back of his neck. If you do this correctly, your right hamstring will slap against his neck.

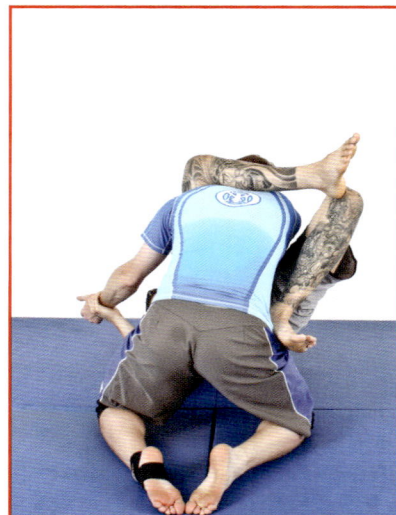

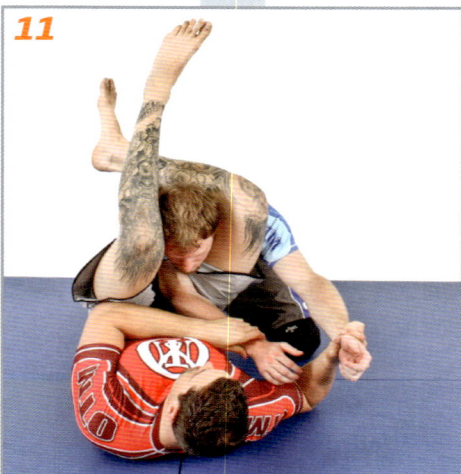

11

I curl my right heel toward my butt and pull my knees toward my chest to collapse Lance's posture. I extend my left leg to begin locking the figure-four.

12

I figure-four my legs and pull on Lance's head with both hands to finish the choke.

DOUBLE-WRIST CONTROL PUSH/PULL WRIST PIN

The biggest problem with using double-wrist control to set up triangles is that every grappler knows exactly what you want to do the moment you control the wrists. Even if your straight shot and horse kick triangles are smooth and tight, your opponent can bury his elbows and shut down your attacks as soon as you begin to move. Do not let this frustrate you, instead, use your opponent's hypersensitivity as misdirection. Pull on one of his arms and push on the other as though you were going for the triangle. His instinct will be to resist your movement and do the opposite to counteract it. If you push, he will push back. If you pull, he will pull back. When he pushes back, yank the arm away, using his energy against him. When he pulls his arm toward him, push it, driving his wrist to his stomach. To be effective, you have to do this combination of movements quickly and with force. You can even exaggerate the technique by pumping your arms back and forth repeatedly before actually attempting the push/pull wrist pin. If you do that, it will look pretty goofy, but it works, which is what matters.

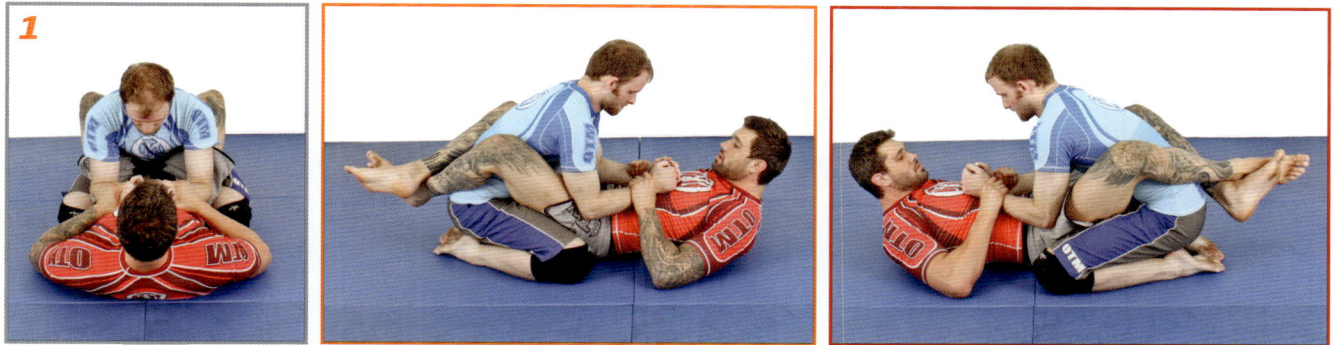

Lance is in my guard at the 45 degrees position, and I am controlling both of his wrists with upward grips.

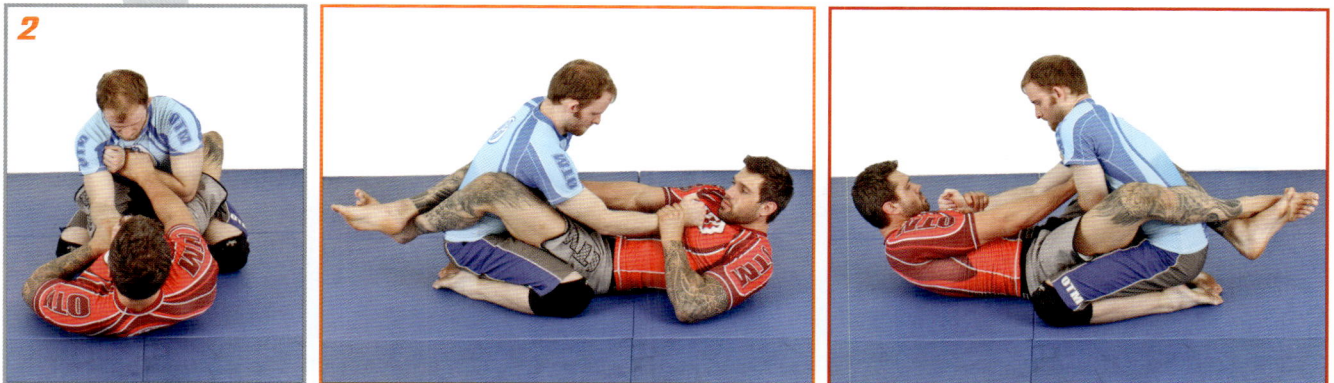

I jam Lance's left arm into his chest with my right hand and yank on his right arm with my left hand.

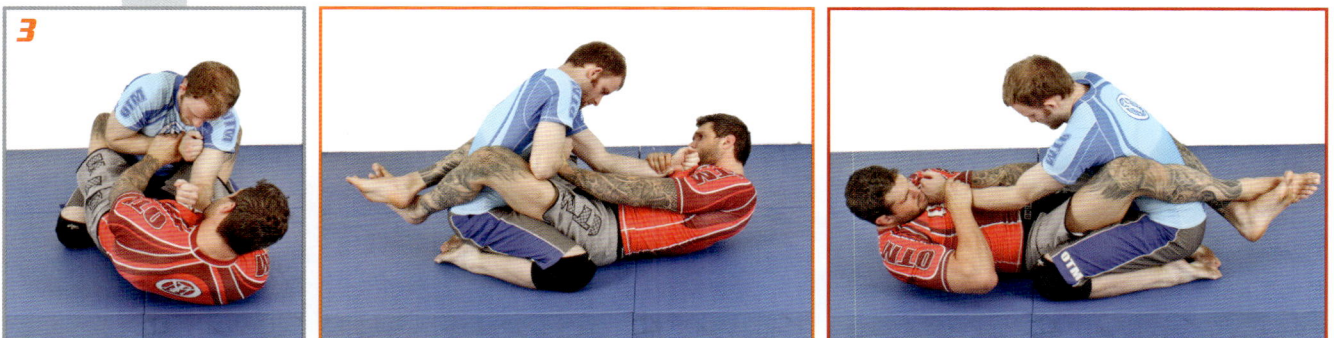

Lance assumes that I am attempting a basic wrist pin triangle. To defend, he pushes his left arm away from his body as he retracts his right arm. I quickly reverse directions. I pull his left arm with my right hand and push his right arm with my left hand, using his own movement to execute a wrist pin. As I do this, I shift onto my right hip and pin his left arm against my chest.

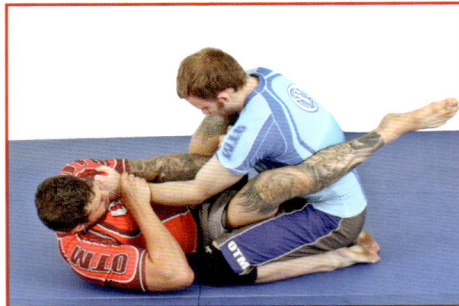

Since Lance's immediate reaction to a hip pop will be to posture out, I maintain control of his wrists and roll my left knee over his right arm to more securely pin it to his chest.

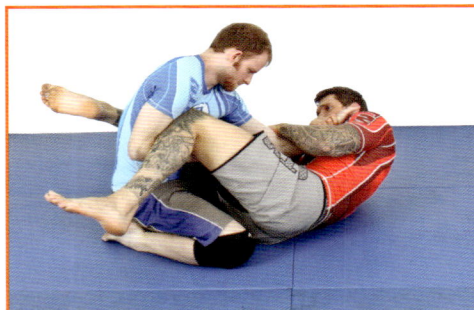

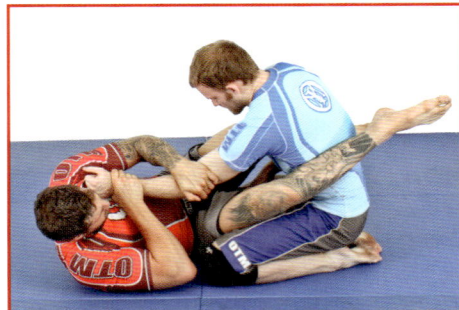

I reach across my body and cup Lance's left elbow with my right hand, establishing a two-on-one grip to compensate for the leverage I lose by not having a foot on his hip.

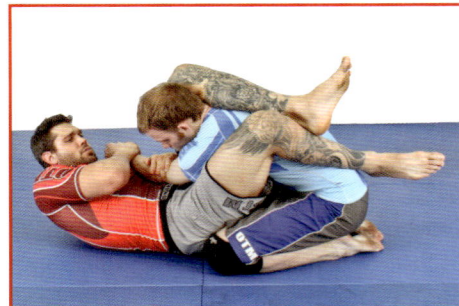

I drag Lance's right arm across my body as I elevate my hips and circle my left leg over his back and across the back of his neck, pulling him into a triangle.

I figure-four my legs and use both hands to finish the traditional triangle.

CROSS GRIP TWO-ON-ONE TRIANGLE

In the gi, sleeves and lapels provide an incredible amount of control. The cross grip two-on-one triangle is very similar to a classic gi-based triangle, but I realize that basic wrist controls will not be enough to control my opponent, so I use a two-on-one cross grip to succeed where double-wrist control may fail. As you will see in the photographs below, the two-on-one cross grip I use in this technique is similar to an arm drag, which is a powerful technique on its own. I use that leverage to control my opponent and establish a threat. He does not want me to take his back, so he is forced to defend that option as I work for the triangle, dividing his attention between two fronts. Although there is a lot of space between you and your opponent, the two-on-one will lock him in place and force him to overextend himself as he tries to defend, giving you the opening to swoop in for the triangle.

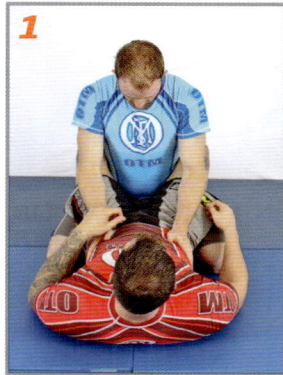

Lance is in my guard.

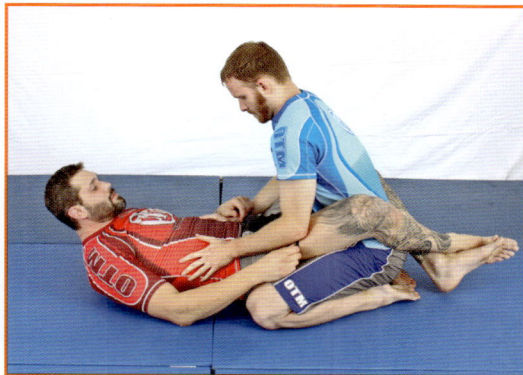

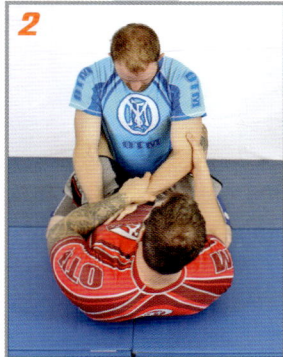

My left hand latches on to Lance's left wrist, establishing a downward grip. My right hand grips his left elbow.

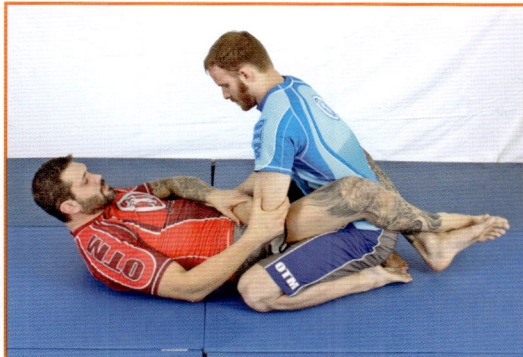

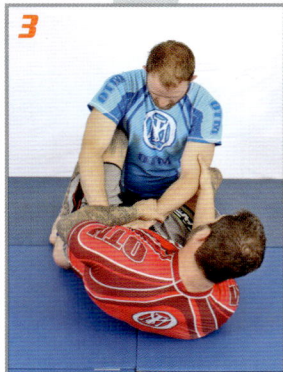

I post my left foot on the mat and shift off-line on to my right hip.

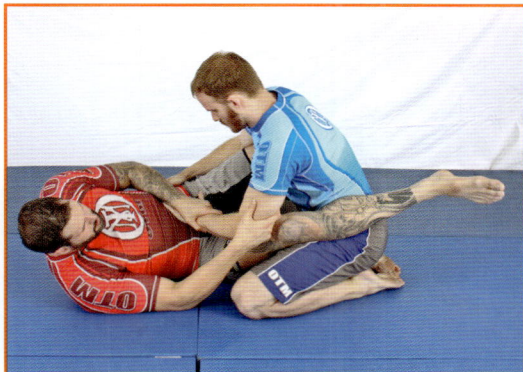

4

I dig my right foot into Lance's left hip, which is key for maintaining control over his body.

5

I straighten my right leg to scoot my hips away from Lance. As my hips create space, I pull on his arm, forcing his upper body to fold over my right foot that is planted securely in his hip. If he doesn't bend, I cannot finish this technique.

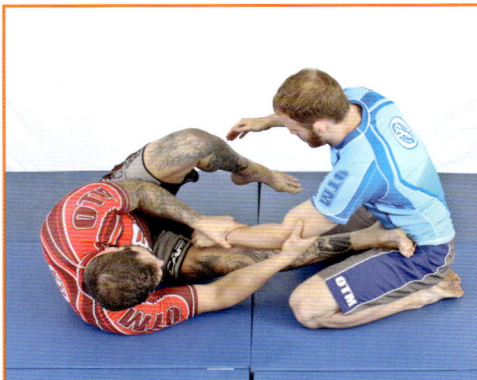

6

As I begin to maneuver my left leg, Lance senses that he is in danger and grabs my left ankle to control my leg.

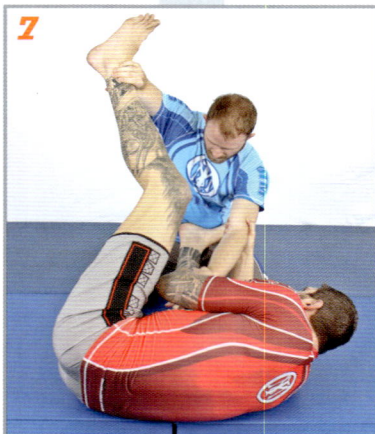

7

I kick my left leg to the sky to extend Lance's right arm.

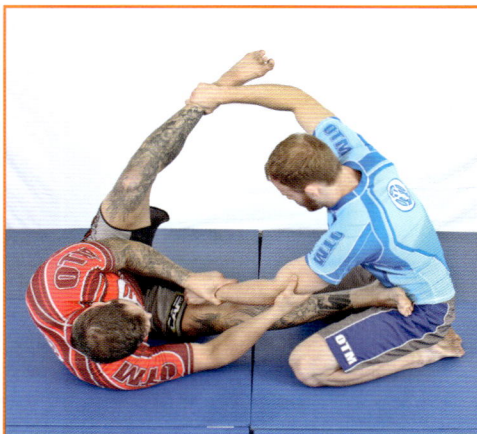

My left foot quickly circles inside of Lance's right arm.

I dig my left foot into Lance's right biceps and push his arm back by extending my left leg.

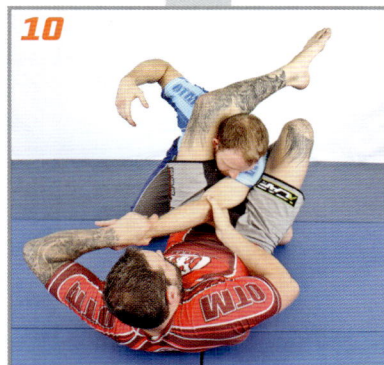

As I push with my left foot, I let it slip off of Lance's right biceps as I elevate my hips toward his neck and pull Lance's left arm across my body as hard as I can. It's important to note that I curl my right leg toward my butt to scoot my hips forward as I pull him into the triangle, eliminating the space between us more efficiently.

I lock my legs for the triangle and finish with an armbar triangle.

HELICOPTER TRIANGLE

In the previous technique, I used a two-on-one cross grip to create space and bait my opponent into a triangle, but as I create space for the cross grip triangle, my opponent could begin to counter. A leg-lock player, for example, may instinctively wrap his arm around my calf, potentially using my triangle attempt as a setup for a leg attack. When my opponent does this to defend the triangle, he may feel as though his grip gives him the advantage, but he is actually giving me his hand. I maintain my original cross grip and reach across with my other hand to grip the wrist of the arm wrapped around my ankle, putting me in perfect position to switch to a triangle on the opposite side. To swivel my hips into position, I need to execute a motion similar to a Granby roll, which is an advanced movement, but the payoff is that your opponent will be caught by surprise, and with both wrists controlled, he will have very few tools with which to defend. I originally saw Rigan Machado teach the helicopter triangle at a seminar, and he was using the gi, but I have had success with it in no-gi, especially if my opponent is wearing gloves.

Lance is hovering at the 45 degrees position.

I establish a cross grip by controlling Lance's left wrist with my right hand. I post my right hand on his left knee.

As I shift onto my right hip, I dig my right foot into Lance's left hip. If I need to create extra space to bring my right foot inside, I push off of his left knee with my right hand.

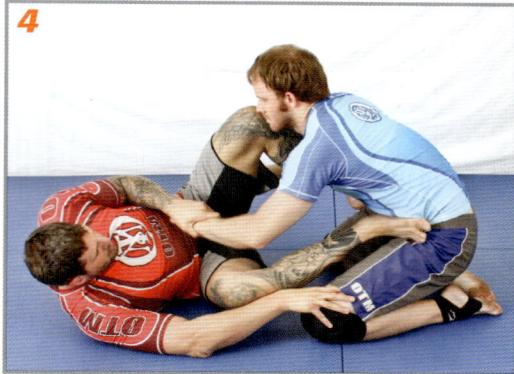

I slide my left knee under Lance's right arm and across his chest as I scoot my hips out.

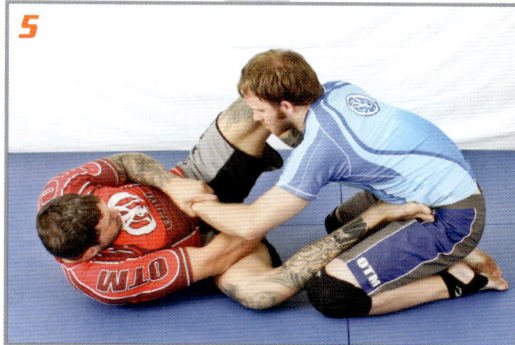

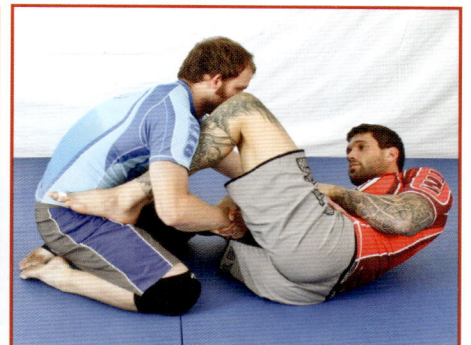

Lance wraps his right arm around my left calf to keep me from moving away and to potentially set up a leg lock. My right hand snakes under his left arm and latches on to his right wrist. I continue to maintain my cross grip.

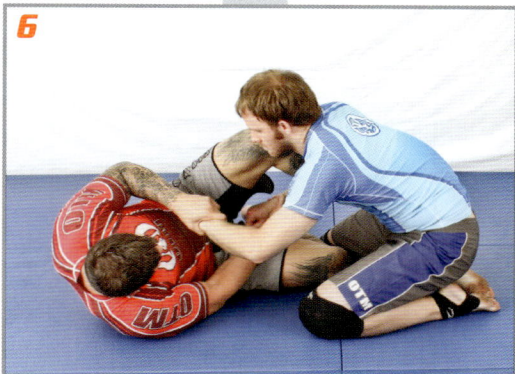

I maneuver my foot to the outside of Lance's right knee and dig the ball of my right foot into the mat.

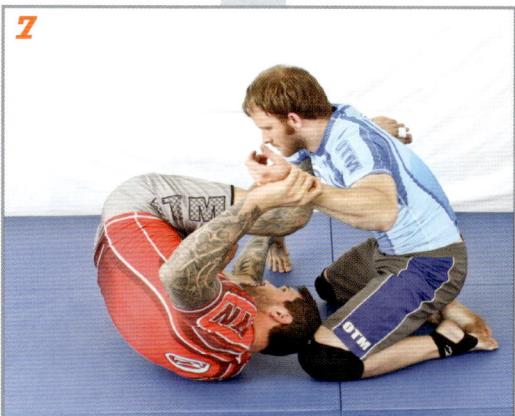

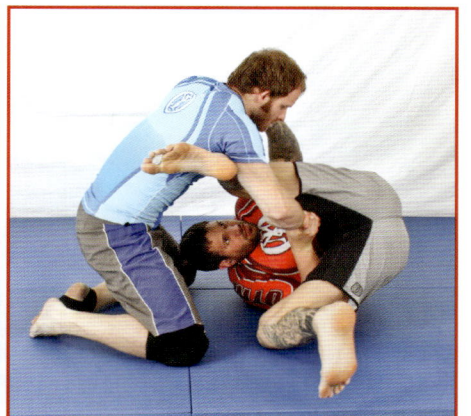

Pushing off of my right foot, I begin to roll over my right shoulder as I pull on both of Lance's wrist to help me roll and to confuse him.

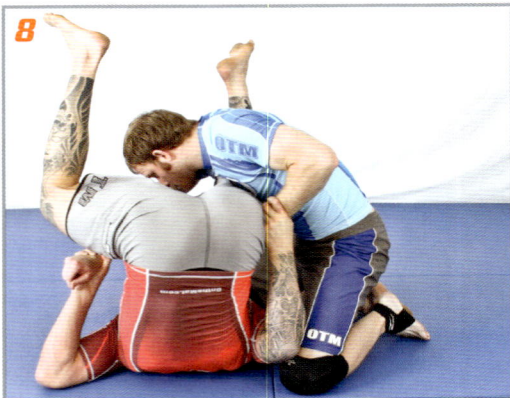

I continue to roll and begin to circle my hips as my body shifts directly underneath Lance's neck.

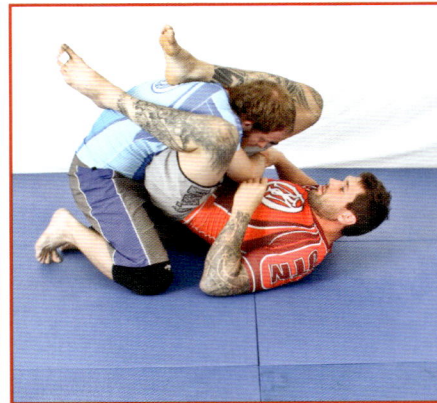

Now that I have rotated 360 degrees, I pin Lance's right arm across my body and release his left arm to begin locking the triangle.

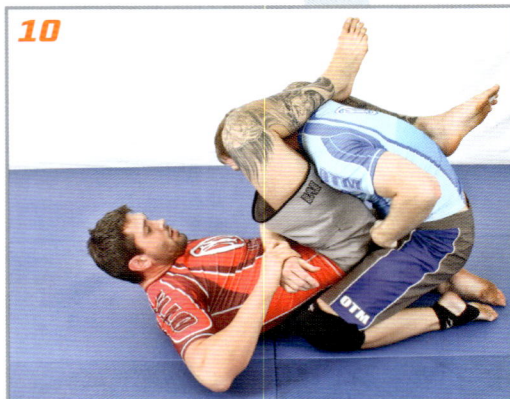

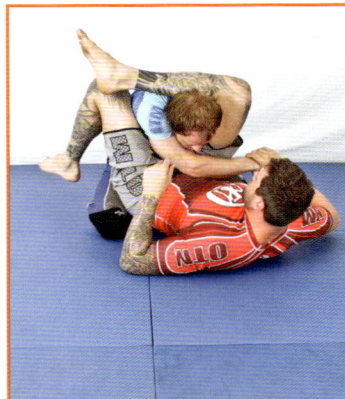

I throw my right leg across the back of Lance's neck, shifting my shoulders toward his left knee to create a strong angle for the triangle. As my right leg moves into position, my left knee pinches into his right shoulder to limit his movement.

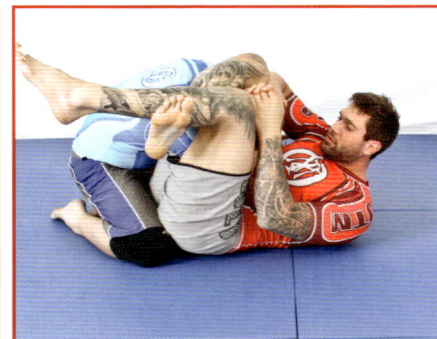

I lock my legs and use both hands to finish the traditional triangle.

DOUBLE BICEPS RIDE STRAIGHT SHOT

When you use double-wrist control or cross grip control, you are assuming that for the most part your opponent is maintaining the 45 degrees position and not trying to drive his weight on top of you. If your opponent is at the 45 degrees position and he is trying to grab your upper body and crowd you, switch to the double biceps ride, which is similar to Brazilian jiu-jitsu's spider guard. By bringing your knees inside, you can keep him in the optimal submission zone. Grip his triceps and pull with your arms, while driving your shins into his biceps at the same time to create tension on his arms from two different directions. That "tug of war" pressure is what will give you control over your opponent. The double biceps ride is not necessarily an ideal form of control because you are not controlling his hands or his head and have very little control over his backward movement. Fighters like Antonio Rodrigo Nogueira, however, have proven that it can be effective, especially in mixed martial arts, where fighters continue moving forward because they want to strike. I do not recommend lingering in this position, because your opponent will eventually realize that moving forward is a mistake. You need to begin attacking right away, and the straight shot is a great place to start. It is a quick leg-through triangle that will catch a lot of fighters off guard.

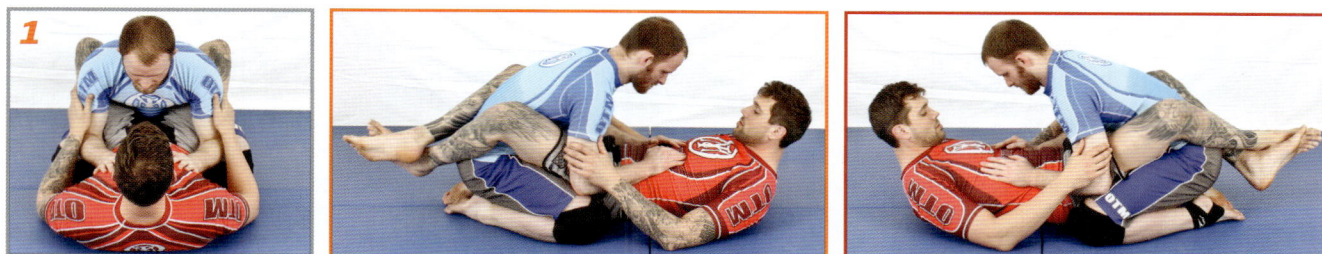

My double-wrist control and cross grip attacks have failed, and now Lance is beginning to realize that he is in the optimal submission zone. He begins to move forward.

I pummel both of my hands under Lance's forearms and to the inside, gripping his biceps.

With my right hand, I push Lance's left arm to the outside and slide my right knee in, positioning his left biceps on the middle of my right shin as my right foot posts on his left hip. To maintain complete control over Lance, my right hand never releases his arm. Instead, as my right leg moves into place, my right hand slides to his left triceps and pulls it into my shin as my shin drives forward, creating tension on the arm.

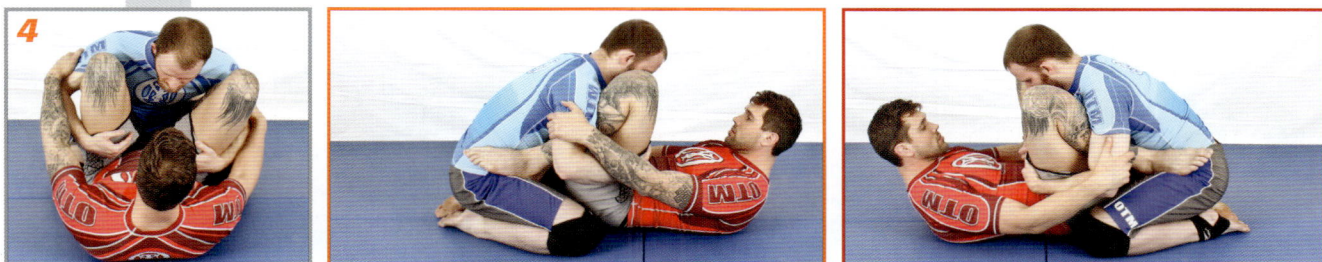

I repeat step three on my left side.

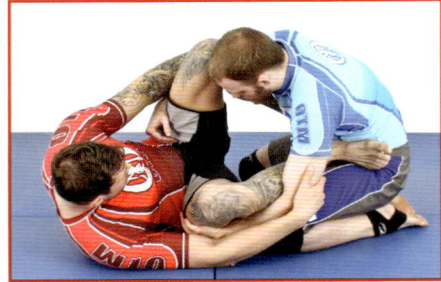

I shift onto my right hip by pressing my feet into Lance's hips. As I move off line in this step, it's important to note that I am moving backward only slightly. A little bit of space is okay, but too much space will ruin the mechanics of my attack.

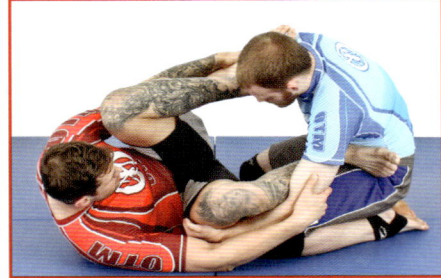

I pull my left knee to my chest, keeping it on the inside of Lance's right arm, and dig my left foot into his right shoulder. I begin to straighten my left leg, forcing his upper body back, encouraging him to drive back in to counter the pressure.

In one motion, I pop my hips forward and pull on both triceps. As my hips travel toward Lance's neck and he falls toward my guard, I slide my left leg off of his shoulder and curl it around the back of his neck. The pull on his triceps and the elevation of my hips pulls his left arm to the inside of my right leg, which is still posted on his left hip. My right knee pinches into his left shoulder.

Although you can potentially lock and finish the triangle in any way that you choose, I prefer to underhook Lance's right arm with my left arm and then lock my hands together to create a sharp angle as I pinch my legs together.

I figure-four my legs and finish the triangle.

DOUBLE BICEPS RIDE TO CROSS GRIP TWO-ON-ONE

I mentioned previously that the double biceps ride does not provide very much control in terms of your opponent's head and hands. When you drive your shins into his biceps and then attempt to transition to the straight shot triangle, he is likely to hug your legs because that is his easiest option. I've seen guard players get frustrated when their opponent hugs their legs because they feel smothered, but they fail to realize that their opponent is choosing to attach himself rather than explode out. By stalling the position in this way, your opponent is actually giving you time to establish additional controls. In this technique, you transition to a double biceps ride with a cross grip to set up the two-on-one triangle, which may have been impossible when you tried it from the cross grip alone because your opponent was moving forward. The overlap of controls—the double biceps ride combined with the two-on-one cross grip—gives you the leverage that you need to create space and clear your opponent's arm for the triangle. As you will see in the photographs below, I do not create as much space in this variation of the cross grip two-on-one triangle as I did in the cross grip section, and that's because my opponent is hugging my legs to counter the double biceps ride. That actually works to my advantage in this case because having his arm on the outside of my leg puts me in position for the biceps push. I do not need to bait my opponent into grabbing my ankle.

1

Lance is in the 45 degrees position, but I am concerned that he is going to posture out of the optimal submission zone.

2

To begin controlling his posture, I grip the base of his skull with my left hand and pull down as I pummel my right hand under his left forearm, shooting it through the inside of his arm to the base of skull.

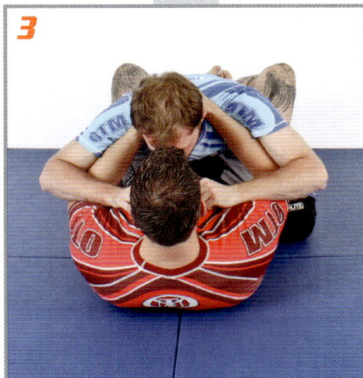

3

As my right hand delays Lance's ability to posture, I pummel my left hand under his right forearm and grip the base of his skull, establishing a double collar tie.

4

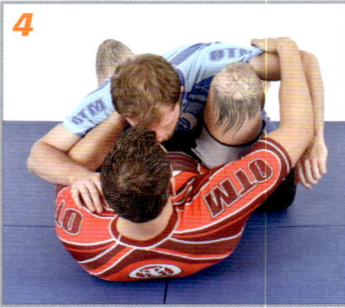

Feeling that he cannot posture, Lance begins to move forward. My right hand slides down to his left biceps and pushes it to the outside as I maneuver my right knee to the inside, posting my right foot on his left hip and positioning his biceps in the middle of my right shin. My right hand shifts to his triceps and pulls his biceps into my shin as my shin drives forward to create two directions of pressure. My left hand is still in the collar tie position should he attempt to posture.

5

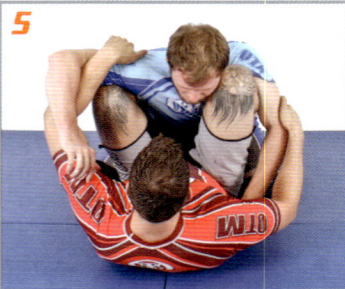

I repeat step four to bring my left knee to the inside, establishing the double biceps ride.

6

Lance hugs my legs and begins to stall the position, not moving forward or backward, stifling the straight shot triangle. I bridge my hips to push him away, and he counters my energy by driving forward.

7

As soon as Lance resists my bridge, I push my right foot into his left hip to shift onto my right hip, creating space and an angle.

8

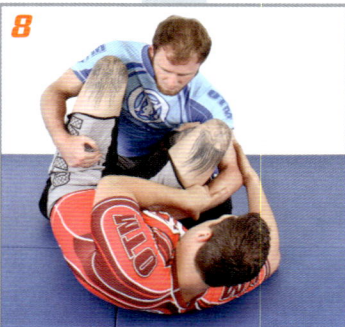

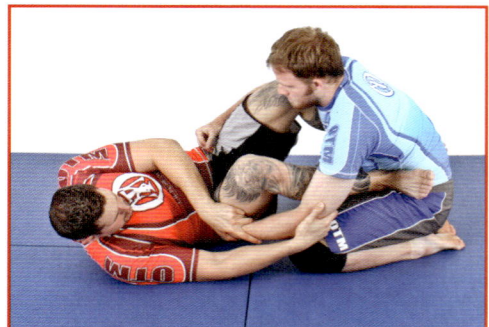

My left hand releases his right triceps and latches onto his left wrist, establishing a two-on-one cross grip.

9

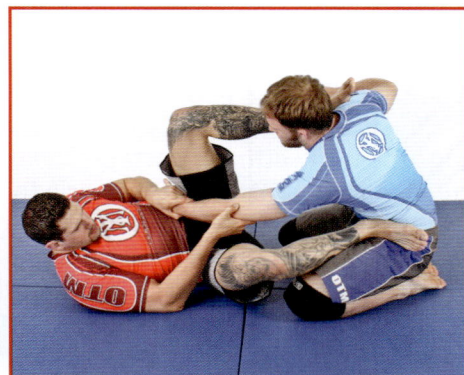

I scoot my hips away. I drag Lance's left arm between my legs with my two-on-one cross grip as I pull my left knee to my chest and post my left foot on his right shoulder. I straighten my leg, forcing him to react to the pressure. It's important that I keep him bent in this step by pulling on his left arm and digging my right foot into his hip. If he postures, I will lose the triangle.

10

When Lance resists my push, I kick my left leg forward and over the back of his neck as I yank his left arm across my body and curl my right leg to scoot my hips toward his neck.

11

I lock the triangle and finish the submission with both hands on his head.

COLLAR TIE PRINCIPLES

The collar tie is an essential tool from guard because it allows you to control your opponent's movement to such a degree that you can create space, while delaying his forward and upward movement, which is a major aspect of setting up attacks from your back. For the collar tie to work properly, you need to control his head. A common mistake is to grip the neck because it feels like a strong grip, but holding the neck does not stop your opponent from arching his back to raise his head toward the ceiling. To control your opponent's posture, you need to cup the base of his skull, giving you the leverage to curl his spine toward your chest. With his posture beat, you can then stop his forward motion by digging your forearm into his chest. By using the collar tie to keep him from coming forward, you can move away, while moving his body low in your guard where it is most vulnerable. For me, since my legs are pretty long, I need to create more space than someone who might be shorter, but creating that space is still important no matter what your body type.

IMPROPER HEAD CONTROL

PROPER HEAD CONTROL

In the photograph on the left, I am controlling Lance's neck. Since my leverage is poor with that grip, he can straighten his back and begin to sit up. In the photograph on the right, I am controlling the base of Lance's skull. From that position, I can force his spine to bend, giving me the leverage I need to control his posture.

CREATING SPACE

As you can see in this series of photographs, I am using a proper collar tie with my right hand to control Lance's posture. To move away and create space, I position my right forearm against his chest in the crook between his neck and shoulder. I then use the collar tie to shift onto my left hip, guiding his head down toward the mat as my hips move off line. With my forearm delaying his forward motion, I scoot my hips away to create space. If I tried this movement without a proper collar tie, he could quickly smother me or posture out.

1

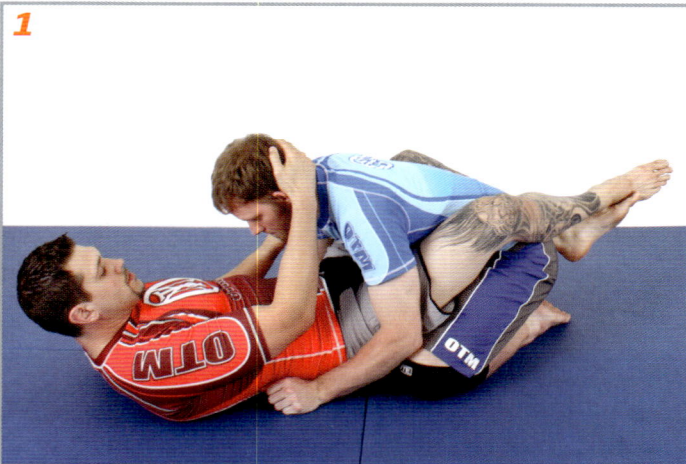

I am controlling Lance's head with my right hand, using a collar tie, and I am controlling his right arm with my left hand.

I open my legs and post my right foot on the mat.

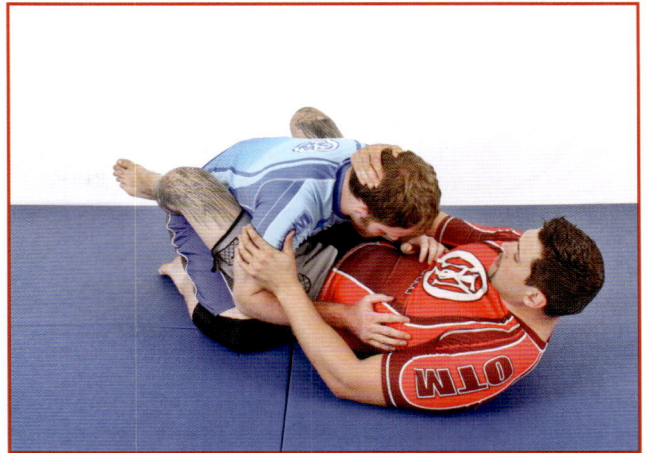

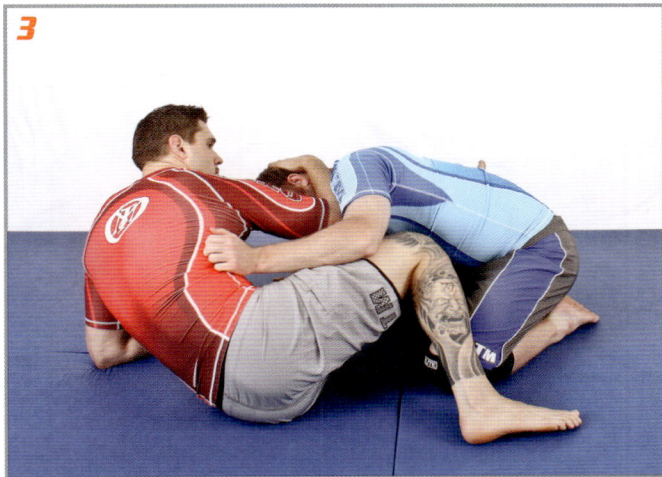

As I come up onto my left elbow, I set my right forearm against Lance's chest without releasing the collar tie. Using the frame I have created with my right arm, I dig my right foot into the mat and escape my hips.

UPWARD AND DOWNWARD WRIST TWIST LEG-THROUGH

The leg-through triangle is the most basic triangle from the collar tie position, and it resembles the other leg-through triangles that we have already covered. The benefit of attacking with the leg-through triangle from the collar tie over double-wrist control or the double biceps ride is that you can delay all three directions of movement. When you have more control over your opponent, your submission rate will increase because you are not relying entirely on timing. However, your amount of control lessens when you open your guard and take a leg off of his back to thread it around an arm to lock the triangle. At that point, only your hand on his head is stopping him from rolling his head down and ducking out of the triangle. Not all opponents will think to move backward, making this triangle an excellent option under the right circumstances. If you feel that your opponent will move away from you, use the leg-walk-up triangle. As you will notice in the photographs below, I demonstrate two variations of the leg-through triangle, one with a downward grip and one with an upward grip. The downward grip variation is best used when your opponent is attempting to posture, and the upward grip variation is best used when your opponent is attempting to stack you. Once you have chosen a grip, the mechanics of the leg-through triangle are essentially the same.

1

Lance is in the 45 degrees position and I have a collar tie.

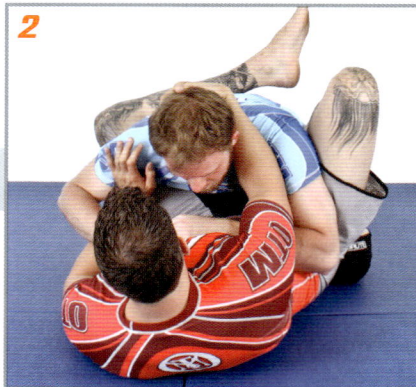

2

I feel that Lance wants to posture, so I decide to set up a downward grip. I pummel my left hand under his right forearm, which should not be too difficult because he is creating space by attempting to posture.

3

My left hand pushes Lance's right arm to the outside, and my left knee slides inside to a position similar to a biceps ride except that my calf remains curled across his back to delay his backward movement. My right foot posts on his left hip.

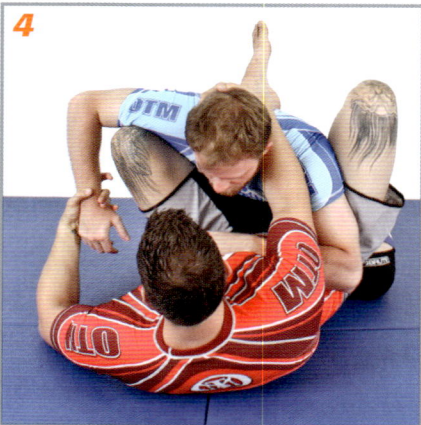

4

My left hand slides down Lance's right arm and latches on to a downward grip. My left knee remains against his right arm to keep his right arm flailed out.

5

I twist Lance's wrist with my left hand and straighten my left arm to force his right arm even farther away from his body.

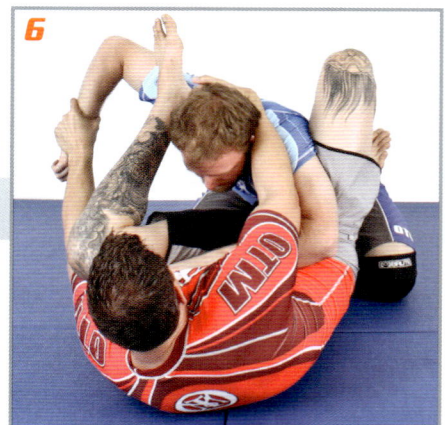

6

I pull my left knee toward my chest and snake my left foot in front of his right shoulder, feeding it through the circle I created with my downward grip. If I need more space in this position, I can use my right foot on his hip to scoot my hips away, but I need to do this as I begin to feed my leg-through. This entire step needs to be done quickly to lessen the chances of his ducking out and escaping.

I throw my left leg across the back of Lance's neck as I elevate my hips and use my collar tie to pull him into my triangle. My right leg remains posted on his left hip and squeezes into his left arm to keep him from ripping it out of the triangle.

My left hand hooks Lance's right leg as my right hand grabs my left shin and pulls down. I use my left arm and my right leg to swivel my hips, creating an angle for the triangle.

I figure-four my legs and finish the traditional triangle.

UPWARD GRIP VARIATION

If I feel that Lance is moving forward, I use the upward grip instead. As I shift my hips off line, I twist his right wrist and press his right arm to the sky, forcing it to bend as though I were applying an upward arm crank. With his right arm up, I can use the collar tie to create additional space (if I need it) so that I can pull my left knee to my chest, threading my left foot over the front of his shoulder. From there, the leg-through triangle finish is the same finish I used for the downward grip variation.

SKY PIN

My legs are longer than most people's, and some techniques are more difficult for me to execute because I have so much leg to swing around or slip through. I have modified my techniques, even simple ones, like the upward grip variation of the leg-through triangle, to compensate. If you are like me, long and not exceptionally flexible, the sky pin approach to the leg-through may be a better option than the traditional approach. Instead of threading your leg-through, bring it over the arm controlling the wrist with an upward grip. The mechanics of the move make it similar to a wrist pin, meaning that it's a difficult technique to counter because your opponent's elbow and hand have already cleared your leg before you release his wrist. To make your transition to the triangle clean and efficient, it's important to bring your leg over the bend of your elbow to ensure that you have completely cleared his arm before you release his wrist. The concept that makes this technique effective—bringing your leg over your own arm to get the triangle to compensate for a lack of space—will work in a variety of situations and positions, not just the collar tie.

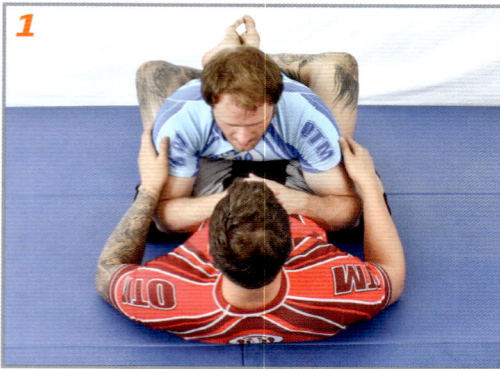

Lance is in my guard at the 45 degrees position.

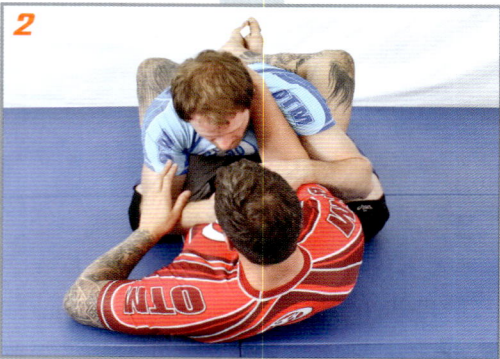

I pummel my right hand under his left forearm and snake it to the base of his skull, establishing a collar tie.

My left hand latches on to an upward grip on Lance's right wrist.

4

I dig my right foot into Lance's left hip and shift onto my left hip, curling my left leg onto his back to delay his backward movement.

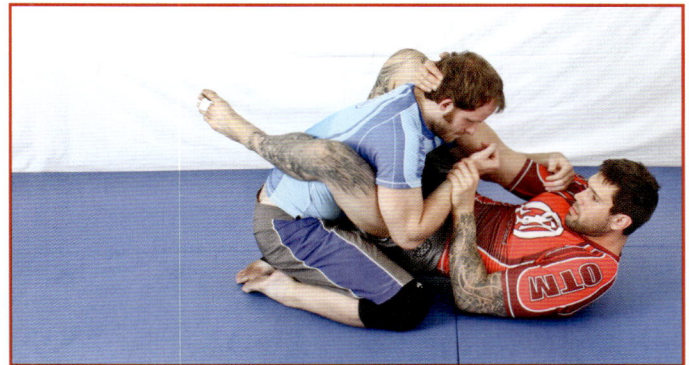

5

I begin to push Lance's right arm toward his head with my left hand.

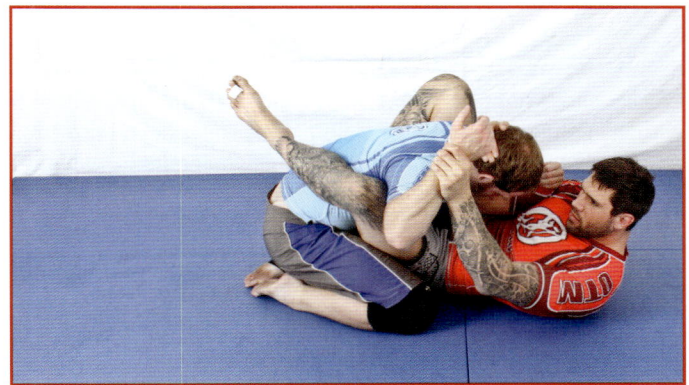

6

I twist Lance's right wrist counterclockwise as I continue to press it toward the sky, forcing his right arm to bend. It's important that I torque his arm as though I were applying an Americana because the pressure of the angle is more powerful and more efficient than a 90 degree angle, which is the angle that many grapplers mistakenly choose.

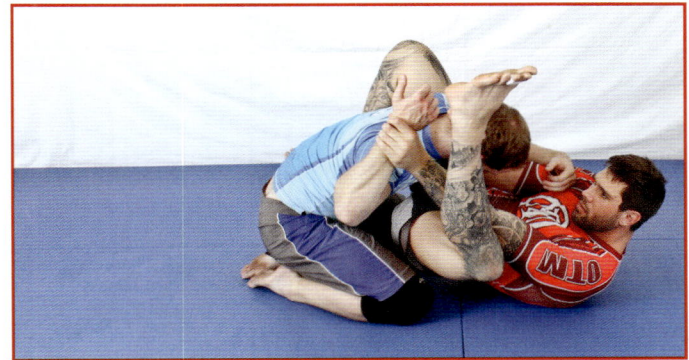

7

I swing my left leg around and over my left arm to ensure that I have successfully cleared Lance's right arm. I have not yet released control of his right wrist.

8

As my left hamstring slaps against Lance's neck, I release control of his right wrist and elevate my hips, using my collar tie to pull him into the triangle.

9

I hook Lance's right leg with my left hand to create an angle for the triangle as I kick off of his right hip and execute a knee pinch with my right leg. I choose to maintain the collar tie in this technique because I feel that I need to swivel my hips a bit to set the triangle, but you can grab your own shin if you prefer.

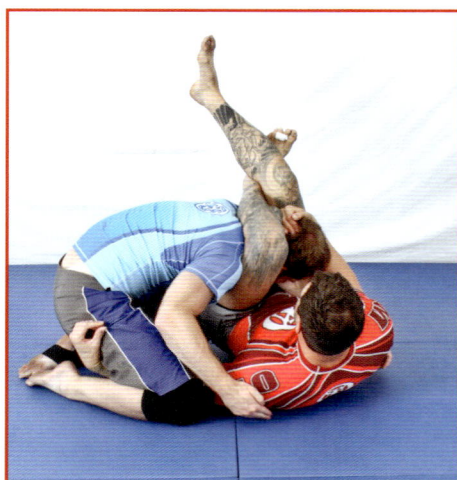

10

I figure-four my legs and finish the triangle.

COLLAR TIE LEG WALK-UP

The weakness of the leg-through triangle from the collar tie is that your opponent could duck out of your guard as you thread your leg-through for the submission. If you suspect that your opponent will move backward to escape the triangle—perhaps he tried it already—use the leg walk-up triangle instead. With the leg walk-up, you can control both his forward and backward movement with your legs, and your collar tie controls his upward movement. The key to that control—which is the same principle that I demonstrated in previous leg walk-up triangles—is to set the heel of your top leg in front of his shoulder, effectively delaying his ability to move forward. Since you establish your top leg before you maneuver your other leg around his arm, you can use a hamstring curl with that top leg to stall his backward movement as well. Your legs, your arms, and your hips all work together to dominate your opponent's upper body. The goal is to reduce your reliance on timing and develop your ability to dictate the action from your guard by understanding and controlling the directions of movement. I was in the process of perfecting this technique when the concept of delaying three directions of movement dawned on me. This technique was my eureka moment.

Lance is in my guard at the 45 degrees position.

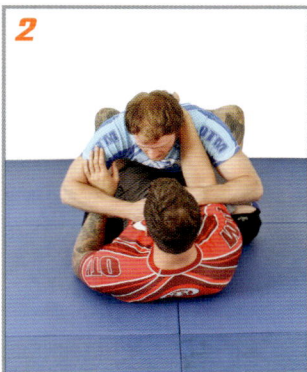

I pummel my right hand under Lance's left forearm and establish a collar tie. My left hand pummels under his right forearm and controls his right biceps.

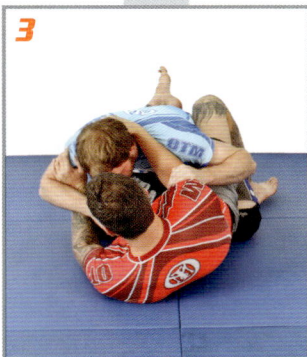

I plant my right foot on the mat and shift onto my left hip as my left hand pushes his right biceps away.

While curling my left leg into Lance's back, I post my right foot on his left hip and pull down on his head with my collar tie. In this position, I am effectively delaying all three directions of movement.

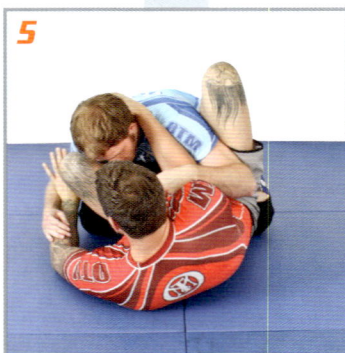

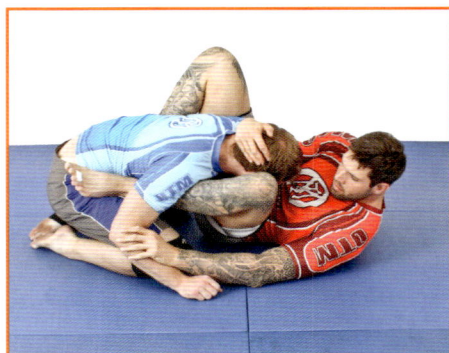

I continue to push Lance's right arm away with my left hand so that I can slide my left knee inside, posting my left foot on his right hip to establish a biceps ride.

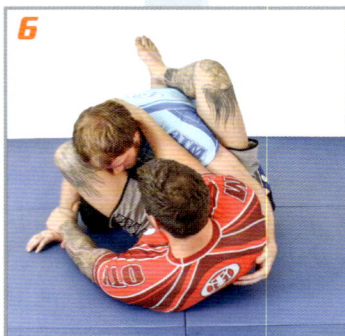

As soon as my left knee establishes a biceps ride, I immediately begin to swing my right leg up his back, keeping my leg heavy and in contact throughout the movement. I execute this movement in one seamless and forceful motion to trick him into posting his right hand on the mat. At the same time, my left hand slides down his right arm to establish wrist control.

I pull my left knee to my chest and snake my left foot out from under Lance's right arm. To prevent him from stacking into to me, I set my left heel in front of his right shoulder as I maneuver my left leg.

8

With my wrist control, collar tie, and right leg curl still in place, I throw my left leg over Lance's right shoulder, curling it into his back as I drive my left hamstring into his neck.

9

To swivel into position for the triangle, I post my right foot on Lance's left hip as I swing my left leg across the back of his neck. If the leg swing does not adjust my hips enough, I can push off with my right leg to create the angle that I need to lock the triangle.

10

I lock my legs and finish the arm-on-the mat triangle. As you can see in this step, this technique will typically force his inside arm to the mat. If you cannot lock the triangle, use your favorite finish from the arm-on-the mat section in the first chapter.

COLLAR TIE ANKLE GRIP COUNTER

Whether I am working for the leg-through triangle or the leg walk-up triangle from the collar tie, I need to be wary of my opponent winning the hand fight—preventing me from controlling his wrists—and latching on to my ankle to block my triangle and set up a pass. When this happens in other 45 degree control positions, transitioning to a counter becomes a race against his guard pass. The collar tie, however, allows me to negate much of his speed because I can stuff his head and delay his forward movement. As I delay his pass with the collar tie, I snake my own arm around my leg and re-grab his wrist, allowing me to break his grip and stuff his arm in one motion. Your opponent practically walks into this triangle by grabbing your ankle, and even if you miss the triangle, your opponent will hesitate to control your ankles later in the match for fear of being sucked into another trap. When I saw Baret Yoshida use this technique in an Abu Dhabi tournament (even though he wasn't able to quite finish the triangle), I knew that I could not pass up adding a technique as slick as this to my arsenal. It is a high-percentage technique that you need to practice if you want a well-rounded triangle game.

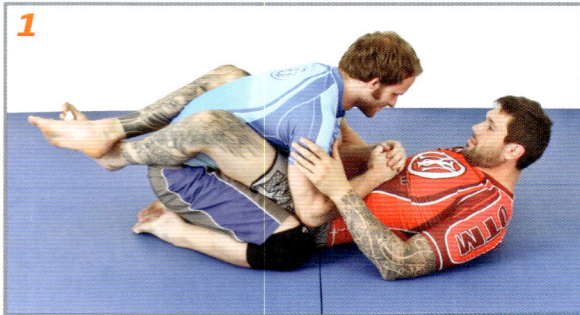

1

Lance is in my guard at the 45 degrees position.

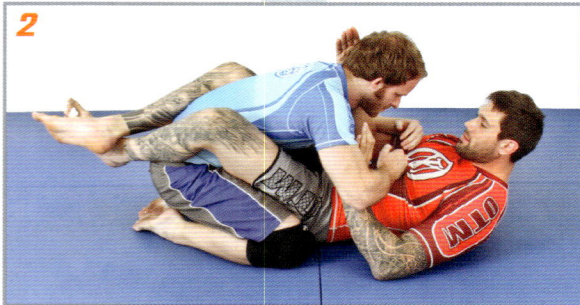

2

I establish a collar tie with my right hand by pummeling it under Lance's left forearm and grabbing the back of his head. My left hand pummels under his right forearm and controls his right biceps.

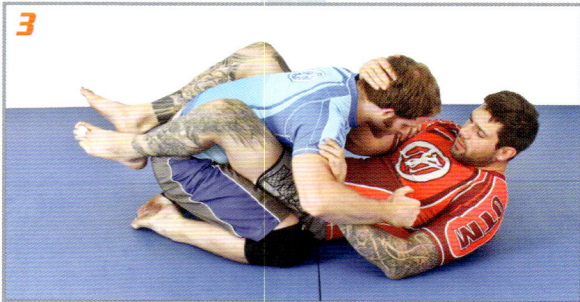

3

I push Lance's right arm to the outside with my left hand.

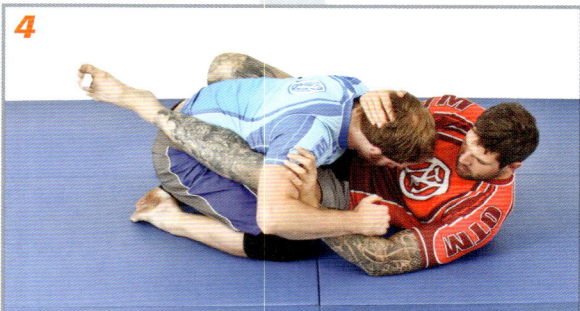

4

I post my right foot on the mat and shift off line onto my left hip. My left leg curls onto Lance's back to delay his backward movement.

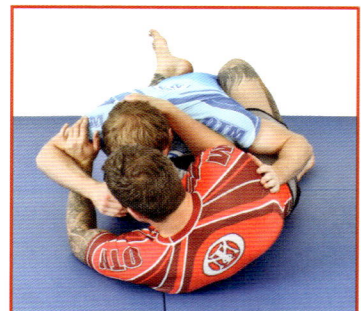

5

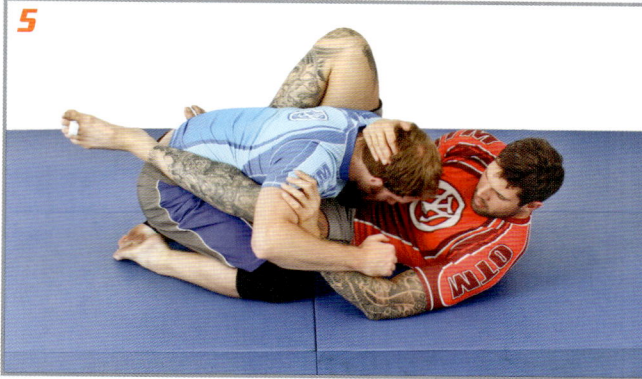

I plant my right foot into Lance's left hip as I begin to slide my left knee inside to establish a biceps ride on his right arm.

6

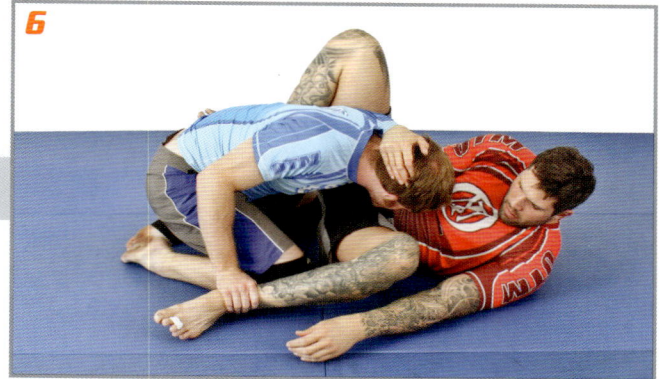

Lance realizes that he is in danger and grabs my left ankle to block the triangle and pins it to the mat to set up a guard pass.

7

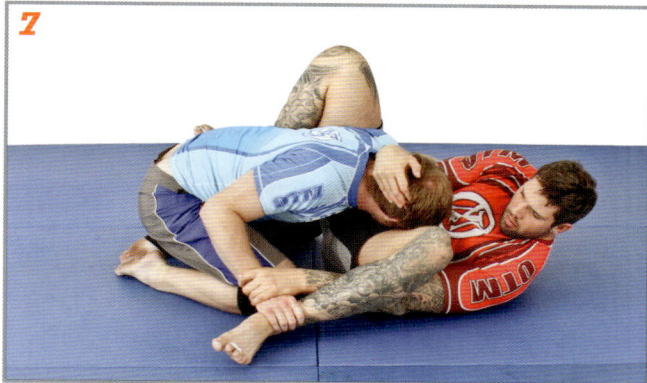

Before Lance can step over my left leg, I quickly snake my left hand under my left thigh and latch on to his right wrist.

8

I kick my left leg to the ceiling to break Lance's grip. At the same time, I elevate my hips and slam my left thigh against his neck to begin establishing the triangle.

9

While still controlling his head and left wrist, I swing my left leg across the back of his neck and pinch my right knee into his left shoulder to create an angle for the triangle.

10

I figure-four my legs and finish the traditional triangle with both hands.

COLLAR TIE TO SANKAKU (INSIDE)

When you use the collar tie and a biceps ride to work for a leg-through triangle or a leg walk-up triangle, your opponent can shut you down in a number of ways. In the previous technique, your opponent grabs your ankle in an attempt to stop you from clearing his arm for the triangle. If your opponent is playing tighter to you, limiting your space and caging your hips, you may find yourself with one knee inside against his chest and your other leg over his back. You will feel close to the triangle because you have almost cleared one of his arms, but with your foot on his hip and your ankle pressed into your own butt, you do not have the space to maneuver for a leg-through or a leg walk-up triangle. I see many grapplers achieve this position only to be frustrated by their opponent's defenses. Invariably, the person on top stalls and then explodes out. The solution to getting the triangle from this position is to swivel to a sankaku. He may be stalling out your more traditional triangle setups, but he cannot easily stop you from swiveling upside down to clear his arm. Although unorthodox, it is extremely effective. If at first you struggle to land this technique, keep practicing; the sankaku is too powerful of a technique to ignore.

Lance is in my guard, lingering in the optimal submission zone.

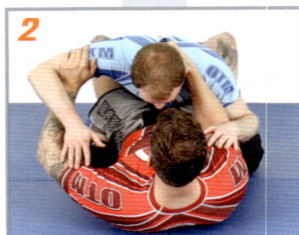

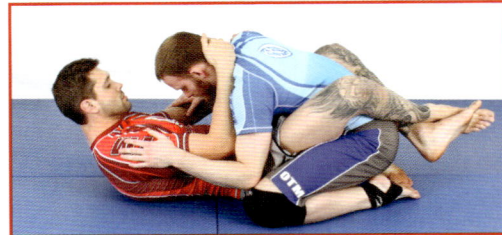

My right hand shoots under Lance's left forearm and establishes a collar tie as my left hand pummels under his right forearm and controls his biceps. I then push his right arm to the outside with my left hand.

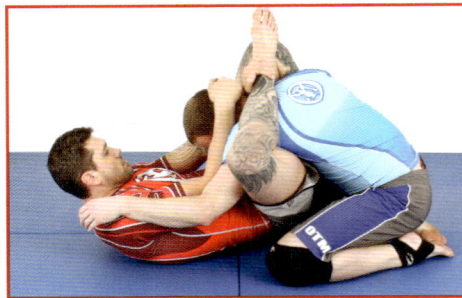

I latch on to my right ankle with my left hand, using a palm-down grip. If Lance chooses to stack me here, he will actually make my transition to the sankaku easier.

I pull my left knee under Lance's left arm to a biceps ride and throw my right leg over his back as though I were working for a leg walk-up triangle. To stop the technique, he locks my left foot into his hip and drives his hips forward to squish my left ankle into my butt, effectively blocking me from threading my left foot out and over for the triangle.

5

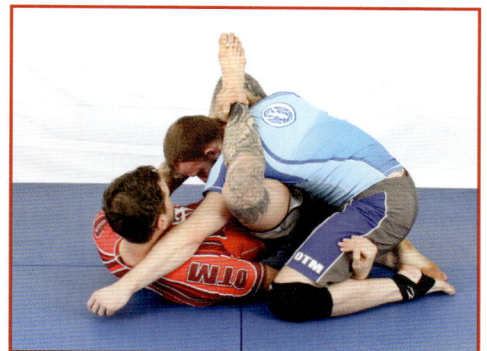

I hook Lance's left leg with my right arm and control his head by pinching it between my left forearm and his left shoulder. To increase the power of the pinch, I straighten my left arm.

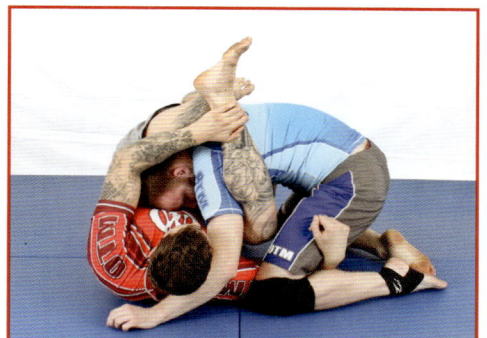

6

I pull my head toward Lance's left knee with my leg hook, beginning to swivel my hips out as I roll onto my shoulders. Notice that my hips are elevated, I am still controlling my own ankle, and my left leg is traveling over the back of his neck, while remaining compact. If I flail my left foot out, he could grab my ankle and escape.

7

I continue to rotate until I have turned almost 180 degrees. I pop my hips up repeatedly and continue to pull on my right ankle until I feel that his jaw line is in line with the "V" of my right leg, a concept we discussed in the sankaku section of the first chapter. In this step, my left thigh is helping to keep his posture down, and I keep my left knee in contact with my right shin as much as possible.

8

I feel Lance's jaw line slip into the "V" of my right leg. I immediately figure-four my legs and control his left triceps with my left hand. I can either pull on his left arm and curl my legs to finish the sankaku from here, or I can use the sweep options that I demonstrated in the first chapter.

COLLAR TIE TO UNDERHOOK WRIST PIN

The previous series of techniques revolve around your ability to force one of your opponent's arms away from his centerline, allowing you to transition to a biceps ride, which gives you the control to then attack with a leg-through triangle or a leg walk-up triangle. If your opponent is hugging his elbows tight to your hips from the beginning, you may not be able to force one of his arms to the outside. In that situation, using a wrist pin is a better choice, but a traditional wrist pin is also likely to fail if your opponent is already committed to defending his arms. To be successful with the wrist pin against a smart opponent, you need to confuse him. Use your collar tie to set up an underhook, which will trick your opponent into thinking that you want an inverted armbar, simultaneously giving you the leverage to stretch him out and rock his elbow off of your hip. When he defends his arm, stuff the wrist for the triangle. Throughout this move, your hips are mobile, which helps to further convince your opponent that you are no longer hunting for the triangle. My students love this technique and have had a great deal of success with it in competition.

1

Lance is in the 45 degrees position.

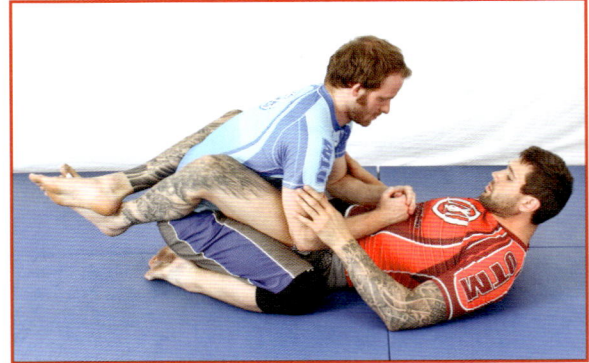

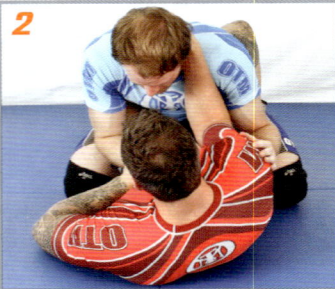

2

I shoot my right hand under Lance's left forearm and establish a collar tie. My left hand latches on to his right wrist.

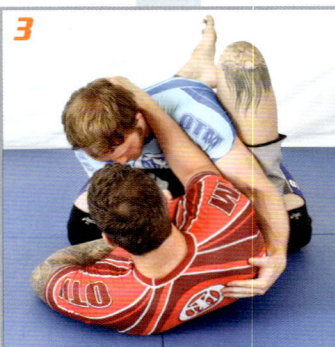

3

I post my right foot on Lance's left hip and shift onto my left hip as I begin to force his right wrist toward his stomach for the wrist pin triangle. He resists by hugging his right elbow to my hip.

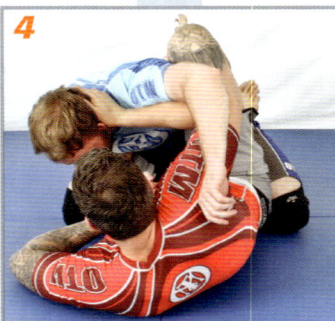

4

Using my collar tie, I push Lance's head down and to my left, almost as though I want to stand. Forcing his head in that direction gives me space to bring my elbow inside of his left armpit. I then flare my right elbow into the air forcing Lance's left elbow to flare as well.

5

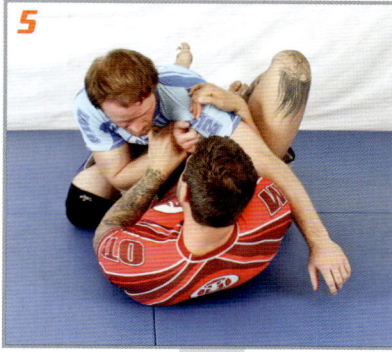

I circle my right hand down and under his left arm to establish an underhook. As I pull on Lance's body with my right underhook, I rock my hips to my right. At this point he may feel that his left arm is in danger, so I continue to force his right wrist toward his stomach with my left hand to capitalize on his confusion.

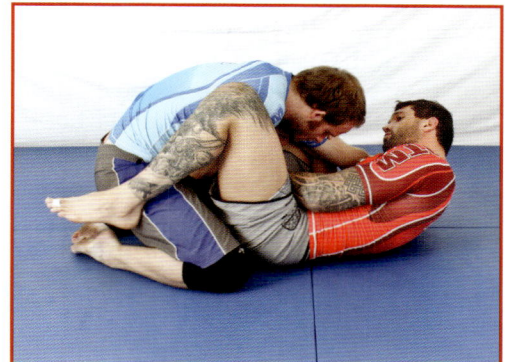

6

I point my left knee outward and swim my left leg around Lance's right elbow, pinching my left knee in front of his right shoulder to begin clearing his arm for the triangle.

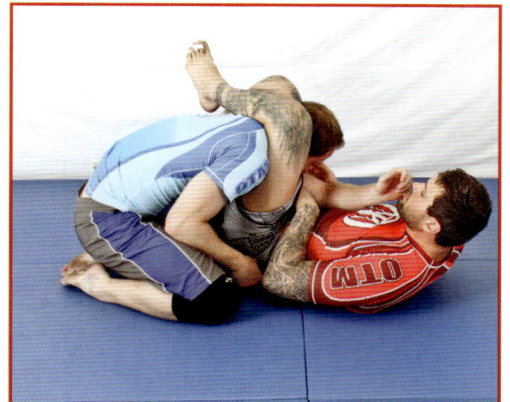

7

I throw my left leg over Lance's right shoulder and across the back of his neck as I use my right underhook to drag his left arm across my body. I post my foot on Lance's right hip and pinch my right knee into his left shoulder to swivel my hips into position.

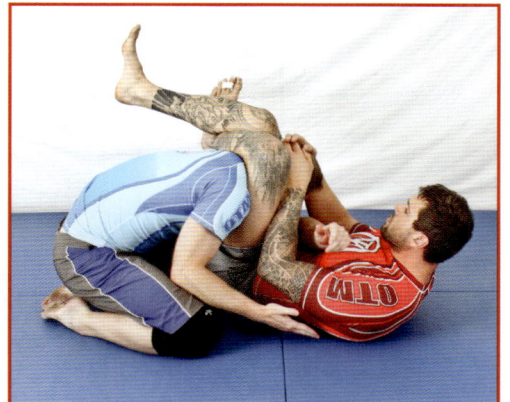

8

I then figure-four my legs and finish the traditional triangle.

DOWNWARD WRIST PIN WITH GRAPEVINE

As I mentioned earlier, using a downward grip is ideal for forcing your opponent to collapse because the pressure you can create is like a decline press, and you can augment that control by moving yourself away to create extra space, even if that space is just an inch. I prefer the downward grip because I like to keep my opponent low in my guard, but a downward wrist pin alone will rarely be enough to land the triangle, especially if my opponent is hugging his elbow to my hip to defend. I need more than upper-body control in this situation; I need lower-body control as well. Gene LeBell emphasized foot and leg control, and he advocated using grapevines because a single grapevine can stall three directions of movement in the guard and also force your opponent low in your guard. When LeBell spoke, I listened. I began to experiment more and more with grapevines, and found them to be just as effective as LeBell had promised, which surprised me somewhat because many guard players ignore the grapevine option. In terms of getting the triangle, using the downward wrist pin and grapevine simultaneously will cause my opponent to drop into a triangle. While my opponent struggles to recover his base, I am already sinking the triangle and setting my finish. Look to use grapevines whenever you can, they will expand the scope of your guard game. Try to use them when a technique focused primarily on upper-body control, like the underhook wrist pin, fails.

Lance is in my guard at the 45 degrees position.

I attempt to pummel my right hand under his left forearm, but Lance hugs my hips. Though it is not ideal, I opt to establish a collar tie with my right hand without having my right arm inside. My left hand then latches on to Lance's right wrist, securing a downward grip.

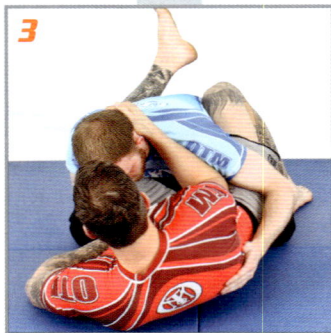

I plant my right foot on the mat and shift off line onto my left hip.

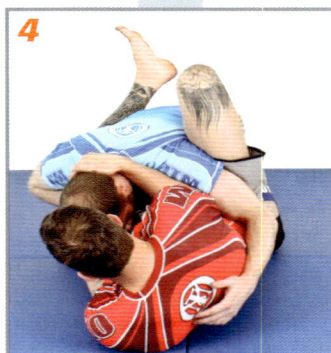

I post my right foot on Lance's left hip and press his right wrist toward his stomach with my left hand to transition to the triangle, but Lance blocks me from clearing his elbow by squeezing it against my hip.

5

My left foot immediately slides down Lance's right side and snakes under his right ankle, hooking a grapevine.

6

I straighten my left leg to collapse Lance's base with my grapevine. As my leg extends, I perform a downward wrist pin. The combination of the downward wrist pin and the grapevine forces his elbow to the inside of my leg, dropping him into a triangle. It's important to note that I am still controlling his posture with a collar tie.

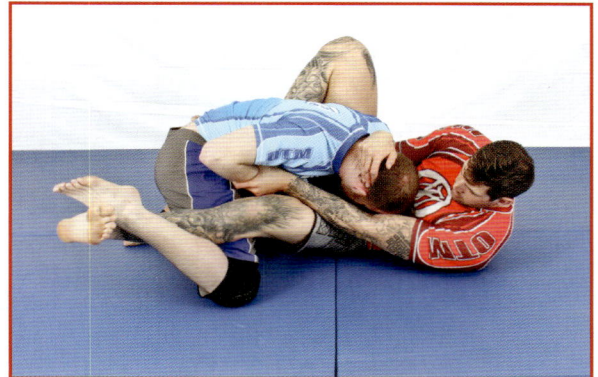

7

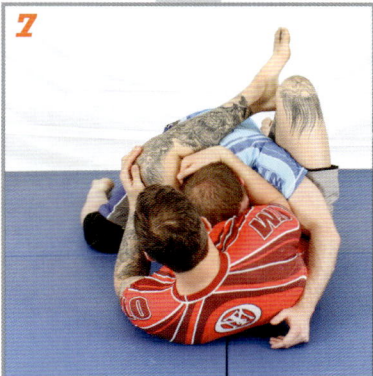

My left leg swings over his right shoulder and across the back of his neck.

8

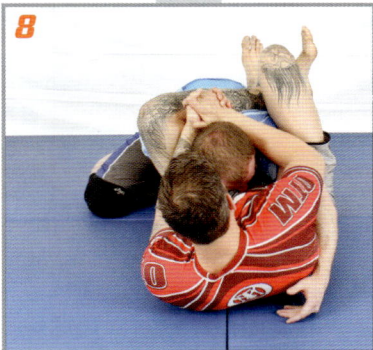

I use my collar tie and my right foot in Lance's hips to adjust for the triangle. I end the fight using an arm-on-the mat finish.

COLLAR TIE CROSS GRIP PULL-PUSH PIN

In the previous two techniques, we have looked at options for setting up the triangle when your opponent hugs his elbows to your hips. The underhook pin used movement and misdirection to secure a pin, and the downward wrist pin with grapevine focused on using a grapevine to collapse his base so that you could clear his elbow. If his elbows are tight and his butt is against his ankles, the underhook or the grapevine may be unavailable. With no other options for controlling your opponent you'll need to resort to mind games. The key to this technique is to trick your opponent into reacting to your pressure with the opposite pressure. If you push him back, his body naturally wants to come forward to correct his balance. If you pull him toward you, he will likely pull away from you. When you develop this approach to grappling, you can keep your opponent mentally off balance. He will never be quite sure about his reactions, resulting in hesitation and making him vulnerable to a sweep or a submission. In this technique, you have established a collar tie, and you use a cross grip to pull his arm as though you were trying to position it for an armbar. When he resists to protect his arm, you push his arm to his stomach, pinning it, so you can climb your legs up for the triangle.

Lance is in the optimal submission zone. I attempted to pummel my left hand under his right forearm to establish an inside collar tie, but his defense is too tight. I settle for a collar tie on the outside of his arm, and my right hand secures a cross grip on his right wrist.

I post my left foot on Lance's right hip and yank his right arm across my body with my right hand.

When Lance resists the drag by pulling his right arm back, I immediately push his right wrist to his stomach with my right hand, augmenting the momentum of his pull with the power of my push. I open my left leg at the same time to ensure that he does not return to hugging my hip.

4

I throw my left leg across the back of Lance's neck to clear his arm as I release my cross grip.

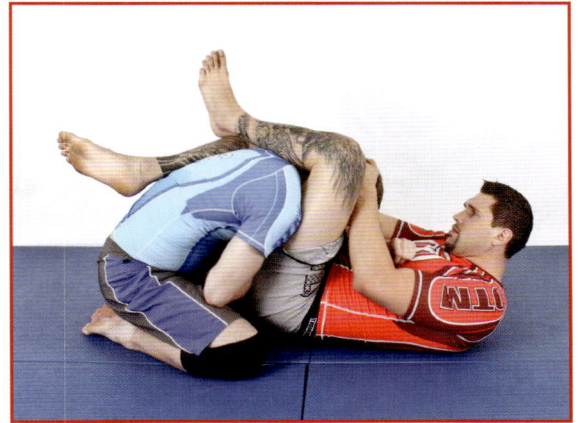

5

My left hand cups the back of Lance's left elbow as my right hand grips his forearm, securing a two-on-one grip.

6

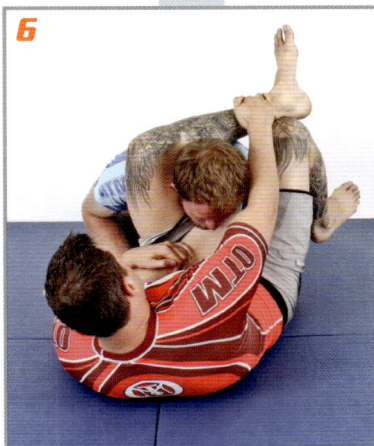

I drag his left arm across my body and grab my left ankle with my right hand, pulling it into position for the triangle.

7

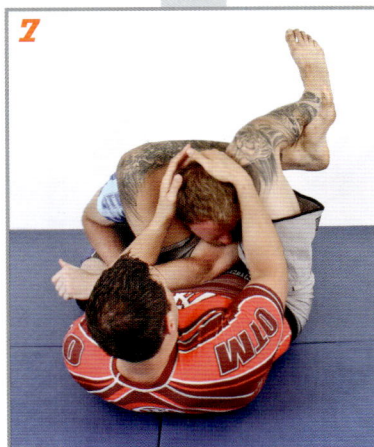

I figure-four my legs and finish the triangle.

LISTER CHOKE TRIANGLE

As your guard becomes more aggressive and you get better at bringing your legs and hips into the fight, your opponent will adjust his defense accordingly, oftentimes focusing entirely on pinning your hips and controlling your legs. When you are fixated on controlling his wrists and clearing an arm to set a triangle, this can be frustrating because it stifles all of your hip and leg movement. However, by loading up his defense on your hips he leaves his neck exposed. If you feel like you cannot move your hips and you cannot control his arms or wrists, attack his neck. The hand choke is probably the simplest and most direct option. I learned this from Dean Lister when I was training in San Diego. I had not been grappling for very long, and he used this choke to confuse the hell out of me. It was an easy choke to defend, but it was a constant distraction. He used it to set up a back take, but after experimenting with it myself, I found that it can also be used to set up the triangle because it forces my opponent to remove his hands from my hips to defend the choke. By anticipating this, you can time your attack and throw your legs over his arms to catch the triangle.

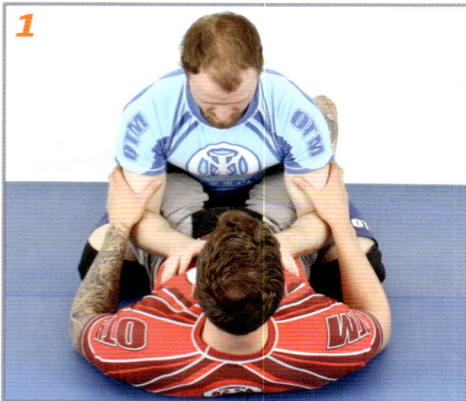

Lance is still in the optimal submission zone, but I cannot control his hands or his elbows.

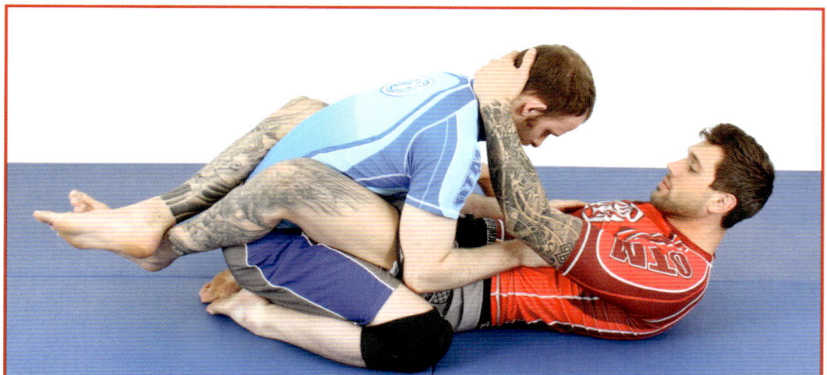

My left hand shoots to the base of Lance's skull and secures a collar tie.

I pull Lance toward me with my left hand and snake my forearm under his chin with my right hand, gripping my left wrist with my right palm facing me.

4

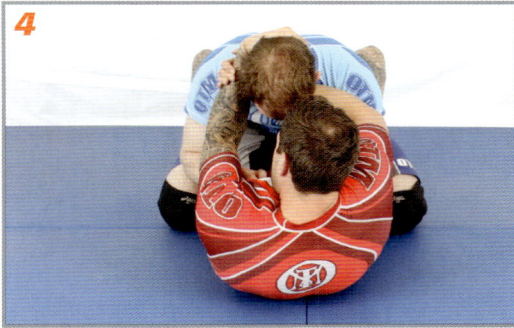

As I pull Lance's head down into my right forearm with the collar tie, I raise my right elbow to begin the choke.

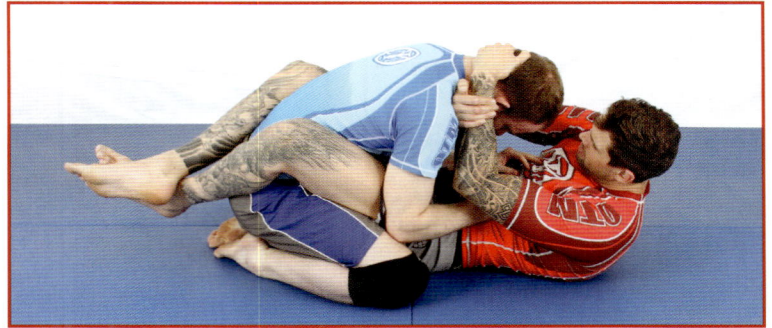

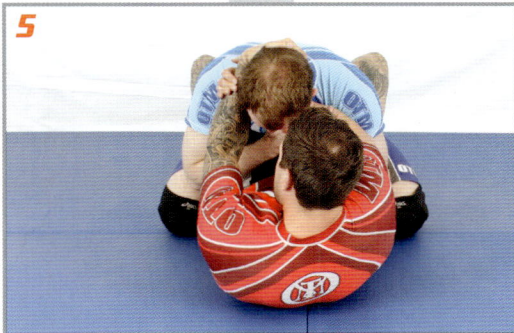

5

Lance begins to defend the choke by digging his right hand between his neck and my right forearm. At this point in the technique, he could actually defend with either arm, so I need to pay attention to which arm he chooses to use.

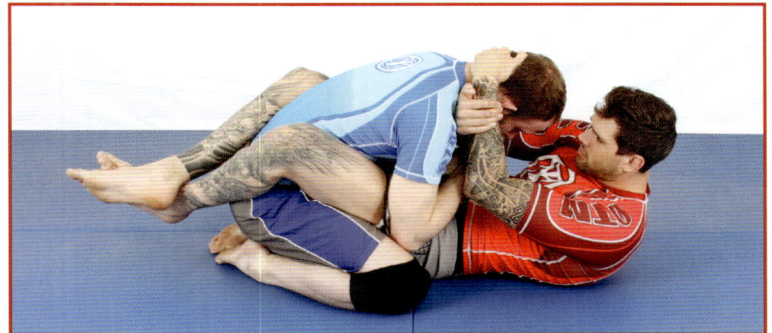

6

I open my guard and swing my left leg out, while still maintaining the threat of the Lister hand choke.

7

My left leg circles around Lance's right elbow to clear his arm.

8

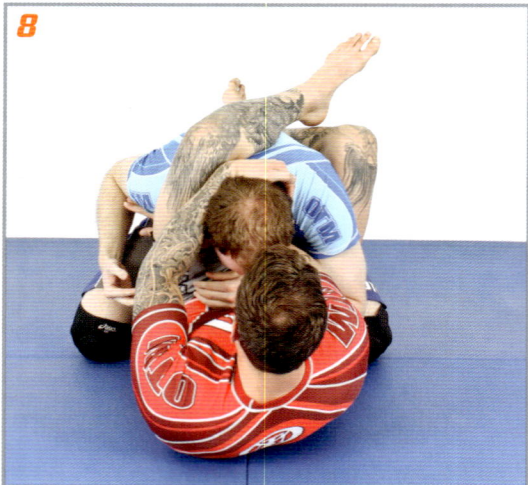

I drive my left hamstring into Lance's neck.

9

I post my right foot on Lance's left hip and pinch my right knee into his left shoulder to angle my hips for the triangle.

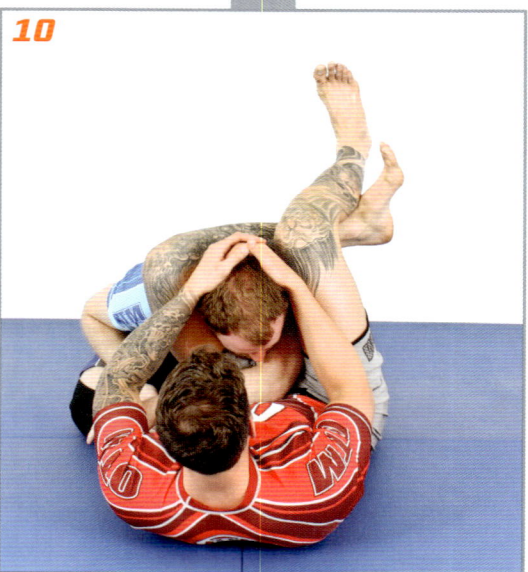

10

I finish the choke by locking my legs and pulling on Lance's head.

CORNER LOCK TO WRIST PIN

When you set the corner lock, your opponent's primary concern will be to defend the arm lock. In the previous technique, I transitioned to the triangle, while my opponent's arm remained mostly extended by clearing his other arm with a leg-through triangle. If my opponent curls his arm toward his chest to protect it from hyperextension, he may pull his elbow out of the triangle when I pop my hips for the leg-through triangle. In this case, I focus my attention on the arm that is being threatened by the armbar, and use my opponent's defensive movement to execute a wrist pin, shoving his hand to his chest to clear the arm. I can then set and finish the triangle. They key to successfully clearing the arm with this technique is pumping your legs to prevent the elbow from getting stuck inside of your guard. As you will see in the photographs below, I use an entry for the corner lock that differs from the previous technique, giving you more options for securing the corner lock. This entry is especially useful if your opponent is controlling your biceps, blocking you from using the underhook collar tie entry. The corner lock that you achieve will be the same in both techniques, meaning that the wrist pin and the leg-through triangle will still work from the corner lock regardless of how you got there.

1

I have Lance in the corner lock position. My left leg is over the front of Lance's right shoulder and my feet are crossed right over left. I have control of Lance's head with my left hand and my right arm is hooked under his left leg.

2

I grab control of Lance's right wrist with my left hand.

3

I pin Lance's right wrist to his chest with my left hand.

4

I scissor my legs straight but keep them crossed and elevate my hips. This creates some space between my hips and Lance's body, while allowing me to maintain control. With my left hand I immediately stuff Lance's right arm into the space created by my leg movement.

5

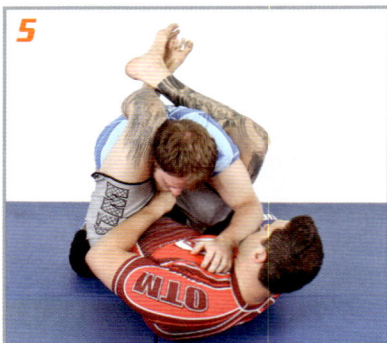

I drop my hips, forcing Lance's right arm out of my guard.

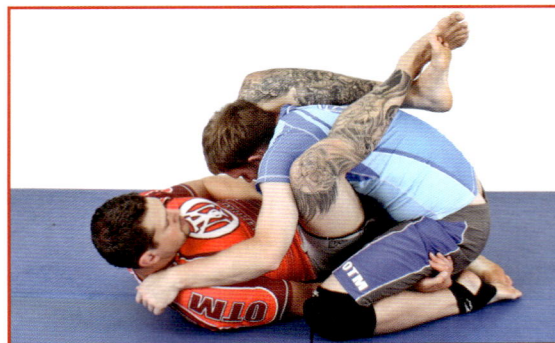

6

My left hand reaches over Lance's left arm and grabs the back of his elbow.

7

I elevate my hips and drag Lance's left arm across my body with my left hand. At the same time I also release control over his left leg with my right arm and then post my right hand on his left knee to help square my hips up to his body.

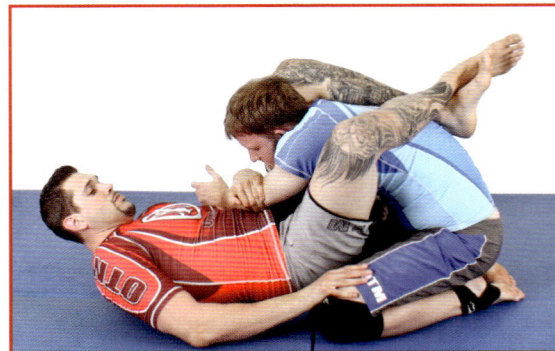

8

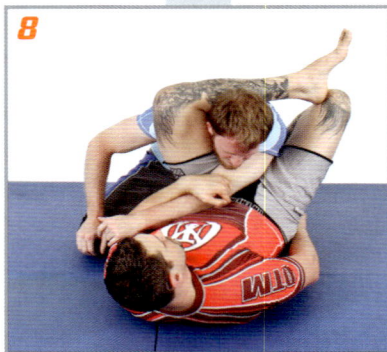

Unlocking my legs, I put my right foot on Lance's left hip and shift my left calf across the back of his neck. I make sure to maintain tight squeezing pressure with my thighs when performing this step.

9

I figure-four my legs, right over left, locking the triangle. I then flex and squeeze my legs and pull on the back of Lance's head to finish the submission.

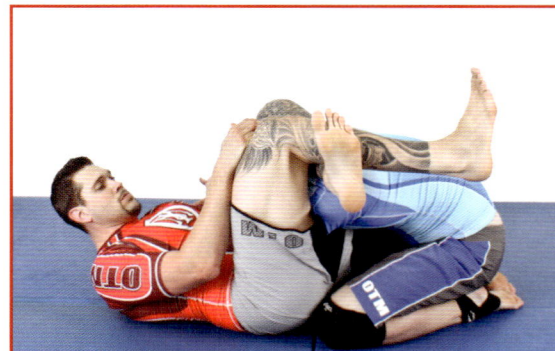

THE BANNER TO SWING BACK TRIANGLE

The corner lock is a strong controlling position that potentially sets up armbars, triangles, and omoplatas. Since this book focuses exclusively on the triangle, I will not be delving into the broad scope of options available from the corner lock, but I do want to show you an unorthodox back take that sets up the swing-back triangle. A former training partner of mine, Sean Spangler, showed this to me as a way to take the back. I really loved it, so I used it to set up my favorite triangle off my back, the swing back triangle. The banner is an advanced technique that requires hip coordination and an understanding of angles and leverage, so do not get frustrated if you struggle with it at first. Keep practicing. Once you get good at taking the back, you can then work for the swing-back triangle. If you glance at the photographs below, you will see that my opponent ends up in the turtle position with me attempting to take his back. Once I get to that position, I fall to my side, which forces my opponent to make a decision. He can either roll with me, giving me his back, or remain turtled, giving me the swing-back triangle. There is no right answer for my opponent.

Lance is hovering in the optimal submission zone and is controlling my biceps with both hands.

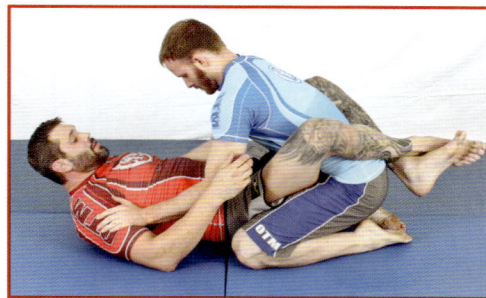

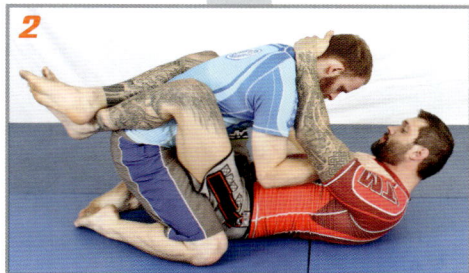

My left hand grips the base of Lance's skull, securing a collar tie.

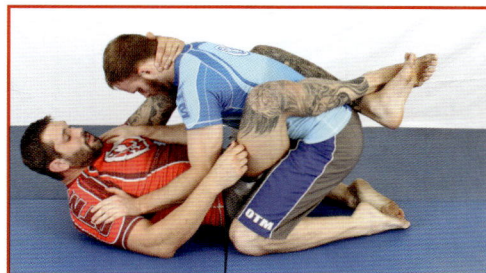

I open my guard, posting my left foot on Lance's right hip and curling my right leg onto his back as I shift my hips off line.

I reach the back of my right hand between Lance and me and hook it on the outside of his right knee. As I snake my right arm into position, I begin to elevate my hips. At the same time, I pull my head toward his left knee, setting my left knee on the back of his head, crossing my feet to lock the position.

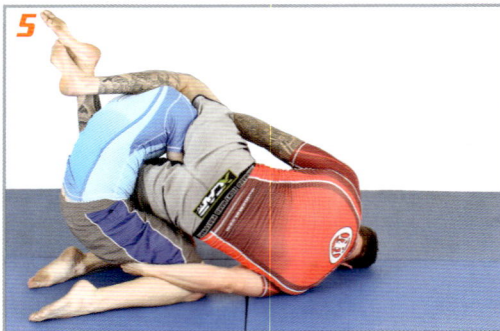

To gain access to Lance's back, I keep my guard closed and bridge my hips into him. As I bridge, my right shoulder stays on the mat, but I straighten my back to remove my head from underneath him.

I unhook Lance's right leg, post my right elbow on the mat, and open my legs to begin scooting my hips toward his lower back. As my hips shift, I pummel my left hand under his left arm and latch on to his left forearm. In this step, I anticipate transitioning to the swing-back triangle, so I do not fight to get the back hooks.

I pin Lance's left arm against his chest by pulling on it with my left hand. I fall to my right, swinging my right leg over his pinned left arm, as I post my left foot on his hip.

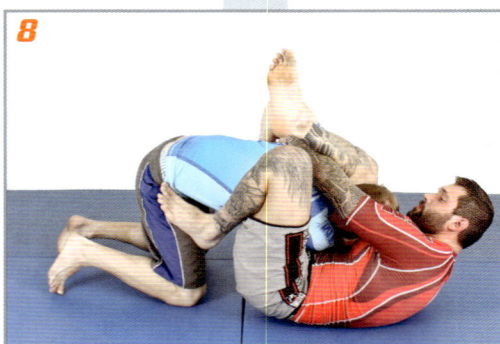

I throw my right leg over the back of Lance's neck as I press my left foot into his right hip to swivel my hips into position for the triangle.

I figure-four my legs and finish the traditional triangle.

CHAPTER THREE

0 DEGREE INTRODUCTION

In the last chapter, you learned how to set up and submit your opponent when they are hovering in your guard. As we get more into the advanced triangle set ups in this chapter, I want to remind you not to overlook what you have already learned in the previous chapter. If your opponent is hovering in your guard, you can quickly submit him with timing-based attacks. Don't do more work than you have to. If it's easy and simple, keep it easy and simple.

But now you must learn to address the problems that occur when grappling high level opponents that rarely hover inside your guard. Now you will need to learn and develop trapping systems. The benefit of these control-based systems is immense to the guard player. They will give you time and the ability to inch your way into a high percentage triangle finish. I have the most success setting up and finishing triangles from the guard with control-based systems like the Irish collar and the shoulder pin. They're two of my favorites, but this book is for every guard player out there that wants to improve his game. I will cover and address many different trapping systems in this chapter. The key is to find the ones that work best for you and apply it to your specific game.

So the question becomes: "When should you apply a trapping system?" There are many answers to that question. It could be a personal preference. Maybe you have a high percentage of success from a certain trapping system, so breaking your opponent down and controlling him would be your optimal choice. It could be because your opponent is a transitional-based grappler so you need to control him as much as possible so he doesn't pass your guard. It could be that your opponent is playing low in your guard and controlling your hips, making it hard for you to push him off to transition into an open guard game. Regardless of the reason, you are now forced to fight at the 0 degrees position, and the way to win is with the utilization of trapping systems.

Trapping systems are a true game of inches. Once you have your opponent tied up, you have to keep him in control as you inch your hips into place. It's a physical battle to control and manipulate your opponent's upper body, while getting your hips off line and in position to win. To be good at these systems you must develop a sensitive feel to the placement of your opponent's weight on your body. You have to develop that feel, so you know if you've made enough space to attack. Cultivating this feel will make you lethal when it comes to utilizing trapping systems, but it can only be learned by practice. I spent many years developing some of the trapping systems in this chapter. When I first started using them I had mixed results, but I kept practicing until I figured out the patterns for success. In this chapter, you will get my opinions on which system or technique set ups work best for me. I even include a couple of set ups from my favorite series of attacks, the lazy Susan. If you truly want to be a guard master, this chapter will help make that a possiblity. The first key is to identify which trapping systems to utilize depending upon the winning or losing of the hand fight.

WINNING THE HAND FIGHT

Ideally, when you attempt to execute a trapping system, you want one of your opponent's arms outside of your body. This could be executed by an overhook, underhook, Irish collar, shoulder pin, and/or rubber guard type scenario. Once you position your opponent in a way that prevents him from obtaining an inside biceps tie, you have made the first step in succeeding to win the hand fight. If you use a tight trapping system it will also bind your opponent's arm to your body. This will prevent him from backing out and posturing, truly trapping him in place. Some opponents will give this hand position away not realizing how much control they are giving up. Others will be more careful and force you to fight to get the arm on the mat control. Regardless,

once your opponent's arm is out of the fight you will have the advantage. With the trapping system in place, you can now begin the game of inches to manipulate your opponent and set up your triangle.

The first system I created was the Irish collar. I designed it to not only be a good trapping system, but also as a staging point to gel all my trapping systems. The Irish collar is a simple way to keep my opponent's posture knocked down, and force my opponent's head to stay tight to my head. It also gives my legs the freedom to push and pull with a closed guard and manipulate my opponent's base with grapevines using leg and foot control. Having his arm trapped outside of my body and his head pinched tight, I can use my elbow and knee together to fight his free arm for the inside tie up. Utilizing a biceps ride I can attain a strong wrist control or even better, set up one of my absolutely favorite over the back grips, the Boston handshake. Once there, it usually is an easy win regardless of the opponent. I can utilize the Boston handshake to attack with a triangle, a double wristlock, use it as a sweep, and even as a way to take my opponent's back. The combination of all of these threats together make it a multidimensional grip that is very reliable. It's one of my go to grips.

My favorite transition from the Irish collar is the shoulder pin. This guard is essentially the ultimate trapping system; the shoulder pin is a high guard version of an overhook. Like an overhook, your opponent's arm is on the mat and out of the fight. Unlike the overhook, the shoulder pin ties your hips to your opponent's upper body by looping your arm over your opponent's arm, and under your own thigh, then cupping the front of your opponent's shoulder with your hand. For added strength, you can lock your hands together and pinch your elbows tight. With my opponent locked firmly inside of my trap, I can force him to hover and simultaneously prevent him from backing out and escaping. Once in a hovering position, I can effectively attack with submissions without much risk.

I've seen many other grapplers toy with this position without much success. The details are critical in this position, by utilizing the wrong grip or moving onto the wrong hip you can ruin your chances of success. Even though this is one of my most effective guard systems, it took me some time to trouble shoot it and make it what it is today. My initial inspiration for the development of my shoulder pin system was from Dean Lister. When I saw him use it to set up a triangle against Alessio Sakara, I knew that he was on to something effective. I spent years developing the techniques and strategies that are now my shoulder pin system, and the process was so frustrating at one point, that I actually gave up on it. But through failure came success and my success with the shoulder pin has done wonders for my guard game.

Your strategy for attacking from the shoulder pin changes based upon which hip is on the mat. If you are pinning your opponent's left arm and are on your left hip, I call that the triangle side because the triangle will be your primary submission. If you are pinning your opponent's left arm and are on your right hip, I call that the armbar side because the armbar will be your primary submission. Since we are focusing on the triangle, we will explore the triangle options from both the armbar side and the triangle side for each variation of the shoulder pin. Both sides are extremely useful if approached correctly, and because it is something that I developed almost entirely on my own, very few of your opponent's will know how to defend it.

I've spent a large amount of time perfecting my shoulder pin game. I've had so much success with this position that the shoulder pin is my guard system of choice, especially when rolling with high level grapplers. I usually use the lazy Susan set up, a technique that you will learn later in this chapter, to position my body perfectly to set up the shoulder pin triangle. I hope you take the time and not only learn these techniques, but quickly apply them to your guard game.

LOSING THE HAND FIGHT

Unfortunately, you can't always win the hand fight. If I'm grappling an opponent who is meticulous about his hand positioning, or who manages to secure and maintain double biceps control, I transition to the rubber guard so I can maintain control of his posture even if I can't force his arm to the mat. In the previous positions, you have some ability to control and manipulate your opponent's hands, though the succession of positions—from the Irish collar to the shoulder pin—assumes that you need more and more tools to control your opponent. Rubber guard comes into play when your opponent is controlling both of your biceps and has shut down your attempts to use other positions by locking your arms in place. Essentially, the rubber guard is nothing more than a posture pin with a leg hook, but the mechanics of the position allow you to dictate the action within your guard and begin winning the hand fight. The rubber guard gives you options for controlling your opponent and forcing his hand to the mat to improve your ability to attack. Since my flexibility is not the greatest, my approach to the rubber guard is a little bit different from how Eddie Bravo approaches it, and I will be focusing on my favorite triangle setups from that position rather than the entirety of the system. If you are not already familiar with the rubber guard and like what you see here, then you should check out the entirety of Bravo's system. If you are a rubber guard player, you may like some of my adjustments.

The primary weakness of the rubber guard is its inability to control backward movement. It is great for dominating your opponent's posture and can even work well against the stack if you are well versed in the system, but the standard rubber guard position does not adequately prevent your opponent from ducking out, especially if you are competing in MMA and cannot wear gi pants. This is not a criticism of the rubber guard. It is just an observation of the mechanics of the position. I have trained with a lot of grapplers that use the rubber guard really well, but the duck out frustrates them. However, if you introduce the grapevine to the rubber guard, that problem disappears, making the rubber guard much more dangerous, especially if the system is part of your usual game plan.

The cuff, the position I cover last in this chapter, is similar to the rubber guard in terms of control, but the position itself immediately threatens the choke. It is based on a technique I learned from judo where you grab the cuff of your own pants to choke your opponent. In the rubber guard, if your right leg is over your opponent's back, you grip your right ankle with your left hand. In the cuff, if your right leg is over your opponent's back, you grip your right ankle with your right hand. Though it may not look like it, the cuff actually requires less flexibility than the rubber guard, and if your opponent stacks, the angle of the grip prevents him from stressing your knee. Like the rubber guard, the cuff will be more effective if your opponent's arm is trapped on the mat, but it is still dangerous with both arms on your body.

I tend to use the cuff more than the rubber guard because I am not very flexible, and if I do use the rubber guard I use it to set up the cuff. The key to establishing a strong cuff is to quickly punch your gripping hand across when you reach to grab your own ankle. If you are slow to set your grip, you opponent could establish a two-on-one grip and use it to pass. Once your grip is established, your forearm in his throat creates a threat, and you have a free hand to begin controlling your opponent's wrist. Immediately crunch into your opponent to increase the pressure of the cuff, and immediately start using grapevines to continue demolishing your opponent's defenses. The cuff will feel awkward at first, especially if you are an avid rubber guard player and are not used to using a cross grip to seize your own ankle, but once you work with the position you'll see just how useful it can be in your skill set.

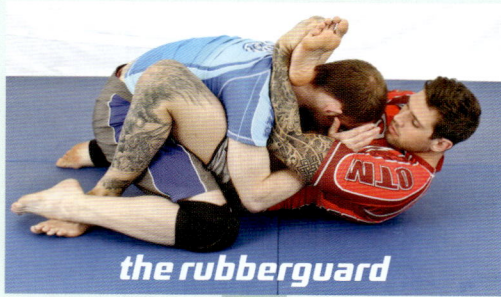

the rubberguard

the cuff

overhook   the Irish collar

0 degrees position

underhook shoulder pin

shoulder pin: triangle side

shoulder pin: armbar side

IRISH COLLAR TO BOSTON HANDSHAKE TRIANGLE

I said before that I want my opponent low in my guard so that my legs can easily climb up his body and lock a triangle. However, at the 0 degrees position moving your hips can be difficult if he is actively pinning you to the mat by stacking and caging your hips. When that happens, maintain the Irish collar, and use a grapevine to stretch out your opponent. As your opponent's base collapses, use your forearm pressure on his biceps to force one of his arms to the outside, giving you the opportunity to transition to the Boston handshake, an over-the-back grip, which is one of the best grips in grappling because you can dominate his posture and his arm with one grip, creating a variety of openings for submissions and reversals. I taught this technique to Ryan Couture and he used it in his first fight for Tuff-N-Nuff. Ryan's opponent took him down, but Ryan set the Irish collar, hooked a grapevine, and latched on to the Boston handshake, climbing his legs up for the triangle almost instantly. His opponent ultimately escaped, but he was wary of Ryan's ground game for the rest of the fight, and his hesitation gave Ryan the opening to sink and finish the rear naked choke later in the bout.

1

I pummeled my hands inside of Lance's arms and secured the Irish collar. I tried the leg walk-up leg-through triangle but he resisted my attempt to force him lower in my guard.

2

My left foot snakes under Lance's right leg and under his right shin, hooking his ankle.

3

I straighten my leg as I shift onto my left hip. The power of the grapevine forces Lance to move backward, and I assist that movement by driving him away with my Irish collar, forcing his head to shift from my shoulder to my solar plexus. I post my right foot on his left hip, giving me the option to escape if he manages to escape the grapevine before I can set the triangle.

4

My right hand grips Lance's right shoulder as my left hand slides to his biceps and begins to press it away.

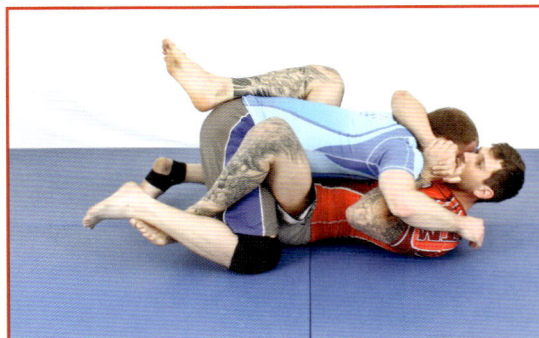

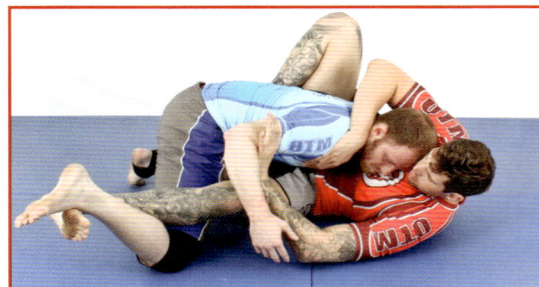

5

I slide my left hand down to Lance's right wrist and drive his hand towards his waist. This gives me the space to reach over his back with my right arm, snake my right hand through the crook of his elbow, and latch on to his right forearm, establishing the Boston handshake. To prevent him from straightening his right arm I pull his arm into his body, pinning it in place.

6

As my left hand releases his wrist, my left leg kicks free of the grapevine and swings in front of Lance's right shoulder, draping across the back of his neck. I maintain the Boston handshake throughout this step.

7

My left hand latches on to Lance's right wrist, forcing it away from his body to limit his ability to defend as my right hand grabs my left shin, pulling it into position for the triangle as I shift my hips.

8

I lock my legs and finish the triangle with Lance's arm on the mat.

COUNTERING THE STACK WITH THE BOSTON HANDSHAKE

The Boston handshake, like all over-the-back grips, is a powerful tool for setting up submissions. To be dangerous with the Boston handshake, you need to hunt for it. You need to apply it from a variety of positions and a variety of setups. You will not always be able to grapevine your opponent. In this technique, your opponent is stacking you, staying high in your guard to shut down your mobility and your offense. The Irish collar can somewhat delay your opponent's forward movement, but if your opponent is strong and aggressive, he can use the stack to power out of your Irish collar. If you anticipate the stack and act quickly, you can use your opponent's forward movement to force his arm into position for the Boston handshake. A lot of fighters instinctively use a similar movement to attempt triangles or Kimuras, but they give up too much control when they try to transition to the submission. With the Boston handshake, you can switch to an unorthodox figure-four, where both of your arms are on opposite sides of your opponent's body rather than the same side, and establish the Boston handshake. Once you have the Boston handshake, you can easily nullify the stack and land the triangle.

I have established the Irish collar and Lance is driving his weight into me. If he is not stacking me, I can still execute this technique by pulling him toward me with my guard.

As Lance begins to stack me, I dig my left forearm into his chest and begin driving it into his right arm to force his right arm away from his body. I lean on to my left hip to give my left forearm more leverage.

My left hand presses Lance's right biceps back as my right hand cups his right shoulder.

I snake my right hand under Lance's right arm and grip my left wrist to secure a figure-four on his biceps. To secure a strong grip in this step, I dig the wristwatch section of my wrist into his armpit, pulling him into me to compress his shoulder just before I lock on to the figure-four. This movement will often encourage the stack as well, which is good for my technique at this point.

While maintaining pulling pressure on Lance's right shoulder with my right wrist, I slide my left hand down to his right wrist.

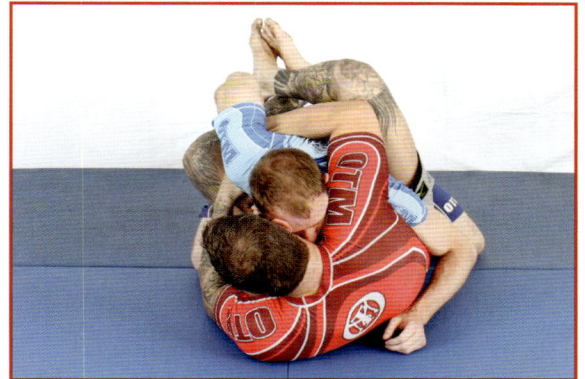

With Lance's body pulled tight to mine, I now establish the Boston handshake by grabbing his right forearm with my right hand. I use both hands to pull his right arm into his ribs to prevent him from straightening his arm to escape.

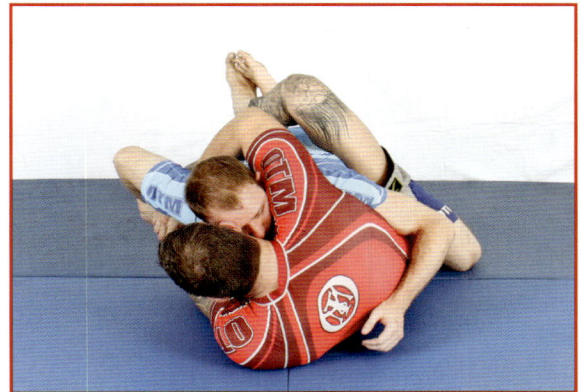

Without releasing my grips, I use both hands to maneuver Lance's right elbow to the inside of my left thigh.

8

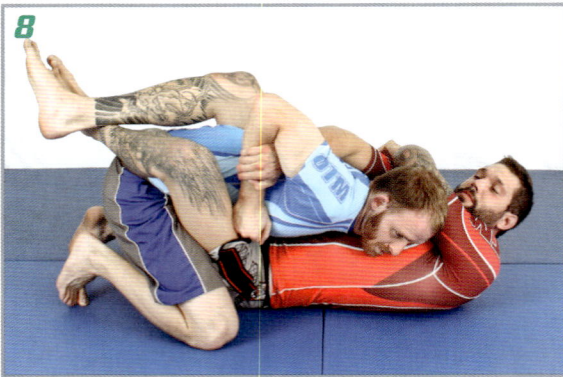

I maintain the Boston handshake as I swing my left arm to the right side of my body.

9

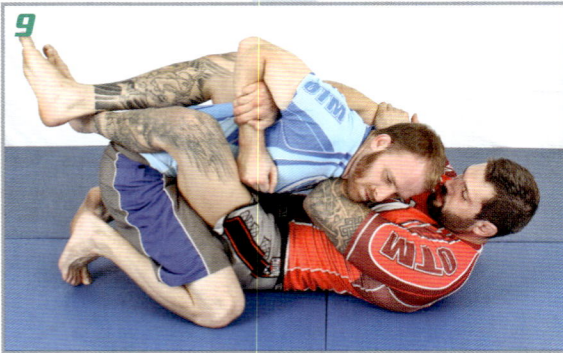

I begin to crossface Lance by driving my left elbow to the center of his chest as my left forearm grinds into his neck. My left hand grabs my right elbow to secure the position. I use the crossface to create space, forcing him to hover in my guard.

10

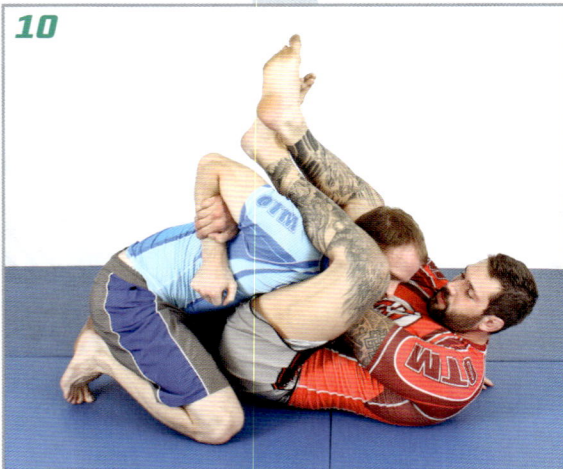

I throw my left leg over Lance's right shoulder as I elevate my hips.

11

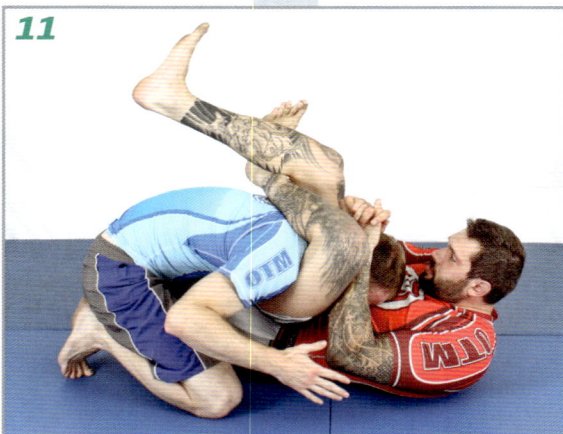

I lock and finish the arm on the mat triangle.

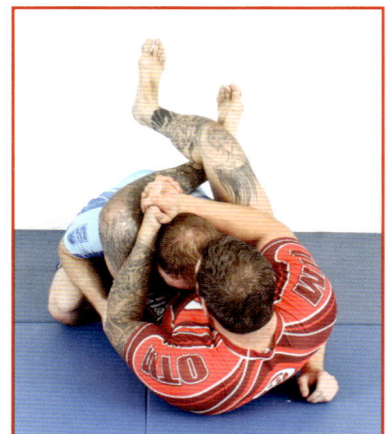

OVER-THE-BACK GRIP HAMMERLOCK OPTION

In the previous techniques, I looked to establish the Boston handshake, which allowed me to pin one of my opponent's arms and control his posture with one hand. Instead of gripping the forearm, I can choose to latch on to the wrist. With the wrist grip, I can pull my opponent's arm behind his back and attack with the hammerlock, an old-school submission that applies pressure similar to a double-wrist lock, or what you may call a Kimura. The hammerlock can sometimes be difficult to finish from guard, but the pressure creates discomfort and forces my opponent to deal with the threat of having his shoulder torqued into tearing. With his arm behind his back, throwing my leg over his shoulder for the triangle is relatively easy. Since I can maintain the hammerlock grip until just before I finish the triangle, my opponent has very few options to defend and is in pain right up until the point my hamstring begins to shut off blood flow to his brain. If you can get the hammerlock grip, do not pass it up, but I tend to prefer the Boston handshake because I feel that it is more secure.

1

Lance is in my guard.

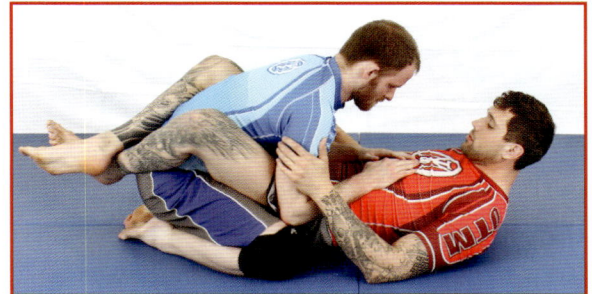

2

As I pull my knees toward my chest, I pummel my hands inside of his arms and force his arms to the outside.

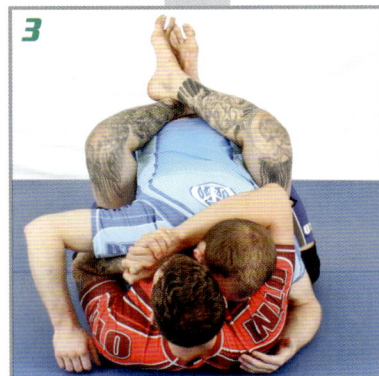

3

I have successfully pummeled both hands inside of Lance's arms to establish the Irish collar.

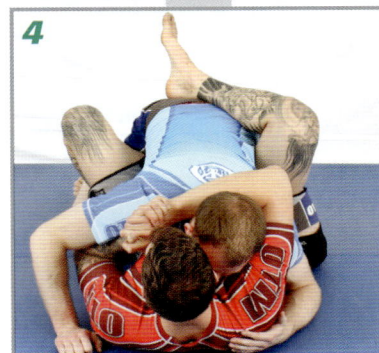

4

As my left foot hooks Lance's right ankle, my left forearm begins to drive into his right biceps to force his arm away from his body.

5

I post my right foot on Lance's left hip and shift onto my left hip as I straighten my left leg, securing the grapevine.

6

I cup Lance's right shoulder with my right hand as my left hand slides down his arm, pressing it away.

7

I latch on to Lance's right wrist with my left hand and immediately force it behind his back, passing his left wrist to my right hand.

8

To secure the hammerlock, my right hand pulls Lance's right wrist into his back. I could potentially finish him with a shoulder lock using this grip, but it is not strong enough to hold for a long period of time.

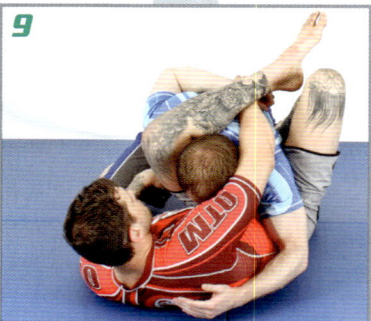

9

With the hammerlock in place, I throw my left leg over Lance's right shoulder, clearing his right arm for the triangle. I do not release the hammerlock until my left leg is across the back of his neck.

10

To finish the submission, I figure-four my legs and use an arm on-the-mat finish to win the fight.

IRISH COLLAR KINGPIN TRIANGLE

I call this technique the kingpin triangle because it is actually the beginning of a technique called the king-pin, a wrestling reversal that ends with your opponent pinned by your legs rather than your arms. As I used the original kingpin in the gym, I found that it was great for attacking an opponent high in my guard in the 0 degrees position, and it created openings for other attacks as well. Though bringing an opponent low in my guard is ideal, I have to accept that I will not always be able to maneuver my opponent into that position by moving myself away or by using a grapevine to drive him down. I can use the Irish collar to establish an over-the-back grip in this scenario, but not in the way that you might think. Since my opponent is high in my guard, my hand cannot reach around his back to grab his wrist or forearm for the over-the-back grip, but my foot can, leaving both of my arms free as I climb my other leg up for the triangle. As you will see in the photographs below, I demonstrate re-grabbing the arm just before you transition to the triangle finish. When you begin to use this technique, you may feel that you can just kick your leg free and set the triangle, and that's perfectly fine. Just know that, if you need to, you can re-grab the arm to make the transition.

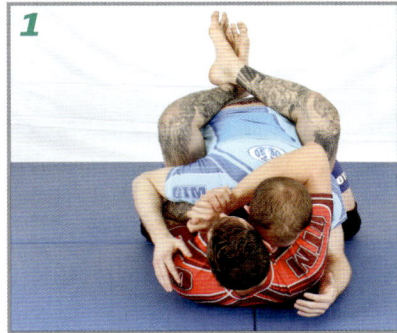

1

I pummel to the Irish collar.

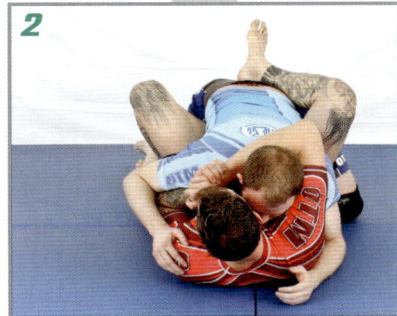

2

I drive my forearm into Lance's right biceps to force his right arm away from his body as I snake my left foot under his right ankle.

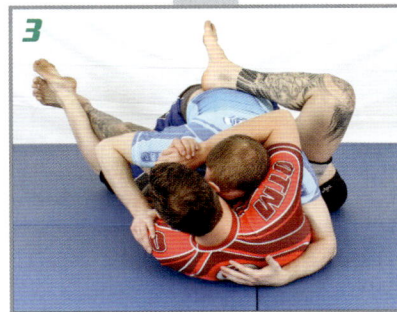

3

I straighten my left leg to lock the grapevine. Rather than post-ing my right foot on his left hip, as I did in previous techniques, I fold my right leg across his lower back. I can do this by choice or out of necessity.

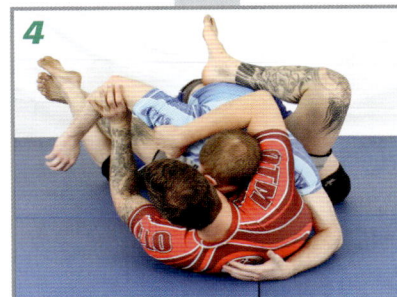

4

I release the Irish collar and cup his right shoulder with my right hand. My left hand begins to press his right arm backward as it slides down toward his wrist.

5

My left hand latches on to his right wrist and forces his arm to bend. My right foot threads under his right arm, hooking it for an unorthodox over-the-back grip.

6

I throw my left leg over his right shoulder, keeping his right arm locked in place with my right foot.

7

I choose to re-grab Lance's right wrist with my left hand to give me additional control as I kick my right leg free and post my right foot on his left hip. My right hand grips my left ankle, pulling my leg across the back of his neck.

8

Since the triangle started with Lance high in my guard, I hook his right arm with my left hand, lock my hands together, and use the combination of the arm hook and my right foot on his hip to shift my hips into position for the triangle.

9

I figure-four my legs and finish the triangle.

IRISH COLLAR TO FOREARM PINCH TRIANGLE

As much as I love to use over-the-back grips, they can be difficult to secure on a skilled opponent. A seasoned grappler will know that he is in danger as soon as you begin using your hands to control his biceps or his wrists. He will instinctively keep his elbows and arms close to his body and out of danger. If your attempts at using an over-the-back grip have failed because your opponent knew to hide his arms, use the Irish collar to trick him into pummeling. He will assume that you are attempting to isolate his arm using one of the previous techniques in this chapter, and immediately snake his arm back to where he believes it is safe. You can then use the Irish collar to pin his wrist with your forearm and lock the triangle. He will not suspect that he is danger in because you are not using your hands to control his arm, and he is using a movement that has beaten your attacks before. Techniques like the forearm pinch can be difficult to learn to use because they require a high level of coordination and finesse because maintaining a position like the Irish collar limits your mobility somewhat, but the future of the no-gi guard is techniques like this one.

1

Lance is in my guard at the 0 degrees position, and I am controlling him with the Irish collar.

2

I lean onto my left hip and shift off line.

3

My left forearm pushes Lance's right biceps away as I post my right foot on his left hip. As I force his right arm away from his body, I slide my left knee in front of his right biceps. In this step, it is important to continue squeezing with the Irish collar to limit his ability to duck out. If he stacks, I can still do this technique, but if he moves away from me, I will lose my opportunity.

4

I continue to pull my left knee toward my chest, setting Lance's right biceps in the middle of my left shin as though I were looking to secure a biceps ride. I maintain the Irish collar even though that means not controlling his right arm with my hands or arms. For this technique, I want him to have the space to pummel back inside.

5

Lance feels that he is in danger and begins to pummel his right hand on top of my left biceps to bring his arm back inside of my legs.

6

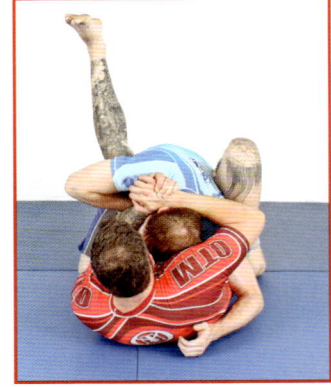

I kick my left leg into the air, creating a ramp for Lance's right arm to slide down. At the same time, I jam my left forearm into his right wrist to create pinching pressure.

7

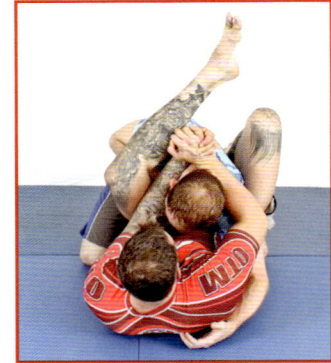

I drop my left leg, while continuing to drive my left forearm into his right wrist, sticking his right arm into his ribs. My left forearm pins it in place.

8

I throw my left leg over Lance's right shoulder, clearing his pinned right arm to begin securing the triangle. I still have the Irish collar in place.

9

I lock my left leg in the crook of my right knee and finish the triangle.

ALTERNATE STEP

The forearm pinch can also be used without first going to the biceps ride. When Lance pummels inside of the Irish collar, I drive my right forearm into his left forearm to pinch it to his ribs. I then throw my right leg over for the triangle. The concept of countering the pummel is the same with or without my knee inside, but sometimes your opponent will not pummel back inside if you are using just the Irish collar.

1

I am controlling Lance with the Irish collar, and his left hand is inside of my right arm.

2

To pin Lance's left arm, I pinch my right elbow against his left arm to drive it into his chest.

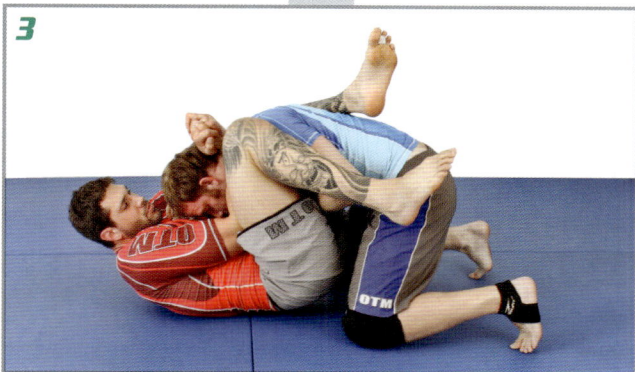

3

Using the Irish collar grip, I push Lance low in my guard as I open my legs and swing my right leg out.

4

I clear Lance's left arm and slap my right hamstring against his neck. Now that I have beat his arm, I can lock my legs and finish the triangle with whatever finish I feel is appropriate.

OVERHOOK LEG-THROUGH OPTIONS

In the 45 degrees chapter, you learned three different approaches to the leg-through triangle: the downward grip variation, the upward grip variation, and the biceps push. The downward grip is useful for bringing your opponent into you to counter his backward movement. The upward grip is useful for relieving pressure, forcing your opponent to move up and back. The biceps push is useful for surprising your opponent once you have "lulled him to sleep" by acting passively. Each option is effective in the appropriate situation, but once a grip is established, the details of the leg-through triangle are relatively the same. Rather than cover the same triangle three times, the photographs below demonstrate the downward grip variation, but you can substitute the upward grip or the biceps push. These are the most basic triangles from the overhook and will be your first options from the position. If your opponent resists having his arm forced away from his body, move on to using pins and forearm pinches.

1

Lance is in the 45 degrees position, and I am overhooking his left arm.

2

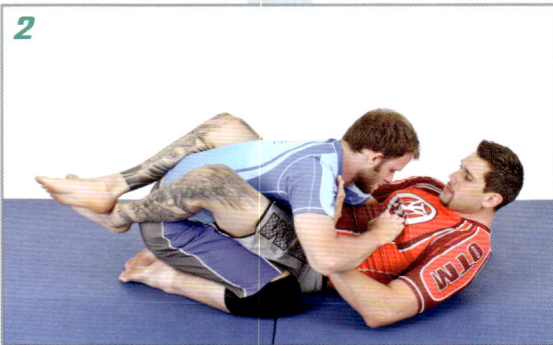

I pummel my left hand to the inside under Lance's right arm and begin to press his right biceps away from his body.

3

My left hand slides down Lance's right arm and latches on to a downward grip on his right wrist. I twist his right wrist counterclockwise and force his arm away from his body. I open my guard and shift onto my left hip. I control Lance's backward movement by curling my left leg onto his back, and I control his forward movement by posting my right foot on his hip.

4

I feed my left leg-through the space that I created in the previous step by cranking Lance's right arm.

5

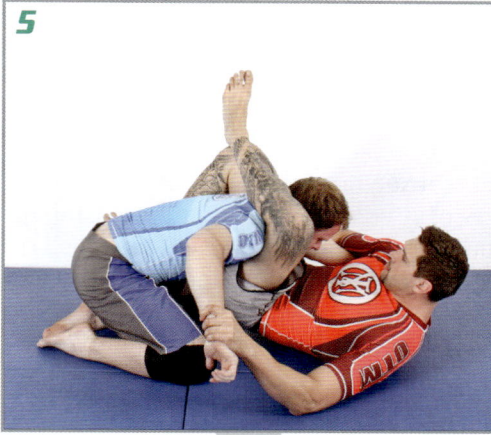

I elevate my hips and set my left leg across the back of Lance's neck and yank on his right arm with my overhook to pull him deeper into the triangle.

6

My left arm hooks Lance's right leg as I angle my hips and lock my legs to finish an arm on the mat triangle.

ALTERNATE OPTIONS

I can also use an upward grip or a biceps push to execute the leg-through triangle. If I feel that I need more control over Lance's upper body, I can release my overhook and wrap my right arm around my right leg and hook the front of his left shoulder with my right hand. I can do this with virtually any overhook triangle.

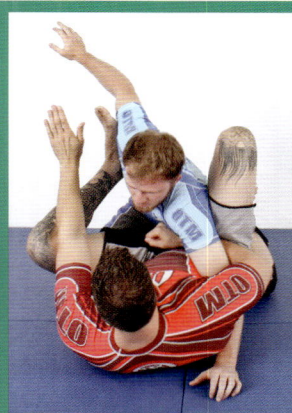

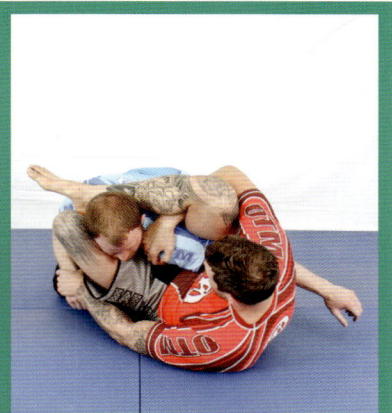

UPWARD GRIP   **BICEPS PUSH**   **SHOULDER PIN**

OVERHOOK PUSH PIN

When you work for a leg-through triangle, especially the downward grip or the biceps push, a skilled opponent will anticipate the triangle as soon as he feels one of his arms being forced away from his body. As your leg maneuvers under his arm, he can block the triangle by hugging it. If you try to continue with the leg-through, your opponent will stall out the triangle until he can escape. To counter the leg hug, pull on his arm with your wrist control and drive your knee into his biceps to create two forms of pressure—pulling and pressing—to control his arm. Then, kick your leg straight and low. The sudden disappearance of your leg will suck his arm to his body, where you can pin it and transition to the triangle. Your opponent's focus on defending the leg-through triangle, which requires him to pull his arm toward his body, makes him vulnerable to wrist pins. You will need this technique if you work the leg-through triangle because your opponent will always defend it.

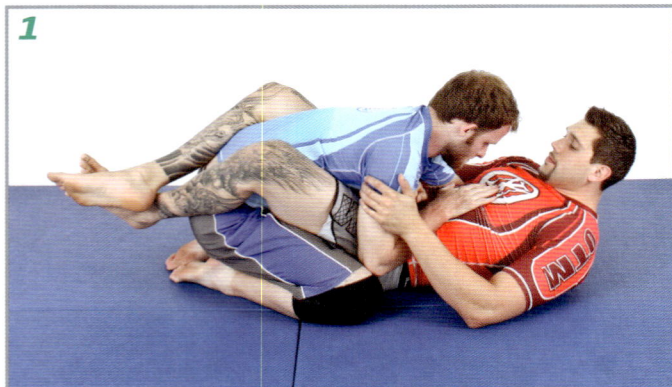

I am controlling Lance with an overhook.

I begin to set up a leg-through triangle by pummeling my left hand under Lance's right forearm and pressing his right biceps away from his body.

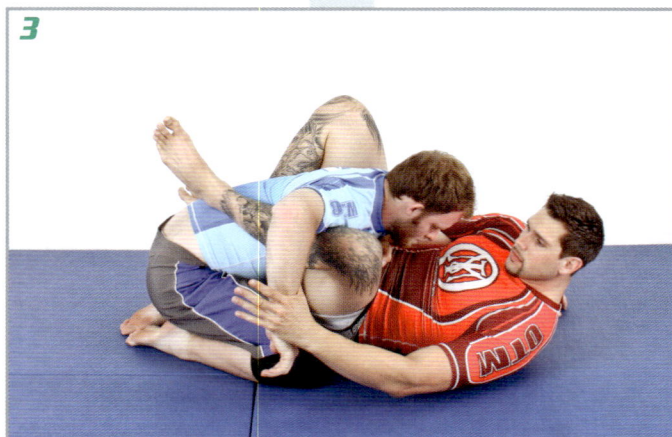

I open my guard, shifting onto my left hip as I post my right foot on Lance's left hip and curl my left leg onto his back. I begin to slide my left hand to Lance's right wrist as I clear my left knee under his right elbow.

4

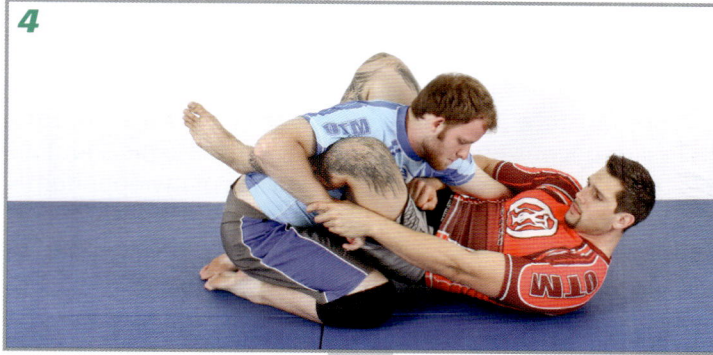

Lance defends the leg-through triangle by hugging my left leg with his right arm. I encourage him to hug tighter by pulling his right arm into my left shin as I drive my left shin into his right biceps.

5

I kick my left leg straight and pin Lance's right wrist to his ribs as my left leg clears his right arm.

6

My left leg swings over the back of Lance's neck, trapping his head and left arm between my legs.

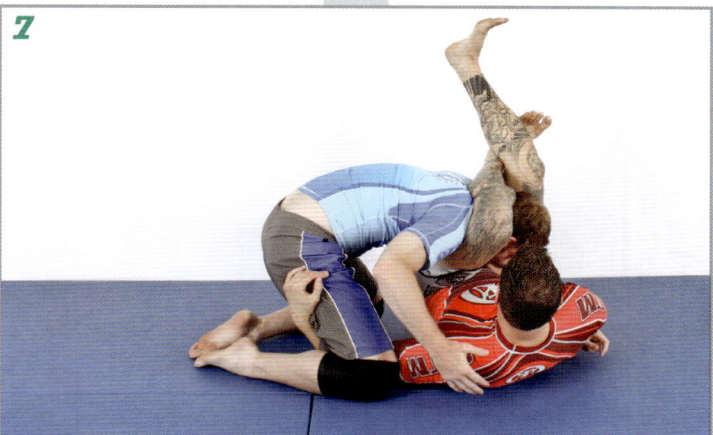

7

I hook Lance's right leg with my left arm and rotate my head toward his right knee. I figure-four my legs to finish the triangle.

OVERHOOK LEG CIRCLE HEEL PUSH

In this technique, like in the previous technique, I am working to finish a leg-through triangle, and my opponent resists by hugging my leg. Typically, I would not hesitate to use the push pin, but if I feel that my opponent is aware of my intentions, I do not want to risk it because he could explode and slam his shoulder forward to escape the triangle before I have a chance to lock my legs. I still drop my leg out of my opponent's grip, but rather than pinning his arm and bringing my leg over the top of his arm (requiring me to release his wrist), I maintain wrist control and circle my leg around digging my heel into the crook of his arm. I pull his arm, while simultaneously pressing with my leg. This takes his arm out of the game completely, giving me a clear, controlled path to the triangle.

Lance is in my guard, and I have an overhook.

I post my right foot on the mat and shift off line.

I set my right foot on Lance's left hip and latch on to his right wrist with my left hand with a downward grip.

My left knee slides under Lance's right arm as I force it away with my downward grip.

5

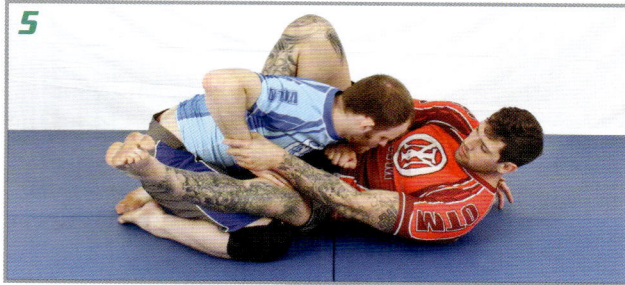

Lance hugs my left knee with his right arm to defend the triangle. I decide that he will explode through push pin, so I kick my left leg straight and begin to circle it outward.

6

Without releasing Lance's right wrist, I maneuver my left leg over my arm and dig my left heel into his right biceps.

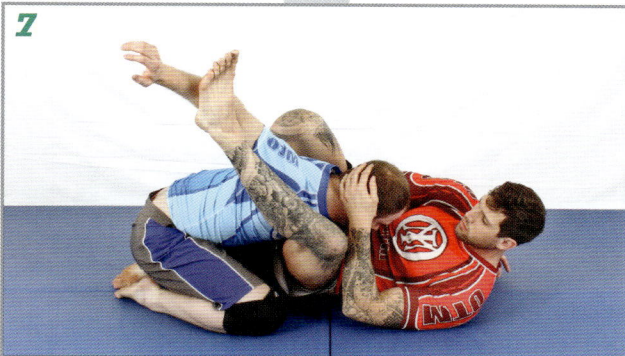

7

I straighten my left leg, pressing Lance's right arm to the ceiling.

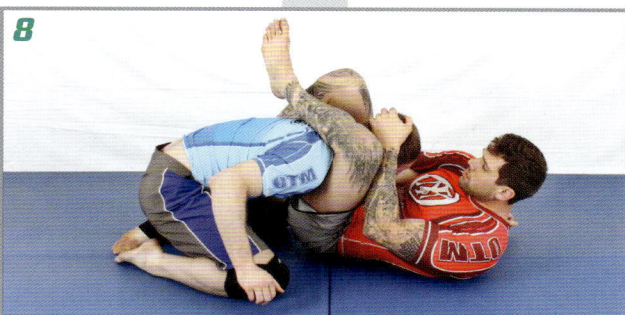

8

I throw my left leg over the back of Lance's neck, clearing his right arm.

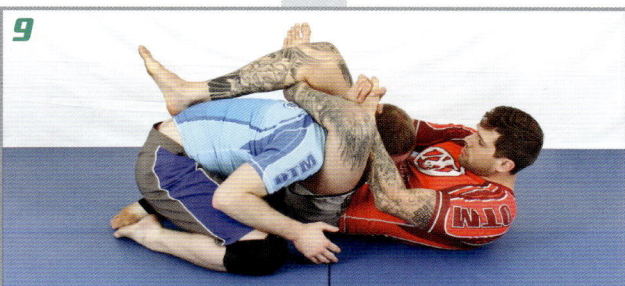

9

I figure-four my legs and finish the triangle.

OVERHOOK WRIST PIN WITH GRAPEVINE

When leg-through triangles fail, work with your opponent's resistance by transitioning to wrist pin triangles, just like you did with the push pin. Though it has been my experience that wrist pin triangles tend to be the most feasible triangles to execute, because they require minimal hip movement and very little flexibility, you should not abandon leg-through triangles. Switch between the two strategies to keep your opponent confused and off balance. The mechanics of the wrist pin allow you to bring your leg over the pinned arm and crush your weight on top of it, which can be easier to do when your opponent is fixated on keeping his arm from flaring out for the leg-through triangle. Earlier in the book, I covered a wrist pin variation where my opponent hugged my hips with his elbow to block the triangle. I used a grapevine to collapse his base, free my hip, and transition to the triangle. The same principle is at work in this technique, except I have overhook control. Just when he feels as though he has beaten my triangle, I grapevine his leg and go for the triangle. That initial false sense of security that my opponent experiences when he hugs my hip makes this technique exceptionally effective.

I am controlling Lance's left arm with an overhook. I figure-four my hands and cup his shoulder for optimal control.

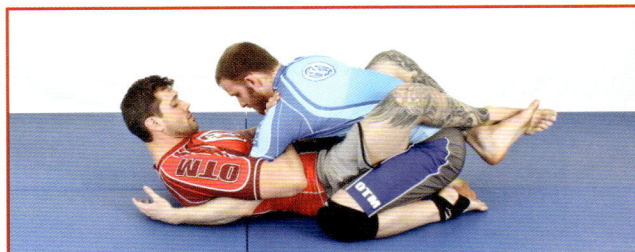

I post my right foot on the mat and shift onto my left hip.

I quickly dig my right foot into Lance's left hip to delay his forward movement as my left leg curls onto his back to delay his backward movement.

My left hand latches on to Lance's right wrist and works to pin his right wrist to his ribs, but he hugs his elbow to the outside of my left thigh to prevent me from clearing his right arm.

5

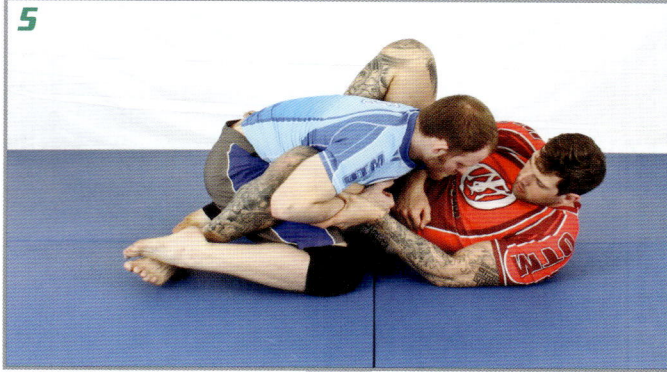

I snake my left foot under Lance's right ankle.

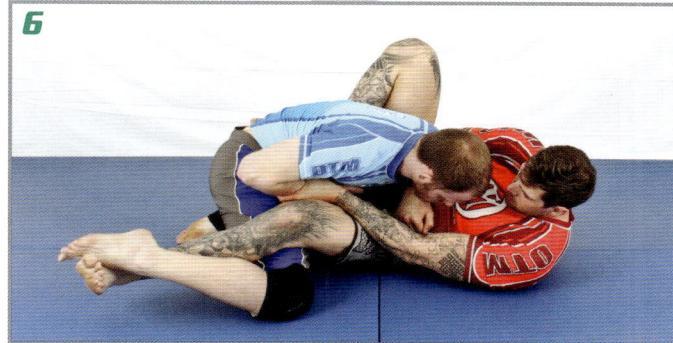

6

I simultaneously straighten my left leg to sink the grapevine as I continue to drive his right wrist toward his ribs, sucking his right arm to his body.

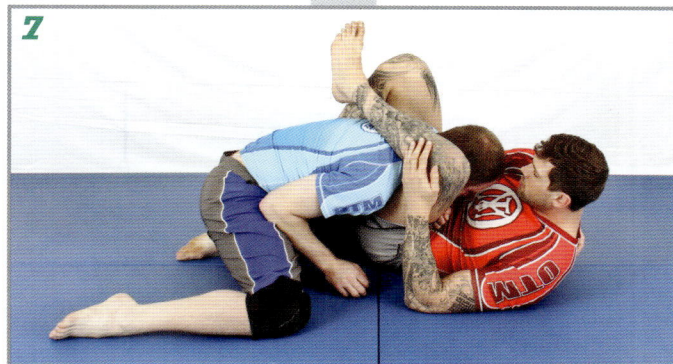

7

I swing my left leg over the back of Lance's neck and elevate my hips.

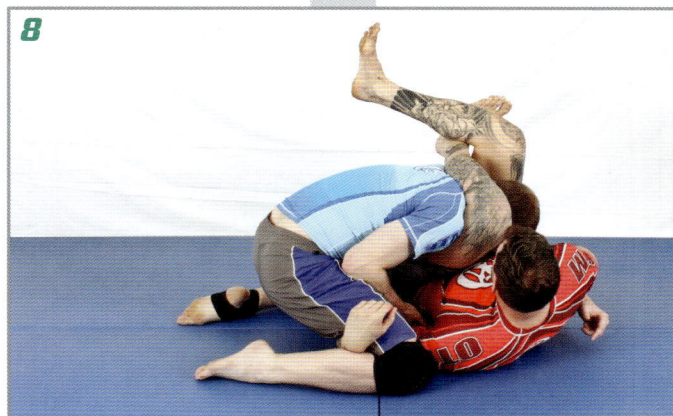

8

I maintain my right overhook as I hook Lance's right leg with my left arm, swiveling my hips into position for the triangle. I figure-four my legs and finish the choke with his arm on the mat.

OVERHOOK WRIST FEED TO FOREARM PINCH

As much as I love to use grapevines from guard to attack my opponent's base and delay his three directions of movement, a grapevine is not always easy to establish, especially if my opponent is sinking his hips into his heels. Trying to force the grapevine when the opening is not there could lead to having my guard passed, so I focus on clearing an arm. A wrist pin, as you have seen in previous techniques, is easily countered by a hip hug. Without the assistance of the grapevine, I need a more methodical approach to isolating and clearing an arm to set the triangle. The wrist feed allows me to control both of my opponent's arms simultaneously by gripping my opponent's far wrist with my overhook arm. I cannot hold the grip forever, because my opponent will immediately start to work free, but if I just throw my legs for a triangle, I will likely lose the triangle as well. The solution: I establish a collar tie to control his posture and use the blade of my forearm to pinch his arm against his body, making my transition to the triangle more controlled, more efficient, and more likely to succeed.

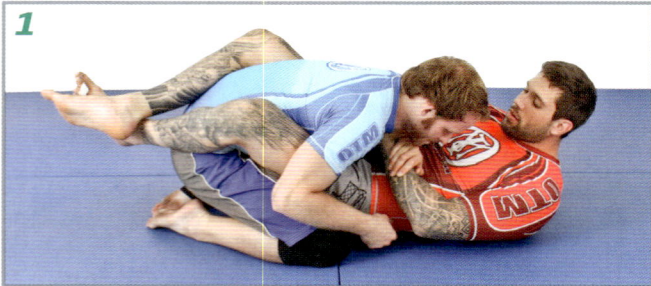

1

I have secured overhook control.

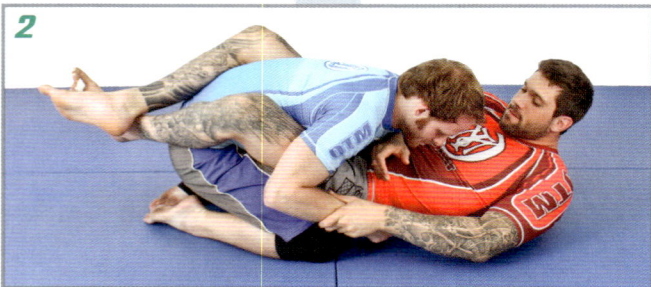

2

I establish a downward grip on Lance's right wrist, keeping my guard closed.

3

I drive Lance's right wrist toward his stomach, attempting the wrist pin triangle. He defends by hugging his elbow against the outside of my hip, and I feel that his butt is too close to his heels for me to use a grapevine. As soon as I feel that the grapevine is unavailable, I feed his right wrist to my right hand.

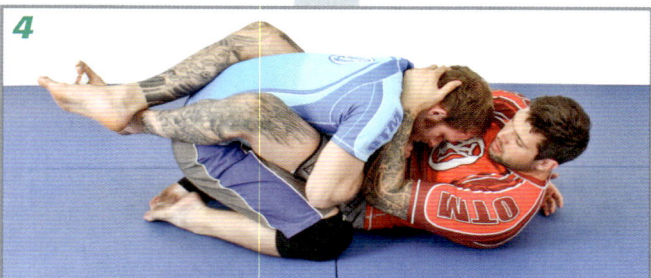

4

My left hand grabs the base of Lance's skull as my left forearm digs into his collarbone.

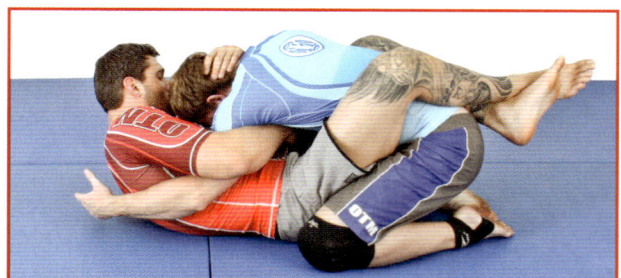

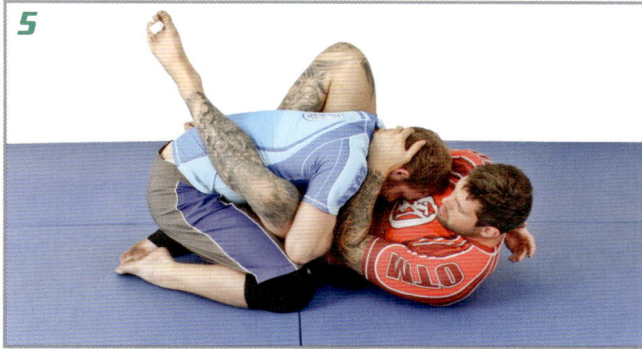

Lance tries to free his right arm by pulling back, inadvertently relieving the pressure on my hips. As he does this, I shift onto my left hip and post my right foot on his left hip.

I drive my right foot into Lance's hip and yank with my right overhook to stretch him out. His body extends. My left forearm drives into his right forearm, pinching his right wrist to his chest as my left leg circles to the outside of his right elbow.

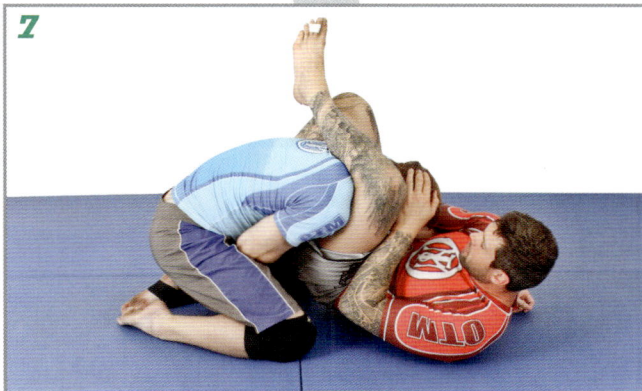

I set my left leg across the back of Lance's neck, clearing his right arm.

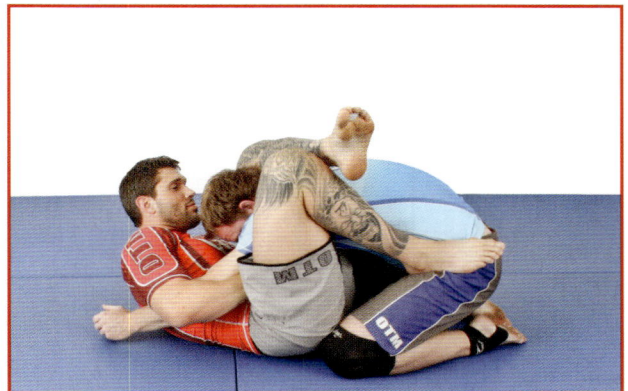

I hook Lance's right leg with my left arm, swivel my hips, and use an arm on the mat finish to end the fight.

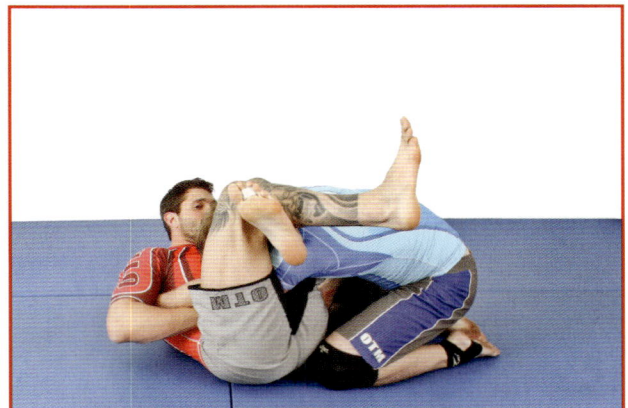

OVERHOOK WRIST FEED TO CORNER LOCK TRIANGLE

The principle that makes the wrist feed work, passing your opponent's free hand to your overhook hand so that you can control two of his arms with just one of your arms, can be used to set up different variations of the triangle and other submissions as well. The weakness of using the forearm pinch from the wrist feed is that if you miss it your opponent is nearly free of the overhook. If your opponent is mobile and explosive, use the wrist feed to transition to the corner lock. The corner lock will give you more control and more options. You can use the corner lock for the triangle, armbars, omoplatas, or sweeps—it is a very dangerous position. The corner lock will succeed where the forearm pinch failed, but setting up the corner lock from the wrist feed does require a bit more movement. It's a trade-off. If you can end the fight quickly with the forearm pinch, do it. If not, secure the corner lock and end the fight from there.

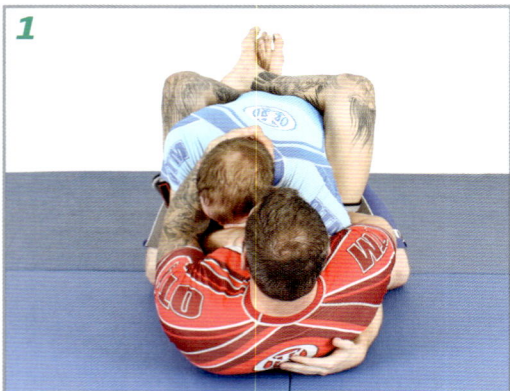

I am controlling Lance with an overhook and a collar tie.

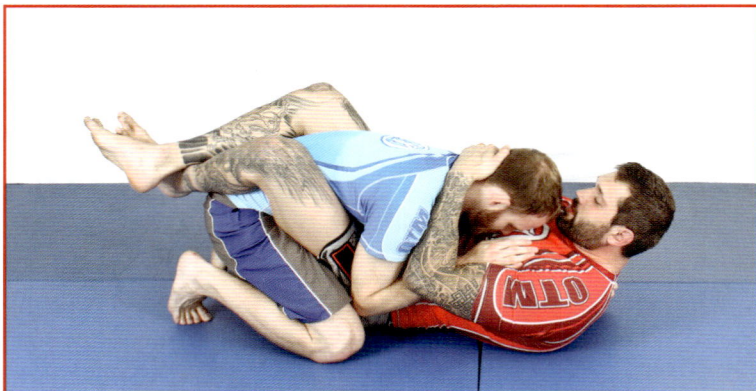

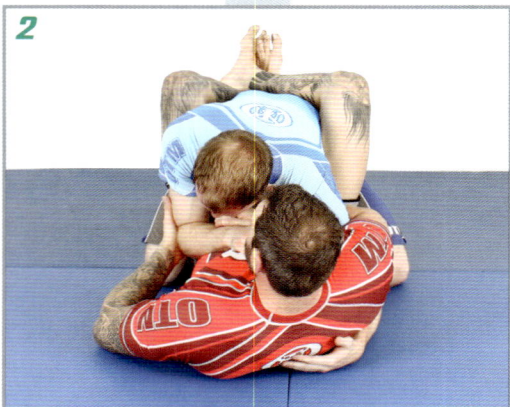

I cup Lance's right elbow with my left hand.

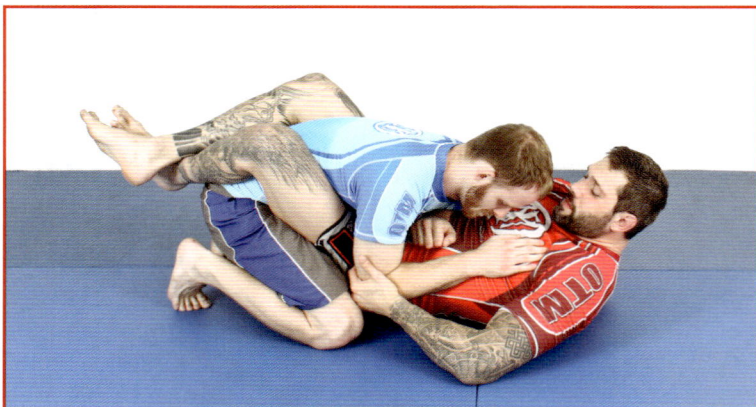

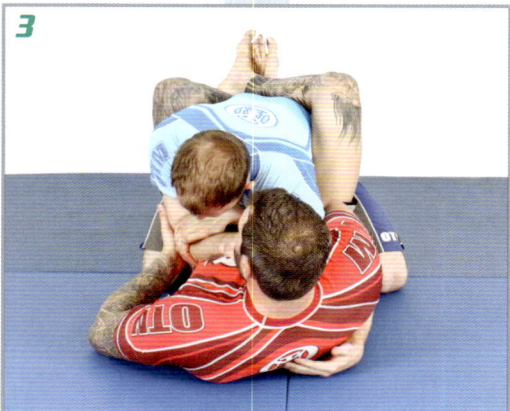

I maintain the overhook as I my right hand latches on to Lance's left forearm, using a thumbless grip.

4

I push Lance away with my guard, straightening my body.

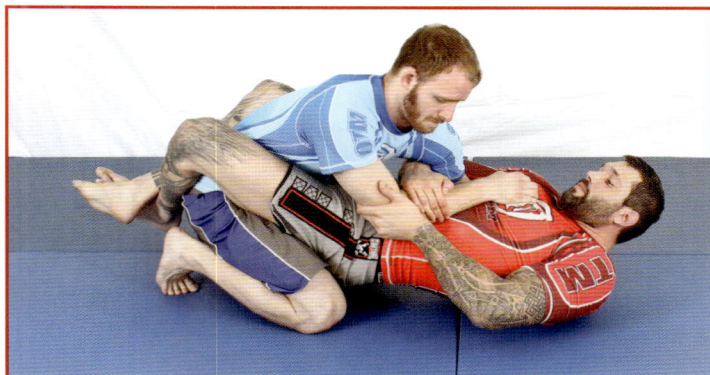

5

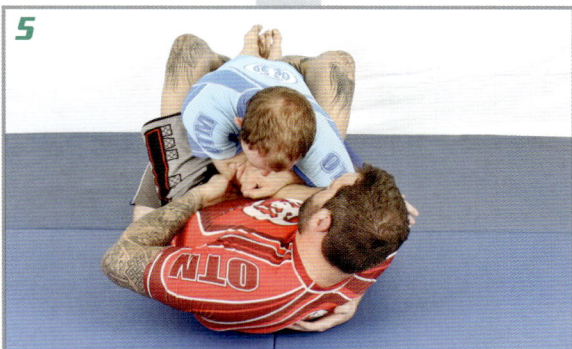

My two-on-one grip yanks Lance's right arm to the center of my stomach as I pull my knees toward my chest. If I need to, I can shove his right elbow deeper with my left hand.

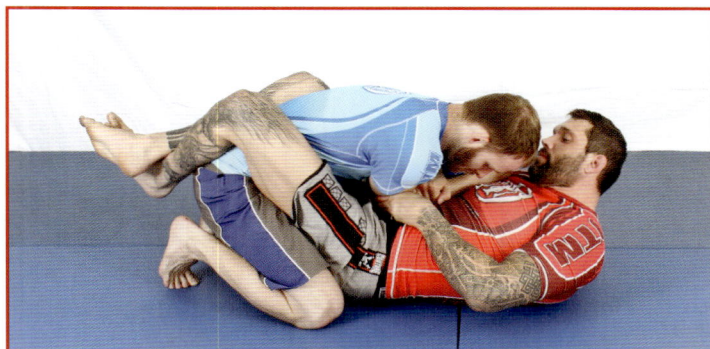

6

My left hand shoots under Lance's chin and cups his left shoulder, positioning my left forearm in a crossface position. If he should attempt to stack me, I will use the crossface to delay his forward motion.

7

I elevate my hips and climb my left leg over Lance's right shoulder and cross my ankles to secure the corner lock. I squeeze my thighs and curl my legs into his back to make the corner lock as tight as possible.

8

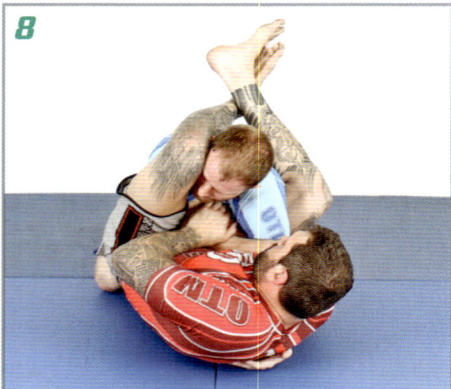

My left hand grips Lance's right biceps. In this position, he assumes that I am looking for the armbar, so he retracts his right arm, trying to free his elbow.

9

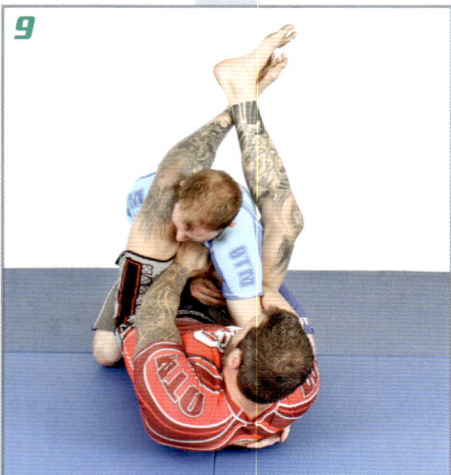

I pump my legs, straightening them and curling them repeatedly. As my legs pump, I push his right arm between my legs with both my hands.

10

As soon as Lance's right arm is outside of my guard, I control his head with my left hand to delay his ability to posture.

11

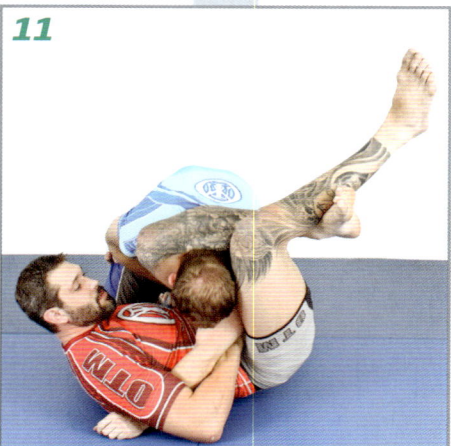

I hook Lance's right leg with my left arm and figure-four my legs, ending the fight by triangle.

THE ANCHOR

The overhook is a great grip to control your opponent's upper body, but you can further increase your control by latching on to his lower body, hooking his leg with your overhook arm. In this position, your body weight traps his arm in place and gives you control of his leg. I call this position the anchor. The angle and level of control that the anchor gives you is ideal for securing a tight, painful corner lock. With this style of corner lock in place, you can attack with sweeps, armbars, triangles, and omoplatas. The key to what option you take depends on how you crossface your opponent. If you crossface high on his head, you use an armbar. If you crossface low, you use the triangle. Though Randy Couture is not known as a guard player, he loves this position and uses it to keep his opponent trapped so that he can focus on attacking. The two drawbacks to using the anchor are that it requires more movement to secure the triangle than other overhook techniques. Additionally, if you fail to secure a deep leg hook initially, your opponent can sprawl and smother the triangle.

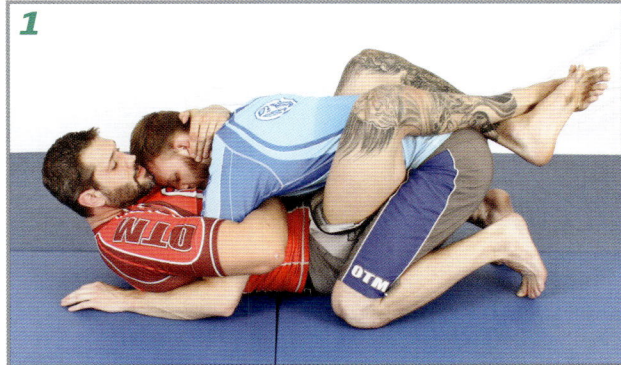

I am controlling Lance with an overhook and a collar tie.

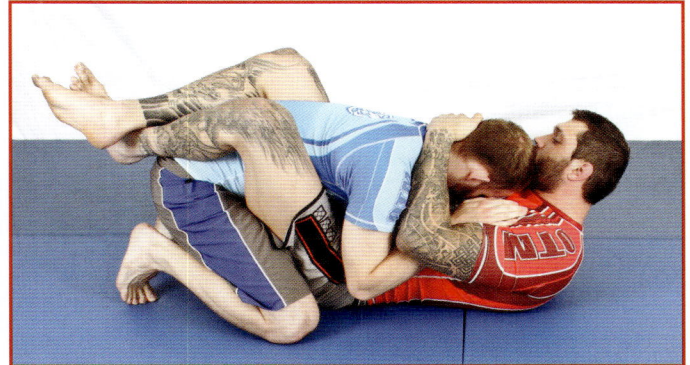

I continue to control Lance's head with the collar tie as my right hand snakes under his left leg, hooking it.

I throw my torso toward Lance's left knee and over his left arm by pulling on his left leg with my right arm. I put my left foot on his hip at the same time. This position should be tight and uncomfortable for him.

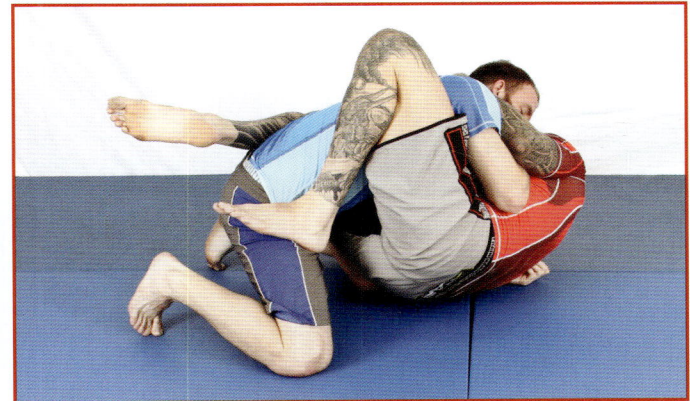

4

My left hand releases Lance's head and maneuvers to the left side of his face. I drive my left forearm across his throat and cup his left shoulder with my left hand.

5

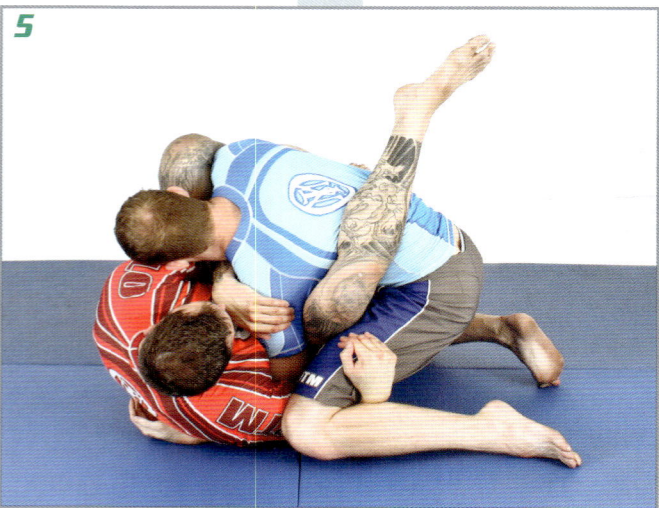

I crossface Lance by using my forearm to crank his chin away. I grind the crossface to make it as painful as possible. As I crossface him, I pinch my left knee in front of his right shoulder to begin climbing my legs up.

6

I circle my left heel to the middle of Lance's back and cross my ankles to secure a corner lock. If I maneuver correctly, I can beat his arm completely with this technique, but sometimes his right hand will be stuck inside, which is fine. I can still lock and finish the triangle even if his hand is inside.

7

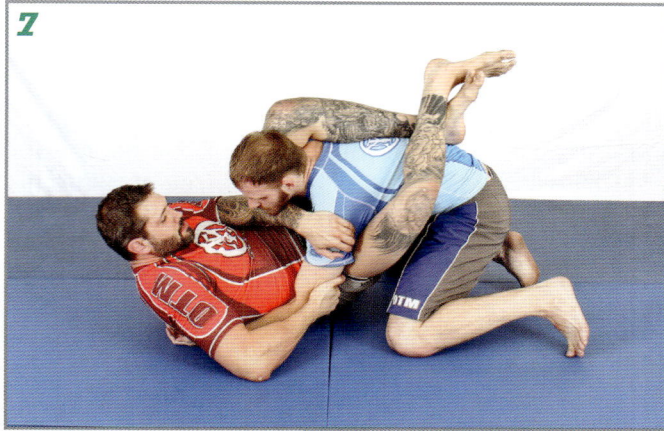

I grab his left arm with both hands and push my closed guard away to stretch him out, allowing me to swivel my shoulders toward my left to give me a better angle for the triangle.

8

I cup the base of his skull with my left hand, while controlling his left elbow with my right hand. I use both grips to pull him deeper into my triangle.

9

My left hand presses Lance's head into the back of my left thigh as I pinch my right knee over his left shoulder.

10

I lock my legs and finish the armbar triangle.

OVERHOOK SCISSOR KNEE PIN TRIANGLE

The anchor is an excellent option for giving you more control in the overhook position, but if your opponent is already pulling away, releasing your figure-four to reach for your opponent's head or leg could give him the space he needs to completely rip out of your overhook. If you can cling to your overhook and figure-four grip, you can counter your opponent's upward movement by using your leg to smash his free arm into his chest, allowing you to clear his arm for the triangle without ever releasing your grip. If your opponent is stacking in, you will not have the space to bring your knee over his arm. If that is the case, you can use any of the other overhook triangles in this chapter. However, if your opponent is trying to move away, the scissor knee pin is a quick and powerful way to land the triangle.

1

I am controlling Lance in the 0 degrees position with an overhook and a figure-four grip.

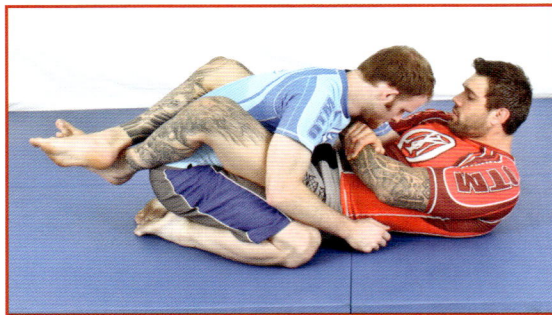

2

Lance begins to pull away from my overhook, creating space. I could also use my left arm as a crossface and drive him away to create space.

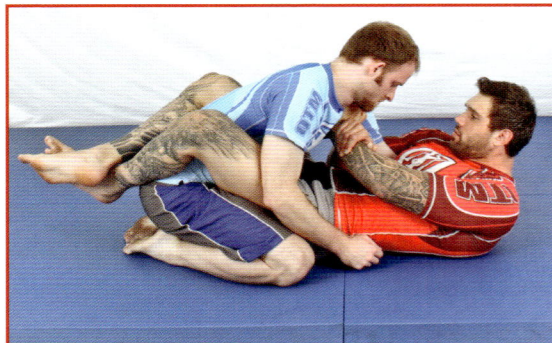

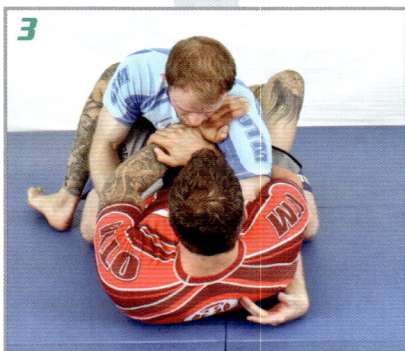

3

My left foot posts on the mat, and I hip out, leaning onto my right hip.

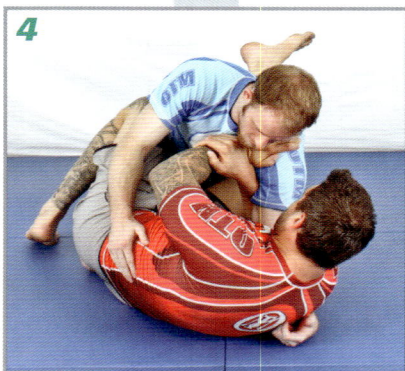

4

I scoot my hips away from Lance to create even more space.

5

I curl my left knee to my chest as I push my right leg down into his left hip to compensate for my inability to post my right foot on his hip.

6

My left knee rolls over Lance's right arm and down his chest, pinning his right arm to his body.

7

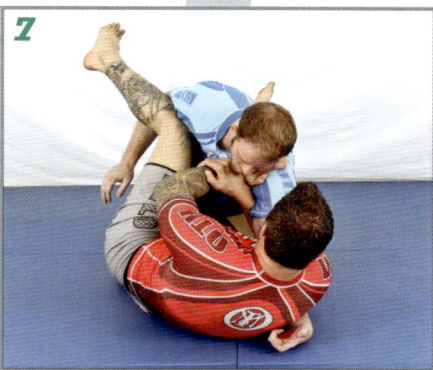

I elevate my hips and push Lance's right biceps with my left knee cap. It's important that I use this motion to force his arm back away from his body. If I do not, he could swim his arm back inside and defend the triangle.

8

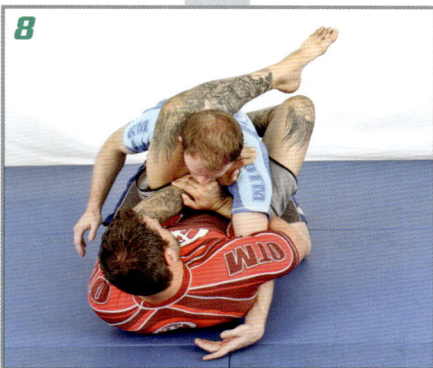

My left foot swivels to the other side of Lance's back, slapping my left hamstring against his neck.

9

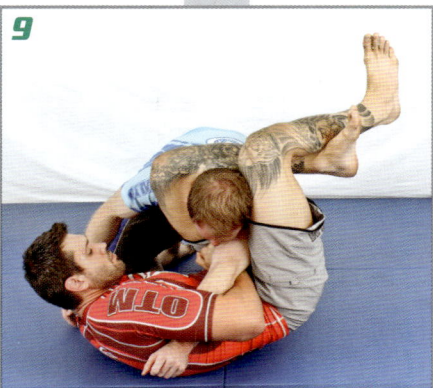

My left arm hooks Lance's right leg, and I swivel to lock my legs and finish the triangle.

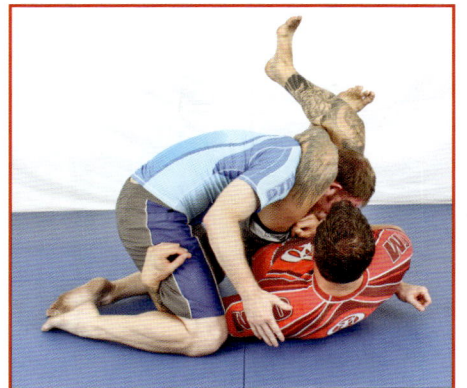

GENE LEBELL'S THREE-FINGER GRIP

Although the entirety of my shoulder pin system cannot fit in this book, I can teach you the core; it's the three-finger grip. I learned the three-finger grip from Gene LeBell, and it is the key to a successful shoulder pin. It's an old catch wrestling grip, I have seen in black-and-white photographs that date back over 100 years, but in all likelihood the three-finger grip is older than that. If you go through all of the work to force your opponent's arm to the mat, hook your own leg, and clasp your hands together with any grip other than the three-finger grip, you will eventually lose the pin, especially if you are sweaty. The three-finger grip allows you to create three directions of pressure. Your arm hooking your own leg hugs into your opponent's arm to trap it to your body. That same arm then pulls down as though you were driving your elbow to the mat and his shoulder to your toes with a movement similar to a triceps extension, which digs the wristwatch section of your forearm into the AC joint of your opponent's shoulder. The final direction comes from rotating your other forearm, starting from the middle of your opponent's chest, into his neck, creating upward pressure with a crossface. This forces your opponent to hover, putting him a precarious position. When done correctly this should be very painful for your opponent which could force him to make mistakes.

If I am working on my right side, my right index and middle fingers separate, creating a groove for my left thumb to slide into. With the three-finger grip established, I can maneuver my forearms freely without losing the grip. If I were to try bringing my wrists together with a gable grip, for example, my grip would begin to slip. With the three-finger grip, my hands remain locked together.

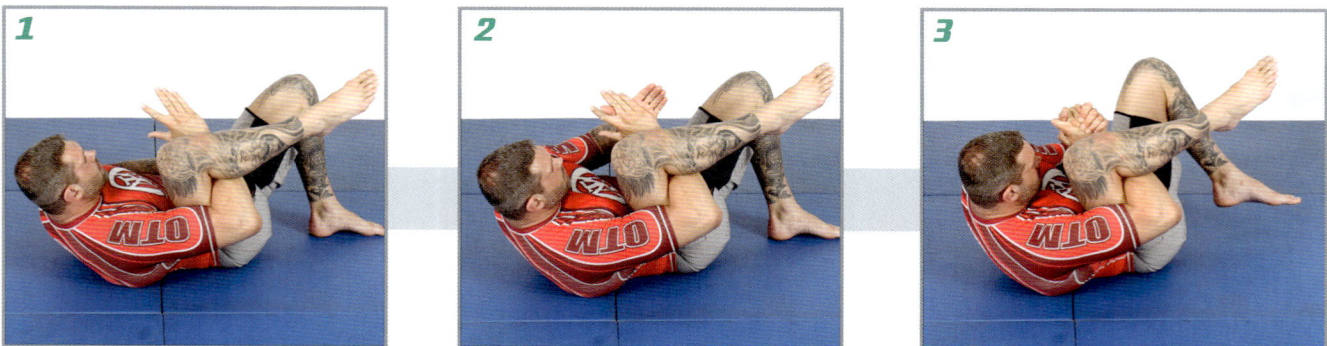

I secure the shoulder pin by sliding my right arm under my right knee and locking my left thumb between the index and middle finger of my right hand. I then apply three directions of pressure by hugging my right knee with my right arm, driving my right elbow down into and toward my toes by performing a triceps extension with my right arm, and rolling my left elbow up.

SHOULDER PIN GRAPEVINE LEG-THROUGH

As you will see in the sequence below, and in the next few techniques to follow, I am attacking from the triangle side of the shoulder pin, leaning on my left hip. If you are new to the shoulder pin, you will likely be most comfortable learning the triangle side first. Though you will learn a variety of other shoulder pin attacks later in this chapter, using a grapevine to set the triangle should be relatively easy if you have been using the other grapevine triangles in this book. When you hook a grapevine from the shoulder pin position, you can actually create hip lock pressure by pressing his head away as your grapevine collapses his base. The hip lock is not consistent in terms of getting a tap, but it is an effective method of distracting your opponent and tricking him into posting his arm on the mat. When he posts his arms, control his wrist and transition to the leg-through triangle.

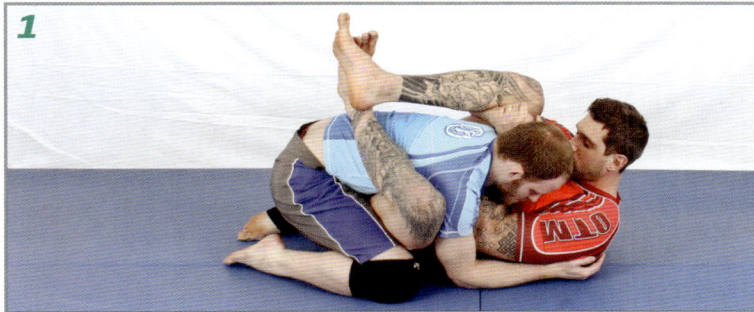

I am locking Lance's left shoulder with a shoulder pin, using my three-finger grip to apply three directions of pressure.

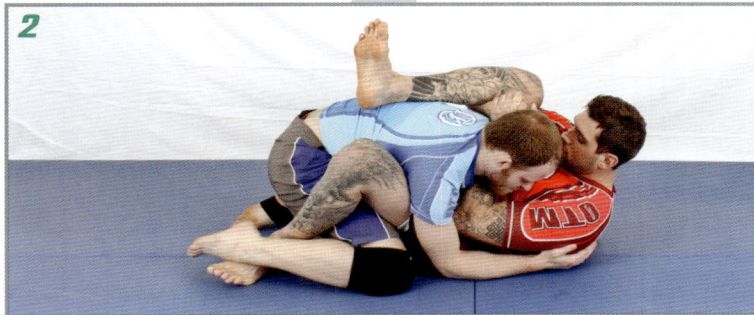

I drop my left leg and lace my left foot under Lance's right ankle.

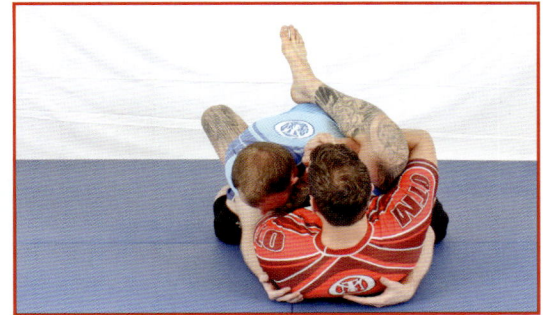

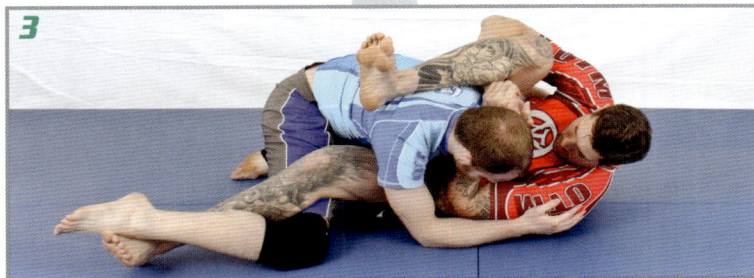

I straighten my left leg to sink the grapevine, collapsing Lance's base to his right side.

I release my three-finger grip and drive my left hand into Lance's face, creating a pinching pressure in his spine. My right hand cups his left shoulder for additional stability as I dig my right heel into the front of his right shoulder.

5

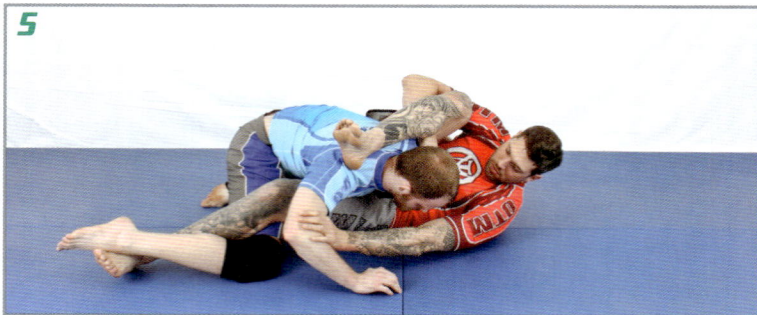

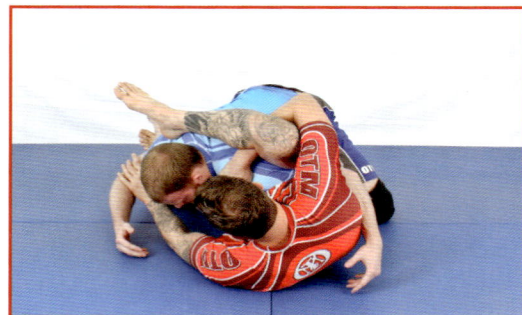

As Lance drives back into me to relieve the pressure on his neck, I slide my left hand down to his right biceps.

6

My left hand continues to slide down Lance's right arm and latches on to his right wrist. I force his right arm away from his body with my left hand.

7

I pull my left knee to my chest, maneuvering it out from underneath of Lance's right arm.

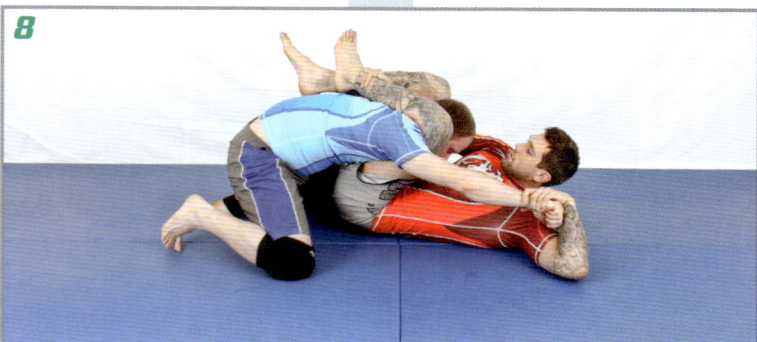

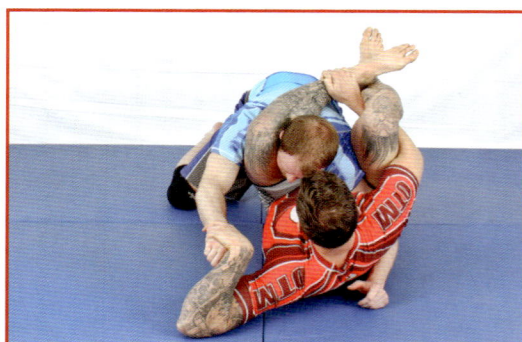

8

My left leg shoots across the back of Lance's neck, clearing his right arm.

9

I secure the triangle and finish the fight.

SHOULDER PIN TO THREE-POINTS POSITION

If you cannot get a grapevine on your opponent because he is sitting on his heels, the next most effective control positions to set up from the shoulder pin is what I call the three-points position. If you attempt to isolate one of your opponent's arms in any other way, you will have to release your shoulder pin. If you release your grip before you have established a replacement control position, your opponent will explode out. As you will see in the sequence below, the three-points position allows you to use your legs to control your opponent. With the three-points position established, you can release your three-finger grip and safely use your free hand to grab your opponent's wrist and fight for a triangle setup because the three-points position controls your opponent's posture, his forward movement, and his backward movement. It is the key to getting triangles from the shoulder pin on the triangle side when your grapevine fails, and if you do not set it up properly, your finish rate will be abysmal.

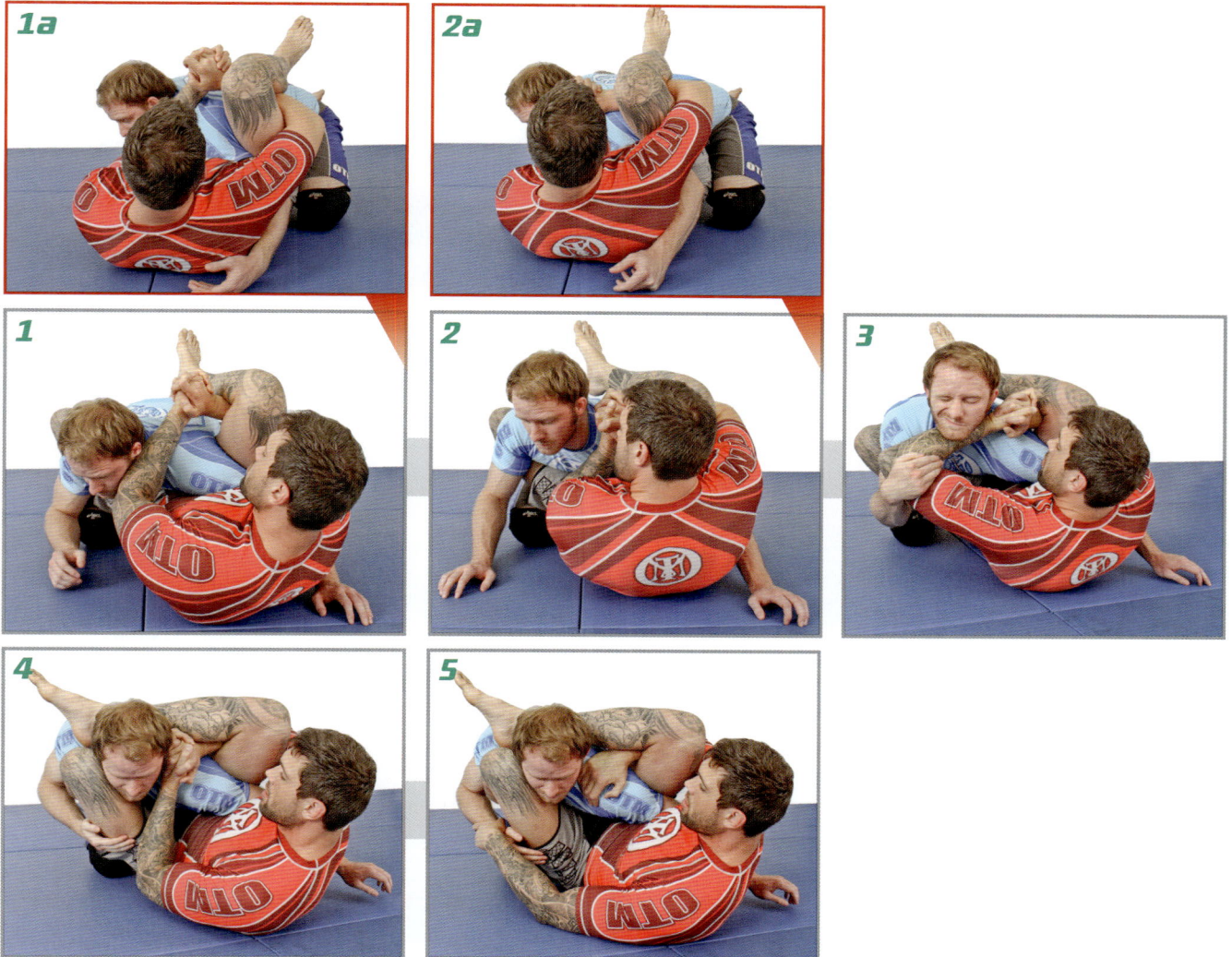

1. I am using a shoulder pin on Lance's left arm to control him.

2. I yank my left hand to pull my three-finger grip over the top of Lance's left shoulder, digging my hands into his shoulder. At the same time, I drive my left elbow into his sternum to hide it and set up a crossface.

3. I violently crossface Lance, lifting his chin into the air. Ideally, I will hook the inside of his right elbow with my left elbow to lift it into the air, but in this case, he assists my lift by reaching to press down on my left elbow to alleviate the pressure of the crossface. Though he weakens my crossface in this step, he creates space between his right arm and his ribs, giving me a path to the three-points position.

4. My left knee slides under Lance's right arm and in front of his right shoulder. My right leg drapes across his back, and my right heel digs into my left knee in front of his right shoulder. I have not released the shoulder pin.

5. I cup Lance's left shoulder with my right hand and grab his right wrist with my left hand, establishing the three-points position.

THREE-POINTS PUSH PIN

From the three-points position, you have a variety of triangle options at your disposal. I prefer to look for the push pin first because the tightness of the three-points position naturally encourages my opponent to hug my leg. A leg-through triangle requires more space and could allow my opponent to duck out. I can counter that escape, but by pinning his arm with the push pin, his head will hit your thigh if he tries to duck out because the space you need to execute the push pin is considerably less than with the leg-through. The mechanics of the three-points push pin are essentially the same as the previous push pin triangles you have learned. You kick your leg straight and low as you pull his arm into that same leg, causing him to hug his own chest to create the pin. That pin gives you a clear path to the triangle that closes the space he needs to duck out.

I have Lance in the three-points position. My right hand cups his left shoulder, and my left hand controls his right wrist. He hugs my left leg with his right arm.

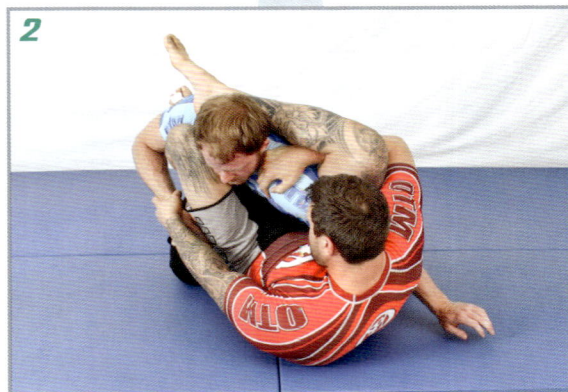

I drive my left shin into Lance's right biceps as I pull his right arm toward my hip.

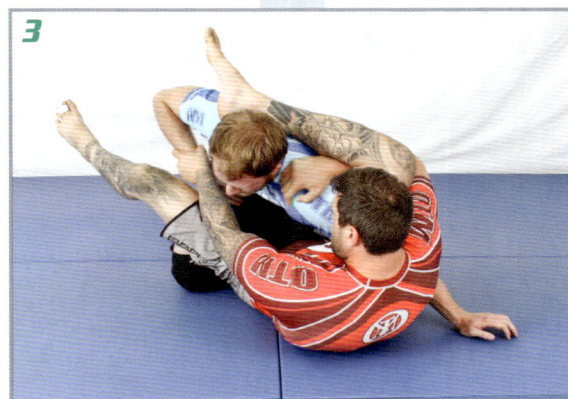

I kick my left leg straight as I press Lance's right wrist to his ribs. The pressure that I created in the previous step assists my wrist pin.

4

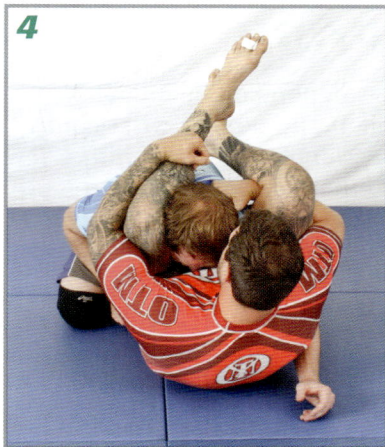

I elevate my hips and throw my left leg over Lance's right shoulder. As soon as my left leg clears his right arm, I hug my left knee with my left arm to stabilize the position. It is absolutely essential that I do not release his wrist until my leg has landed on his shoulder, so there is a moment where my left leg is actually on top of my left arm.

5

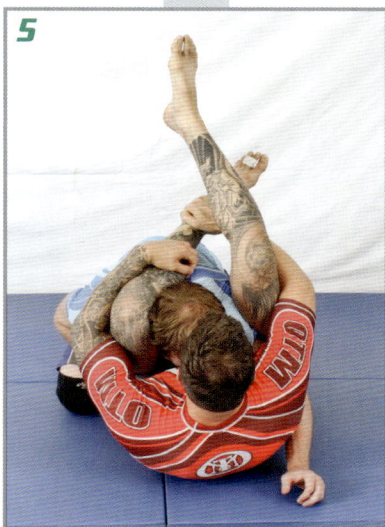

I grab my left ankle with my right hand to begin cinching an arm on the mat triangle finish.

6

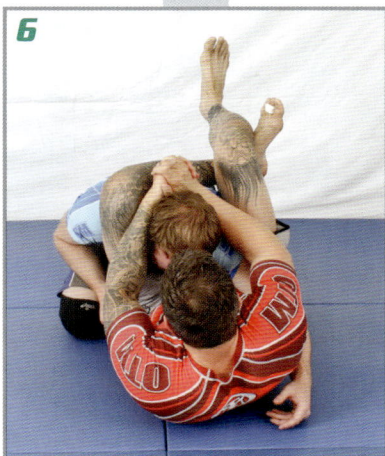

I pull my left leg across the back of Lance's neck with my right hand, cinching my left ankle in the crook of my right knee, locking the triangle. I finish the fight with a basic arm on the mat finish.

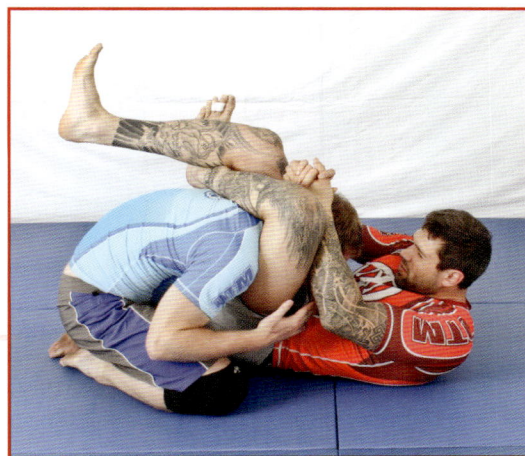

SHOULDER PIN UNDER GRIP OPTION

As slick as the push pin triangle from the shoulder pin may be, I cannot always depend on being able to establish wrist control on my opponent's far arm from the three-points position. If I do not get wrist control, which is common in this position, my opponent can begin to shut down my triangle attempts with a few different counters. If my opponent hugs my knee, I can use the push pin, so that counter is not an issue. However, If he grabs my ankle I need to fight that grip as soon as possible or my opponent may be able to slip free and force the omoplata. In this technique, I reach around and under my leg to grab his wrist from underneath. I pull his arm toward me as I kick my leg straight to break his grip and then feed my leg over for the finish. The power of my leg alone should be enough to free my ankle, but the under grip that I establish in this technique actually creates wrist lock pressure as I kick my leg, motivating my opponent to release his grip. Normally I would utilize the triangle or Nicksick finish in this position due to the length of my legs, but here I'm using the teepee finish just to demonstrate the alternate finishes shown in this book.

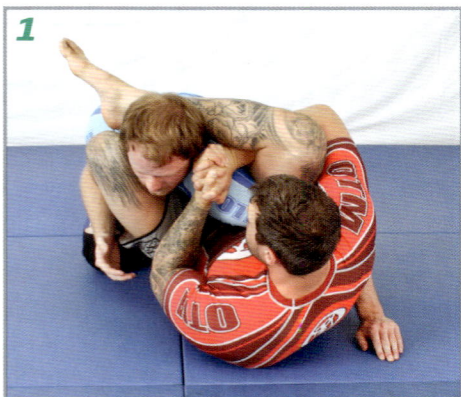

Lance is locked in the three-points position. I am controlling his left shoulder with a three-finger grip.

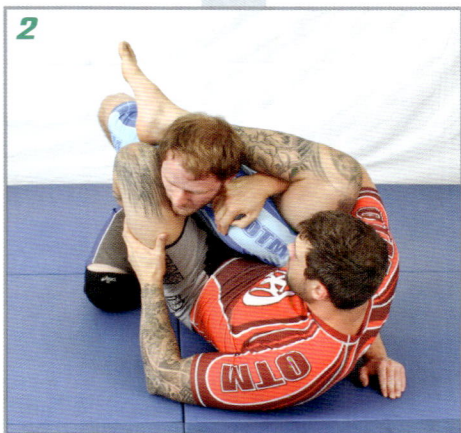

Before I can control his right wrist, Lance begins to counter my position by reaching his right hand back and grabbing my left ankle.

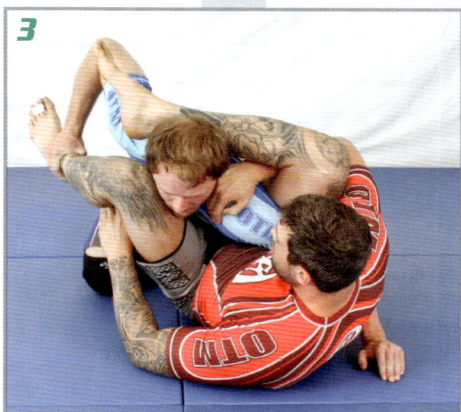

I work quickly to counter Lance's grip by straightening my left leg to force him to fully commit to the grip. I then pull my left knee to my chest to drag his right hand within reach.

My left hand loops under my left leg and shoots inside, latching on to his right wrist. Notice that my right heel is still in front of his right shoulder, delaying his forward movement.

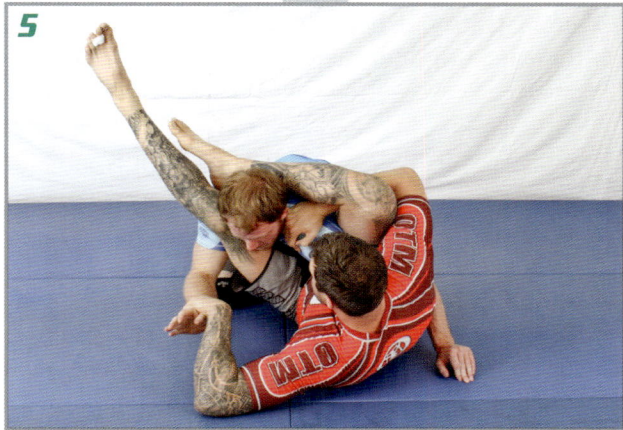

With my left hand controlling Lance's right wrist, I pull down on his right arm and kick my left leg straight into the air. This combination of movement creates wrist lock pressure and he releases my ankle.

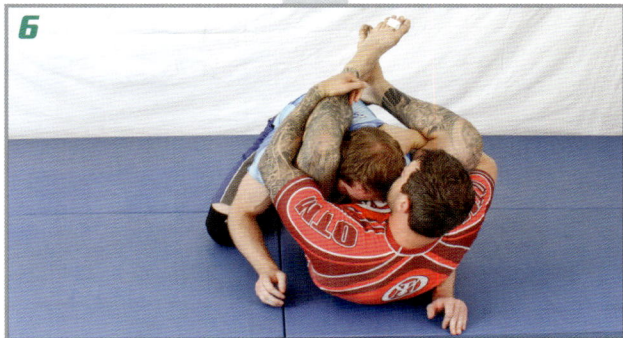

My left hamstring slaps against the right side of Lance's neck, clearing his right arm and locking his head and left arm between my legs. I hug my left knee with my left arm to stabilize the position.

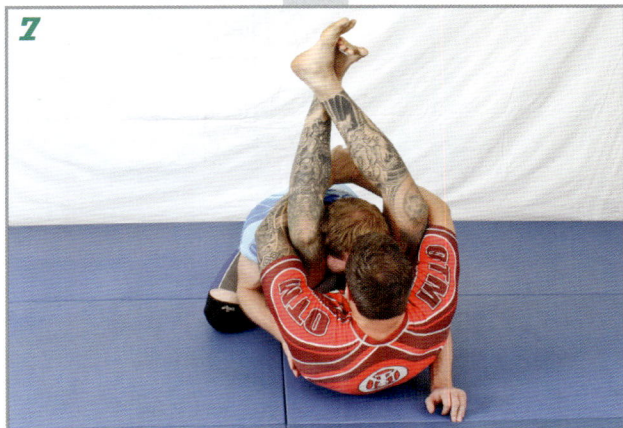

By maintaining the 0 degrees position, Lance has left his neck between my thighs, making the teepee my preferred method of finishing from this position.

SHOULDER PIN SHIN GRIP OPTION

In the previous technique, I used an under grip to break my opponent's control of my ankle so that I could finish my choke. Sometimes, depending on how your body type matches up with your opponent's, his wrist may be out of reach. When you are faced with that dilemma, you can still break the grip by exploiting his body mechanics. First, latch on to the lower portion of your shin that is draped across your opponent's back, locking a modified tie around his neck and upper body to give you additional control in the position. Then, kick your leg to break his grip. For this technique to work, you can't just kick your leg straight or swing it wide. Your opponent's hand will just follow your ankle. Kick it up diagonally, toward the ceiling and to the outside as well. Your opponent's shoulder has a wide range of motion in front of his body and to his side, but the range of motion behind his body is limited and weak. If you execute the kick properly, his arm will bend into a position similar to an upward pin. His shoulder will reach its limit, stop rotating, and his grip will break to protect his arm. In the photographs below, as I did in the previous technique, I demonstrate finishing with a teepee because the nature of this position drives his neck between my thighs and makes gripping the teepee easy, but you can always transition to the triangle if you would like.

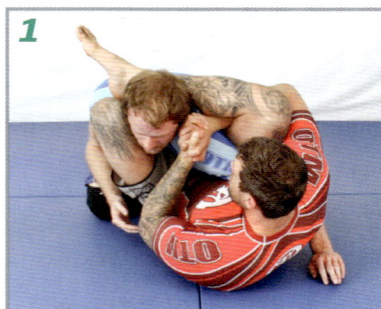

1

Lance is locked in the three-points position. I am about to release my three-finger grip and grab his right wrist for the push pin triangle.

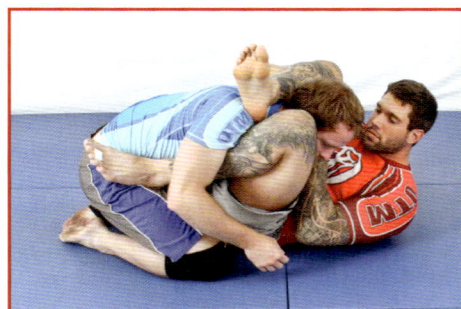

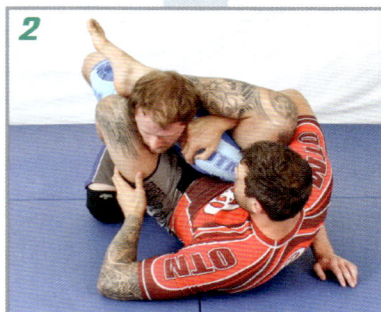

2

As my left hand reaches to grab Lance's right wrist, he pulls his right arm back and latches on to my left ankle, attempting to escape the position.

3

I attempt the under grip option by looping my left arm under my left leg, but my left hand cannot reach his right wrist.

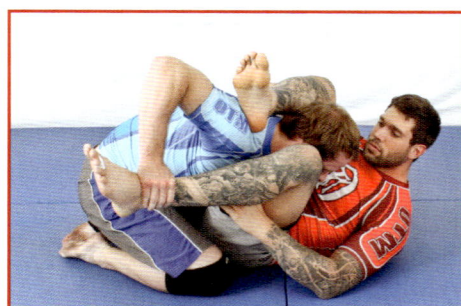

4

My left arm immediately shoots between my legs and grabs my right ankle. I pull down with my left hand to lock Lance's upper body in place.

5

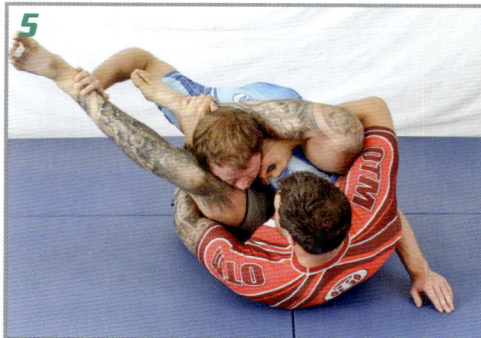

I kick my left leg straight and out to my left. If you look closely at the bend of Lance's right arm, his shoulder is torqued as though I were applying an upward arm crank.

6

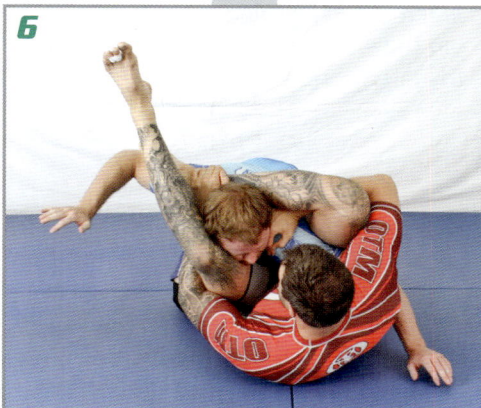

While keeping my left leg straight, I swing it toward Lance's right shoulder as I continue to pull down on my left ankle to limit the mobility of his upper body. The angle of my leg swing and the pressure of my right leg curling into his upper back forces his right arm to bend into a weak position. He must release my ankle or have his shoulder ripped.

7

My left leg locks over Lance's right shoulder as my left hand releases my left ankle and snakes across his back to grab my right hand. I cross my ankles and squeeze my knees to stabilize the position.

8

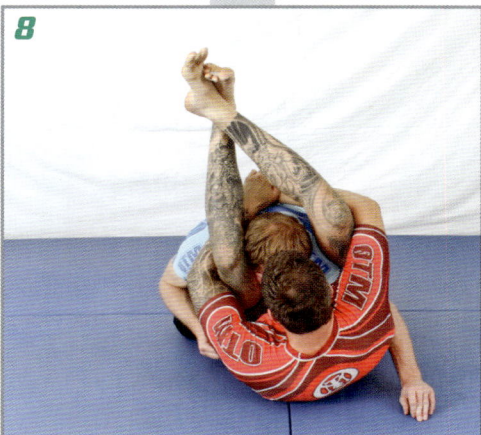

I finish Lance with the teepee.

THE SAFETY PIN

The three-points position is a high-percentage technique for forcing your opponent into a weak position where he can very easily make mistakes. However, there are two behaviors that can prevent you from ever achieving the three-points position. Your opponent can be so wild and explosive that you fear losing control by opening your guard, or he can lock himself into position to stall out your shoulder pin, hoping for the referee to stand the fight up or for you to abandon the three-finger grip. The safety pin allows you to keep your guard closed so that you can maintain control of an explosive opponent, and it allows you to improve your position against an opponent who is trying to stall the match. The key to the safety pin is where you place your hands. You use a collar tie to feed your opponent's neck to the hand that would usually cup his shoulder. Most opponents will choose to stack during this transition to counter your control by punching their shoulders through your guard. If they do stack, you will easily land the triangle. If they stall, your grips will make them weak enough that you can force the triangle. You can use a variety of grips—a downward grip, an upward grip, a throat jam pin, or a biceps push—to land the triangle, so choose the grip that works best for the situation.

1

I am using a shoulder pin on Lance's left arm to control him. I would use the three-points position, but he is explosive, and I don't want him to escape.

2

I crossface Lance with my left forearm as I flare my left elbow into his right biceps, forcing his right arm away from his body.

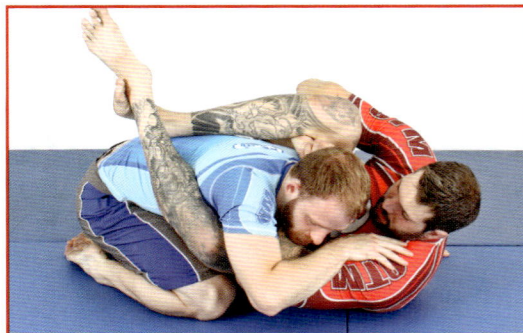

3

My left knee slides under Lance's right arm.

4

I quickly cross my left ankle over my right to prevent Lance from escaping, and I squeeze my legs together to maintain my position. It's important that I cross my bottom ankle over my top ankle for maximum control.

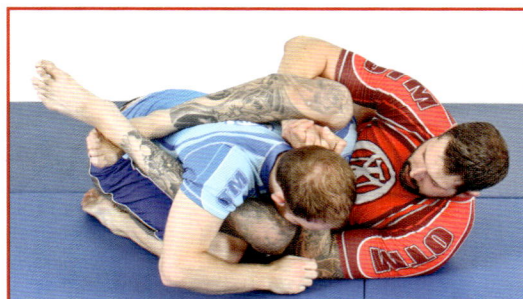

5

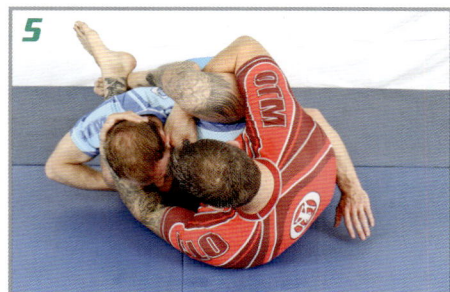

I cup Lance's left shoulder with my right hand as I grab the base of his skull with my left hand. I pull his head into his left shoulder with my left hand to prevent him from circling away to escape.

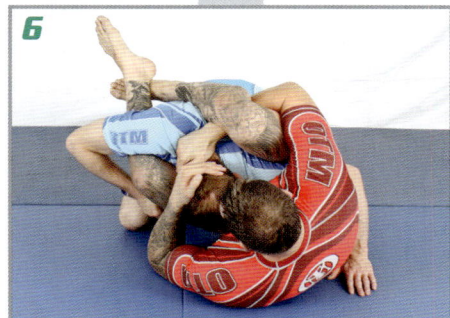

6

I shoot my right hand to the back of Lance's neck, digging my fingers into his tendons. My left hand maintains the collar tie. This is the safety pin position.

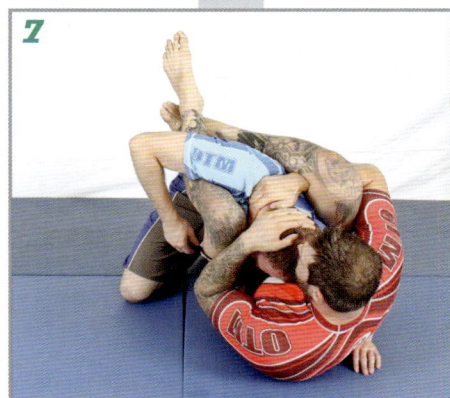

7

Lance, feeling that he cannot posture and that the pressure of the crossface is gone, begins to stack into me. I can also pull my knees to my chest to encourage him to stack.

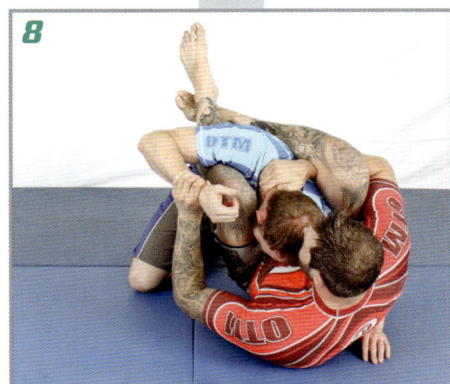

8

I maintain control of Lance's neck as my left hand secures an upward grip on Lance's right wrist. My guard is still closed.

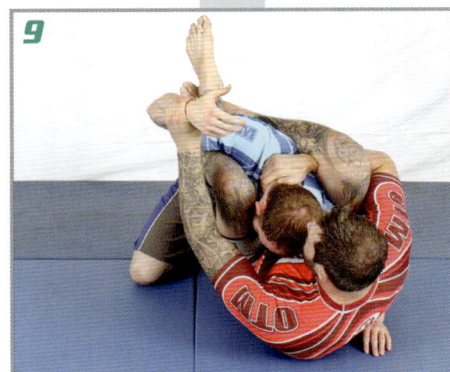

9

I crank Lance's right arm into an upward pin, bending his arm as though I wanted to apply a shoulder lock.

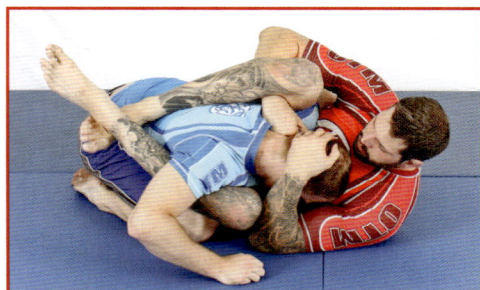

10

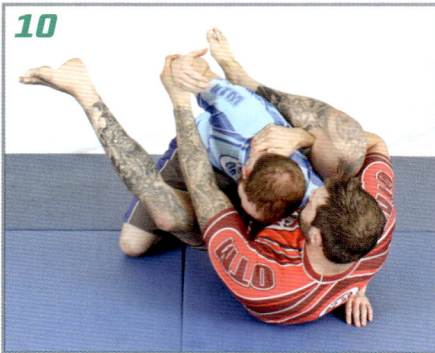

I open my guard and swing my left leg around Lance's right arm as I elevate my hips.

11

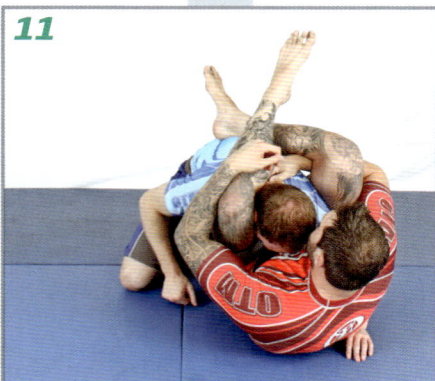

I slam my left thigh into Lance's neck, clearing his right arm. My left arm hugs my left knee to stabilize the position.

12

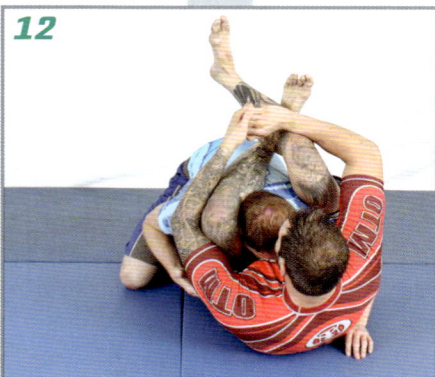

Rather than fight to maneuver my hips, I pull my left shin to the middle of my right calf and lock the Nicksick to end the fight.

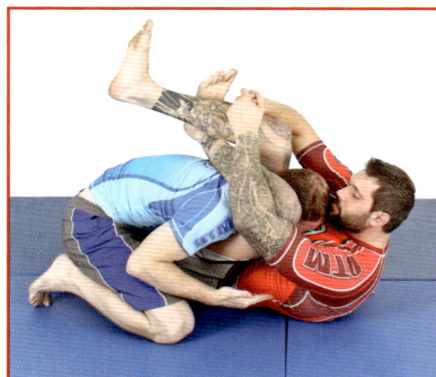

ALTERNATE GRIP: LEG CIRCLE HEEL PUSH

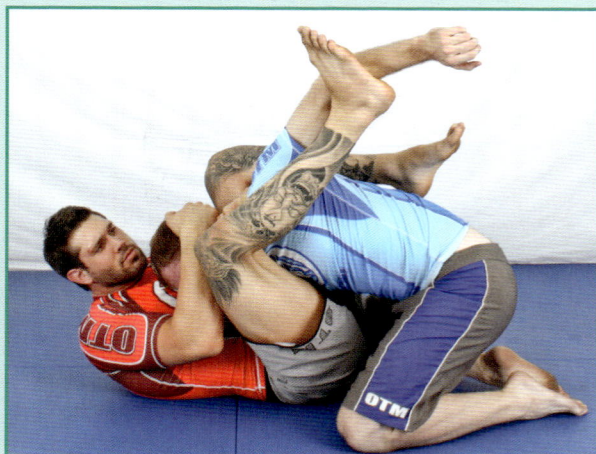

If I use a downward grip to clear Lance's arm from the safety pin, I need to combine it with a biceps push because of how little space there is in this position.

LAZY SUSAN SERIES TO SHOULDER PIN TRIANGLE

Any guard player will tell you that attaining traps or control over a good hand fighter is very difficult. The lazy Susan is a great option against great hand-fighters, forcing them to open up their base and let you take control of the grip. The lazy Susan starts with a feinted Pendulum sweep. I dive my arm under my opponent's leg and then drive him laterally in an attempt to sweep. I'm genuinely trying to execute a successful sweep. However, because my opponent's arms are free, he will post his hand on the mat to stop the sweep. With his arm isolated from the body, I now have a split second to bring my legs up, trap his arm, and lock down a shoulder pin control. As my opponent begins to shift his weight back to his knees and settle his base, I release control of his leg, secure biceps control, and slide my knee under his arm. Once this position is locked in I can be patient, make adjustments, and slide my leg all the way free and eventually lock in the triangle. The key to getting this concept work is to be aggressive and focus on creating the perfect body position for your opponent to get tied up and submitted. When rolling with top level world champions, this is my go-to guard setup. I focus on selling the sweep, quickly locking in my control, and making the position a perfect one.

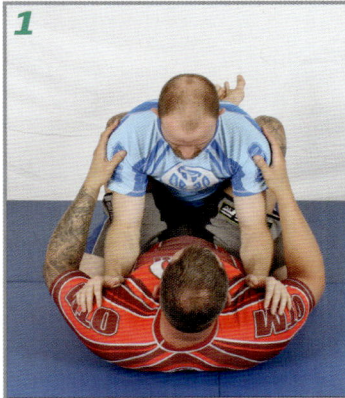

Lance is in my guard at the 45 degree position with both of his hands controlling my biceps.

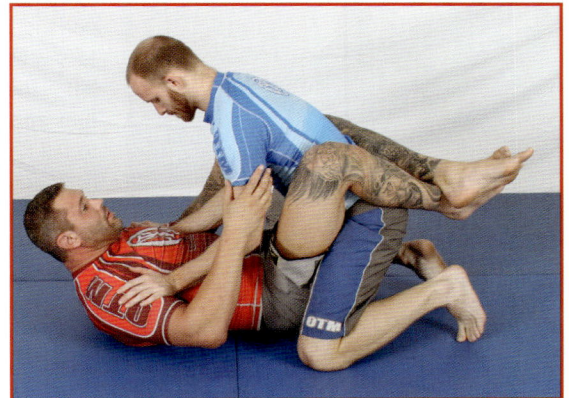

I reach up with my left hand to grab control of his head and begin sliding my right arm underneath of his left leg.

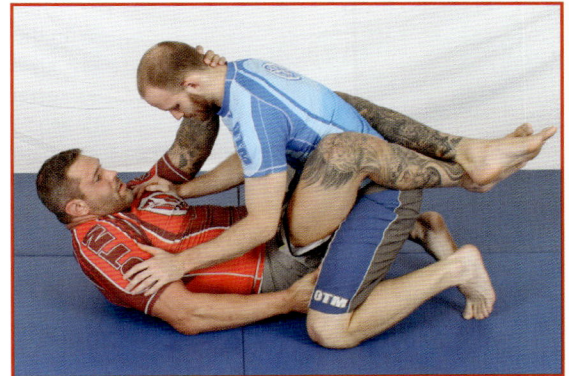

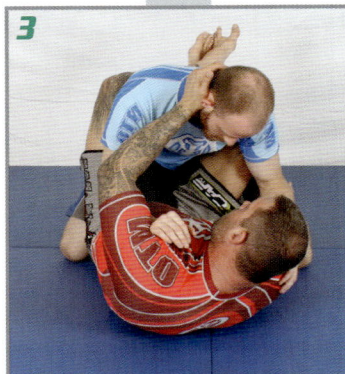

I cup the back of Lance's left leg with my right hand and pull myself to my right. Notice that my guard is still closed and my opponent is still in line with my body.

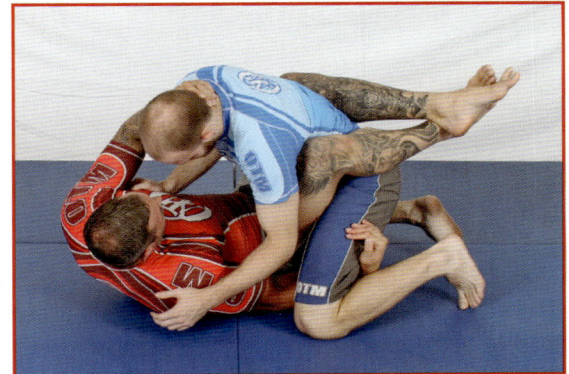

4

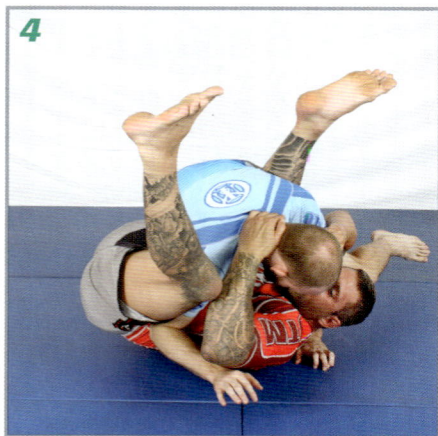

I quickly open my legs and pull my head to my opponent's left knee.

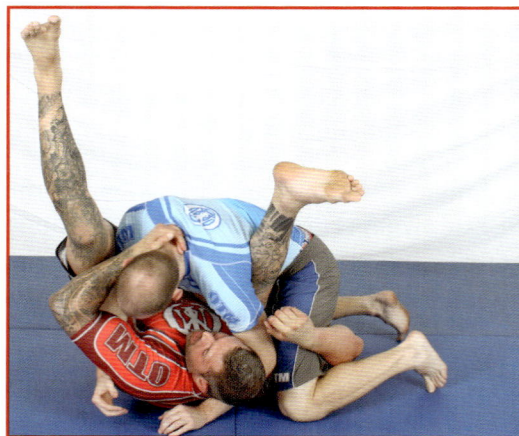

5

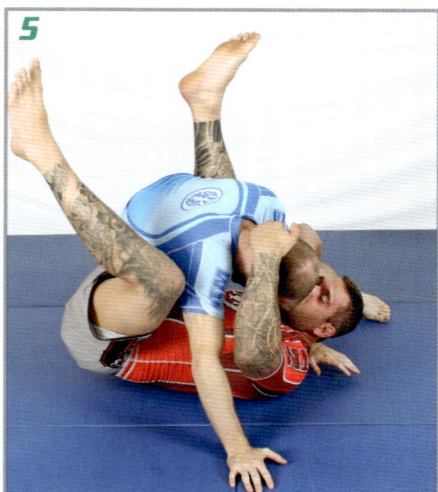

I drive my legs away, simultaneously lifting up on my opponent's left leg, attempting to sweep my opponent to my left. This generates momentum and causes my opponent to fall forward and to his right. He quickly counters this movement by using his free right arm to post wide on the mat.

6

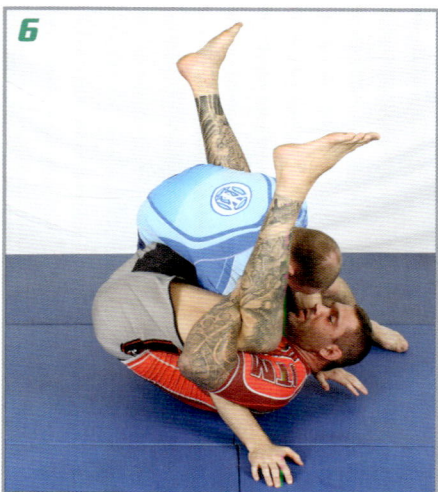

With the sweep stopped, I now quickly seize his extended arm to secure control of his upper body. I do this by driving my left leg towards my chest, releasing my left hand from his head, wrapping it behind my left knee, and cupping his right shoulder. I need to quickly get my left leg over his shoulder before he regains balance.

7

With Lance's right arm pinned high to my body, I can release my leg hook and quickly secure an inside biceps tie with my right hand. This gives me the space I need to slide my right knee under his left arm.

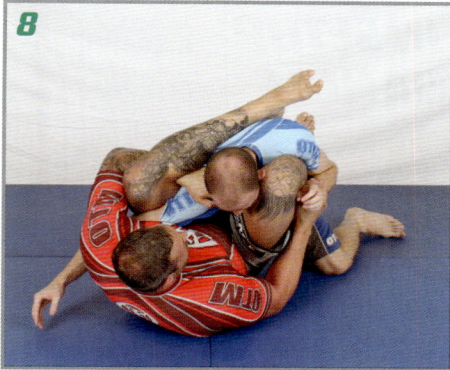

With the shoulder pin position secured, I can now begin attacking with my triangle attack. I switch my biceps tie to a upward wrist control on Lance's left arm.

I use the upward wrist control to crank Lance's arm towards the ceiling, opening space under his left arm.

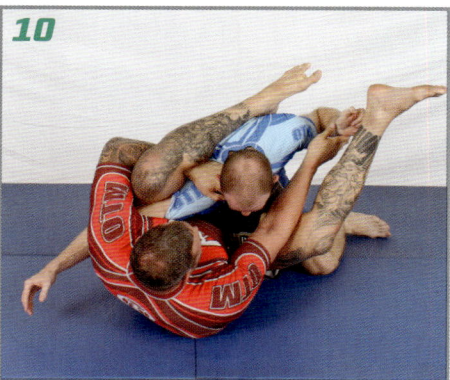

Once his arm is cranked up, I throw it clear and swing my right leg wide around my opponent's left arm.

With his left arm cleared, I lock my right foot under my left calf and finish the triangle with the arm on the mat Nicksick finish.

LAZY SUSAN TO SHOULDER PIN SETUP TO BOSTON HANDSHAKE TRIANGLE

I use the lazy Susan to shoulder pin setup more often than any other setup. If you're precise with the setup and secure the arm correctly, it gives you a ton of control. It's the type of move that I can utilize even when my training partners know it's coming, simply because it starts so fast and finishes with such a strong control. However, there are times when I prefer to transition out of the shoulder pin and into this technique, utilizing the Boston handshake to clear my opponent's arm and finish the triangle. If I'm unable to get the upward grip from the shoulder pin triangle and I feel like he's going to go omoplata and escape my triangle, I prefer to utilize the over the back grip and secure the Boston handshake triangle. The shoulder pin setup puts you in a good position to attain a downward grip and set up the Boston handshake. Often, when training, I do this switch when I don't feel that my original setup finish is going to be 100% effective. It's worth it to me to take the extra steps to get a solid triangle finish. Once I secure my over the back grip, it's a simple matter of clearing the arm and locking on the choke.

Lance is in my guard at the 45 degree position with both of his hands controlling my biceps.

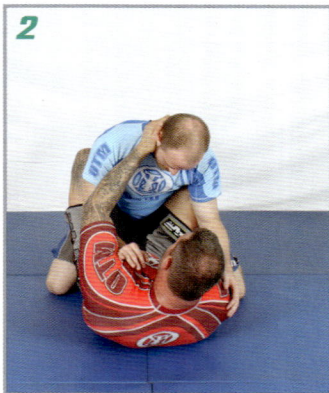

I reach up with my left hand to grab control of his head and begin sliding my right arm underneath his left leg.

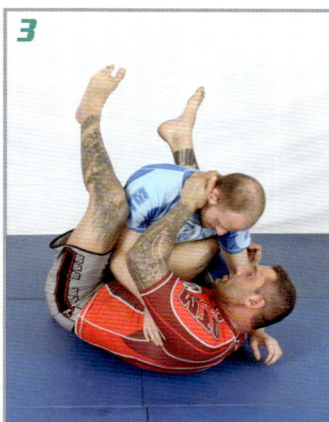

I dive my arm hook deeper under Lance's left leg and swing my hips to create the momentum for the sweep.

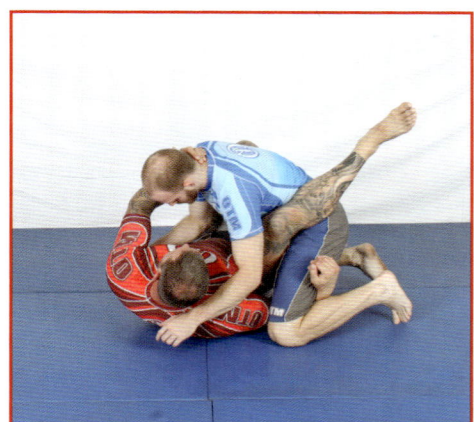

4

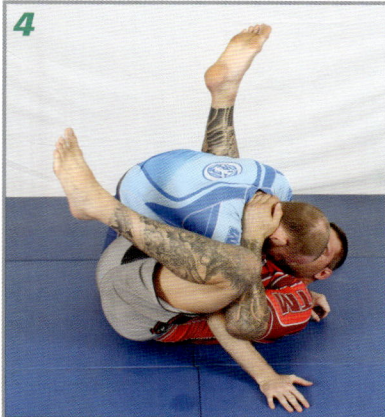

I hoist Lance's leg up, committing to the sweep. Because my right arm is so deep I'm able to secure his left arm with my right hand. Lance posts with his right arm to keep himself from being rolled.

5

With the sweep stopped, I now quickly seize on his extended arm to secure control on the upper body. I do this by driving my left leg towards my chest, releasing my left hand from my opponent's head, wrapping it behind my left knee, and cupping Lance's right shoulder. I need to quickly get my left leg over his shoulder before he regains his balance.

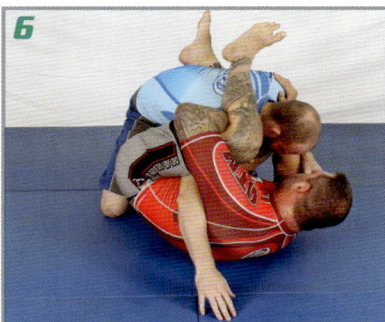

6

With Lance's right arm pinned high to my body, I can release my leg hook and quickly secure an inside biceps tie with my right hand. This gives me the space I need to slide my right knee under his left arm.

7

With the shoulder pin position secured, I switch my biceps tie to a downward wrist control on his left arm.

8

I extend my right leg, bringing Lance's left elbow away from his body. This creates a pocket of space, while still maintaining control of his wrist.

9

I release my shoulder pin control with my left hand and throw my arm over Lance's neck and back. I then lock a one-on-one grip on his left forearm with my right hand still controlling the left wrist. At this point, I curl my leg back against his body.

10

With both hands controlling Lance's left forearm and wrist, I now drop my leg and pull both arms upward, jamming Lance's left arm high and tight, binding to his body. Notice that my left foot is on his right hip. If you're unable to establish this foot placement, go to the Irish collar section to see alternate controls to prevent your opponent from stacking into you.

11

I release my right hand from Lance's left forearm, allowing my left hand to completely control it. I now press against Lance's right hip with my left foot and then bring my right leg over his left shoulder.

12

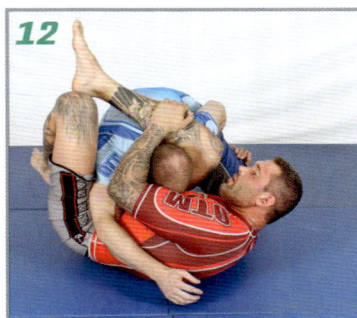

I grab control of my right shin with my left hand and, pivoting off Lance's hip, I dive my right arm under Lance's left leg.

13

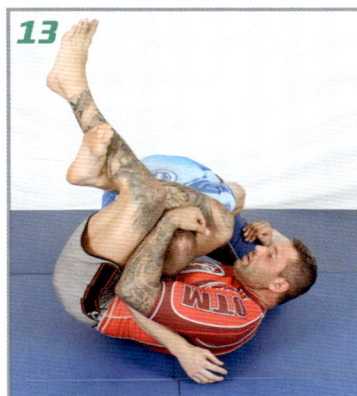

I figure-four my legs and pull Lance's head down into the choke while maintaining control of his left leg. This will finish the triangle.

SHOULDER PIN TO CHIN LIFT (THE CHUCK ZITO)

The best way to beat the shoulder pin is to pin and smother your opponent's hips. If he knows that, and he is starting to stall your attacks, you need create space and establish a threat. The chin lift is the most effective solution for this problem. It is violent and, in my experience, it is a great tool for mentally breaking your opponent because the pain, discomfort, and the feeling of being bullied can be too much for some fighters. As you use the chin lift to press your opponent's weight off of your hips, bring your leg over and around his arm to set the triangle. To use this attack, you do not need to control his wrists, which makes for an especially sneaky triangle. As you will notice in the photographs below, I demonstrate the chin lift from a standard shoulder pin, but the chin lift is just as effective from the three-points position. If using this move in the gym hurts your friendship with training partners, blame me and carry on using it. Do not feel bad for taking advantage of simple, direct, and effective technique. I nicknamed this the Chuck Zito just because I I wanted to call a technique the Chuck Zito; he's the original American bad ass.

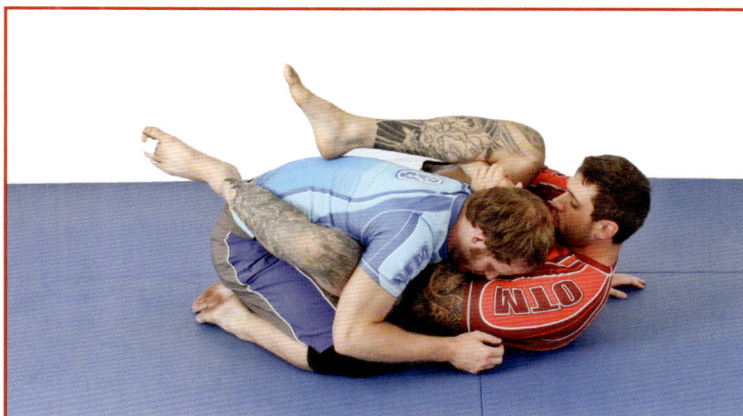

My hands are locked into a three-finger grip over Lance's left shoulder, securing the shoulder pin.

I circle my left forearm up Lance's chest into his neck, beginning to lift his chin.

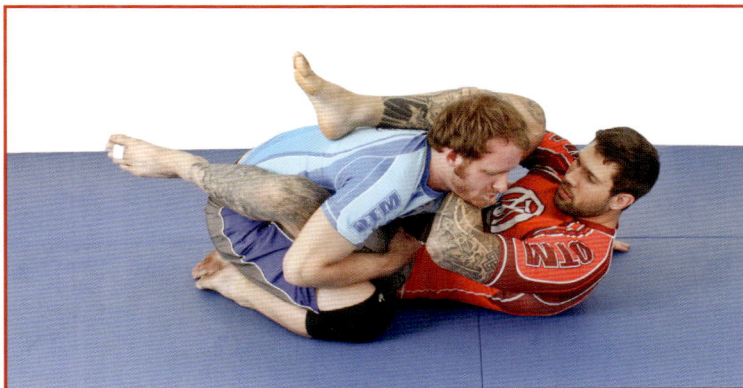

I release my three-finger grip and cup Lance's left shoulder with my right hand.

4

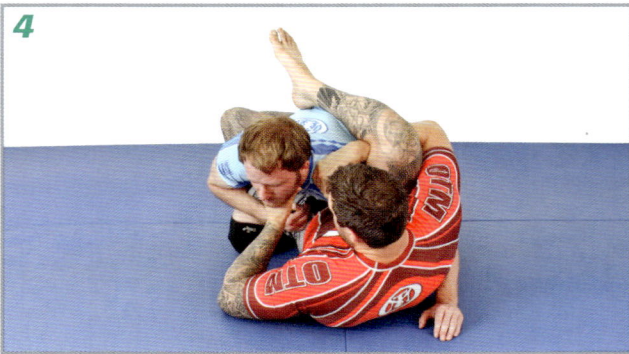

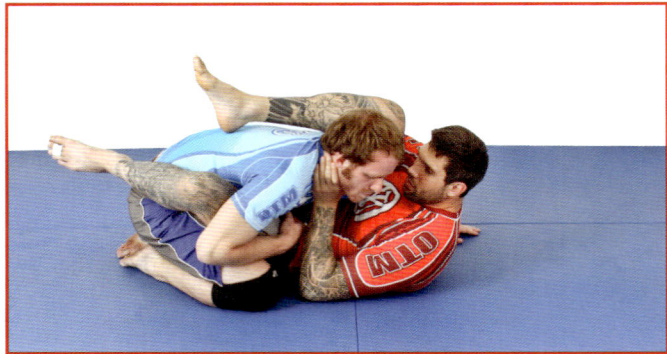

My left hand grabs Lance's neck.

5

I lift Lance's head by pressing my left hand into his neck. As you can see, he is now in the 45 degrees position, the optimal submission zone.

6

My left knee circles over Lance's right arm and pins it to his ribs. If he reaches to relieve the pressure on his neck, this same movement will work, I will just bring my knee higher.

7

With Lance's right arm pinned, I begin transition to the triangle by grabbing the base of his skull with my left hand, releasing his neck to begin pulling him into the triangle.

8

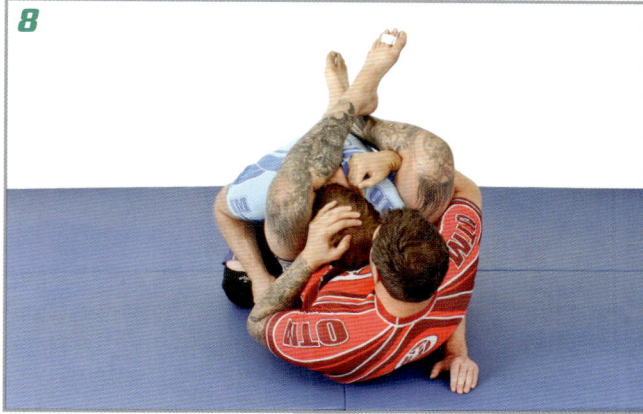

I throw my left leg over the back of his neck, clearing his right arm.

9

My right hand snakes under my right leg and grabs my left ankle, pulling it toward Lance's left shoulder for the triangle.

10

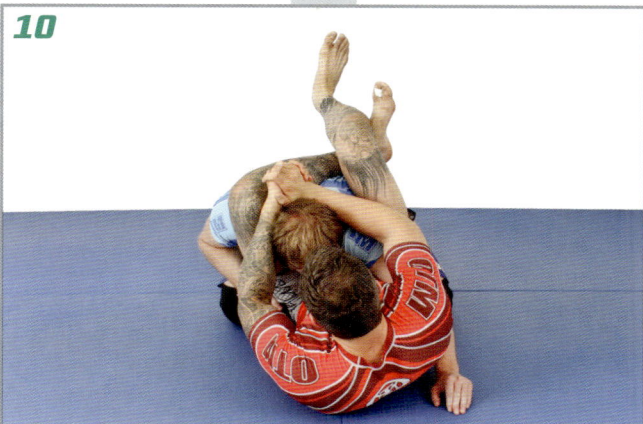

I use both hands to finish the triangle with Lance's arm on the mat.

COIL ROLL TRIANGLE

A truly desperate opponent will not stall. He will do anything he can to escape. Sometimes, your opponent will turn away from you, hoping that you will abandon the shoulder pin to attack with an omoplata, or you could decide that you want to bait your opponent into escaping the omoplata to force him to move in a predictable direction. Many fighters are very good at escaping the omoplata and would rather fight to escape the omoplata than the triangle. The safety pin can negate this option if you can lock it in, but if your opponent is determined to give you his shoulder, you may not be able to trap his head and control his neck. As he turns away, giving you the omoplata, he will roll forward to unwind his arm and escape the submission. You could take the top position, but I prefer to trick him to fall back into the triangle. This is a dynamic move that involves forcing your opponent to scramble. It takes practice and awareness to execute properly, so do not give up on it if it fails at first.

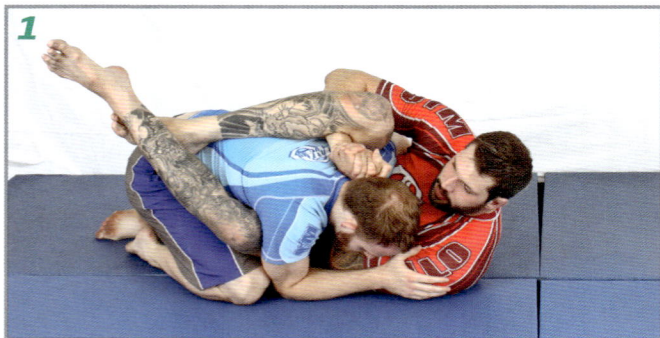

1

I am controlling Lance with the shoulder pin.

2

I use the crossface to push Lance's head away from my chest.

3

I release the three-finger grip and cup Lance's shoulder with my right hand, while gripping my right shin with my left hand. I begin to slide my left hand down on the shin, crossfacing Lance and creating additional space between our bodies.

4

I pull my left arm back and then pull it under my body to prop myself up. My right foot is still on the right side of Lance's head, keeping his head trapped. If I put my foot in front of his face, he could roll too quickly and escape.

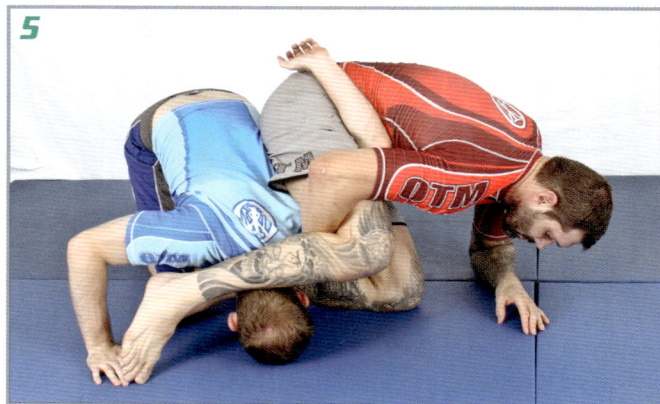

5

I start to twist my body as I rotate my right knee towards the mat. This puts a lot of pressure on Lance's left shoulder.

6

I've now driven my right knee to the mat, while maintaining control of Lance's right hand. I use my forehead as a point of balance if needed. At this point, if Lance does not begin to roll over his left shoulder, he's in danger of getting injured.

The torque of my twist forces Lance to begin rolling forward. I am still cupping his left shoulder tightly with my right hand.

Lance lands on his back to complete his roll. I continue to rotate my body in the same direction, beginning to turn my chest toward the sky.

As Lance attempts to escape, I raise my leg and reach forward with my left hand, catching Lance's head.

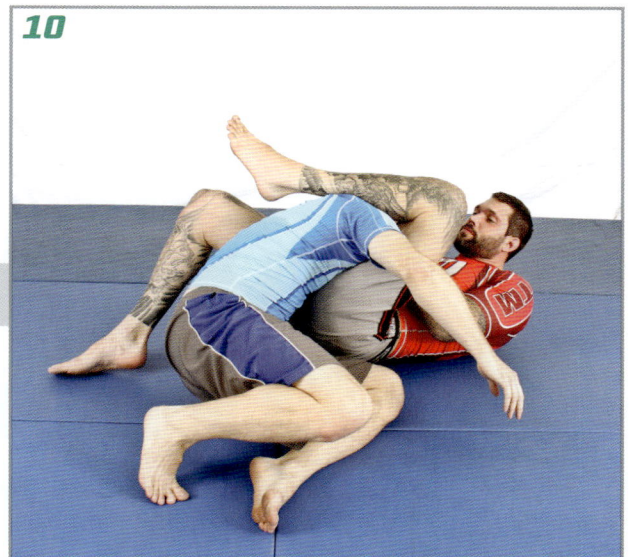

As my back turns to the mat, I pull Lance's head between my legs with my left hand. I set my left leg across the back of his neck as he moves between my legs.

I figure-four my legs and finish the triangle.

SHOULDER PIN TO KNEE PINCH TRIANGLE

From the armbar side of shoulder pin, my crossface is extremely powerful, and I can constantly threaten the armbar to force my opponent to make mistakes. I demonstrated the triangle side first because most grapplers will instinctively fight from their left hip when they get the shoulder pin, especially if they are learning to transition to the shoulder pin from the overhook. When you begin to work from the armbar side, you need to remember that your strategy changes. From the triangle side, the majority of your triangle setups will require you to feed your leg under your opponent's arm. From the armbar side, the majority of your triangle setups will require you to bring your leg over your opponent's arm. As you bring your leg over his arm, imagine that you are an octopus and that you are crushing him to death. Your squeeze needs to be consistent and strong for you to be effective. This technique, the knee pinch triangle, is a simple way to begin attacking from the armbar side. If it fails, it will open up other options.

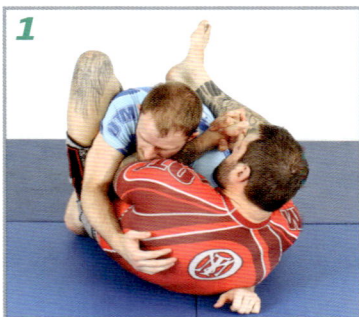

1

I am controlling Lance with a shoulder pin. I am on my right hip, and my left foot is driving into his right hip to stretch him, immediately making him uncomfortable.

2

I drive my left forearm into the center of Lance's chest, then slide it towards his jaw and raise his chin. It's very important that my forearm catches underneath his jaw. The combination of movement in this position—the crossface, the shoulder pin, and the hip stretch—is incredibly painful for Lance and frees my hips.

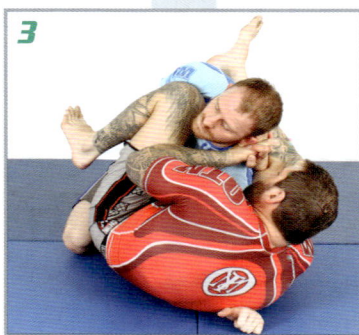

3

I crunch into Lance as I curl my left leg to my chest. My left knee then drives into his right arm, pinning it against his chest. I continue to use the crossface to keep him in position.

4

My left knee rolls over the front of his shoulder, pinching into his neck as my left foot flares outward to clear his right arm. My right foot then points toward my left knee to cinch the position.

5

I throw my left leg across the back of Lance's neck and momentarily cross my ankles for stability.

6

I begin to lock the figure-four by shifting my hips and controlling Lance's head with my left hand, but he begins to duck out to escape.

7

I squeeze my knees together as my right hand slides to his left elbow. I squeeze my right arm against my ribs to pinch his left hand in my armpit.

8

Lance begins to resist the armbar by driving forward to bend his left arm. I delay the stack by pressing his head into his left shoulder with my left hand. At the same time, I adjust my triangle position by posting my right foot on his left hip and pinch my right knee into his left shoulder as my left leg folds across the back of his neck.

9

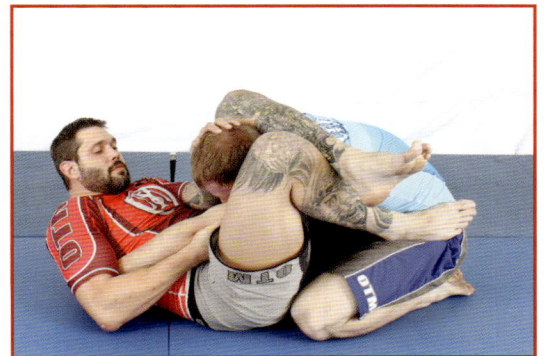

I figure-four my legs and finish the armbar triangle.

SHOULDER PIN PULL BACK

When I'm working from the armbar side of the shoulder pin, my opponent will sometimes feel my triangle attacking coming, and will pull his head away as I shoot for the triangle. He can to turn his body away forcing me to attack with an omoplata in an attempt to escape the triangle. Many grapplers are skilled at escaping the omoplata, making it more of a transitional situation than a submission attack. There's one last triangle I can attempt before abandoning the position and attacking with the omoplata. There's some subterfuge involved in this technique. As my opponent twists his body to escape the triangle, I quickly snag his head and pull him back into the choke. The key here is creating friction with your free leg, dropping it on your opponent's head to slow down his spin. As long as you keep pressure on your opponent's neck, and you're on the correct hip, it will give you time to swing your leg over his shoulder and finish the attack. An alternate way of utilizing this setup offensively would be to trick your opponent into utilizing an omoplata escape, and then using this setup to pull him back in for a triangle choke. I will do this sometimes when my opponent is purely holding and stalling my shoulder pin system.

1

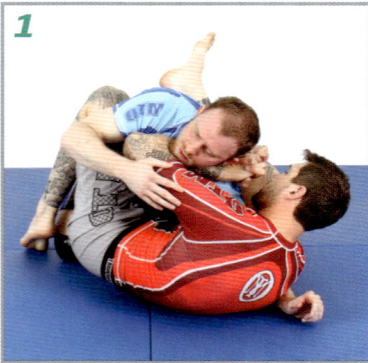

I am controlling Lance with a shoulder pin, and I have just shifted onto my right hip, the armbar side. I am using my left forearm to crossface him and to force his right shoulder to hover.

2

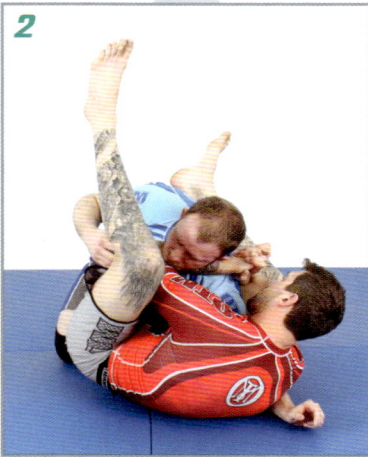

I throw my left leg into the air, elevating my hips as I attempt to clear his right arm for the triangle.

3

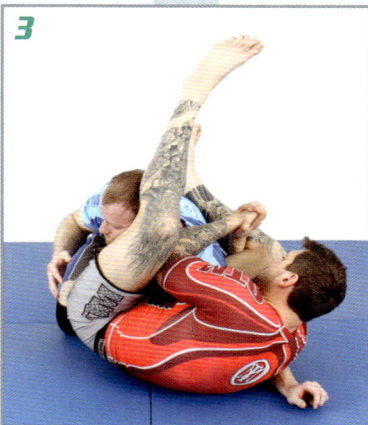

I overshoot the triangle. My left leg passes to Lance's left shoulder, leaving only his left arm between my legs.

4

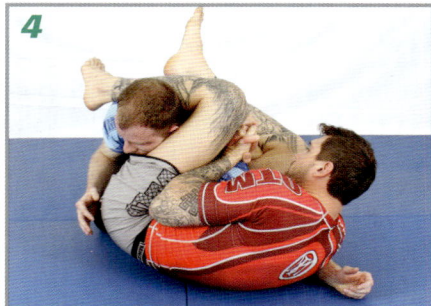

While remaining on my right hip, I set my left leg on the back of Lance's neck and curl my left heel toward my butt to stabilize the position. My right hand cups his left shoulder for additional control.

5

My left hand reaches between my legs and grabs the back of Lance's neck. My right leg slides down his back a bit to stifle his ability to roll forward.

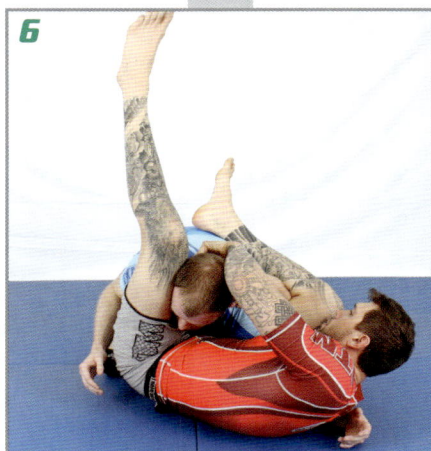

6

I yank Lance's head between my legs with my left hand as I swing my left leg out to the side.

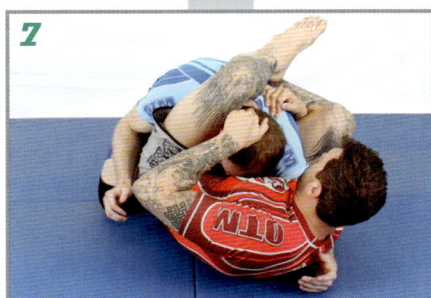

7

I slam my left hamstring into Lance's neck, using the momentum to swivel my hips out.

8

I can now begin locking the triangle. If I need to maneuver my hips even more, I can underhook Lance's right arm to adjust and tighten the triangle.

BEATING COUNTERMOVEMENT FROM THE SHOULDER PIN

Finishing the triangle from the shoulder pin will often be a battle no matter how smooth your setup. Shoulder pin triangles can be challenging to finish because you lock the triangle over your opponent's shoulders, which makes him wider. He will want to create space between his head and the shoulder that is trapped between your legs to reduce the pressure on his neck. The most effective way for him to accomplish that is to turn his body and drive his head across your body to pry your legs apart with a cross-body style of pressure. To prevent that, hug your own knee and adjust your hips. The best way to counter your opponent's escape attempt is to stop it from happening in the first place, so immediately hug your own knee as soon as you clear his arm for the triangle. Then work to finish the choke.

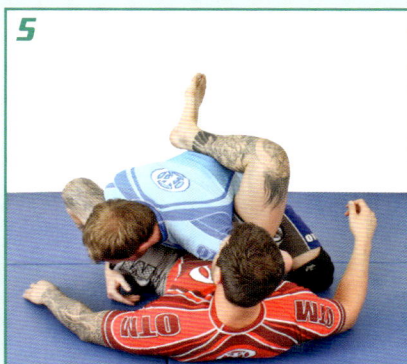

I am close to locking and finishing the triangle. Lance breaks my legs open and escapes by hugging my right leg with his left hand as he rotates to his right and drives his left shoulder across my body.

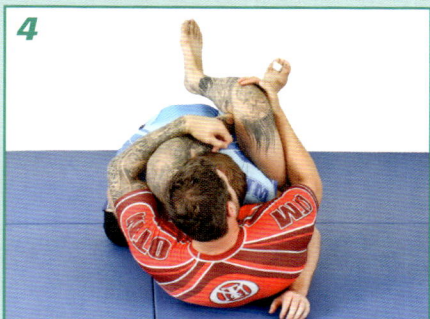

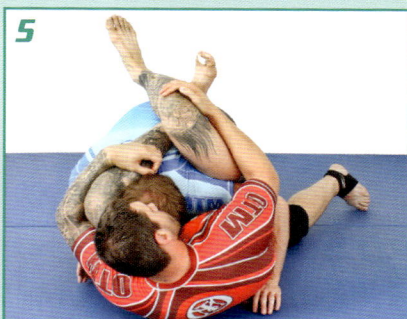

The correct way to counter Lance's escape is to immediately hug my left knee with my left arm and squeeze my knees together. My right hand then grabs my left ankle and pulls it under my right leg. I lock my legs together and hug my knees with both arms to stabilize the position.

TACTICAL ENTRY TO THE UNDERHOOK SHOULDER PIN

The underhook shoulder pin uses the same three-finger grip as the traditional shoulder pin, but you secure it from an underhook rather than overhooking your own leg. The underhook shoulder pin may not be as secure as the traditional shoulder pin but it is far more mobile. If you want to create movement rather than stifle it, whether you are a submission grappler who is down on points or a fighter that wants to get off of his back as soon as possible, the underhook shoulder pin allows you to play a more dynamic guard. Keep in mind that you must be willing to work quickly; if you move slowly, your opponent will blast through the guard. To be effective with the underhook shoulder pin, apply the same three directions of pressure with the three-finger grip as you did from the traditional shoulder pin, and try to keep his trapped arm from traveling up to your shoulder. Having it lower is better, and having it bent backward is best. There are many setups for the underhook shoulder pin, but this entry assumes that your opponent is dominating your biceps in a tight 0 degrees position. The key to creating the space that you need to pummel is in the subtle movements of your elbows, so follow the photographs closely. Once you have the underhook shoulder pin secured, attempt the knee pin triangle and then transition to the corner lock series if he defends.

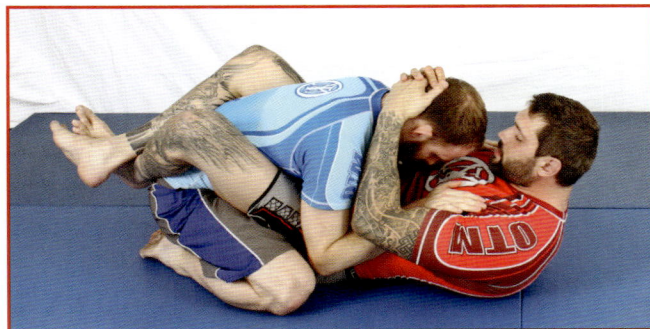

I have a double collar tie on Lance's head, while he has double biceps ties.

My left hand continues to control Lance's head as my right hand slides across my chest and secures an upward grip on his right wrist. Notice that this positions my right elbow inside of his left biceps.

I pull Lance's right arm with my cross grip and pinch my left elbow into his right elbow to force his right arm toward my centerline. As I obtain my right cross grip, I subtly drive my right elbow forward, placing my elbow inside of his left elbow.

4

I swim my right arm underneath Lance's left arm, obtaining a deep underhook.

5

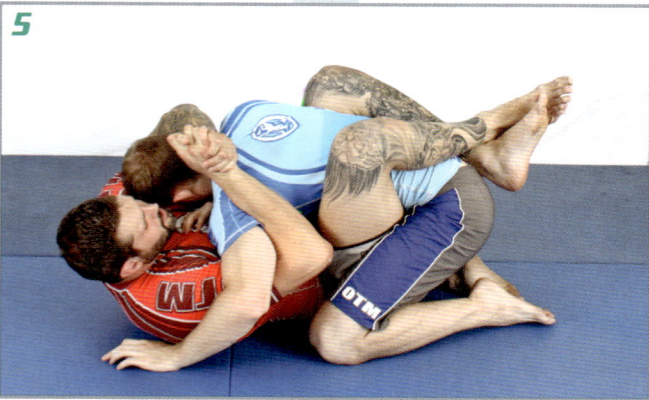

My left hand releases Lance's head and quickly grabs my right hand to secure a three-finger grip. My left arm is still around the back of his head, delaying his ability to posture.

6

I grind my left forearm over Lance's head and down his face, setting it on the left side of his neck. I apply the three directions of pressure with my three-finger grip to secure the underhook shoulder pin as I open my guard and shift onto my right hip.

LEG SCISSOR ASSIST TRIANGLE

Here, I demonstrate pummeling in to the underhook shoulder pin, but you can use the elbow shuffle to set up this technique as well. You saw this style of triangle in the shoulder pin section, but you may have more success with this variation because you can create more space when your legs are free. The power of your leg makes it relatively easy to smash your opponent's arm against his body for a pin, and since you can maintain your underhook shoulder pin throughout the technique, you have a great deal of control to augment the power of your knee. I tend to look for this triangle from the underhook shoulder pin first. If my opponent defends the knee pin, I transition to the corner lock series that I demonstrate in the next technique.

Lance is beginning to win the hand fight from the 0 degrees position by controlling my biceps with both of his hands.

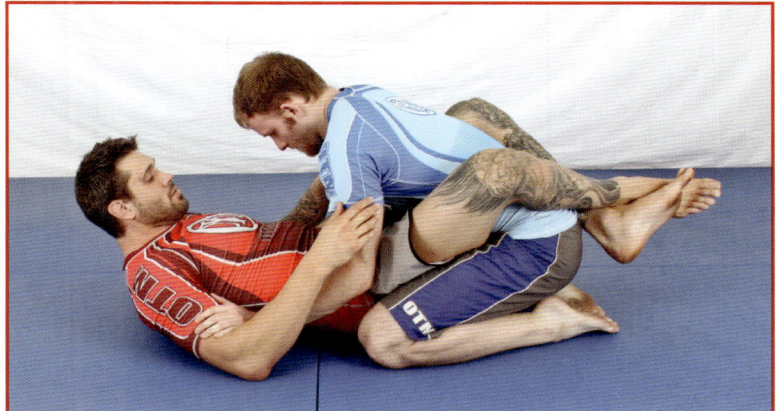

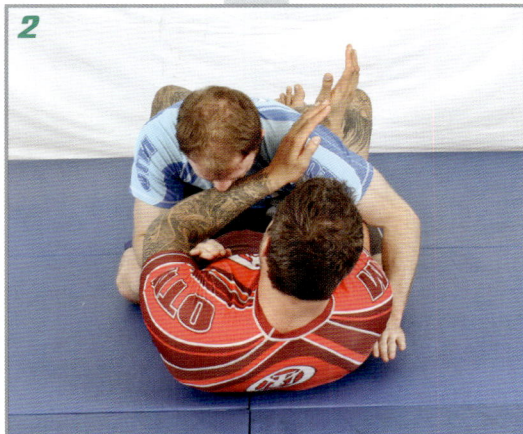

I maneuver my right arm under Lance's left armpit.

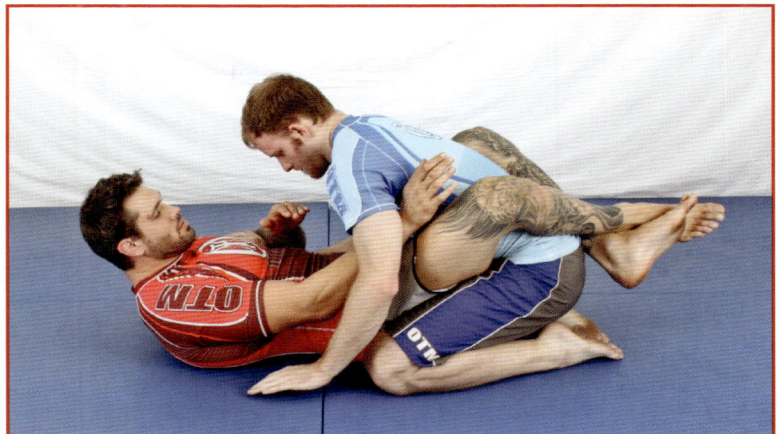

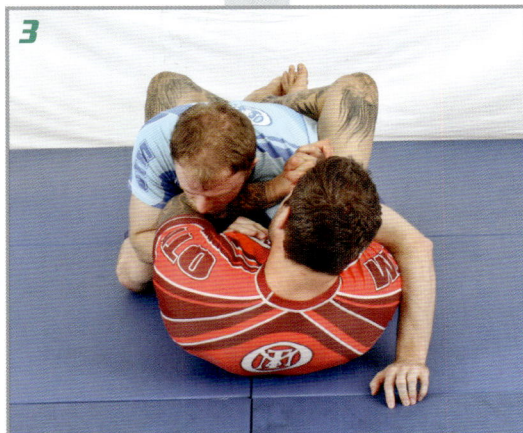

I lock the three-finger grip and apply the three directions of pressure to begin cinching the underhook shoulder pin.

4

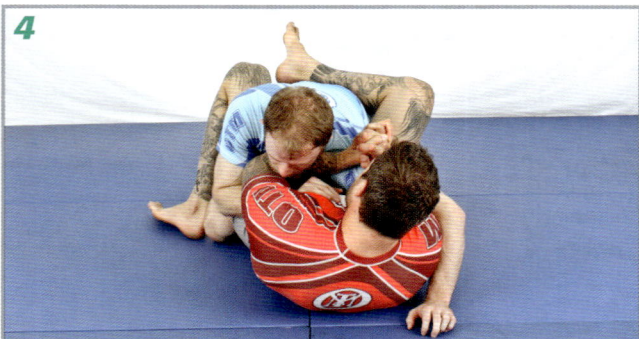

I post my left foot on the mat.

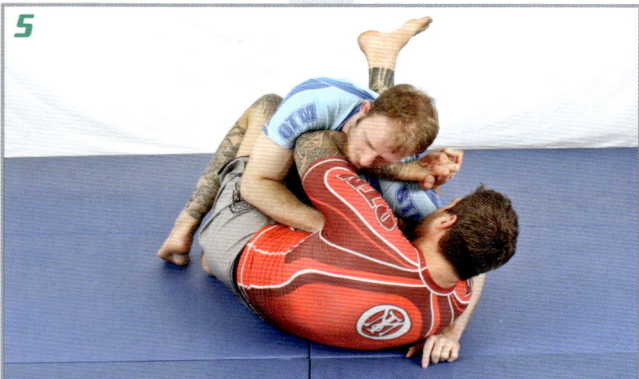

5

I shift onto my right hip, cross-facing with my left elbow to create space. My three-finger grip is still tight.

6

My left knee rolls over the front of Lance's right shoulder. I am still cross-facing with my left elbow to force him to hover.

7

My right knee rotates down to Lance's right biceps. I dig my left knee cap into his right biceps and drive his right arm back with my left leg. This position pins his right arm in place and prevents him from pummeling it back inside.

8

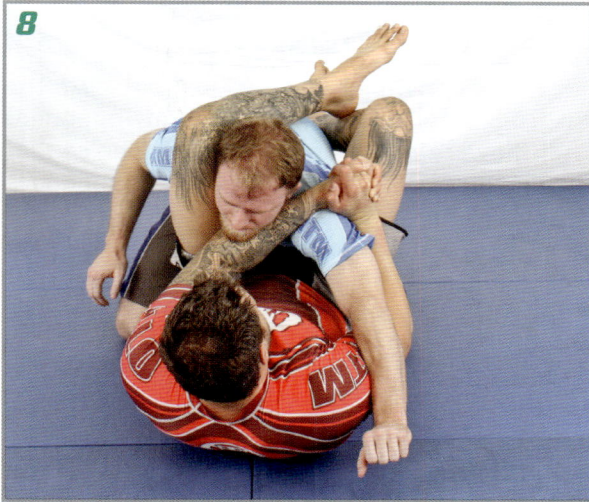

I quickly pop my hips into the air, throwing my left leg across the back of Lance's neck.

9

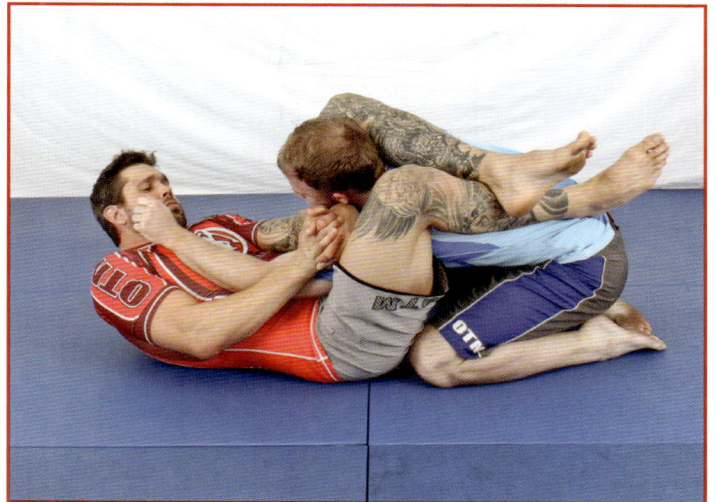

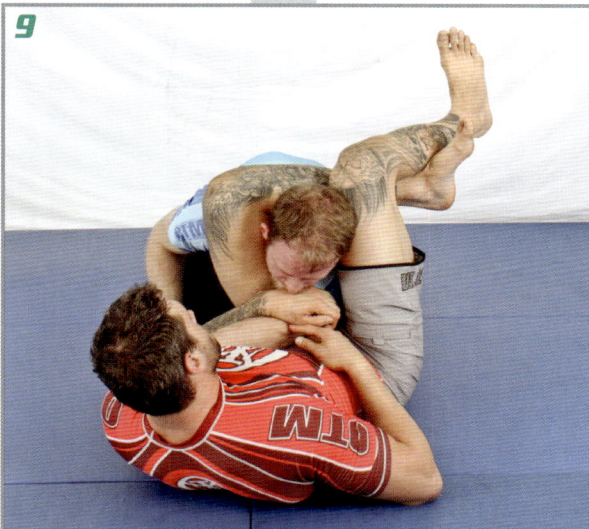

I ride the momentum that I generated in the previous step and swing my left foot under my right leg. At the same time, I drag my three-finger grip down Lance's left arm and pull his left arm across my body.

10

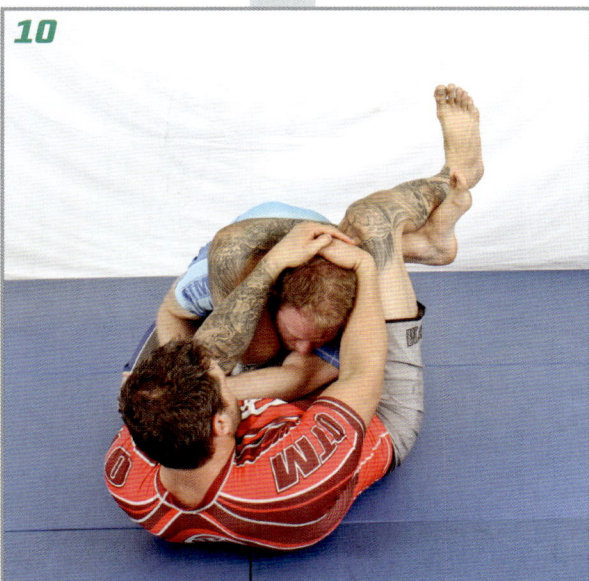

I lock my legs and finish the traditional triangle.

RABBIT HOLE WITH WRIST PIN VARIATION

Generally, I prefer to adjust my guard strategy to account for my opponent's body position, but I like the underhook shoulder pin enough that I will sometimes force it from other positions bringing my opponent to the 0 degrees position. Many no-gi grapplers, whether or not they are aware of the strategic choice that they are making, would rather fight from the 0 degrees position instead of a position where their opponent is postured to strike or stand. They feel comfortable working in close quarters, and will try to force a 0 degrees situation as soon as possible. If you are one of those grapplers, add this transition to your arsenal. It uses an attempted arm crag to create an underhook shoulder pin that ultimately ends in a series of corner lock submissions. When you use the underhook shoulder pin, this corner lock submission series will arise often, regardless of how you set up the position, so familiarize yourself with it now.

Lance is postured inside of my closed guard.

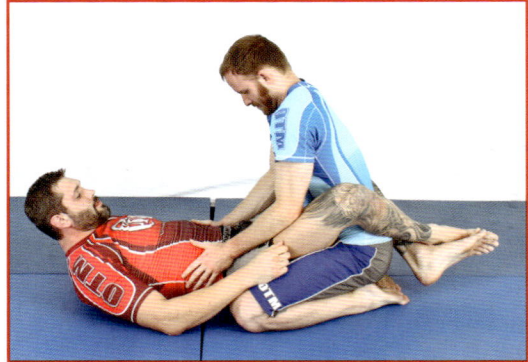

My left hand grips Lance's left wrist as my right hand latches on to his left elbow.

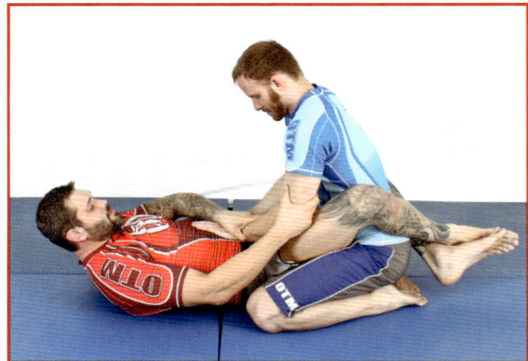

I drag his left arm across my body as I crunch my knees toward my chest.

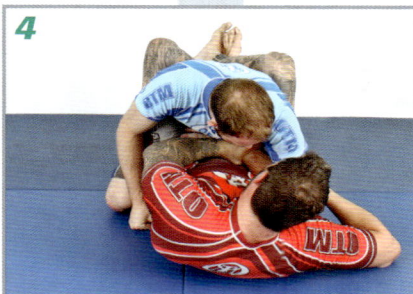

Lance pulls his left elbow to my right hip to prevent me from taking his back. I go with his counter and pin his left wrist to my right hip with my left hand, locking his arm in a bent position.

5

I shoot my right arm through the hole created by Lance's bent arm.

6

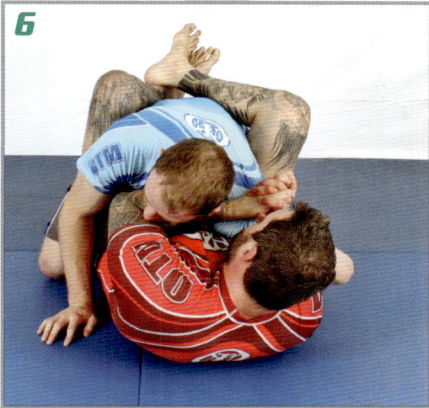

My left hand releases Lance's wrist and grabs my right hand, immediately securing a three-finger grip to lock the under-hook shoulder pin.

7

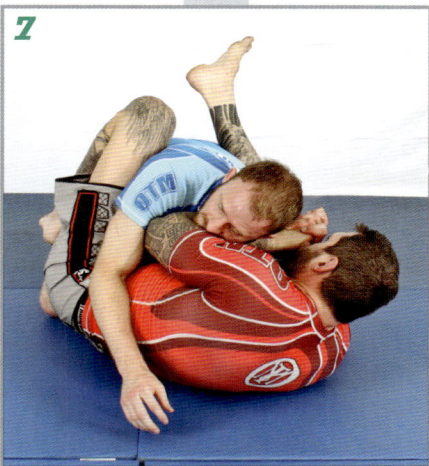

I open my guard and shift onto my right hip, while cross-facing Lance with my left elbow.

8

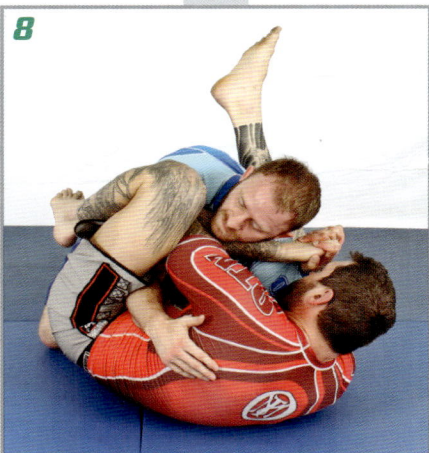

I initiate the knee pinch by setting my left knee against the front of Lance's right shoulder.

9

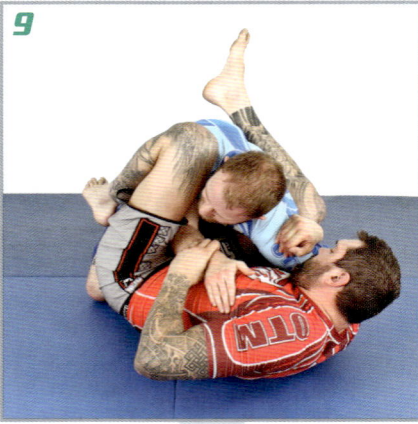

I break my grip and grab Lance's right wrist with my left hand. It's important that I keep my right underhook tight, cup the shoulder, and keep my legs flexed.

10

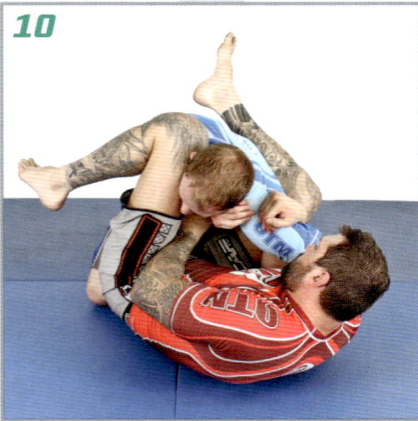

I shove Lance's right wrist to his neck and pinch my left knee into shoulder to close off any space.

11

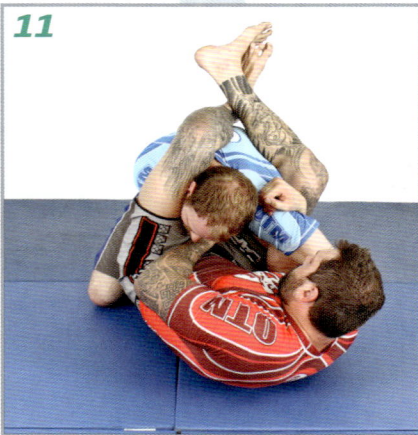

I cross my right foot over top of my left ankle to secure the corner lock.

12

I relock the three finger grip, slide it down Lance's left arm, locking my right wrist in place just above his left elbow.

13

I extend my legs, driving Lance away, while clocking my body to my left. This puts pressure on his left shoulder, forcing him to tap out from the shoulder lock. It's important to keep his elbow pinned tightly to my chest to maintain control of his arm.

14

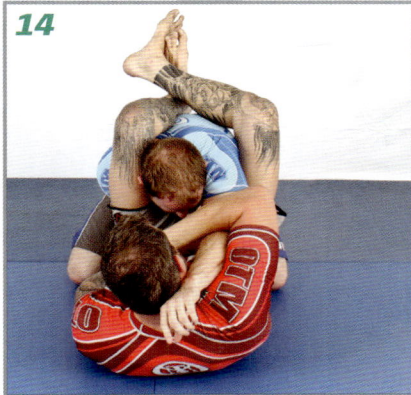

Lance slips the neck lock by rotating his left thumb to the ceiling and sliding his left arm to my shoulder.

15

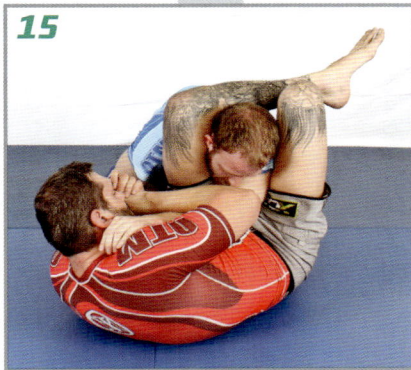

I post my right foot on Lance's left hip and swivel my hips as I swing my left leg across the back of his neck. Notice that I'm keeping my hands locked tight to maintain control of his left arm.

16

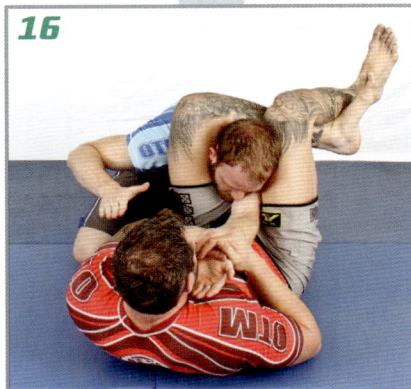

I figure-four my legs and rotate his palm to the sky to finish the armbar triangle.

SHUCK AND SWITCH

In the traditional shoulder pin section, you learned that you could attack the triangle from either side, but your strategy changed based on what hip you were attacking from. The same concept is true of the underhook shoulder pin. If you are facing your opponent's trapped arm, you focus on beating his far arm with your legs. If you turn onto your other hip and face away from his trapped arm, your primary method of attack is threatening the back take by using your grip to shuck his trapped arm across your body. When your opponent fights to keep you on your back, you switch your underhook shoulder pin to the opposite side and begin attacking. Should your opponent fail to retract his arm, it's very simple to switch and lock on an armbar. If your opponent retracts his arm, you can react to his movement by slapping your hips up high and locking in the triangle. Although there's a lot of transition in this technique, the ultimate goal is to stay one step ahead of your opponent's counters and eventually lock in the triangle choke.

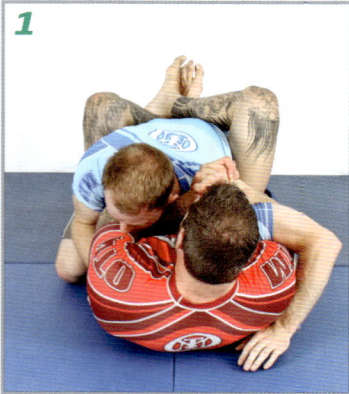

I am locking Lance's left shoulder with an underhook shoulder pin. I attempted to fight from my right hip to clear his right arm for the triangle, but I failed.

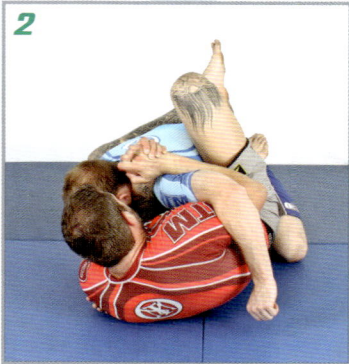

I unlock my legs and shift onto my left hip. I then put my right foot on my his left hip and extend my right leg, stretching out his body. This separates the shoulder and could force him to tap due to the pain from the separation of his left shoulder.

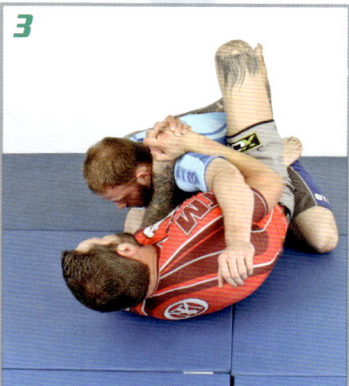

To create enough pressure to pop Lance's left arm across my chest, I drive my right foot into his left hip and yank on his left arm with my three-finger grip as I arch my back. He will feel like his arm is being pulled out of its socket.

4

Lance's left arm passes across my body as he tries to relieve the pressure on his shoulder. To secure his left arm, I drive my right forearm into the back of his left triceps to wedge his arm into my left hand.

5

As Lance attempts to drive his left arm back to the other side of my body, I hug him to my chest by cupping his right shoulder with my right hand.

6

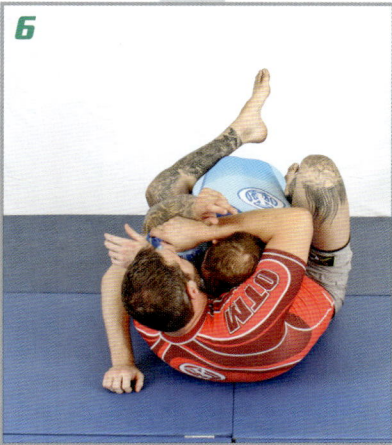

My left hand shoots under Lance's right armpit as he continues to drive his left shoulder across my body to block me from transitioning to his back.

7

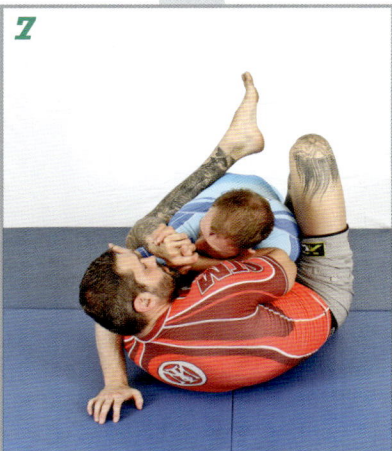

I lock the three finger grip on Lance's right shoulder.

8

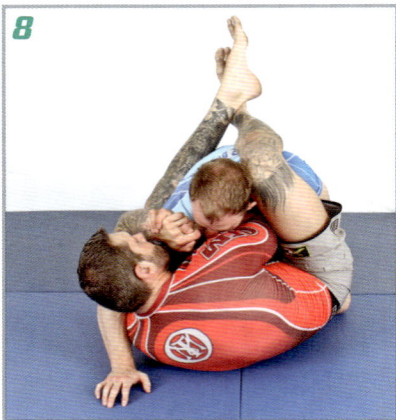

I hop my right leg over Lance's left shoulder and cross my ankles to establish the corner lock. Lance yanks his left arm out of the corner lock to protect it from an armbar. By constantly switching from attack to attack, I have forced him to over-defend his arm.

9

I uncross my feet and post my left foot on Lance's right hip. I push off his hip and rotate my body to my right, while maintaining tight control of his right arm by gripping his elbow with my right hand and hugging his forearm with my left arm.

10

I figure-four my legs and finish with an armbar triangle.

CHIN RIDE SWEEP TO REVERSE TRIANGLE

The biggest obstacle that you will encounter when working the shuck is the inability to establish an underhook shoulder pin on his other arm once you have passed his trapped arm across your body. A small shift in position can make it unreachable, especially if your arms are not exceptionally long. The solution for this problem is to grab the strongest leverage point within your reach: your opponent's chin. This is not a friendly technique, but it is effective. You can use this grip to twist his head, forcing him to roll to his back, which is an effective way of transitioning to the back or to the mount. I use it to set up a triangle because I expect my opponent to instinctively resist the reversal, and I use that resistance to sink a reverse triangle. As you can see in the sequence below, this technique requires a great deal of movement and coordination. You will need to practice this move for your technique to be smooth and effective.

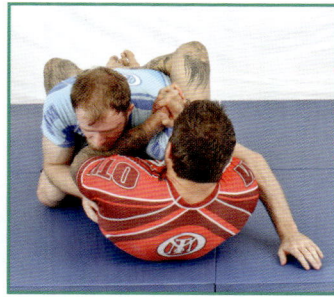

I have an underhook shoulder pin locked on Lance's left side.

I open my guard and plant my right foot on Lance's left hip. Utilizing the pressure of the shoulder pin control, I begin to shuck Lance's left arm towards my head.

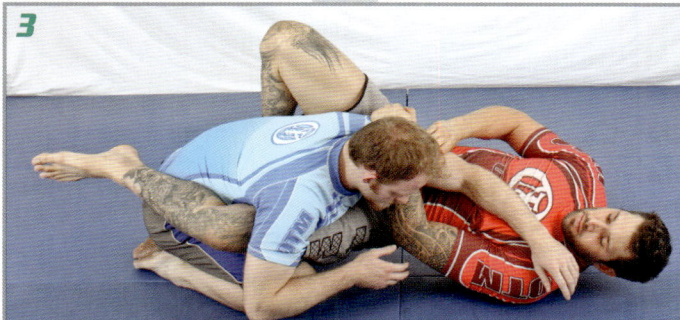

I bridge my hips upward, giving Lance's left arm the space to slide off my shoulder and down my chest, crossing my center-line.

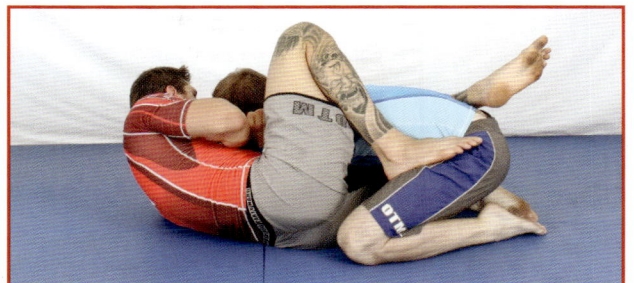

I use my left hand to pull Lance's left arm completely across my center-line. I then press on Lance's left triceps with my right hand, squeezing his arm to my chest and preventing him from ripping free.

5

I reach over Lance's head with my right arm, locking my right hand onto his chin and pulling his head tightly to my chest.

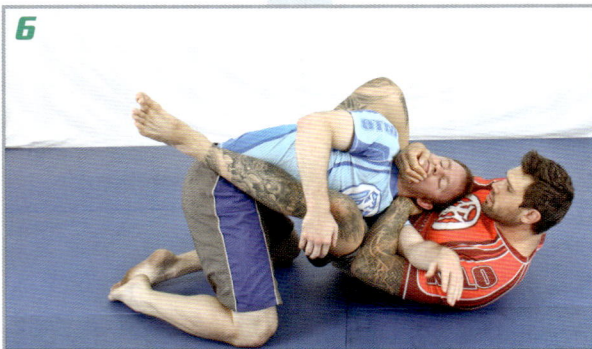

6

I pull on Lance's chin, driving my right elbow to the mat to begin rolling him to my right. To help him roll I swing my legs to my right, adding momentum to the roll.

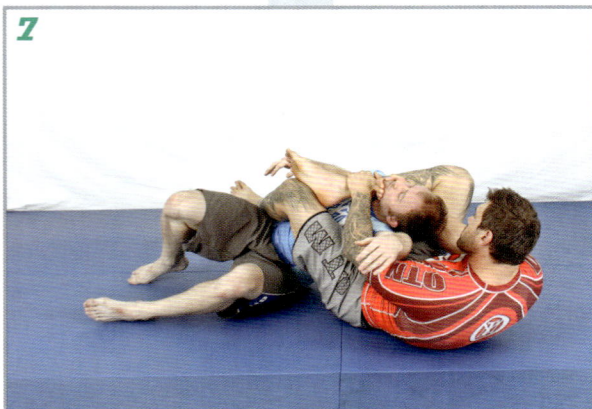

7

As Lance rolls to his back I throw my right leg over his right shoulder and quickly catch my ankle with my left hand. Notice that I maintain control of his chin throughout the movement.

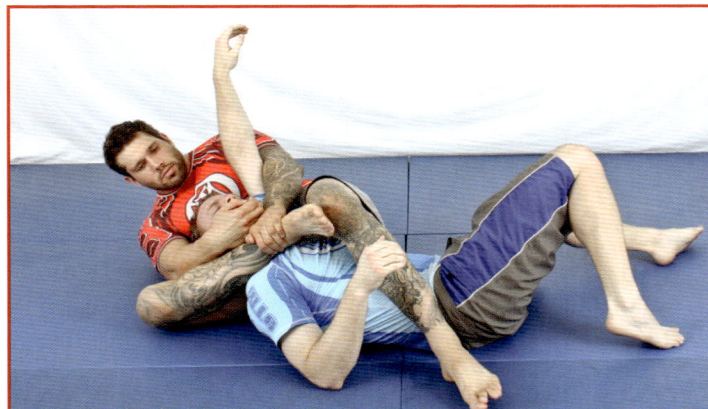

8

I figure-four my legs and tuck my left foot underneath of Lance's body to prevent him from peeling off my leg. To finish the choke, I lean forward, driving my hips into the back of Lance's head. For extra power, I could hook either of his legs with my left arm and pull it forward, cradling him and putting him to sleep.

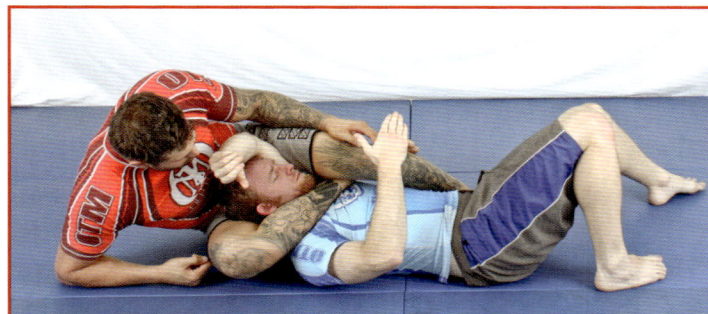

EDDIE BRAVO'S MEAT HOOK TRIANGLE WITH GRAPEVINE

To maintain the rubber guard position, you hook your arm around your opponent's head and over your own ankle, while freeing your grip hand to fight the wrist for a triangle. The problem with hugging the rubber guard with the meat hook is that you are sucking your opponent against your hips to control him, but you are also reducing your own mobility. If you are flexible, you could maneuver your free leg around his arm for the triangle, but even then, if he hugs your hip, your ability to move your leg will be determined by his strength rather than your flexibility. I prefer to use a grapevine to collapse his base, while using a wrist pin at the same time. I have nothing to lose by using the grapevine in this position; it ruins his base, controls the three directions of movement, prevents him from passing, and drops him into the triangle. The rubber guard alone is a great position, but when you start mixing it with grapevines, your opponent will have no idea what is going on, and he will feel helpless. If your opponent's butt is tight to his heels, blocking the grapevine, curll his upper body toward you using your rubber guard to lift his hips and create space.

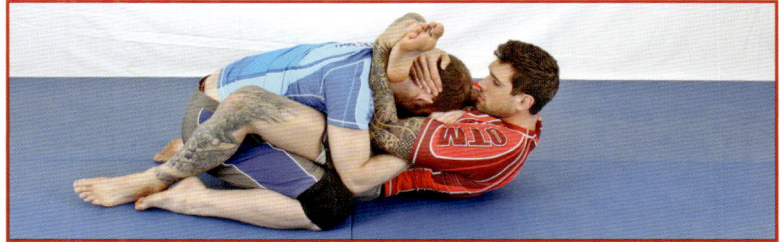

I am controlling Lance with the rubber guard, gripping my right ankle to fold my right leg across his upper back to control his posture. I crunch forward and control his head with a collar tie for additional control. If I were playing the rubber guard system, I would immediately try to pass his hand to the mat, but he is defending against that move.

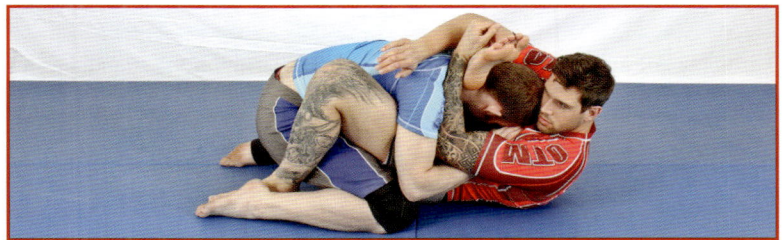

I lean forward and wrap my right arm around Lance's head and over the lower portion of my right shin. My right hand digs into the tendons of his neck to secure a grip. I focus on squeezing my chest to my leg to hug him tightly to help delay his backward movement.

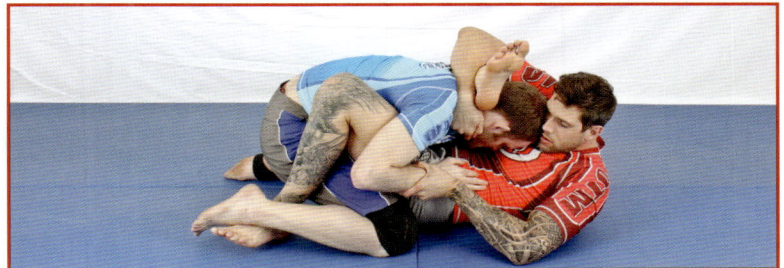

Once my right hand is securely gripping Lance's neck, my left hand releases my ankle and latches on to a downward grip on his right hand. My right foot snakes under his right ankle.

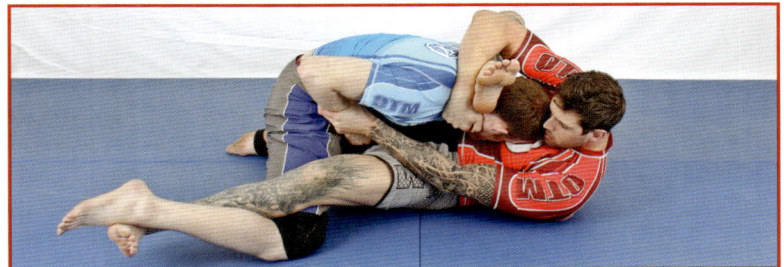

I simultaneously extend my left leg to sink the grapevine and press Lance's right wrist to his hip with my left hand. If I execute these movements at the same time, he will fall forward into the triangle. Notice that my grapevine naturally shifts me onto my left hip, which makes strengthens my attacks.

5

My left leg releases the grapevine and swings over Lance's right shoulder.

6

I grab my left ankle with my right hand to begin cinching the triangle as my left hand controls Lance's head.

7

I lock my legs and finish Lance with his arm on the mat. You can use any finish variation that you prefer.

ALTERNATE TRANSITION

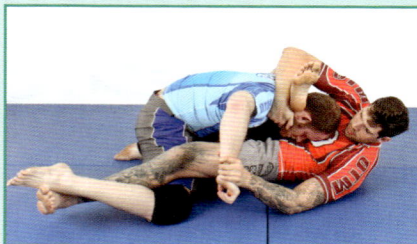

If you cannot execute the wrist pin and grapevine simultaneously, you can grab his wrist once it hits the mat and execute a leg-through triangle or a push pin triangle to clear his arm completely.

RUBBER GUARD CROSS-GRIP PULL-PUSH PIN WITH GRAPEVINE

The meat hook is a good way to work for the triangle from the rubber guard, but if your opponent knows the system, he will know that the triangle is your primary attack when you throw your arm over to free your grip hand. If he is stubborn, he can stall the position and block your grapevine. You can still get the triangle from the rubber guard position, but you need to be more deceptive. Establish a cross grip from the basic rubber guard position and yank on his arm to make him think that you are trying to set up an armbar. When he pulls his arm back to resist, switch directions and drive his wrist toward his stomach to pin it for the triangle. Your initial yank should pull him forward somewhat, lifting his butt off of his heels, allowing you to sink the grapevine as you drive back for the pin. When done properly, this is a smooth setup that does not require a lot of movement, but you need to be wary of your opponent trapping your hand when you attempt the cross grip. Moving quickly and confidently is important when you use this technique.

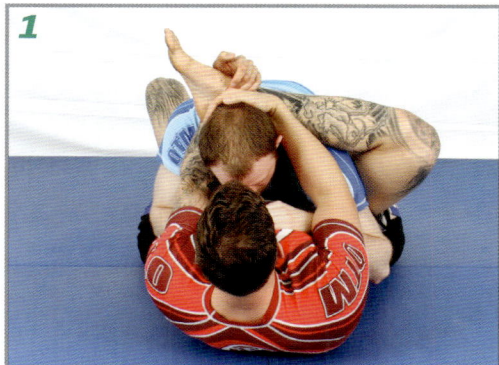

I am controlling Lance with the rubber guard. He shut down my meat hook attempt, so I am using the basic rubber guard with a collar tie to limit his movement.

My right hand releases the collar tie and grab Lance's right wrist, securing a cross grip. Notice that my left foot has snuck around his right leg and hooked underneath of his right ankle.

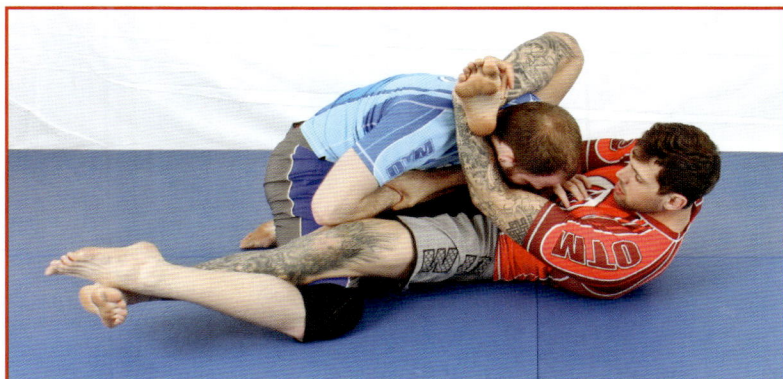

I yank Lance's right arm across my body with my right hand. When Lance instinctively retracts his right arm to defend against the armbar, I push his wrist toward his stomach with my right hand and extend my left grapevine. The combination of movements pins his right wrist to his stomach and shifts me onto my left hip.

4

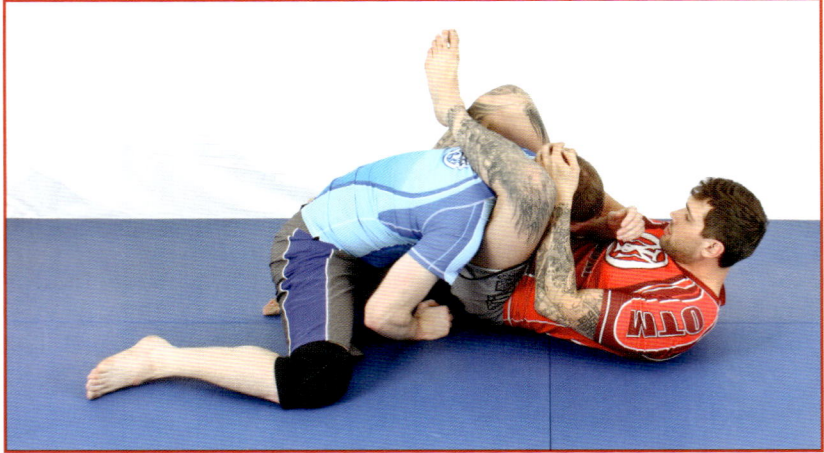

I throw my left leg over Lance's right shoulder to begin locking the triangle. I control Lance's head with both hands as I post my right foot on his left hip and adjust the angle of my hips to set my right leg across the back of his neck.

5

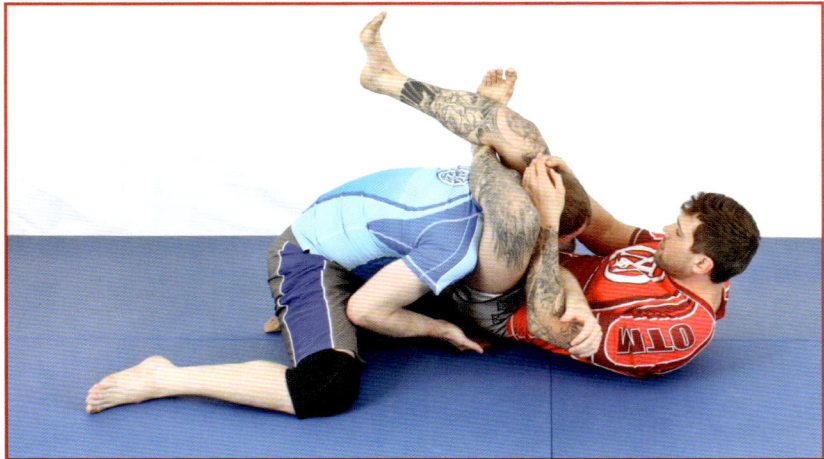

I lock the triangle and finish the fight.

ALTERNATE OPTION: WITHOUT THE GRAPEVINE

1

2

3

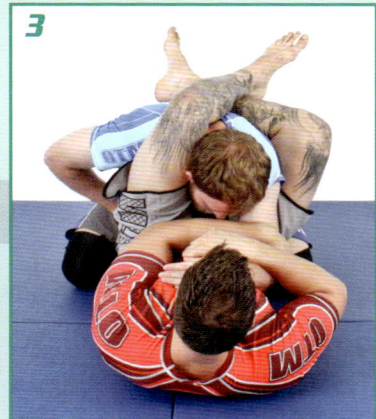

I can also use the pull-push pin without the grapevine, but I need to force Lance low in my guard by pressing my left foot into his right hip. When I shove his hand to his stomach for the wrist pin, I flare my left knee out so that my own leg does not block the pin.

THE RELJIC GOGO TRIANGLE

Combining attacks can be critical in setting up successful attacks. This technique is a great way to setup a gogoplata submission, and use your opponent's defense to transition into a triangle. When I was training Goran Reljic for a fight in the UFC, he showed me this rubber guard entry into the gogoplata as his favorite triangle setup. My flexibility is not phenomenal, but Reljic's is, and this setup works well for him. You attack your opponent with the gogoplata, which is not necessarily a high-percentage submission to begin with, and you use his defense to establish wrist control and transition to a triangle.

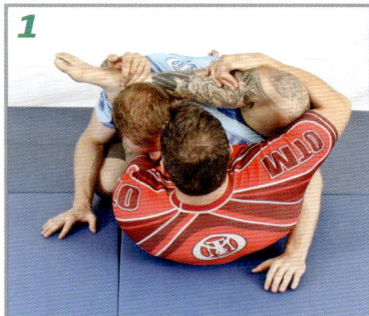

1

Lance is locked in my rubber guard, and I am hugging my right knee with my right arm to trap his left arm on the mat.

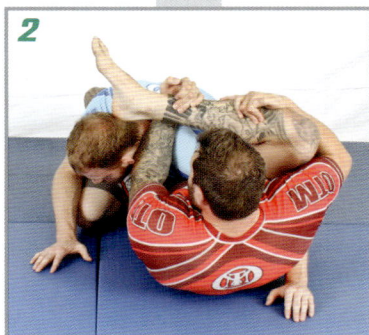

2

I roll my left arm over Lance's head to the left side of his face. I dig my left forearm into his jaw line to create crossface pressure. This stretches him out and gives me extra space.

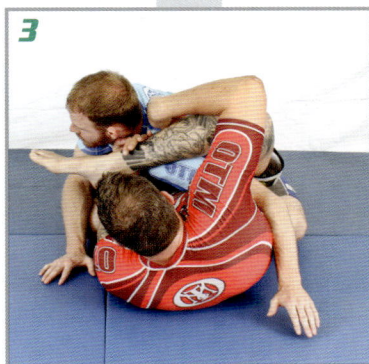

3

I continue to crossface Lance with my left arm as I pull my left foot down and under his chin.

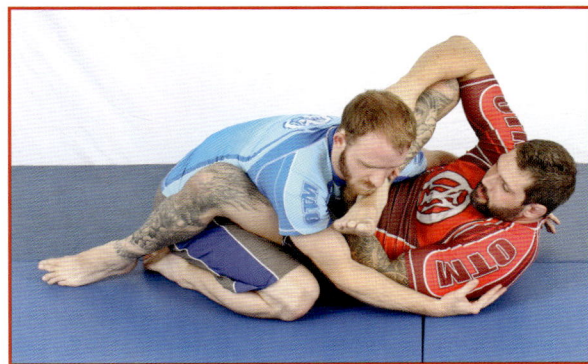

4

I slide my right shin under Lance's throat and control his posture by wrapping my right arm around the back of his head and gripping my right wrist with my left hand.

5

Lance grabs my right foot with his right hand to defend the gogoplata. He uses his grip to press my shin away from his neck.

6

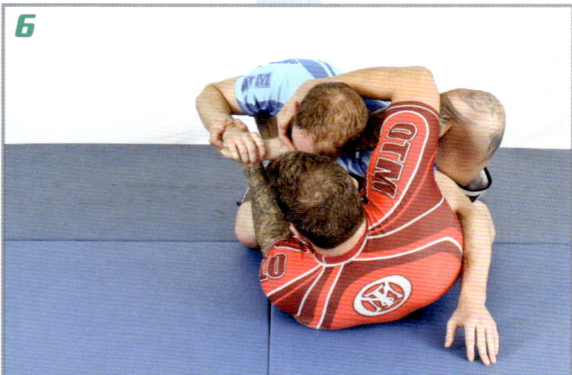

As my right arm cups Lance's head, my left hand latches on to his right wrist with an upward grip.

7

My left hand straightens Lance's right arm and forces it away from his body.

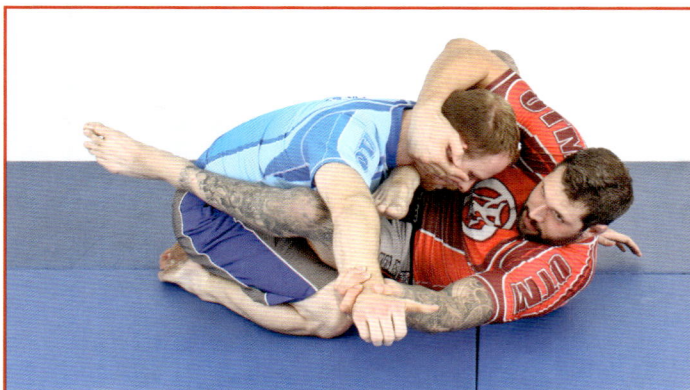

8

I pull my left knee to my chest, bringing my left leg under Lance's right arm.

9

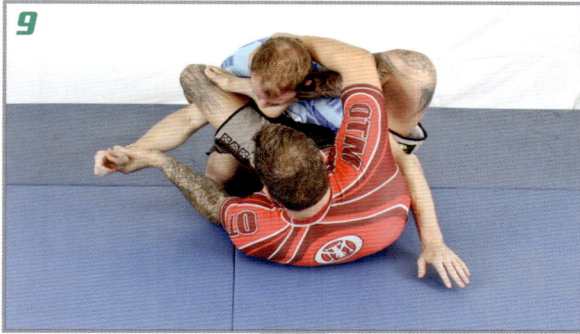

I drape my left leg over Lance's right arm and curl my left heel to his thigh. I cannot hop directly to the triangle because my right foot is still on the other side of Lance's head.

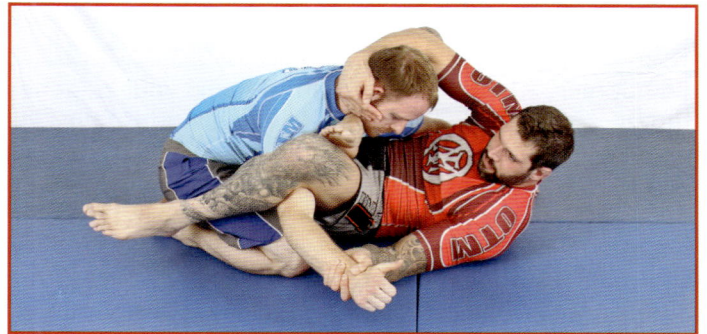

10

I swing my legs to the left to relieve the pressure on my right leg and begin to lift my right foot over his head.

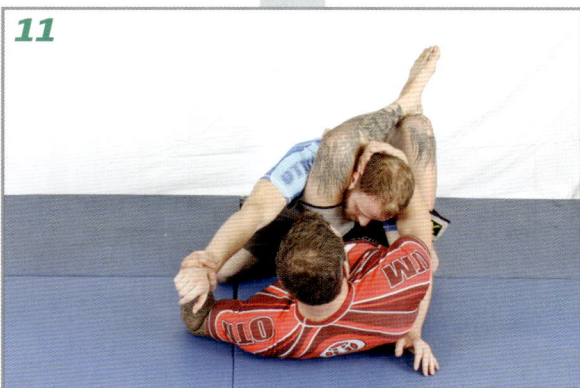

11

My legs swing back to the right as I pull Lance's head into my guard with my right hand.

12

I lock the figure-four and finish the triangle with Lance's arm on the mat.

THE CUFF CHOKE TRIANGLE

Sometimes, when you establish the cuff your opponent will interpret the forearm against his throat as a threat, so he begins to turn away, tucking his chin. That movement can actually be painful for him, like a neck crank, but he will be difficult to choke. Before you do anything else, set a grapevine to delay his movement. You could then fight his wrist with your free hand, but with your opponent already maneuvering to escape, he might slip out before you can lock the submission. Instead, reach across with your free hand to the other side of his neck and latch on to your shin. Squeeze your forearms together to create choking pressure. With both of your forearms driving into his throat, he can no longer turn, which means that it is now much more difficult for him to wiggle free of your position. His free arm will reach to push or pull your arms off of his neck, which exposes him to a leg circle triangle. The principle at work here is the key to having a dangerous guard: you create a threat that your opponent must address, which compromises his position. If your arms do not create a strong enough threat, you can swing your free leg to the other side of his head and apply pressure to the cuff choke. Using this combination of attacks works best when your opponent's arm is on the mat, but it can still be effective if it is not there.

I have the rubber guard and decide that I need to transition to the cuff to force Lance into a weaker position.

I quickly drive my right arm across my chest and grab Lance's right wrist with my right hand. I drop my left foot under his right ankle at the same time.

I simultaneously press Lance's right arm from his body with my right hand and straighten my left leg to secure the grapevine. It's important to note that I used the leverage of the grapevine to shift onto my left hip to strengthen my position.

4

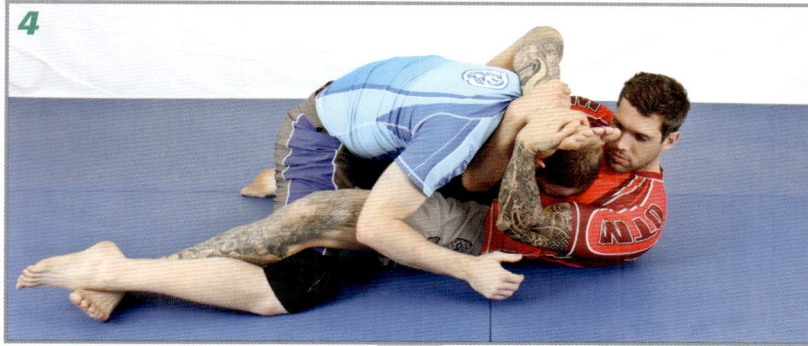

With my grapevine still locked, I wrap my right arm around Lance's neck, grabbing my right ankle with a cross grip. Notice how my right hand grips to the inside of my left arm to make the cuff as tight as possible.

5

Lance begins to turn to his right to escape the cuff. I immediately latch on to my right shin with my left and grind my left forearm into his neck, squeezing my arms together like a vice grip to create a choke.

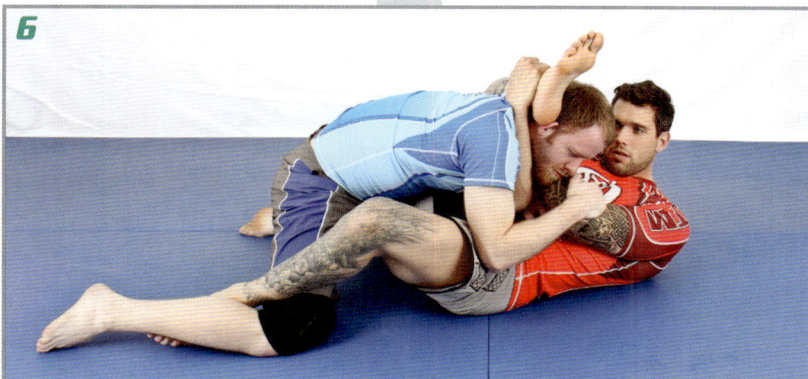

6

To relieve the pressure on his neck, Lance grabs my left biceps and attempts to pry my arms apart.

7

I post my left foot on the mat and scoot my hips away from Lance.

8

I circle my left foot over Lance's right arm and dig my left heel into his right biceps.

9

I press Lance's right arm back with my left leg.

10

I figure-four my legs on Lance's right shoulder and finish the reverse arm-in triangle by driving my left forearm into his neck.

ALTERNATE FINISH

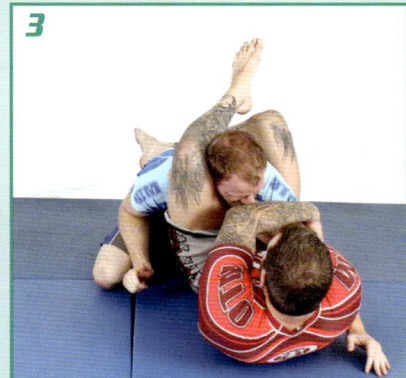

1

2

3

1) Lance tucks his chin and resists the pressure of my forearms. He does not fight the position hard enough to give me the leg circle triangle. 2) I elevate my hips and swing my left leg around Lance's head. I slam my left hamstring into the left side of his neck and retract my right arm to drive his carotid artery into my left leg. As I dig my right forearm into his neck to finish the leg assist cuff choke, he rips his right arm out to begin defending the choke. 3) As soon as Lance retracts his right arm, I roll my left thigh around Lance's head and over his right shoulder. I can now lock and finish the triangle.

CHAPTER FOUR
90 DEGREES INTRODUCTION

In the previous chapter, you learned how to triangle choke your opponent with control based trapping systems. Even though these systems can offer a high percentage of successful set ups and finishes for submissions, they are not 100% fool proof. Grapplers that have effective defense inside the guard could break through your controls and escape to a postured position. If they do, you can still attempt to break your opponent back down to a 0 degrees position and try to trap and submit him once again. If that attempt fails, it's probably time to switch to the sit up guard. In grappling, you might have the luxury to wait and continually try to break your opponent down, but in MMA the longer you wait to transfer into the sit up guard, the more damage from strikes you may receive. It's because of this that you are now seeing UFC fighters like Martin Kampmann quickly pop up to the sit up guard position. Athletes like Martin are having more success with transitioning to more dominant positions and getting submissions from the sit up guard. Simply stated, if your opponent sits up in your guard, then you sit up with him.

While doing this you are jamming your opponent keeping him from winding up and throwing powerful strikes down on top of you. This puts your opponent on the defense and limits the damage done to you.

When your opponent is postured, it's important to identify whether or not your opponent is sitting down on his heels. If he is, then he is primed for attack via the sit up guard, if he is not, then you will have to adjust to one of the guard systems in the next couple of chapters.

THE SIT UP GUARD

The sit up guard is a very important system when answering the problems caused by an opponent's posture. No matter which system of attacks you use from the sit up guard, it's pivotal that you consistently threaten your opponent with a hip bump sweep. This forces your opponent to defend the sweep, giving you the time and opportunity to set up and finish a triangle choke.

The sit-up guard is composed of four control systems linked together by the hip bump sweep. This chapter is organized sequentially to show you how you might transition from one system to the next with relative ease. These systems can be mixed and matched allowing you to adjust them based on your personal preference.

These systems within the sit-up guard are designed to have their own threat built in. So by combining this with the threat of the hip bump, you actually have two active threats in place for each control position. One active threat can be enough to trick your opponent into giving up a submission; two active threats increase your odds of success dramatically.

The first control system you will learn is the double wristlock grip, or you may know it as the Kimura grip. From the double wristlock grip, you actively threaten with the double wristlock submission. This, with the hip bump sweep added, is a nice combination. The double wristlock is a powerful shoulder lock that all fighters, regardless of experience level, respect. It's important to me that you do not view the double wristlock as a mere submission, but that you view it as a two-on-one grip control. Like many other two-on-one grips, you can utilize the double wristlock as a control to manipulate your opponent in many different ways. One example of its versatility would be how Karo Parisyan successfully used it for judo throws in many of his MMA fights.

The next control position you will learn is the headlock grip. I call this position the headlock grip rather than the guillotine grip because the guillotine submission is not my only option from this position. Regardless of those options, the very act of wrapping your arms around your opponent's head will usually make him think that you're chasing after a guillotine choke. Because the guillotine choke can be such a painful submission to endure, many grapplers have an innate phobia of being caught in it. That same fear works to your advantage and gives you a small variety of triangle set ups to finish your opponent. Most of those set ups will come from blending the headlock grip with a half stock/ cow catcher grip to make the proper angle and adjustment for locking in the triangle finish. You can even take the half stock grip option and make it a control based system called the lock 'n stock.

The lock 'n stock is a half stock with an over-the-back two-on-one grip. The lock 'n stock sets up neck cranks, arm locks, guillotines, front face locks, sweeps, and of course triangles. I love using it because it offers a good mix of control and attacks. The lock 'n stock will be a new position for many of your opponents, and the variety of attacks and suffocating control may likely overwhelm them. However, like most powerful positions, the lock 'n stock is not always easy to achieve. Trying to transition directly to it from a generic closed guard can be even more difficult. The sit-up guard puts you much closer to the lock 'n stock, but the headlock grip will do most of the work for you. The reason is that your opponent will usually bring his hands up to protect his head and neck from attacks, exposing himself to the half stock. Once you have established a half stock, the lock 'n stock grip is easy to attain. This will be how you usually secure the lock 'n stock control.

The last sit-up guard control position in my system is the octopus guard. This unorthodox position is the brainchild of innovative grappler Eduardo Telles. I have studied grappling footage of Telles in competition. He is a unique grappler that has succeeded by being strong in areas that others consider to be weak position. I like to study people that are creative and overcome grappling obstacles by thinking outside the box. The octopus guard is one of those innovations I find interesting, even though it's not an option that I rate highly on my list.

To establish the octopus guard, essentially, you pass one of your opponent's arms across your body and sit up into him. Once you have established the position, you have a variety of attacks and sweeps that you can use. The triangle setups that I demonstrate from the octopus may not mirror how Telles would use the octopus guard. My body type and catch wrestling background has an undeniable influence on how I work the position, but Telles is still the inspiration. I suggest that you experiment with the octopus guard and incorporate it into your game. It may frustrate you at first (it certainly frustrated me), but it is an option that might be worth your time practicing.

sit-up sweep

double wristlock grip

90 degrees
position

octopus guard

lock 'n stock

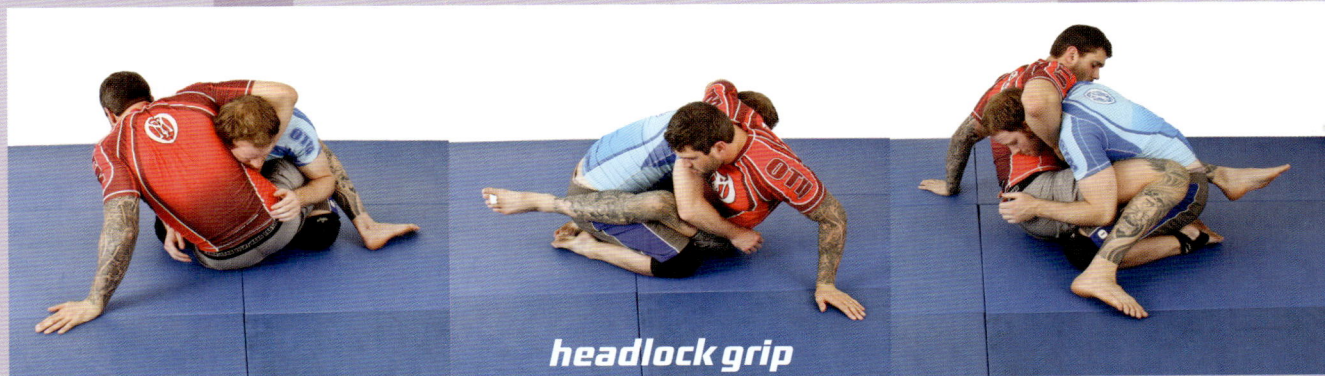
headlock grip

HIP BUMP TRIANGLE

To have an effective sit up guard game you must first have an effective hip bump sweep. The hip bump sweep is the focal technique when utilizing the sit up guard, if it is overlooked you will immediately start having problems executing any submission set ups. The hip bump triangle uses the threat of the hip bump sweep to maintain control of your opponent and combines it with a high percentage triangle finish. There are a few ways of working a hip bump triangle, but I find this particular option to be the best, because it prevents your opponent from doing most of the typical counters you might see when working from the sit up guard position. Most opponents will stiff arm your body to the mat, sometimes posting on your throat or they might grab control of the arm that you're posting on to sit up and then rip it out from underneath you sending you back to the mat. The solution to this problem is the cross grip. The cross grip control's your opponent's wrist, disabling him from executing these types of counters, while giving you some protection. Then you can hip bump your opponent off balance and then float your hips high for the triangle finish. If you're like me and built like a mountain gorilla, it may take a little time to get the hang of this, but it will pay off in the end if you stick with it.

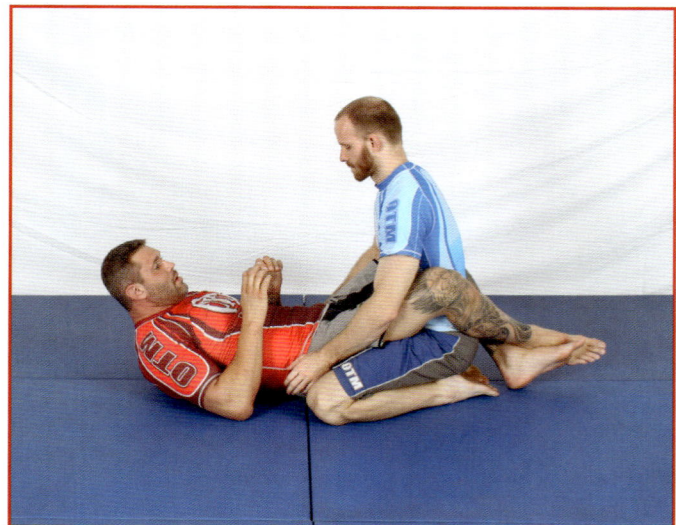

Lance is maintaining the 90 degrees position by posturing and sitting on his heels.

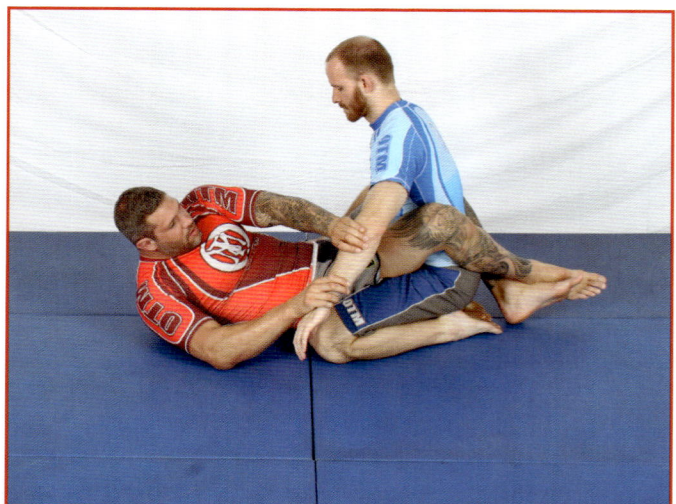

With both hands, I grab control of Lance's left wrist and forearm.

3

I unlock my feet, plant my right elbow and left foot on the mat, and sit forward, while keeping my left arm extended, pushing Lance's arm away from his body.

4

I lift my hips, bumping my hips forward, pushing Lance's arm far away from his body and pinning it to the mat.

5

I elevate my left leg, while twisting my torso, putting pressure on Lance's shoulders, and driving him towards his posted left hand. By ensuring my belly button is facing the mat, I put more pressure on him, locking him in place.

6

I draw my right knee to my chest as I continually drive Lance towards his posted left hand.

Once my right leg clears my opponent's arm, I release control of his wrist and grab the back of his head.

As I fall back to the mat, I hook under Lance's left arm with my right hand, while maintaining my grip on the back of his head. I then post my left foot on Lance's right hip to make a better angle to finish the choke.

I figure-four my legs, maintain control of Lance's arm, and pull down on his head, while squeezing my legs, finishing the triangle.

DOUBLE WRISTLOCK GRIP TRIANGLE

The downfall of the sit-up guard is that it does little to delay your opponent's movement. An active threat, however, can make up for that weakness. The hip bump is a threat, but once your opponent defends the hip bump, he will feel confident in his base and begin to work to escape the position. You need a threat that you can constantly maintain as you work for other attacks. The double wristlock—or Kimura—is that threat. In this technique, you combine the hip bump with a double wristlock setup. When your opponent counters your sweep by driving back in, you transition to a figure-four grip. I want you to think of the double wristlock as more than a submission. It is a powerful two-on-one grip. With that power, you can pin his arm and transition to the leg walk-up triangle, while he focuses on defending the double wristlock and the hip bump. If he attempts to counter the double wristlock, and you cannot overpower him, transition to the hip bump triangle option or use one of the subsequent techniques.

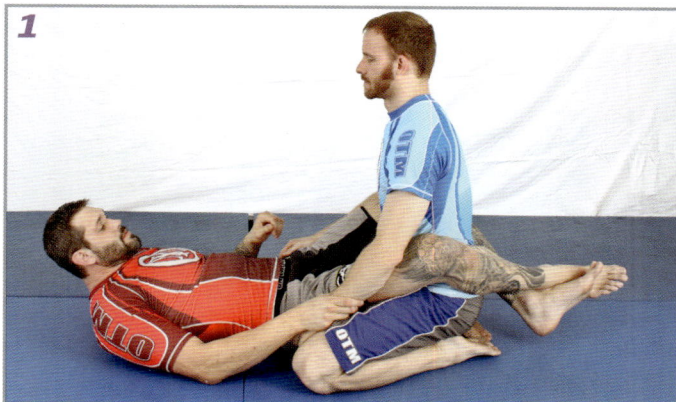

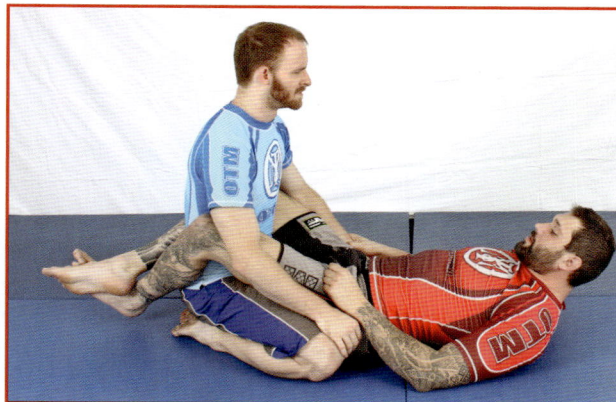

Lance is maintaining the 90 degrees position by controlling my hips and keeping his back straight.

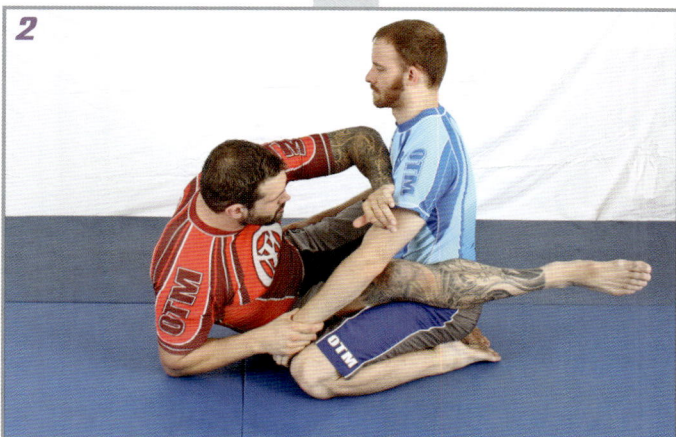

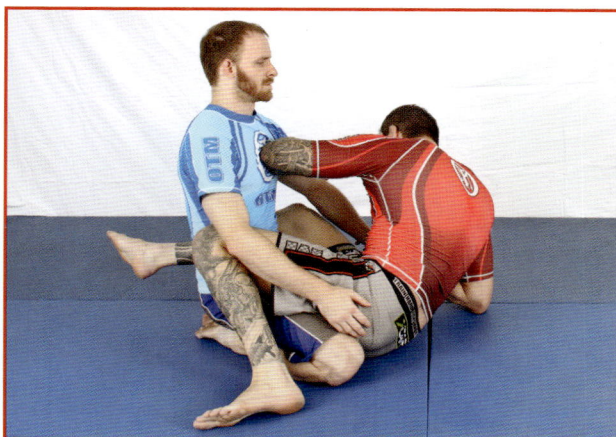

My right hand grabs Lance's left wrist. I twist it clockwise to force it off of my hip. At the same time, I post my left foot on the mat and create space by shifting onto my right hip. I sit up onto my right elbow as I drive my right forearm into his chest to push him to my right.

I elevate and twist my hips, slamming them into Lance for the hip bump. He drives back into me to defend the sweep. I immediately snake my right arm over his left arm and down to my wrist to establish the double wristlock grip.

4

I sit back, attempting to finish the double wristlock by twisting Lance's left arm behind his back and to his head. As I work to finish the double wristlock, I post my left foot on his right hip.

5

Lance defends the double wristlock by sliding his left hand over my leg. My left hand releases my right wrist and latches on to his left wrist. As soon as I establish my grip, I pull my left elbow toward his right shoulder to pin his left forearm against his ribs. My right hand is now free.

6

While still locking Lance's left arm against his ribs, I lie back and throw my right leg over his left shoulder.

7

I adjust my hips for the triangle, controlling Lance's head with my left hand throughout the process, and finish the fight.

FIGURE-FOUR TO SWING BACK SETUP: OPTION 1

To defend the double wristlock threat, your opponent will often give you a path to his back. I will show you the three most common routes. Earlier in the book, I used the threat of a back take to set up the swing-back triangle, and I do the same from the double wristlock options. The principle is the same: I expect my opponent to defend his back, momentarily forgetting my submission options from guard. Then I swoop in for the triangle finish. If he does not defend the back take, I will set my hooks and finish with the rear naked choke. In this technique, my opponent defends the double wristlock by bringing his trapped arm to his stomach and locking his hands together in between our bodies to protect his shoulder. I release my double wristlock, slip my arm out, and switch my hip by pivoting on the mat. I strike the back of his triceps with my elbow to completely turn him. When I begin to take his back, I leave my leg across his belt line as though I were going to apply a figure-four body lock, and I drape my arm over his chest as though I were looking for a rear naked choke. The ultimate goal of the following three techniques is to acquire a one-on-one grip on my opponent's arm, which will allow me to finish with the swing back triangle, shown on page 203.

1

I am controlling Lance's left arm with a double wristlock grip.

2

Lance defends the double wristlock submission by locking his hands together between our bodies. This puts me in danger of getting countered.

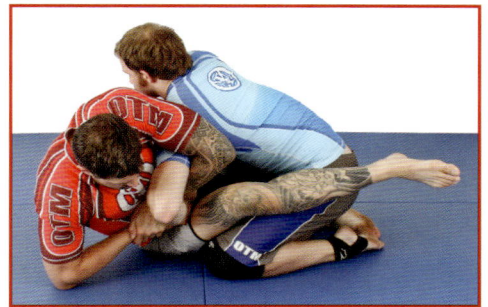

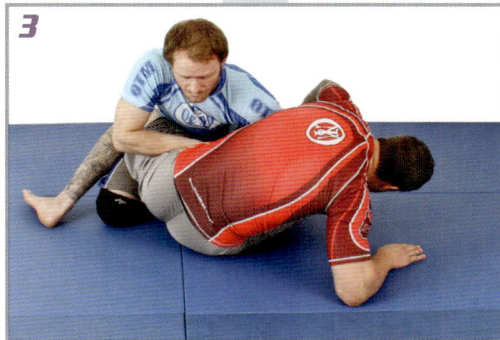

3

I release the double wristlock and lean forward to help snake my left arm free.

4

As soon as my left arm is free, I extend my right arm and balance on my right hand. I then dig my left elbow into his left armpit.

5

I slam my elbow into Lance's left armpit, aiming it down toward the mat to launch him forward. At the same time, I shift my hips out to my right, giving him a clear path forward.

6

I post my left hand on the mat for balance as I drape my right arm over Lance's back.

7

As I throw my right leg over Lance's back, I press my chest into his upper back and snake my right hand under his right armpit.

8

I grab Lance's right wrist with my right hand, securing a one-on-one grip, while dropping my weight onto Lance's back.

FIGURE-FOUR TO SWING BACK SETUP: OPTION 2

Picking your back take setup from the double wristlock depends entirely on how your opponent defends the position. In the previous technique, your opponent clasped his hands together at his stomach to protect his shoulder. In this technique, your opponent defends by looking for a body lock, hugging you. I see many grapplers frustrated by this defense, but those grapplers fail to see that when an opponent hugs your body, his hands can no longer defend his lower body. In this situation, I execute what wrestlers call a switch. I place one arm on the mat and scoot my hips out, driving the back of my other arm into my opponent's armpit, slamming him forward into the mat like I did in the previous technique. The key to this movement is an understanding of off-line concepts. The power for the switch comes from shifting off of my opponent's centerline, and I need to plant my hand on the mat and move my hips to do that. As I did in the previous technique, I set my leg across his belt line and establish wrist control. From here, I can work from the back, or I can attack with the triangle on page 203.

I have secured the double wristlock grip on Lance's left arm.

Lance counters the double wristlock by locking his hands around my waist.

I post my right hand on the mat and lean to my right. I roll my left hand between Lance's legs and dig my left elbow into his left armpit.

4

I use my arm as a lever to force Lance forward into the mat. I simultaneously switch my hips to help drive his shoulder down.

5

I swing my chest toward Lance's back as I continue to rotate my hips.

6

As I set my chest on Lance's upper back, my right hand snakes under his right armpit, and I post my left hand on the mat.

7

I reach under Lance's arm and secure the one-on-one grip on his right wrist. I bring my right leg over his back which is still on the outside of Lance's right hip.

FIGURE-FOUR TO SWING BACK SETUP: OPTION 3

In the previous two techniques, my opponent clasped his hands together in an attempt to defend the double wristlock. If I can pry his arm away from his body before he can lock his hands together or hug me, I have a good chance of finishing the lock. At this point, with his arm traveling quickly to a painful position, his most reliable escape is to straighten his arm in an attempt to rotate his wrist out of the shoulder lock. This is a common escape. If successful, my opponent will have defeated my double wristlock, but he has given me his back. The key to executing this transition is to keep control of his wrist and to slam your elbow down on top of your opponent's shoulder as soon as your head and arm slips through the hole. If you release the wrist too soon, he can rip his arm free and return to a neutral position.

1

I am working to finish the double wristlock on Lance's left arm.

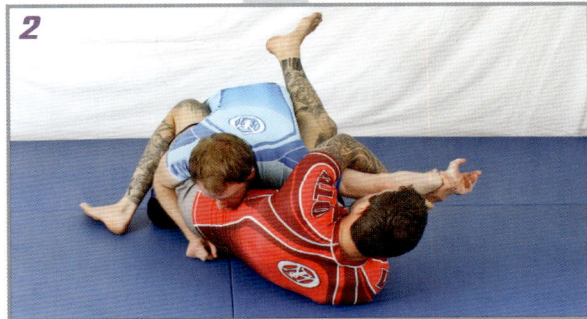

2

I begin cranking the double wristlock. Lance begins to straighten his arm to counter my submission attempt.

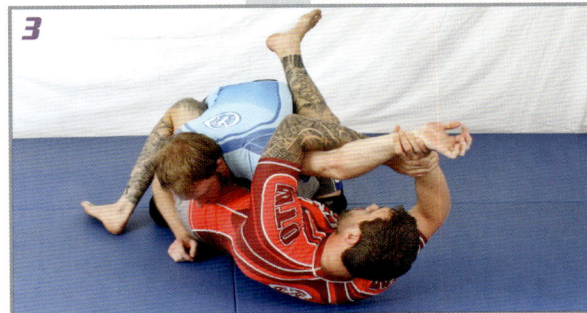

3

I use the figure-four to slide Lance's arm closer to my head.

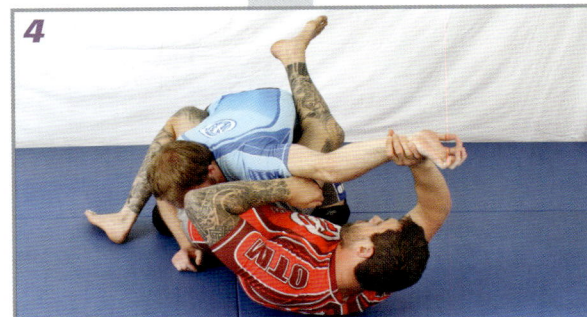

4

I release my grip with my left hand and begin to swim my left arm underneath Lance's left arm. Notice that I maintain control of his left wrist with my right hand.

5

My left elbow swims under Lance's left arm and my head follows.

6

I one arm row my left arm into Lance's armpit and triceps, forcing him down to the mat.

7

Once I have Lance's arm pinned, I release my right grip on his wrist and begin to twist onto my left hip.

8

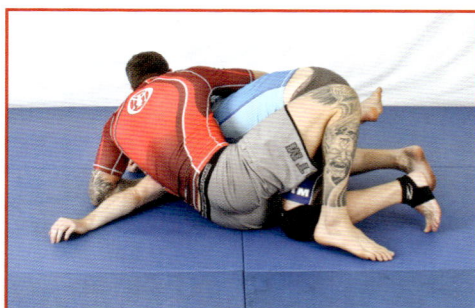

As I set my chest on his upper back, my right arm threads under his right armpit.

9

I secure the back position by throwing my right leg over Lance's back and controlling his right wrist with my right hand, obtaining a one-on-one grip.

SWING BACK TRIANGLE

Now that you have taken the back using one of the previous three options, you can surprise your opponent with a swing-back triangle. Though this technique may look dynamic, it will not be timing based if executed properly. The key to establishing control of your opponent is the over-the-back grip, which, as I mentioned earlier in the book, is one of the best grips in grappling, so you do not need to rush this technique and risk sloppiness. With the over-the-back grip in place, swing back to guard, while posting your near foot on your opponent's hip. The foot on his hip keeps him from moving forward, and a quick shoulder press will drive him lower in your guard, allowing you to set a deeper triangle. As you will notice from the photographs below, I do not swing back underneath my opponent. For the swing back to be effective, you must fall in front of him as you swing your leg around his trapped arm.

I am on Lance's back. My left leg is across his belt line and my right hand has secured a one-on-one grip.

As I slide forward, I press Lance's right shoulder with my left hand, which I will continue to do throughout this transition to push him lower in my guard.

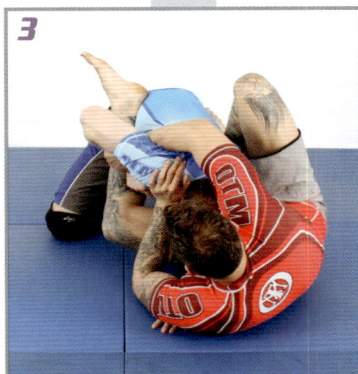

I land on my left side and post my right foot on Lance's left hip, while pressing him away by extending my right leg. I'm simultaneously pulling him tightly into me with my right one-on-one grip.

4

While maintaining the over-the-back grip, I swing my left leg over his shoulder and into the side of his neck.

5

As an option, for more control, I re-grab Lance's right wrist with my left hand as I grab my left shin with my right hand, keeping my right foot posted on his hip.

6

I lock my legs and finish the traditional triangle with both hands on the back of Lance's head.

HEADLOCK TO ARM DRAG TRIANGLE

When I establish the headlock grip, I always try to latch on to one of my opponent's wrists with my free hand to give me the freedom to jump between the double wristlock attack and the headlock series, while protecting myself from a side choke pass or a cradle. For this technique to work, I have to obtain control when my opponent attempts to peel my hand off of his throat. Once he sets his grip and attempts to free himself from my headlock grip, I maneuver my leg outside and around his arm. I then transition from the headlock grip to a two-on-one grip, pulling my opponent's inside arm across my body as I fall back to lock my legs for the triangle. With so much movement involved in setting the triangle, timing becomes an issue. Move quickly, and maintain a firm, tight grip with your hands as long as you can. Two key details will also make this attack more effective: grab the biceps when you work the drag, not the triceps, and set your foot on his hip to stretch him out and to keep him bent over, making him more vulnerable to the triangle.

1

I have established the headlock grip by sitting up into Lance and wrapping my left arm around the back of his head as though I were looking to establish a guillotine. My right hand controls his left wrist to limit his options for defending and countering.

2

Lance digs the fingers of his right hand into my left forearm to protect his neck. As he does that, I shoot my right foot to his left hip and drive my left shoulder into the back of his neck to limit his movement.

3

I continue to press my left shoulder into his back as I circle my left knee in front of his right arm and slide it up to his shoulder. As my left knee moves into position, I release my headlock grip and immediately grab his left triceps with my left hand.

4

Instead of falling straight back, I swivel to my left as my back travels to the mat, allowing me to swing my left leg over Lance's right arm and across the back of his neck in one movement. I pull his left arm across my body with both hands as I fall.

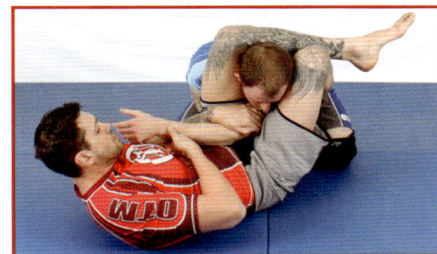

5

I lock my right leg under my left knee and finish the triangle.

HEADLOCK AND HALF STOCK TO SANKAKU

I learned this technique from Karo Parisyan. I saw him land it in the gym, and I asked him how he set it up. He said, "I have no idea." That's Karo, he has a good "feel" for grappling and just makes things happen. We recreated the position and reverse-engineered the technique that Karo spontaneously invented. It has been a part of my game ever since. As you will notice in the photographs below, this technique capitalizes on the controlling power of the half stock—a reverse nelson, which is an underhook where your arm goes across the back of your opponent's neck before threading under his armpit—to set up a wrist pin sankaku. I love using the half stock because it allows me to control my opponent's posture and one of his arms with only one of my arms, leaving one of my hands free to work for a pin. This sankaku entry is quick and, like all sankakus, requires a certain level of hip coordination. If you feel like you need more control over your opponent, or you are not comfortable with sankakus just yet, use the next technique instead.

I am in the headlock grip position. My right arm is wrapped around Lance's head, threatening a guillotine. I am leaning on my left hip, and my left hand is posted behind me for balance.

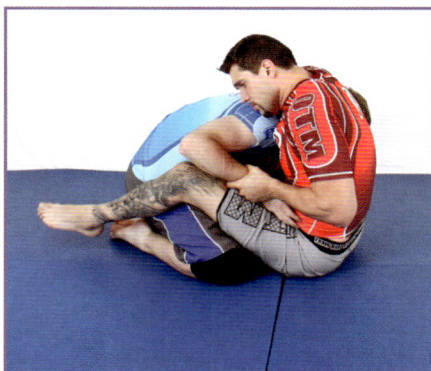

I crunch forward to continue to threaten with the guillotine as my left hand latches on to Lance's right wrist. Once I have established wrist control, I shift my hips and orient myself vertically.

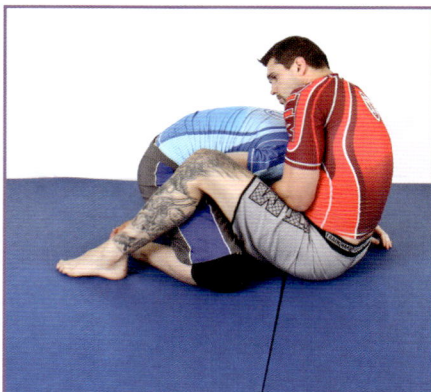

As I begin to scoot my hips away, leaning onto my right hip, I press Lance's right wrist to his stomach, pinning it, and shoot my right hand under his left arm, securing a half stock.

4

I fall toward my right as I hip out even more, keeping my left thigh tight to Lance's side to block his right arm from escaping my pin. I push his head down with my left hand to delay his posture and pull on his left triceps with my right hand to set up my hip swivel.

5

Using my grip on Lance's left triceps, I rock onto my right shoulder and swing my left thigh to the back of his head as I curl my right foot toward his armpit.

6

I continue to roll for the sankaku, rotating my hips onto Lance's back, driving my left knee to the outside of his left armpit. My right foot is now in the perfect "V" position for the sankaku, aligning my right thigh and calf with the "V" shape of his chin. My right hand is still controlling his left triceps.

7

I reach between my legs with my left hand and grab my right shin, pulling it tight into Lance's armpit as I fold my left leg over my right ankle to lock the sankaku. I can now pull on Lance's triceps to finish the choke from the position.

LOCK 'N STOCK

The lock 'n stock is a half stock with a two-on-one grip. The problem with the lock 'n stock is that it can be difficult to set up because your opponent will fight you by threading your arm under his armpit. However, when you are aggressive with the headlock grip, he will forget to defend the half stock, especially if he is thrashing so much that you are hesitant to use the sankaku. The half stock alone is effective for reversals and neck cranks, but transitioning to the lock 'n stock by reaching for an over-the-back grip gives you the benefits of both the half stock and an over-the-back grip simultaneously, making the lock 'n stock an extremely powerful position. Once you have locked his arm behind his back, you have many attacks to choose from. In this technique, you use your over-the-back grip to pin his arm and transition to a triangle. This technique is very similar to the other over-the-back setups that you learned earlier in the book, but the addition of the lock 'n stock makes this triangle controlled and difficult to defend against.

1

I have secured the headlock grip. My left arm is wrapped around the back of Lance's head threatening the guillotine, and I am using my right elbow to maintain my seated guard.

2

Lance snakes his right hand between our bodies and digs his fingers into my left forearm to defend the guillotine.

3

I quickly circle my left hand out from under Lance's neck and shoot it under his right armpit, immediately cranking his right shoulder into the air by driving my left arm across his back.

4

I switch to my left hip so that I can reach my left arm even deeper into his armpit, and I reach over his back with my right hand.

5

My right hand grabs Lance's right wrist and my left hand grabs my right wrist, securing a two-on-one over-the-back grip, the lock 'n stock. It's important that I point his right elbow to the sky by maintaining pressure on the lock 'n stock.

6

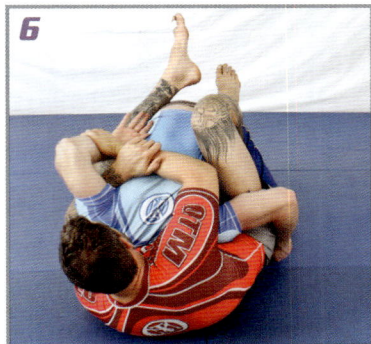

I return to the saucer back position. In crunching forward to saucer my back I pull with the lock 'n stock to hug Lance tight to my chest.

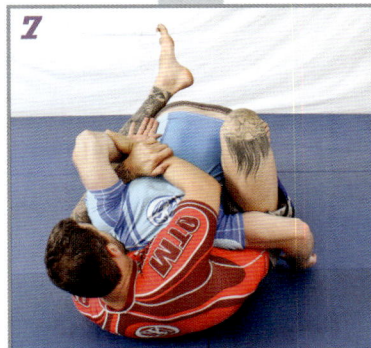

7

I place my right foot on Lance's left hip to help delay the forward motion of the stack.

8

My left hand releases my right wrist and presses on Lance's right shoulder to force him low in my guard. My right hand is still controlling his right wrist.

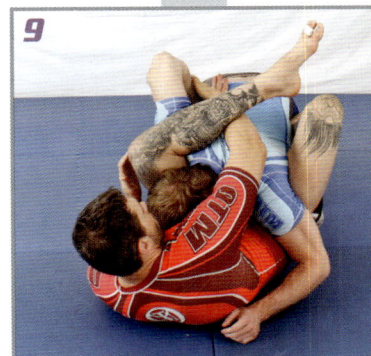

9

While maintaining my over-the-back grip, I throw my left leg over Lance's shoulder and across the back of his neck.

10

I figure-four my legs and finish the triangle.

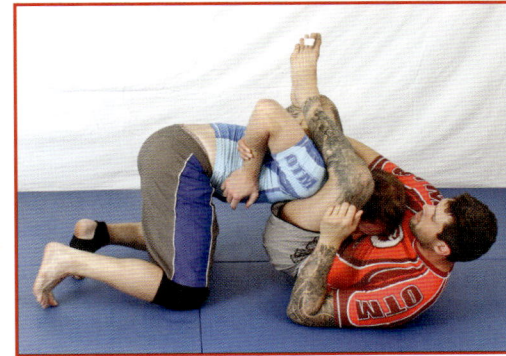

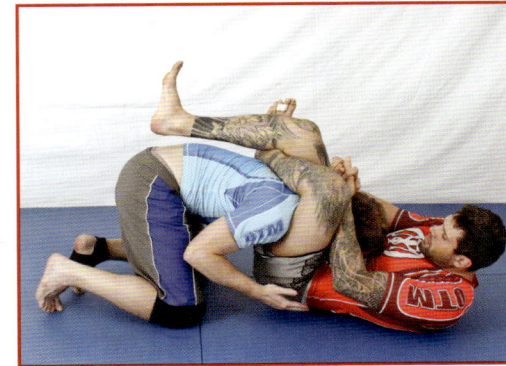

EDUARDO TELLES' OCTOPUS GUARD TRIANGLE

The concept of the octopus guard is alien to many grapplers, but the position itself is common. You have probably landed in octopus guard before, after a scramble or after an arm drag. I typically set up the octopus guard by using an arm drag to attack an opponent who is maintaining the 90 degrees position, but you will see that the octopus guard puts your opponent into a 0 degrees position, so look to set up the octopus guard from that position as well. In this technique, you use the octopus guard to transition to a half stock. Once I trap his far arm over his back, I simply open my legs and lock them around his neck. With his arm tied up in the half stock, your opponent is unable to fight your hands, making it easy to apply the submission. There is a bit of timing involved in applying this triangle, but the position is solid. As long as I keep my grip tight, my opponent's only good counter will be to stack. Unfortunately for him, this will give me a path straight to his back.

Lance is maintaining the 90 degrees position.

My left hand latches on to Lance's left wrist as my right hand grips his left elbow.

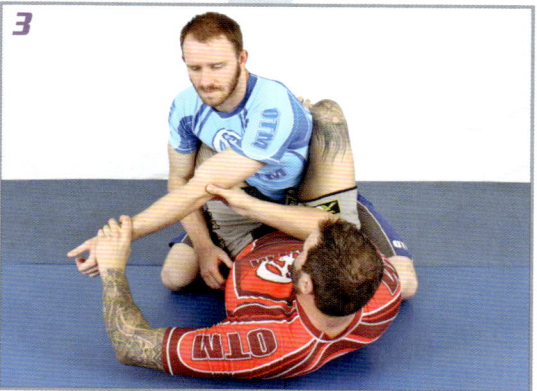

I bridge my hips to push Lance away. When Lance leans forward to adjust his balance, I pull my knees to my chest and yank his left arm across my body with both of my hands, forcing him to fall into me.

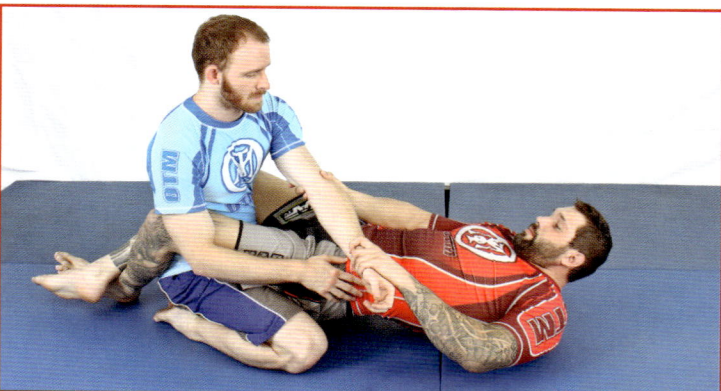

4

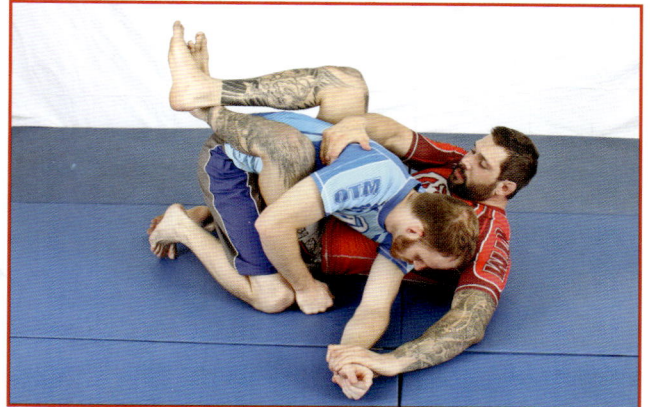

As Lance falls to the mat, I reach across his back with my right arm and control his lat, maintaining control of his left wrist with my left hand. Notice how his head is off to the side rather than directly over my chest.

5

I maneuver my left elbow over the back of Lance's neck.

6

I slide my left arm under his right armpit and start to lock my hands together, securing the octopus guard.

7

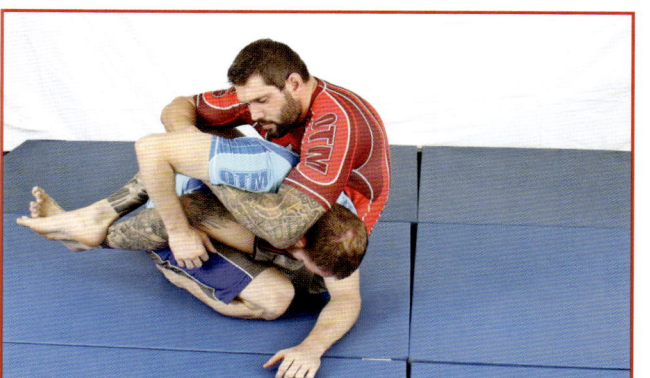

My right hand grabs my left, securing a finger roll grip (or what you might call an s-grip).

8

I pull Lance's arm away from my left leg, hugging Lance as tight as possible. I then pop my hands lower on his right arm, hooking the crook of his elbow rather than his biceps. By shifting lower on his arm, I can apply more pressure and pull his arm even farther back.

9

I unlock my guard and swing my left leg out wide.

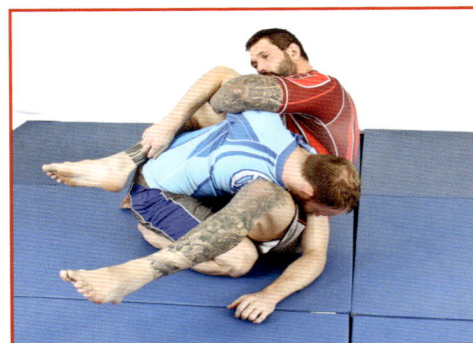

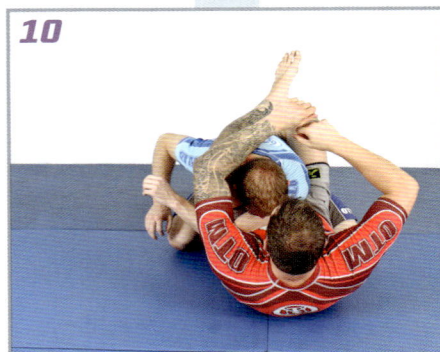

10

I release my grip and fall to the saucer back position as my left leg slaps against Lance's neck, clearing his right arm.

11

I adjust to finish the triangle.

OCTOPUS GUARD TO SWING BACK TRIANGLE

The strength of the previous technique is that it is quick, violent, and powerful. Its weakness is that it requires timing, and there is a brief moment where you release your grips and fall back for the triangle. In that instant, you have no control over your opponent, which could result in him ripping out of your attack. If your opponent has a tendency to explode out of your attacks or you prefer to use a more controlled attack, use the half stock to transition to the Boston handshake, an over-the-back grip that you learned earlier in the book. By securing the Boston handshake, you can maintain control over your opponent as you transition to the triangle, reducing the chances of his escaping. I prefer this grip for several reasons. The first is that one hand is free during the transition, allowing me to use it for balance or to threaten my opponent's neck. The second is that, if my transition fails, I can use the one on one to drag my opponent down, and use my free hand to pop up and take the back and immediately attack with the rear naked choke.

1

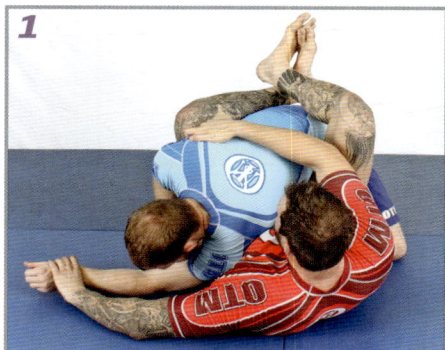

I have forced Lance's left arm across my body. I grip his right lat with my right hand to stabilize the position.

2

I lock an s-grip, securing the octopus guard

3

I sit up, keeping my chest tight to Lance's upper back

4

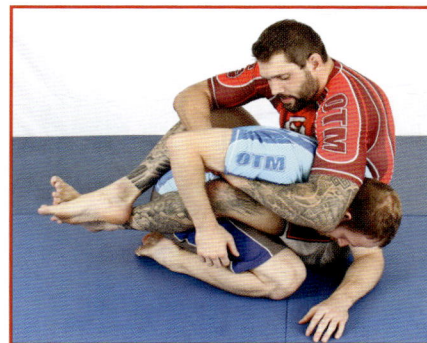

I break my s-grip, keeping my left arm tight to Lance's shoulders, while gripping his right wrist with my right hand.

5

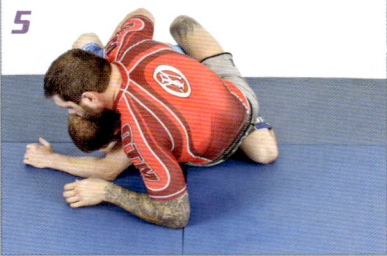

I plant my left elbow on the mat, while posting my right foot on Lance's right hip to delay his forward movement and force him lower in my guard.

6

I pin Lance's wrist to his body and swivel back underneath of him.

7

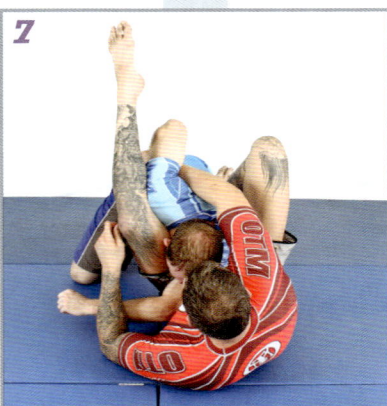

My left leg clears Lance's right arm as I rock to a saucer back position.

8

My left leg clears Lance's right arm and curls over his back.

9

I figure-four my legs and finish the triangle.

CHAPTER FIVE

THE FORWARD LEAN INTRO

When you work the sit-up guard aggressively, your opponent will reconsider maintaining the 90 degrees position. This can be mentally crippling to your opponent, because the 90 degrees postured position tends to be what most grapplers—jiu-jitsu fighters especially—consider the ideal position to achieve within the guard. Out matched by your sit up guard, your opponent usually will attempt to drive you back down to the mat. By doing so, he will transfer his body temporarily into the forward lean position. Quite often the force required to collapse your sit-up guard will be enough to bring his butt off of his heels. When he does this, his body will be committed to forcing you back to the mat. That leaves your opponent extremely vulnerable to getting swept with a side scissor sweep. To take advantage of this vulnerability you must adjust your hips and legs into the side scissor position quickly before he runs you completely flat. Once in the side scissor position you need to get to work on applying a sweep and/or submission. If you hesitate too long, your opponent will regain his balance and posture out, or he will fight his way

back down to smother and control your hips. If this does happen, your side scissor game has failed and you must move on to the appropriate system to deal with your opponent's body position.

The Side Scissor

When I first started grappling, the side scissor was my most successful guard system. It was fast, aggressive, and allowed me to escape from the bottom position rather easily. Later on, when my interest in submitting from the guard increased, I realized I needed to learn and develop other guard systems that gave me more control of my opponent. Later, I became more of a fan of trapping guard systems, but I never stopped using the side scissor. The side scissor is very effective when the timing and situation is right. To do this, it's important to keep in mind the limitations of the side scissor. The side scissor is not the same manner of control as the Irish collar or the shoulder pin, where you can tie up and hold your opponent in one place. Instead, the side scissor is very similar to the sit-up guard in that your opponent is mostly free to move in any direction he wants. Typically, your opponent will be moving forward to the O degrees position when countering the sit up guard. That pressure sets up the scissor sweep, which is your active threat from the side scissor position. That active threat is your method of control because your opponent is forced to defend the threat before launching attacks of his own. When defending that threat he creates openings to set up the triangle.

The reason why the side scissor is so effective against the forward lean position is because your opponent's chest is positioned in front of his hips, meaning his centerline is extended horizontally rather than vertically. The side scissor is ideal for attacking this situation. If your opponent's hips were forward, lifted off of his heels and his chest up, the issue would be a vertical one and not horizontal. In that case, utilizing the K-control guard system would be your best option. When your opponent is in the forward lean position, the side scissor can easily disrupt and weaken his base. This forces your opponent to use his hands to maintain his balance rather than using his hands to win the hand fight. Use this opportunity to tie up his upper body and quickly set up and finish the triangle choke. If for some reason he does not defend the scissor sweep, utilize the sweep to gain the top position.

forward lean position

side scissor guard

DOUBLE WRIST CONTROL SIDE SCISSOR TRIANGLE

Even though I'm a huge fan of trapping systems to control your opponent and lock on a triangle, there are times when a quick speed-based technique will be successful in finishing your opponent. Here, I'm utilizing a double wrist control grip from the side scissor to control my opponent. I go for a quick scissor sweep, which my opponent counters. By adjusting his weight momentarily to counter the sweep, I can plant my bottom foot on his hip and press away, breaking his posture and putting him in a bad position. Then I simply pin his wrist to his hip, clear my leg over his shoulder, and lock down the triangle. This choke works great if you apply it in the window of time when your opponent is hovering and his base is compromised. I recommend this triangle for all levels of grapplers. Once you nail the timing, the quick sweep/submission combination can be very difficult to counter.

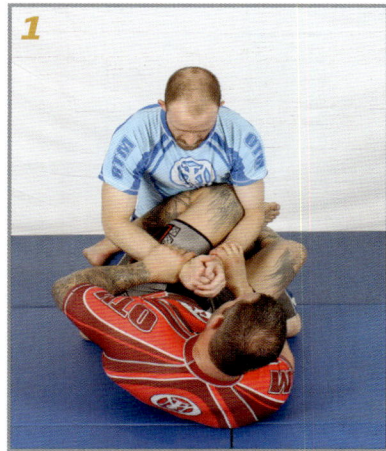

I have double wrist control and have Lance in my side scissor guard.

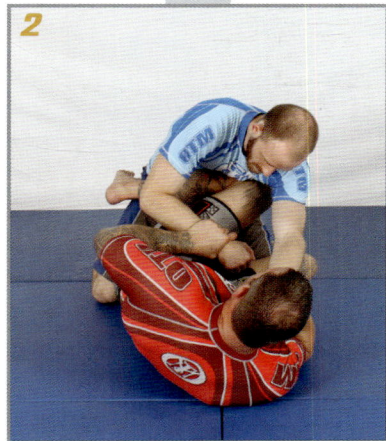

I pin Lance's right wrist to my left thigh and pull his left wrist high to my chest, while scissoring my legs to feint a sweep.

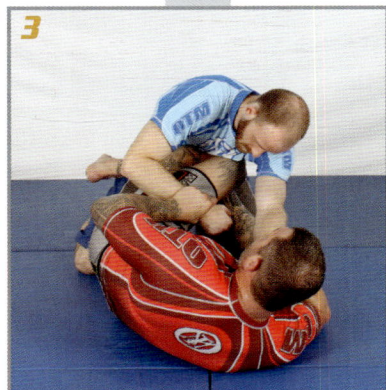

From here I put my right foot on Lance's hip

4

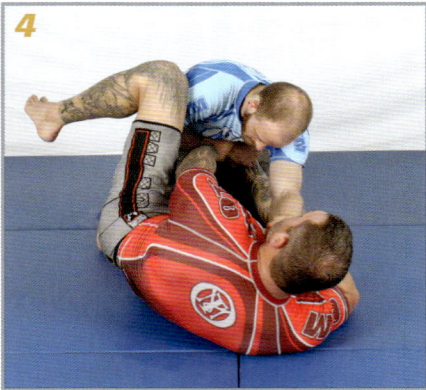

I extend my right leg, while pulling on Lance's left arm. This stretches him out and keeps him low, while I slide his right wrist off my left thigh and pin it towards his body.

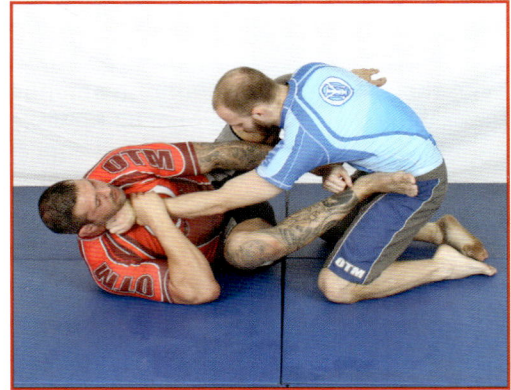

5

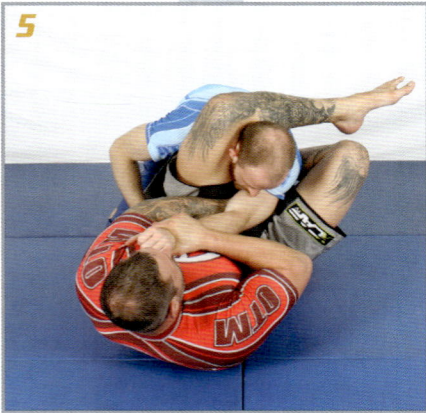

I throw my left leg over the back of Lance's neck, while squaring my hips up with his.

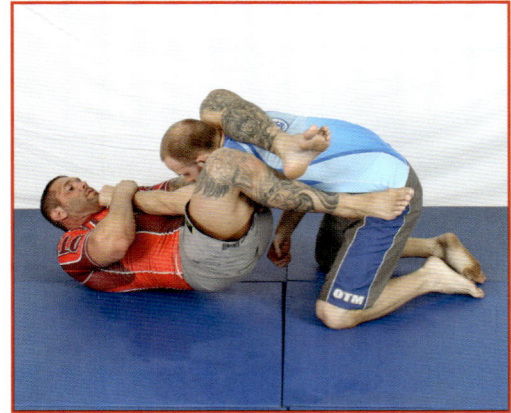

6

I figure-four my legs and finish with the triangle armbar.

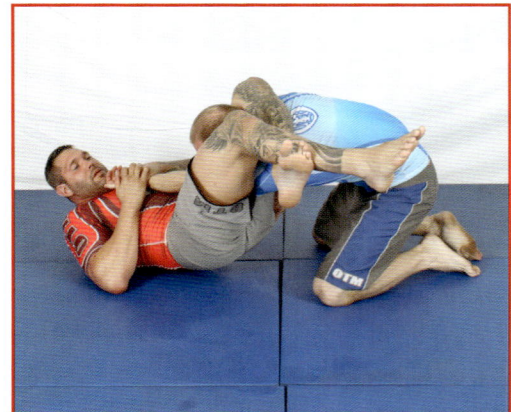

SCISSOR SWEEP ATTEMPT TO WRIST PIN

In this technique, I use my active threat, the scissor sweep, to trick my opponent into giving up a wrist pin. Whether I am faking the scissor sweep, or my opponent blocks the reversal, I need commit to the technique and off-balance my opponent. This technique is simple misdirection, and my opponent needs to believe that I want the sweep. His priority will be to maintain his balance, and he will not see the triangle coming until it is too late. Like all side scissor attacks, this technique is quick and efficient. With the collar tie, you will have adequate control of his head, and an upward grip will give you enough power to manipulate his arm as he defends the sweep. If you are struggling to control his wrist, use the next technique.

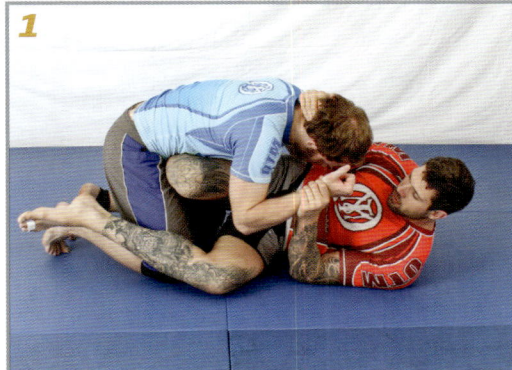

I am in the side scissor position. My right hand is controlling Lance's head with a collar tie, and my left hand has latched on to an upward grip on his left wrist.

I pull Lance forward with my collar tie and my wrist control, loading his weight onto my right leg.

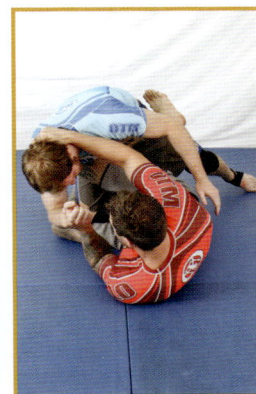

I scissor my legs, initiating the sweep.

4

As Lance recovers from the sweep, I stuff his right arm toward his chest with my left hand.

5

I open my legs as I drive Lance's head down with my collar tie.

6

I elevate my hips as I throw my left leg over Lance's right shoulder.

7

I lock the triangle and finish the choke.

SCISSOR SWEEP TO LEG-THROUGH TRIANGLE

In the previous technique, I established an upward grip and faked a scissor sweep to set up the wrist pin. If I am unable to establish or maintain wrist control, I can assume that my opponent will post his free hand on the mat when I hack his legs for the scissor sweep. By leaning on his hand to maintain his base, my opponent temporarily pins his wrist in place, giving me the opportunity to transition to a leg-through triangle. The key to this technique is the leg across my opponent's belt line and a strong collar tie. The leg across his belt line keeps pressure on his hips to force my opponent to maintain the forward lean position, bent over my leg. When I fake the sweep, I use the collar tie to push myself away from my opponent, giving me the space I need to thread my leg-through for the triangle. I typically use this technique when I cannot establish wrist control. When my opponent posts his hand on the mat to defend the sweep, I can easily establish a downward grip and continue attacking with wrist control.

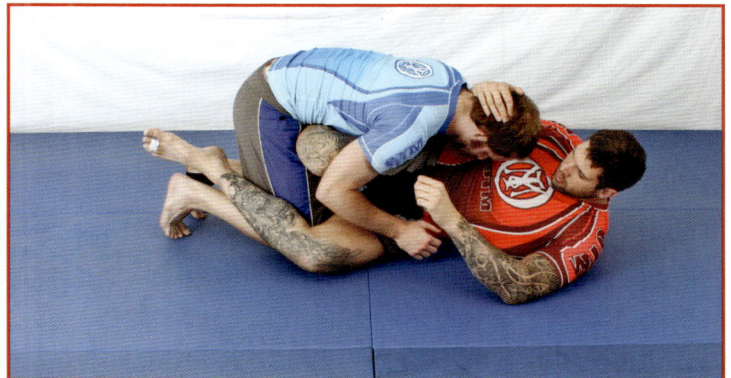

I am using the side scissor position against Lance's forward lean. I have a collar tie with my right hand. I was not able to establish wrist control, and he is beginning to reach toward my legs to set up a guard pass.

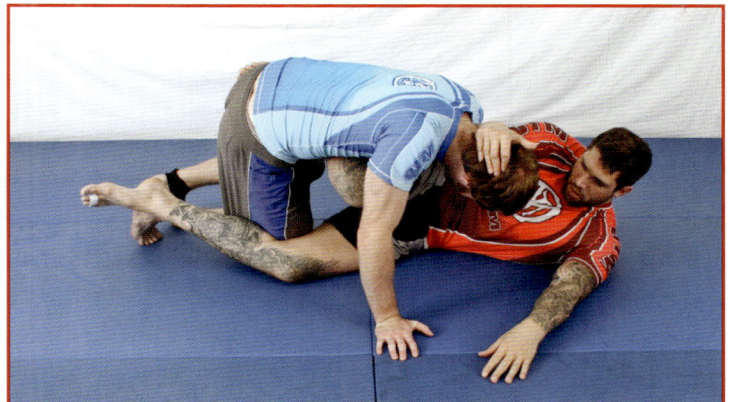

I scissor my legs to attempt the sweep. Lance posts his right hand on the mat to maintain his base.

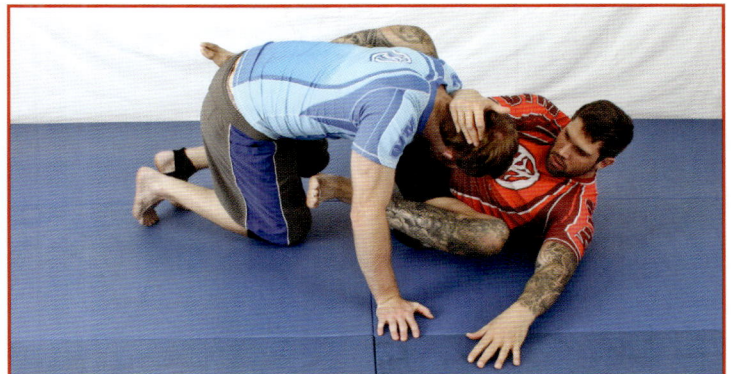

I continue to drive Lance to my left with my collar tie, forcing him to lean on to his right hand. As I do that, I open my legs and pull my left knee toward my chest to begin clearing his right arm.

4

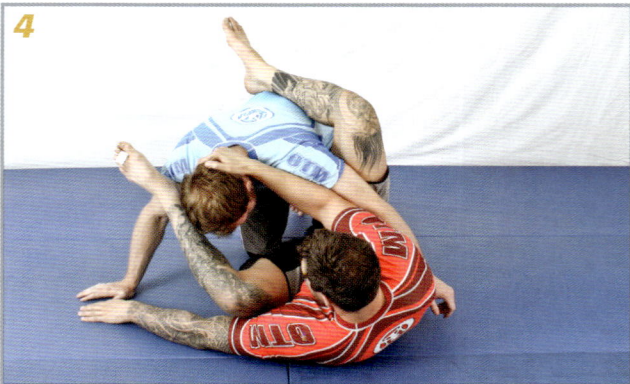

I thread my left leg over Lance's right shoulder.

5

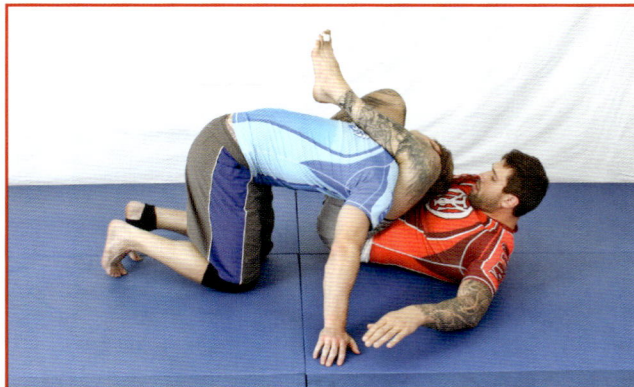

My left leg swings over the back of Lance's neck.

6

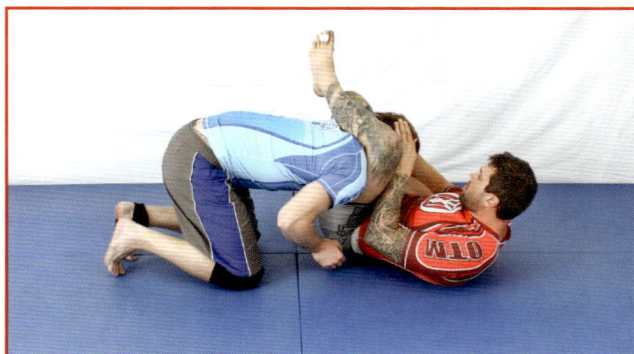

I pinch my right knee in front of Lance's left shoulder to angle my hips for the triangle.

7

I figure-four my legs to set the triangle.

TWO BIRDS, ONE STONE

This is one of the smoothest triangles I have ever developed. If my opponent is moving quickly and is driving into me, eliminating the space that I need to use the previous series of techniques, I use a whizzer, which is essentially an overhook, to give me more control. I can also bait him to drive into me by attempting to stand. If he begins to stack, I would transition back to the collar tie and work to push myself away. With the whizzer set, I can use a technique similar to the wrist feed that you learned from overhook control: I pass my opponent's wrist from my free hand to my whizzer hand, locking up both of his arms with one of my arm—two birds with one stone. If I position myself properly, I don't even need to grab his wrist to pass it, I can just reach my whizzer hand through and latch on to my opponent's wrist. Though my whizzer grip is useful, the real key to this technique is my leg work. The leg across my opponent's belt line dictates everything. As I pin my opponent's wrist to the inside of my thigh, I kick and extend the leg across his belt line to flatten him out, forcing him to fall into the triangle. If you are struggling with this technique, your leg work is probably to blame, so pay close attention to the details in the captions below.

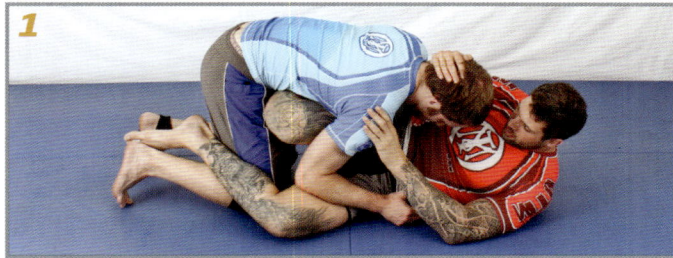

I am in the side scissor position with a right collar tie on Lance's head.

I pull my left elbow underneath and sit up.

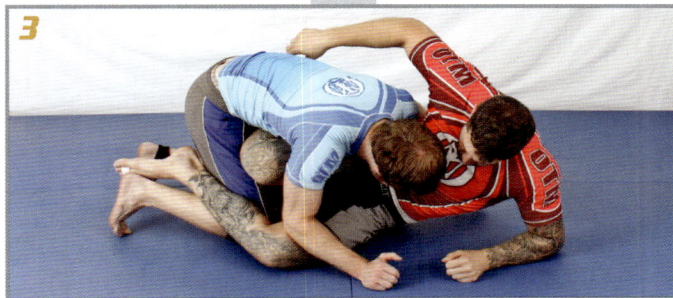

I release the collar tie with my right hand and reach over Lance's left arm.

I establish an overhook with my right arm by shooting my right hand under Lance's left armpit. Without stopping, my right hand continues to drive toward the mat, reaching for his right wrist. As my right hand moves into position, I stretch him out by pushing him away with my right knee.

5

My right hand latches on to Lance's right forearm.

6

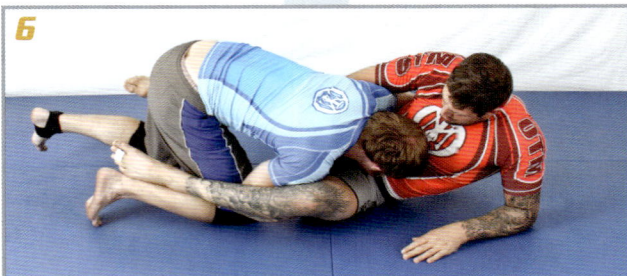

I pull Lance's right arm to my right thigh with my right hand, pinning it to the inside of my right thigh. With the pin set, I begin to straighten my right leg.

7

My left leg slaps against Lance's neck as I return to the saucer back position.

8

I lock the triangle and finish the triangle.

SIDE SCISSOR WALK-UP

For the two birds-one stone to work, you have to establish control of his free arm with your whizzer hand. If you struggle to grip his wrist, your opponent can drive his weight on top of you, collapsing your legs and flattening your hips. At this point, it's too late to use the collar tie to create space. To salvage the position, maintain your whizzer and latch on to his wrist with your free hand. Circle your leg around your own arm and dig your heel into his biceps. As you press his biceps away, straighten the leg across his belt line and walk it up his back like you would in a leg walk-up triangle, digging your heel into his shoulder when you drape it across his upper back. With your top leg in place, you can kick off of the biceps and lock the triangle. Remember, the leg circle is what makes this technique work. Because you will not have the space to thread your leg-through, you need to go around his arm.

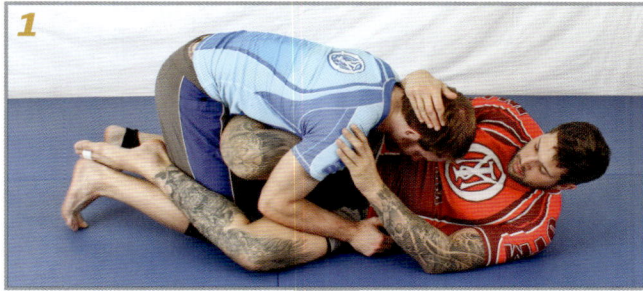

I am in the side scissor position with a right collar tie on Lance's head.

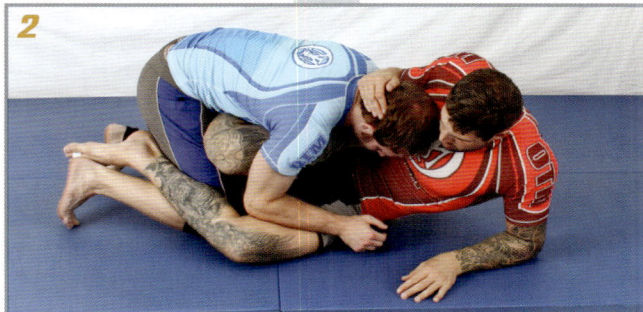

I pull my left elbow behind and underneath me to prop myself up.

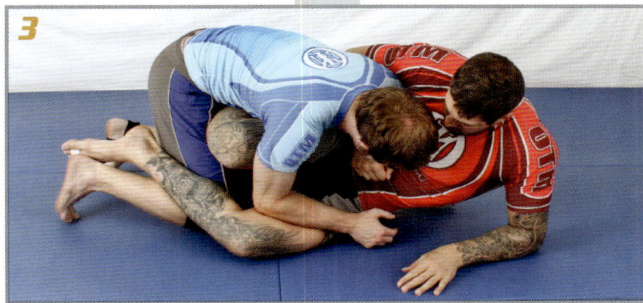

My right arm wraps around Lance's left arm securing an overhook.

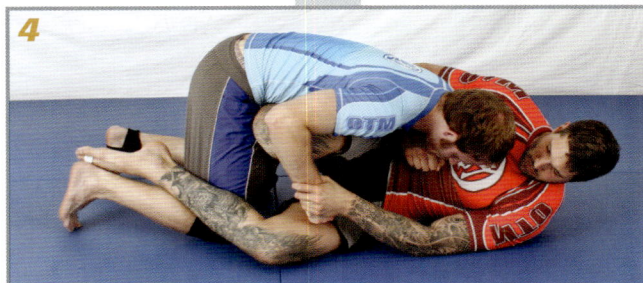

I roll back onto my left side and latch on to his right wrist with my left hand. I then twist Lance's right wrist with my left hand and force his right arm away from his body.

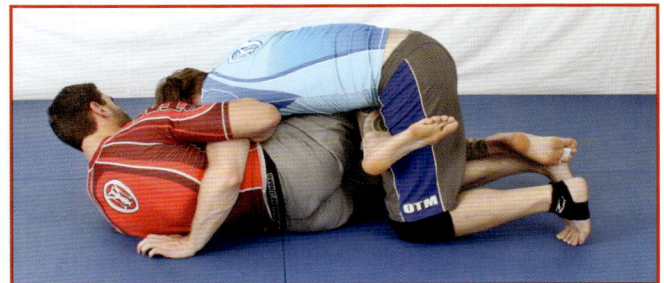

5

I circle my left leg over my left forearm without releasing Lance's right wrist.

6

I set my left heel into the crook of Lance's right arm, and press it away as I pull his right arm toward me with my left hand, creating a push-and-pull dynamic to control his arm.

7

I maintain control of Lance's right arm as I climb my right leg up his back and set my right heel in front of his right shoulder to delay his forward movement.

8

I release Lance's right wrist, while extending my left leg, pushing his arm away. Once his arm is cleared, I throw my left leg over his right shoulder.

9

I adjust my hips and figure-four my legs to finish the triangle.

CHAPTER SIX

HIPS FORWARD INTRODUCTION

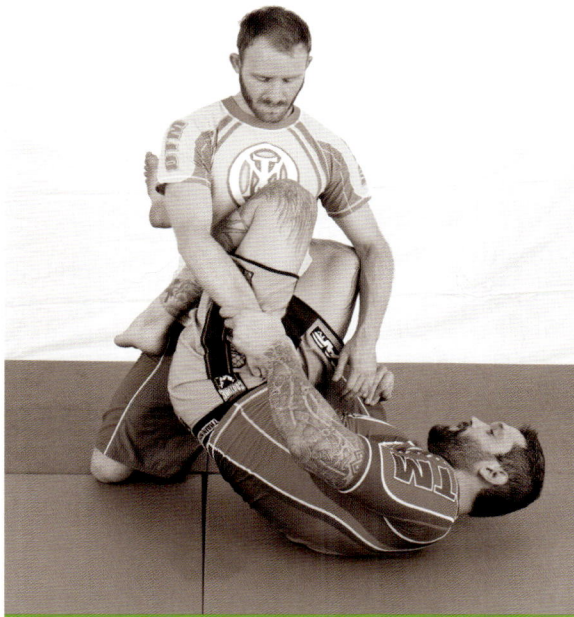

When I designed this book, I organized and systemized it in a way that coincides with an actual grappling scenario that happens quite frequently from the guard position. So I want to review with you the steps necessary for transition in my guard systems based on how my opponent is adjusting his body position in my guard. The following steps are just one example of how to flow your guard systems together step by step.

Step 1

Your opponent is in the 45 degrees position, hovering over you. He is not fully postured or pinning you down. His body position is in the optimal submission zone. Here, I can utilize basic and fundamental triangle attacks. Most of these attacks will be timing based so make sure you use your speed to help lock in the triangle.

Step 2

Your timing based set up didn't work, and you have either broken down your opponent, or he realized he was in danger and drove into you, flattening you to the mat. Either way you are now at the 0 degrees position. Here you can utilize your trapping systems. Always work towards whichever trapping system works best for you. For example, if you have the best results with the shoulder pin, then focus on utilizing that system first.

Step 3

Trapping systems can be tricky to escape, so once your opponent feels you starting to tie him up he will most likely want to escape your trap. Let's say he ducks out and sits on his heels at a postured position. You might want to try and break him down again, but if he is being strictly defensive and you're pressed for time, the best adjustment for attacking is to utilize one of the sit up guard techniques. From the sit up guard you threaten the hip bump sweep and, as he defends you, adjust your tie ups and attempt a triangle.

Step 4

Your opponent stays in control and pushes you back down to the mat, but he does not follow you down. Instead, he is leaning forward with his hips up, no longer in a seated position. You quickly adjust your legs and hips to move into the side scissor position. You threaten your opponent's balance with the side scissor sweep, and, as your opponent defends, you attack with one of your triangle set ups.

Step 5

The opportunity for a triangle finish does not happen. Instead your opponent stays in balance and postures completely away, with his hips all the way forward. Without your opponent bent at the hip, the side scissor guard game becomes harder to play and not optimal for his current body position. So you quickly hook one of his legs with your arm and adjust your body into the K-control position.

K-control

Quite often, people ask me how I got a black belt in Brazilian jiu-jitsu without ever wearing a gi. What they don't understand is that I'm not a black belt in Brazilian jiu-jitsu. I am a black belt in the Hayastan Grappling System, founded by living legend "Judo" Gene Lebell and grappling master, Gokor Chivichyan. They have one of the toughest grappling schools in the country. Their gym in Los Angeles is called the Hayastan Academy. I moved out to Los Angeles just

to train at that gym. My dream was to be the best grappler I could possibly be and I knew that the Hayastan Academy was the only place where that dream could come true. They broke me down and rebuilt me. It was intense and it seemed like the only easy day was yesterday. While I was there, I trained regularly with Manvel Gamburyan and Karo Parisyan. They both helped train me, but it was Karo that took me under his wing and truly taught me how to grapple.

Hayastan grapplers play the guard game differently than most BJJ-style grapplers. Since they are always looking for leg locks, they have to use a unique style of guard to be able to get at their opponent's legs, so they submit them with knee bars and heel hooks. They hook one of their opponent's legs with one of their arms, and use a sort of vertical side scissor with their legs, keeping their opponent's body weight from smothering their hips. Most of the Hayastan grapplers back then just used this style of guard to set up leg locks, except for Karo. He was actually using it to set up triangles. This style of guard didn't have a name back then. I'm not certain if they even have a name for it now. Karo was my coach and he taught me his concepts for making the guard position work and how to set up triangles from it. Over time, I added things to Karo's style of playing the guard and organized it into my own guard system. I later decided to name the guard system K-control, after the man who gave me my black belt, Karo Parisyan.

K-control, in general terms, is a sort of side scissor (where your top knee is in your opponent's diaphragm rather than across his belt line), while hooking one of your opponent's legs with one of your arms. The hooking of the leg creates a hard angle giving you an immediate advantage for off balancing your opponent. This, paired with an adjusted side scissor leg position, allows your hips to be off line, mobile, and easily elevated for submissions. K-control is a transitionally based system, allowing you to attack your opponent's entire body from head to toe. Even when your opponent is fully postured with his hips in a forward position he is still vulnerable to submission attacks when you utilize K-control. You can bend your opponent posture by off balancing him with explosive bucks with your hips and by lifting the leg you have hooked with your arm. This will force your opponent to deal with the threat of being off balanced and cause him to bend at the hips or even post on the mat. Once his upper body is in range of your hips you can attack him with armbars and triangles. Regardless if your opponent is bent at the hips, you can always use K-control to attack his lower body with leg locks. When you use these attacks in combination, going from high to low or low to high, you can confuse your opponent and trick him into giving up a submission or sweep quite easily.

An example of attacking high to low would be when you're climbing your legs up for a triangle, but your opponent instinctually postures and moves his upper body away from your hips. But by doing so, he now exposes his legs to submission attacks like knee bars and heel hooks.

An example of attacking low to high would be when you're hooking and moving to isolate and submit one of your opponent's legs, but he bends down and contracts his body to defend the leg lock, exposing his upper body to submission attacks, like triangles and armbars.

Since K-control can be used as a strong sweeping position, you can constantly threaten your opponent's balance to make him increasingly

vulnerable to submission set ups. The K-control system is complex and can set up dozens of submission combinations. I have spent many years of my life structuring and formulating the K-control guard system so that it can be taught to and understood by my students. In this chapter, you will learn many effective set ups to nail a triangle finish on your opponent from this very unique guard system.

Grips

From K-control, you have three different grip options: the mirror grip, head control, and the cross grip. I will cover the specifics of each grip later in the chapter, but you need to know that these grips can work in any sequential order. By transitioning from the mirror grip, to head control, to the cross grip; or from the cross grip, to head control, to the mirror grip; you work to break your opponent's posture down at all times and encourage him to hover over you where he is vulnerable. For example, I tell my students to think of this sequence as 1-2-3 or 3-2-1 so that they can keep in mind to chain their grip sequence when needed. While you are working to attack from a variety of grips, your method of control will be the constant threat of a sweep. With the leg hook set and your knee in your opponent's diaphragm, you need to constantly attack his balance for the position to be most effective. These concepts will make more sense to you when you learn some K-control techniques in this chapter.

K-CONTROL GRIPS

You can secure a variety of grips from K-control. Technically, you can secure two variations of the mirror grip, the head grip, and the cross grip. For the mirror grip and the cross grip, you can secure a downward or an upward grip. For the head grip, you can establish what looks like a collar tie where your palm is facing toward you as you cup the back of your opponent's head, or you can cup the back of his head with your palm facing away from you, which is not ideal but useful if you cannot reach the collar tie. Regardless of what variation you choose, the mechanics of each technique will not change significantly. However, the grip you choose will alter your attack. Since K-control is likely an entirely new position for you, familiarizing yourself with the proper uses of grips now will make it easier for you to learn the techniques that follow. It's important to learn to switch grips aggressively so when you're in a fight or competition, you can switch your attacks rapidly without getting stuck.

MIRROR GRIPS

If I secure an upward grip on Lance's right arm with my left hand, I want to pin his right arm to my left thigh. If I am controlling that same arm with a downward grip, I want to pin it slightly lower on my left thigh, closer to my hip.

HEAD GRIPS

The first head grip is ideal. Having my palm facing me gives me more strength and more control, but I can still make the techniques work with my palm facing away from me. I create a push-pull effect by pulling on the head and driving my knee into his sternum. To keep him more stable, I angle his head slightly towards the leg hook.

CROSS GRIPS

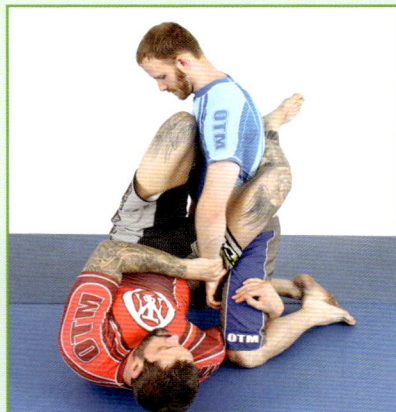

In the first photograph, I am controlling Lance's left arm with a downward cross grip (my pinky close to his hand). With this grip, I have the most control if I pin his left arm to my left hip. If I have a upward grip (my thumb closest to his hand), I pin his left wrist to my right hip.

K-CONTROL TO PENDULUM TRIANGLE

I constantly instruct my students to chain sweeps with submissions for optimal results. This is a prime example of a strong sweep opening up my opponent for the triangle choke. In this technique, I lace my arm deep under my opponent's leg to secure K-control, reaching through and grabbing control of the same side arm as well. This locks down one side of my opponent's body with one arm, leaving me with a free hand to seize control of my opponent's free wrist. Once I have my position secured, I can lift my opponent's leg with my leg hook and execute a pendulum sweep. Because I have control of my opponent's wrist, he has no choice but to post his elbow on the mat in an attempt to regain his balance or roll over to his back. If he manages to stop the sweep, I can keep his arm glued to the mat as I feed my leg under his arm and apply the triangle. This is a great technique to apply in the early stages of K-control development. It's a good position to keep your hips free when underneath of a strong top control player. Because of the grips, it's very difficult for your opponent to free his hands and land strikes in an MMA situation. And, as you fine tune the technique, it becomes very difficult for your opponent to stop both the sweep and the submission in succession.

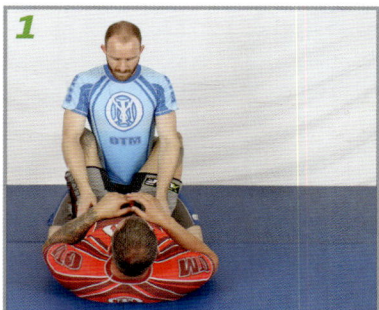

1 Lance is in my guard with full posture and his hips forward.

2 I hook my right arm under Lance's left leg, while reaching up with my left hand to secure a downward grip on his right wrist.

3 I slide my left leg in front of my opponent's chest, while lifting up on his left leg.

4 I pin Lance's right wrist to my left hip. I continue raising Lance's left leg with my right arm. As my arm continues to snake under his leg, I reach forward and grab control of his left arm, cupping his arm with my right hand. As I do this, I pinch my head to my right to help keep both of his limbs more secure.

5

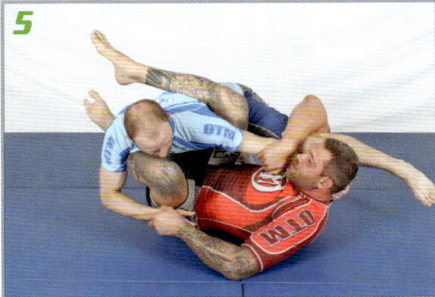

Once both of his arms are secure, I swing both of my legs to my left, pushing them into his body. As I crunch forward and elevate Lance's left leg, I pop my hips to my right, shifting my weight under his center of gravity.

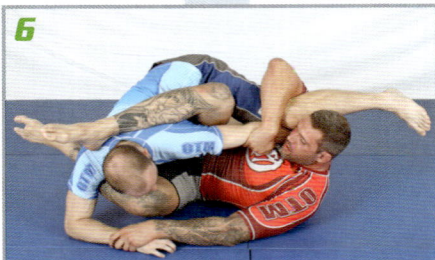

6

I allow Lance to stop the sweep by placing his right elbow on the mat, preventing himself from rolling over to his back. Notice that I retain control of his right wrist as his right forearm is flat on the mat.

7

With the space under his right arm now opened and his posture lowered, I slide my left leg under his right arm, while keeping control of both his right wrist and his left elbow.

8

With my leg now clear from his arm, I cross my feet, right over left, and lock my legs. I then pull Lance back into me using my grip on his right wrist. This upsets his balance, buying myself some time for the adjustment.

9

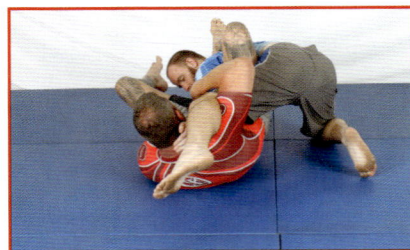

Once I have Lance's right arm cleared, I release my control on his right wrist and switch my left hand to his left elbow and drag his left arm across my body. I release my leg hook, placing my right hand on Lance's left thigh. This lets me push myself to my left, putting myself in line with my opponent and giving me a better angle to close my triangle.

10

Once back in line with my opponent, I triangle my legs, place both hands on my opponent's head and squeeze my legs together for the finish.

K-CONTROL TO ANKLE PICK TRIANGLE

Off-balancing your opponent is the key to K-control. If one off-balancing attempt does not give you a sweep or a submission, immediately off-balance your opponent again. In this technique, you attempt to sweep him over using the previous technique, but he manages to stay upright rather than fall over. To accomplish that, your opponent has to drive his weight in the opposite direction of the sweep. When you feel that your sweep has failed, turn your leg hook hand palm down, cup his ankle, and sweep him the other direction. You can keep jumping back and forth between sweep attempts in this manner until he makes a pivotal mistake. Your opponent will be frustrated and confused by your K-control if you stay aggressive. If you relax and simply hold position, he will pass, so work quickly and methodically.

1

Lance is in the hips-forward position, and I am in a strong K-control position.

2

I bridge my hips into Lance and then pull my knees toward my chest to trick him into driving into me. When he does, I latch on to an upward grip on his right wrist.

3

I attempt to set up the leg-through triangle by bridging my hips into the air and then swinging my left knee into Lance's right arm to sweep him, but his balance is too good. He maintains his base without posting his right elbow on the mat.

4

As Lance drives his weight to his left to reestablish a stable position, I push my upper body away from the leg hook with my left knee, and I rotate my right palm to the mat cupping his left ankle.

5

To topple Lance, I yank his left heel toward me with my right hand as I keep a firm grip on his right wrist with my left hand, driving my left knee into his chest. He falls toward his left hip and instinctively plants his left hand on the mat to defend the sweep.

6

I continue to press my knee into Lance's chest, forcing him to continue leaning on his left hand as I curl my right knee toward my chest, snaking my right foot out from under his left arm.

7

I elevate my hips and kick both of my legs to the sky, locking my legs in a figure-four when my hips reach Lance's neck.

8

I finish Lance with an armbar triangle.

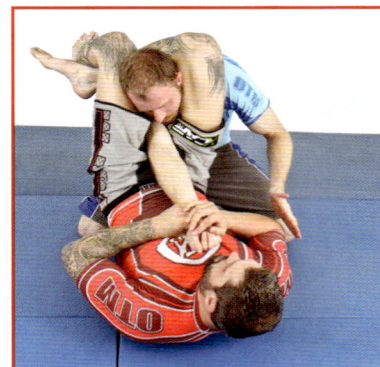

K-CONTROL MIRROR GRIP WRIST PIN TRIANGLE

When working a fast open guard like K-control, you want to take every opportunity to control your opponent. In this technique, you will see how I tie up half of Lance's body with just one of my arms. While this type of control is ideal, your opponent will do everything he can to prevent this from happening. The key to this set up is to make your opponent extend his arm toward the leg you have hooked without letting him escape the position. To do this, you need to do a combination of movements. As you begin to hook and pull your opponent's leg to your shoulder, you post your other hand on his rib cage or armpit and straighten your arm, pushing your opponent's upper body toward the leg you have hooked. When these movements are combined, your opponent will start to feel off balanced and bend his body to the side, bringing his arm and leg closer together. You now quickly adjust into the K-control position to lock your opponent in place. As you adjust, elevate the leg of your opponent with your arm, reaching up to control his arm as well. Once in this position, your opponent can easily be submitted via triangle. Should you have problems with this set up, the answer will most likely be to lift your opponent's leg higher and create more of a sweeping pressure. Keeping this in mind will make this a high percentage triangle set up from K-control.

Lance is postured completely in my closed guard.

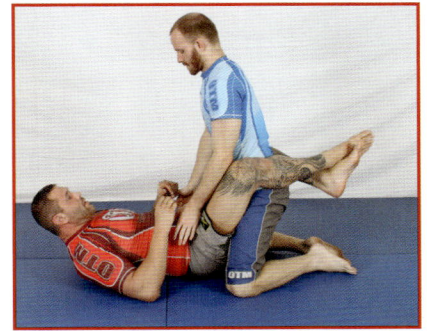

I grab Lance's latissimus muscle with my left hand, while reaching under his left leg with my right arm.

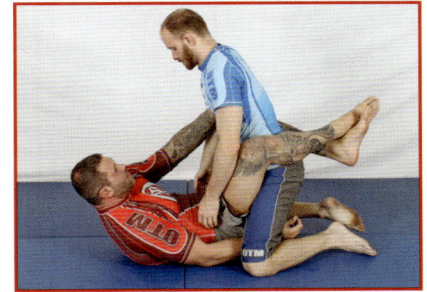

I push Lance towards his left with my left hand as I drive my right arm deeper under his left leg, bringing his left leg deep onto my shoulder. Because of the pressing motion, Lance's hand begins to move towards the mat to regain his balance, allowing me to seize his left arm with my right hand as well.

To keep Lance from smothering me, I bring my left knee to my chest, moving into K-control.

5

I remove my left hand from Lance's lat and move it to his right wrist, pinning it to my left thigh.

6

I kick my left leg straight, while pressing Lance's right wrist to his stomach. As I do this, I elevate Lance's left leg, keeping him off-balance.

7

I cross my right foot over my left and pinch my knees and curl my legs.

8

I place my left hand on the back of Lance's left elbow as I bridge my hips slightly towards the ceiling.

9

I drag Lance's left arm across my body as I release control of his leg and post my hand on his left thigh. This helps me square my hips up with Lance's body.

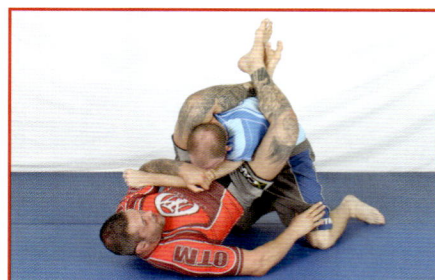

10

I figure-four my legs, place both hands on the back of Lance's head, and finish the triangle.

K-CONTROL TO ARM CLEARING SCISSOR

The head grip is the strongest K-control grip, but is also the hardest to get because your opponent's head will typically be farther away than either of his wrists. If you started with the mirror grip series, your opponent may give you the head grip as he works to free his wrist, so keep on an eye on his head. If it comes within reach, latch on to a collar tie, especially if your opponent is defending your attacks with the mirror grip. When you do get head control, you can use the power of your legs to slam in a triangle. With his posture beat by your collar tie and his base weakened by your K-control, you can force him to hover over you, putting him in a position very similar to the optimal submission zone. I will typically use the sankaku first because K-control makes the transition easier, but the knee pin triangle will likely be more accessible to the grapplers that are just learning my system. In the photographs below, you will see that I use an ankle pick to help me adjust my hips. While the ankle pick works great from K-control, you can use it from any position to help you swing your hips to the other side to lock the figure-four.

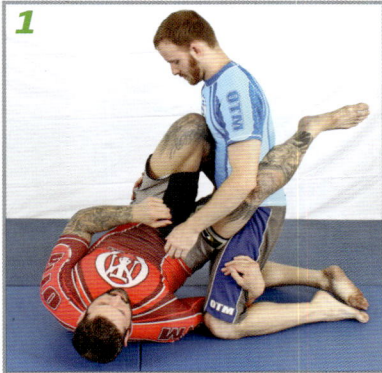

1

Lance is trapped in my K-control.

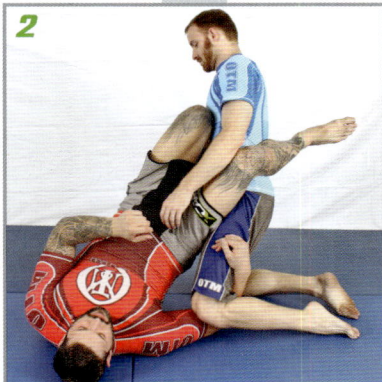

2

I push Lance away with my legs to get him to drive back in.

3

When Lance leans into me, I curl both legs in to suck his upper body close to mine. My left hand grabs the base of his skull, securing a collar tie, as soon as his head is within reach.

4

Lance senses that he is in danger, so he cups my left leg with his right hand.

5

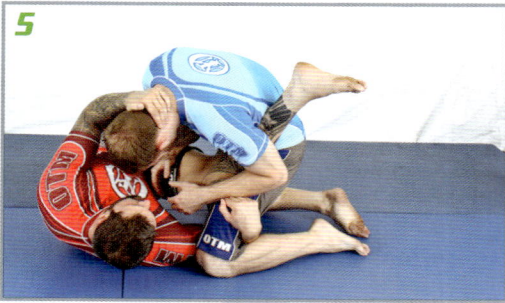

I drive Lance's head toward his left knee with my collar tie as I straighten my left leg and roll my left knee over the front of his biceps.

6

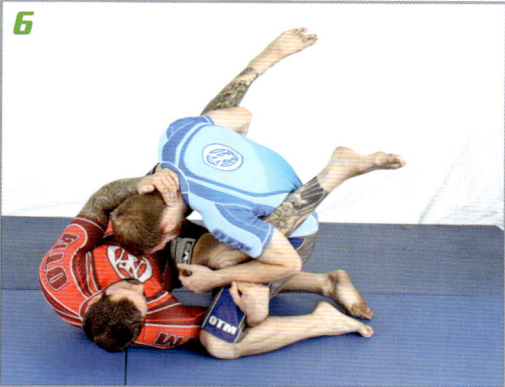

I bridge my hips toward Lance's neck as I press my left knee into his right biceps, pushing his right arm away.

7

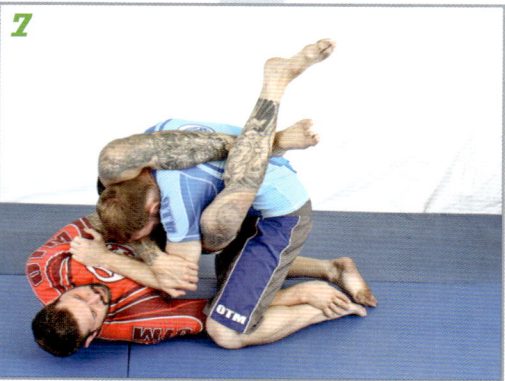

I throw my left leg over Lance's right shoulder and cross my feet. I rotate my right hand palm down and cup Lance's left ankle, while my left hand grabs control of Lance's left elbow.

8

I pull Lance's left ankle toward me with my right hand as I simultaneously pull his triceps across my body. At the same time, I straighten my body and extend my legs. This causes him to fall to his hip, and I'm in a better position to finish the triangle.

9

I place both hands on Lance's wrist, roll his palm up, and finish the triangle armbar.

K-CONTROL HEAD GRIP SANKAKU

As I said before, the sankaku is my favorite attack from head grip K-control. If you have K-control, you are already halfway to a sankaku. Because of the awkward angle between our bodies, my opponent's balance will be upset before I even begin to move. As he floats in my guard trying to correct his base and keep his balance, he'll very likely lose sight of the sankaku attack, even as I'm applying it. When you look at the photographs, you will see that I flick my foot out from under my opponent's arm as I drive my knee over top of his shoulder. The key to succeeding with this motion is to keep the leg bent. This will prevent your opponent from grabbing your foot. If you apply the technique quickly, you will have his arm cleared and begin applying pressure to the choke before he can stabilize himself.

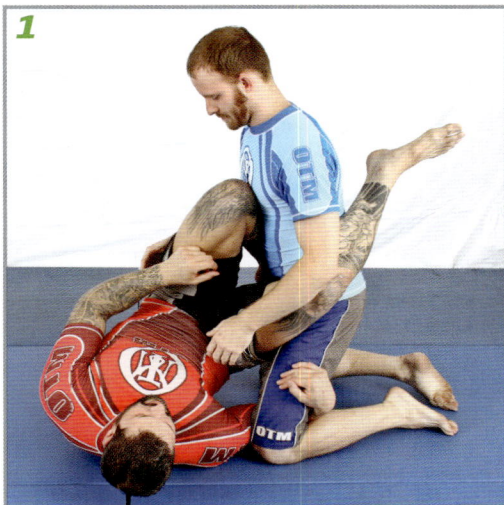

Lance is in my K-control.

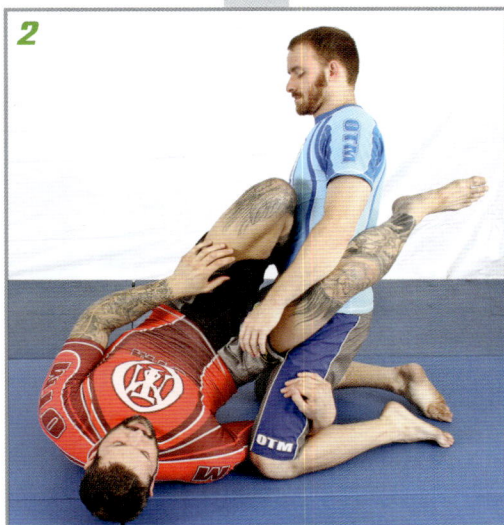

I bridge my hips into Lance to drive him away.

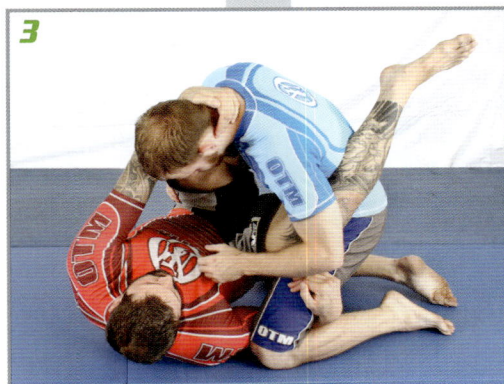

When Lance presses back into me to regain his balance, I grab the back of his head with my left hand, securing a collar tie.

4

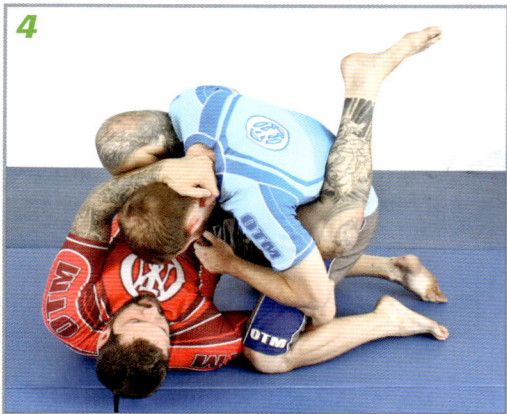

I drive my left knee up into the side of his neck and over his right shoulder. I am rough and aggressive with this transition.

5

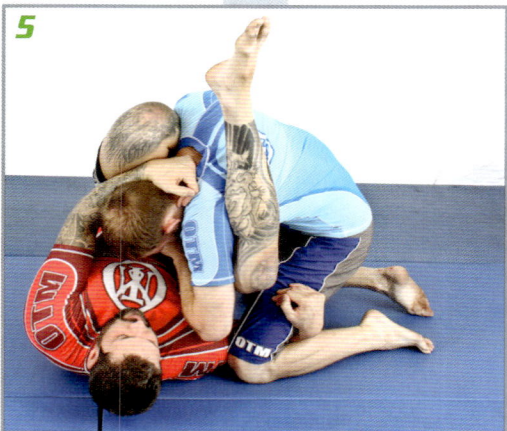

I slide my right leg up Lance's back.

6

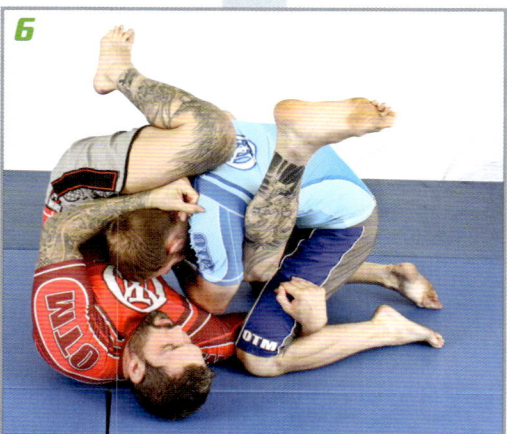

To free my left foot, I curl my left heel to my butt and violently pop my hips to the left. As soon as I free my left foot, I drive my left knee across the back of Lance's neck toward my right foot.

7

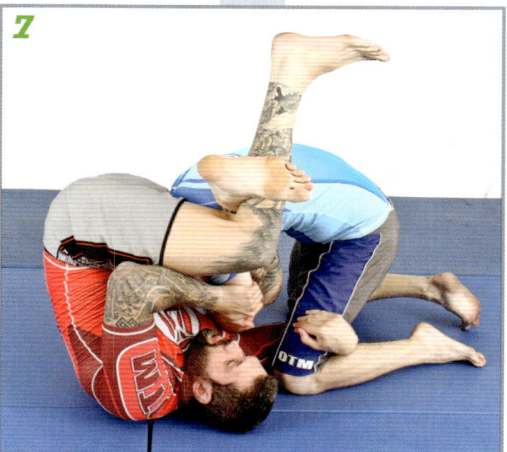

I pop my hips and spin underneath Lance, allowing me to place my right knee in line with his chin. From there, I lock my right foot in the bend of my left knee, securing the sankaku. I can finish Lance here by pulling on his left triceps and squeezing my legs; or I can use one of the other sankaku finishes that I taught in the first chapter.

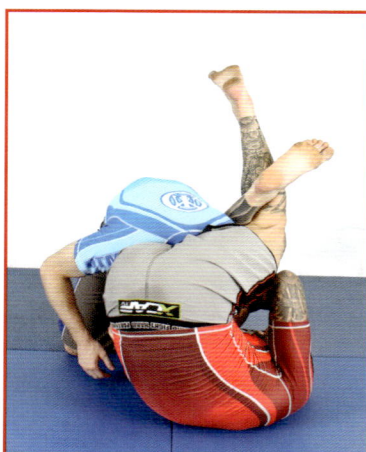

LEG PRESS SWEEP

In this technique, for example, you use your cross grip to dig your bottom foot (the one that was curled around your opponent's back) into your opponent's near armpit. From this position, your leg is like a coiled spring, and you use it to launch him away from you. He will post without thinking and swing back into you to regain his balance. This setup may be similar to the omoplata to triangle setup where you use the threat of the omoplata to trick your opponent into swinging back into your guard resulting in the triangle. In my experience, very few experienced grapplers will ever turn back toward you to defend the omoplata. They will just roll forward to unwind their shoulder. With the armpit sweep, they do not see the triangle coming because the sweep is powerful and somewhat unorthodox.

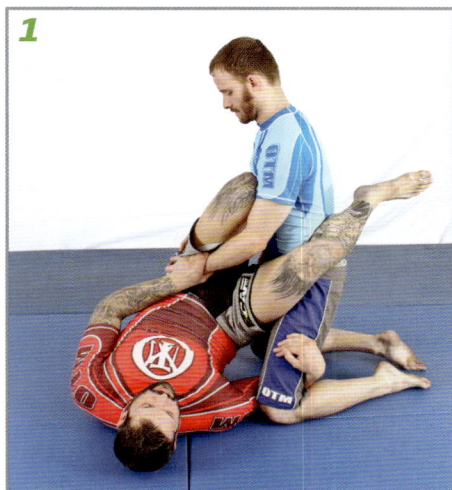

Lance is maintaining the hips-forward position, and I have K-control. I grab Lance's left wrist with my left hand a downward grip and immediately pin it to my hip.

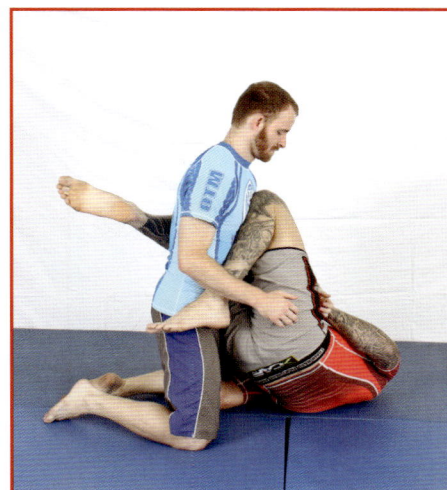

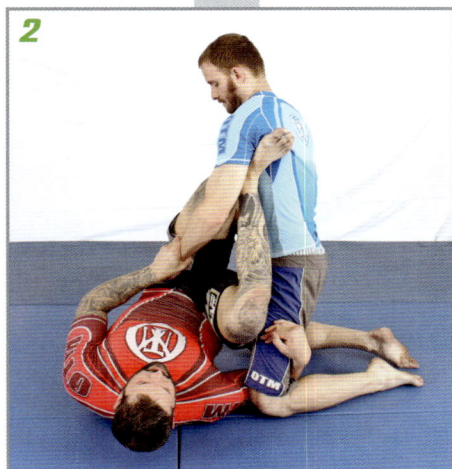

I pull my right knee toward my chest and dig my right foot into Lance's left armpit.

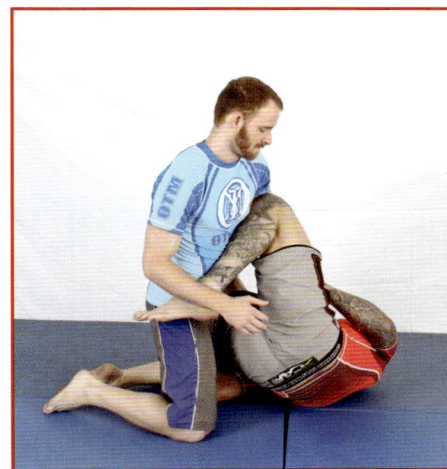

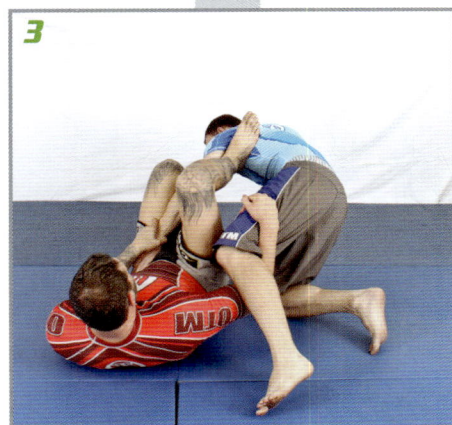

I push Lance to my left by extending my right leg and lifting his left leg with my right arm. He instinctively posts to defend the sweep.

4

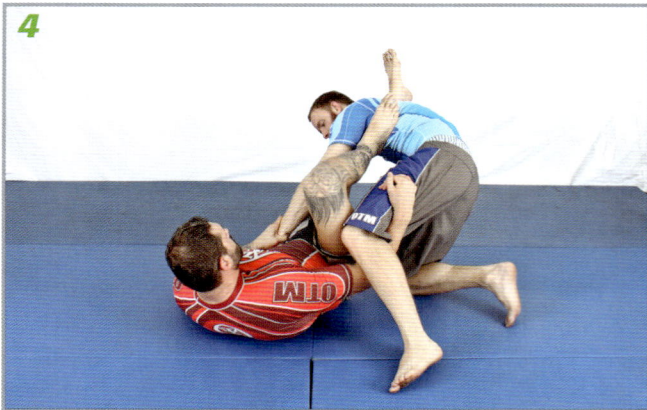

To capture Lance's neck, I straighten my left leg and hook his head with my left foot as I press my left shin into his neck.

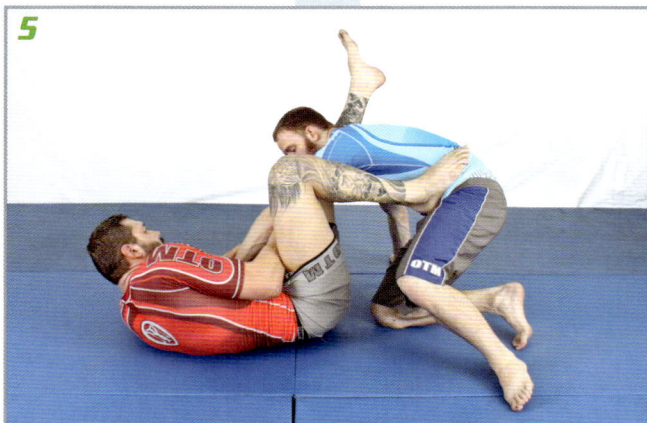

5

I swing my hips into position for the triangle by releasing Lance's left leg and grabbing his left triceps with my right hand as I post my right foot on his left hip. I then elevate my hips and extend my left leg to the sky to generate momentum.

6

My left leg slaps across the back of Lance's neck as I drag his left arm across my body.

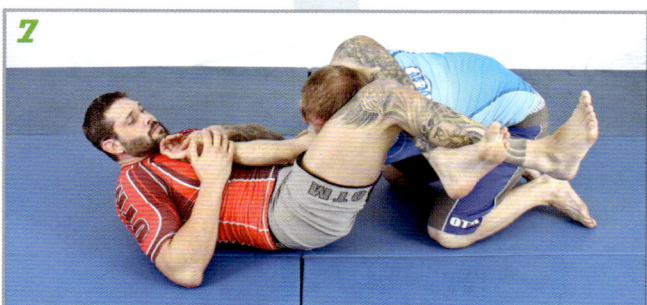

7

I figure-four my legs and finish the armbar triangle.

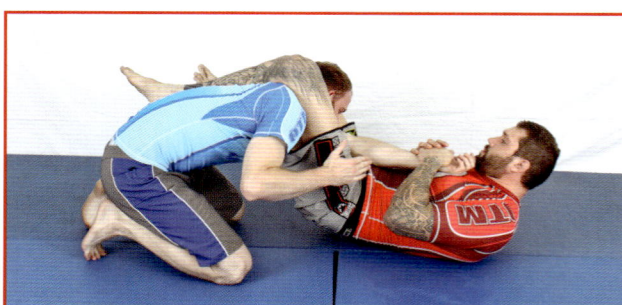

LEG PRESS TRIANGLE

On multiple occasions, I have talked about the value of having two different directions of pressure—pushing and pulling—on one limb. That dynamic makes it easier to dominate and manipulate that limb, which is important for this technique as you clear the arm for the triangle. This concept comes into play when you have the cross grip in K-control. In this technique, like in the last technique, you dig your bottom foot into your opponent's near armpit. Rather than sweep him over, you press him straight up, while you pull on the cross grip. In this scenario, the push pull pressure dominates one of his arms and locks his upper body in place, giving you enough control to set the triangle. You can transition to the sweep if your opponent resists the leg press. The key to this technique is the space between me and my opponent. There's too much pressure and too much space for him to turn back in before I swing over his far arm and lock in the triangle.

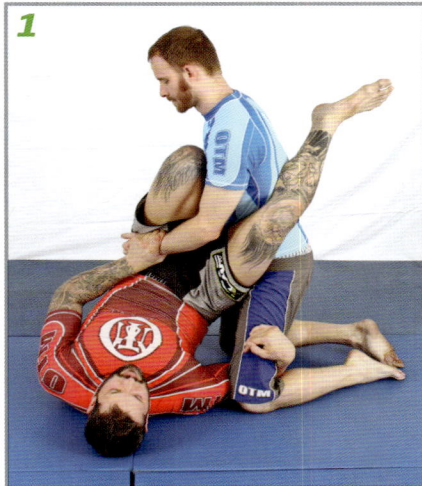

I have established K-control, and I am controlling Lance's left wrist with a cross grip, pinning it to my left thigh with my left hand.

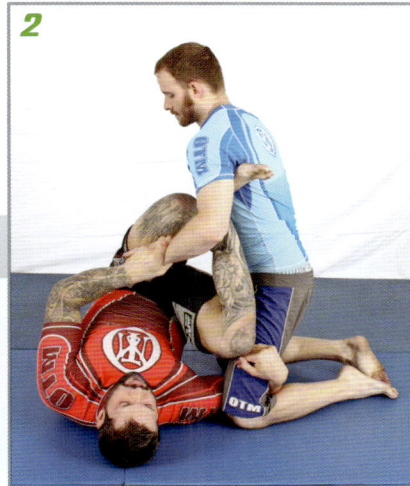

I curl my right knee toward my chest and set my right foot in Lance's left armpit.

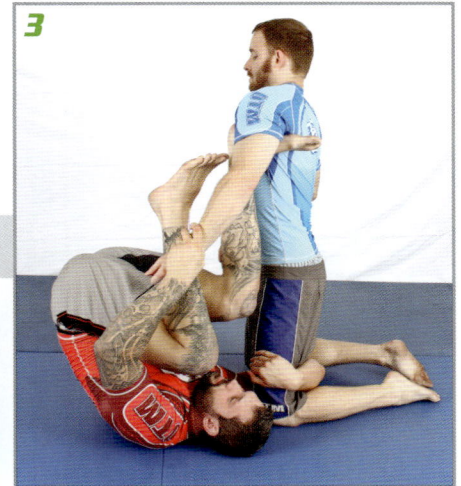

I rotate my shoulders directly underneath my right knee and press Lance to the sky by extending my right leg.

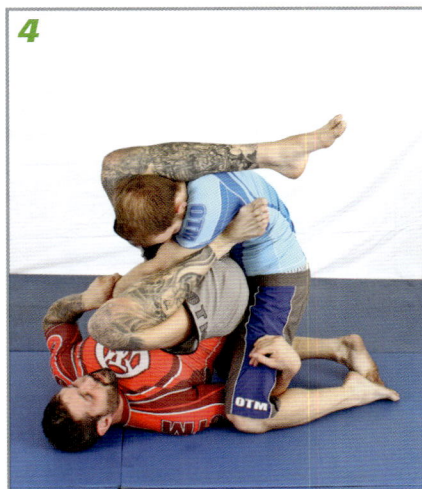

I swivel my hips back to my left as I retract my right leg to pull Lance's body toward my hips. As he falls, I set my left leg over his right shoulder and across the back of his neck.

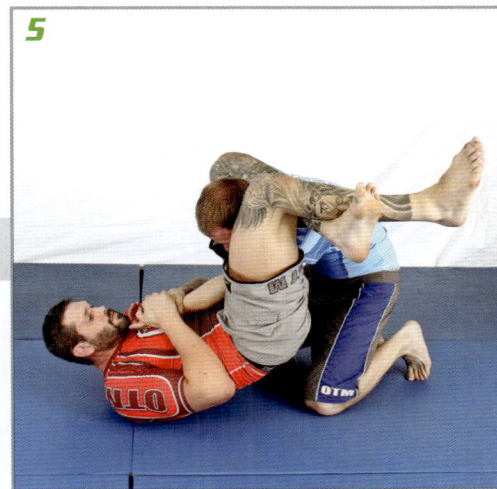

I figure-four my legs and submit Lance with an armbar triangle.

OUT AND BACK TRIANGLE

As I mentioned in the armpit sweep, I tend to avoid using omoplatas to set up triangles. If you like to use the omoplata to set up the triangle, and there are certainly some fighters out there that are good at that, do it if it works for you. Personally, I am more successful swinging into what looks like the start of an omoplata, but rather than chopping his shoulder with one of my legs, I lock my ankles behind my opponent's head and use my leg hook to sweep my opponent backward, the opposite direction of an omoplata. Although most fighters are prepared to defend the omoplata, very few are prepared to defend pressure in the opposite direction. If they fail to defend, you can sweep and land in side control. By forcing my opponent to defend the sweep, he gives me an opening to swoop back in for a triangle. When I swing back in, I make a short circle and lock in my legs. From there, I simply adjust and finish. It should be noted that if I hang out too long in this position, my opponent could rip his arm free. By applying sweeping pressure, and then immediately moving to the attack, I increase my chance of success.

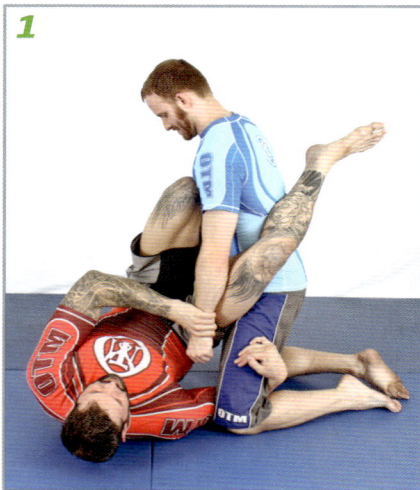

1

I have Lance in my K-control with an upward cross grip on Lance's left wrist with my left hand and I'm pinning his wrist to my right hip.

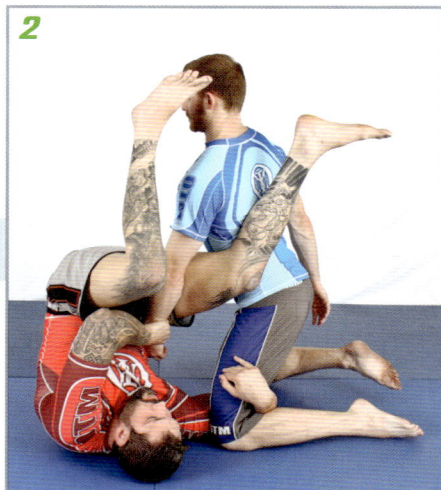

2

I swing my left leg out to my left as I rotate my hips so that I am on my shoulders next to Lance. I keep my hips elevated and extend my legs.

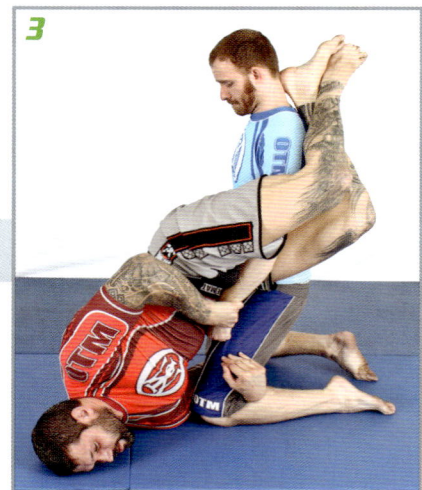

3

I cross my ankles and bridge my hips forward as I begin to roll over my right shoulder. From this position, Lance cannot control my ankles, which is what makes this setup particularly effective.

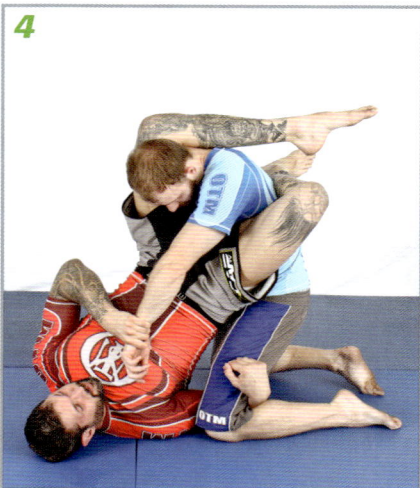

4

When Lance sinks his weight to resist the sweep, I curl my right heel into his upper back and swing my left leg over his right shoulder, rotating my shoulders back to a more traditional guard position.

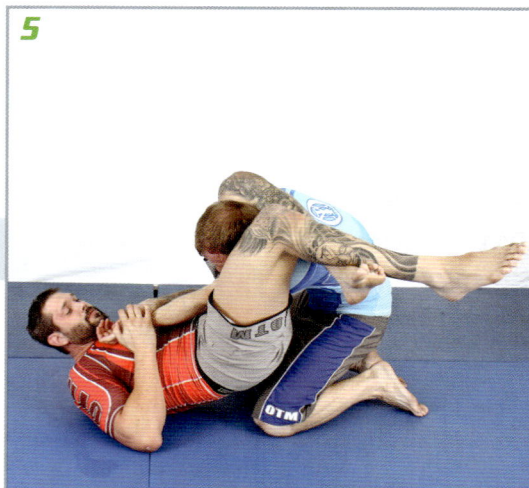

5

I lock my legs and finish the armbar triangle.

CROSS GRIP KNEE INSIDE SWEEP TO TRIANGLE

This is a quick and easy option to attack my opponent if he's postured. Here, I pin my opponent's wrist to my hip, drive my knee into his triceps, and abduct my knees. As my legs spread apart, this cranks my opponent's shoulder forward. I combine this pressure with lifting his leg causing him to fall flat towards his face. If my opponent is quick enough to post on the mat and stop the sweep, I do a quick foot-switch to slide my leg around his neck and cinch in the triangle. If he's not quick enough to post his hand and face plants, I'll simply sit up and take the back. This is a great solution to fighting an opponent with a strong base in K-control. I use a sweeping motion to open the triangle attack, and, if my opponent defends that, I can take my opponent's back, making this a very versatile and fast attack allowing me to finish my opponent. Big movements can have big problems, and the quick adjustment will let me put my opponent away quickly.

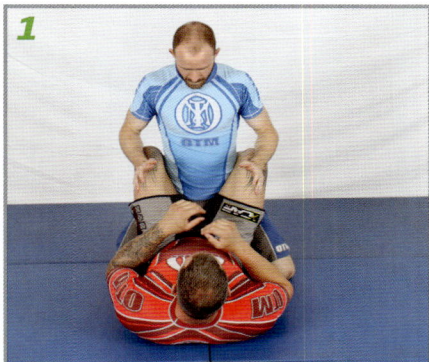

1

Lance is in my guard with full posture and his hips forward.

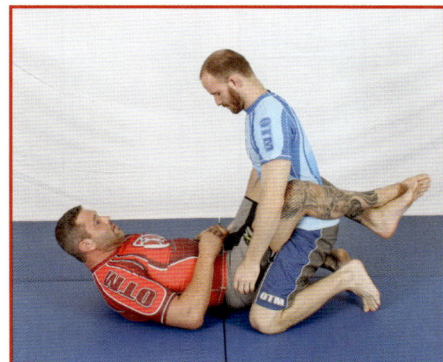

2

I unlock my legs, hook my right arm underneath Lance's left leg and grab his left wrist with my left hand. As I do this, I pivot offline, moving my head closer to his left knee.

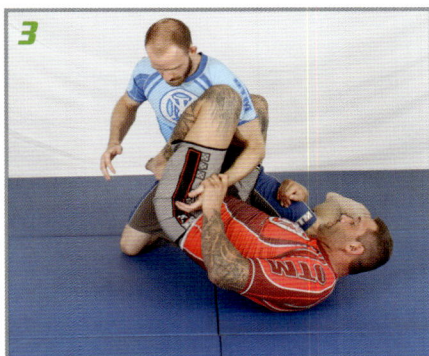

3

I pin Lance's wrist to my left hip, while I simultaneously lift up on his left leg with my right arm, moving to the standard K-control position.

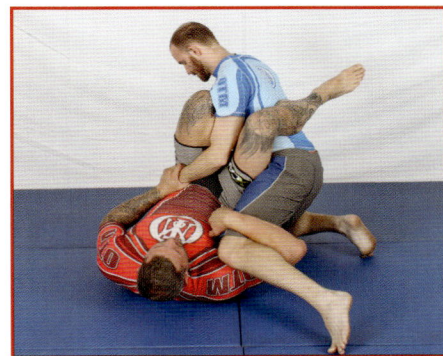

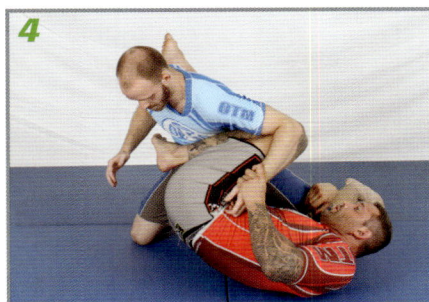

4

I pivot away and under to get my left knee under Lance's left triceps.

5

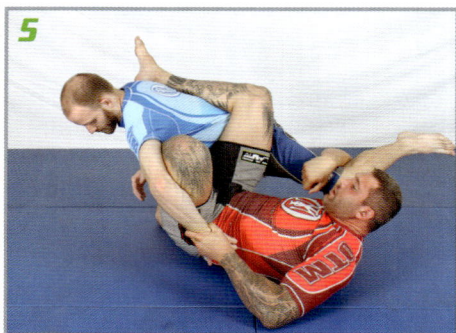

I spread my legs apart, while driving my left knee forward as I maintain control of Lance's left leg with my right arm.

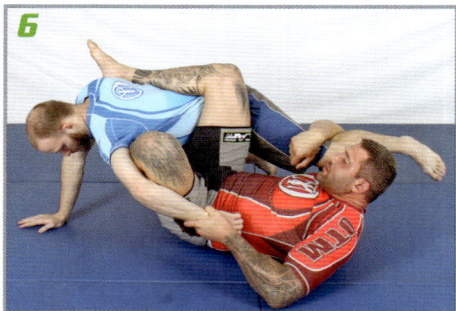

6

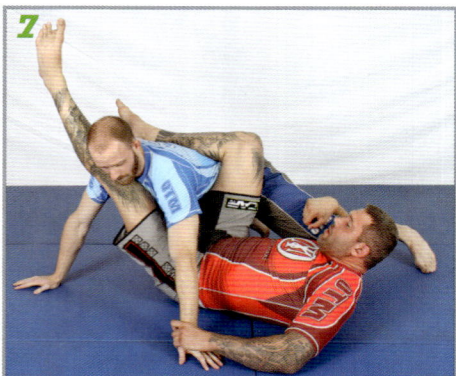

Lance has one of two choices: he can either fall forward and allow me to move up and complete the sweep; or use his free arm to post on the mat to stop his momentum. In this situation, Lance chooses to post his right hand on the mat.

7

With Lance's right arm extended and his posture lowered by my sweep attempt, it gives me the space needed to slip my left leg back in front of his body and under his neck. Notice that I still have control of my opponent's wrist to keep him from ripping his arm free.

8

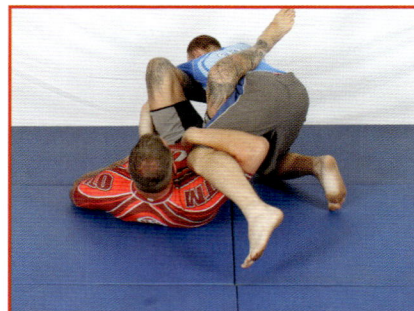

I now release Lance's left leg, bringing myself back in line with my opponent. This allows me to reach up with my right arm and hook my own left shin, pulling my left leg tight around his neck. As I move back in front of hium, I simultaneously pull his wrist to my left, dragging his left arm across my body.

9

I lock my right leg over my left shin, release my opponent's wrist, and place both hands on the back of his head. I pull down on his head, squeeze my legs, and finish the choke.

K-CONTROL ANKLE PICK TO MOUNTED TRIANGLE

The K-control can be an effective sweeping position even if I do not have any grips. If for some reason I cannot establish a mirror grip, a head grip, or a cross grip, I can sweep my opponent and use the scramble to set up a mounted triangle. You can bypass the other gripping options and make this your go-to K-control attack if you prefer, but keep in mind that this technique is not risk free. Without an additional grip, you are relying on speed and timing to successfully set the triangle. As you have probably guessed from reading the rest of my book, I tend to prefer having as much control over my opponent as possible so that I can better anticipate and eliminate his ability to defend. I recommend using this technique when your opponent is running from your grips. If you can land the mounted triangle, great; if not, you can use the ensuing scramble to reset your guard or to transition to a top position.

1

I have K-control and have been unable to establish a secure grip on Lance. I decide to sweep him instead.

2

I push Lance to my left by lifting his left leg with my right arm and by bridging my hips into his chest.

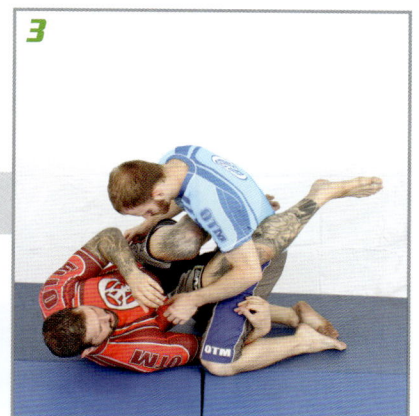

3

I momentarily relax my pressure to allow Lance to shift back to my right.

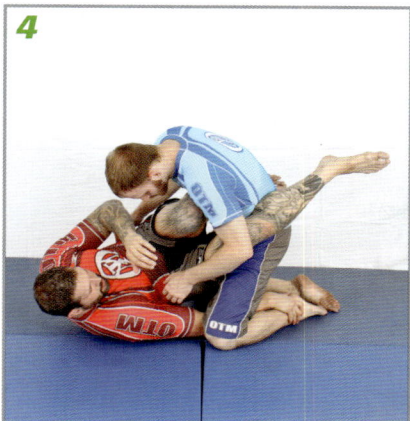

4

I quickly cup his left ankle with my right hand.

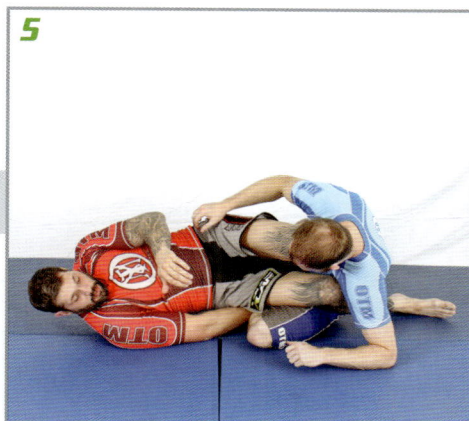

5

I sweep Lance by straightening my back as I simultaneously press him to my right with my left knee and pull his left ankle toward me.

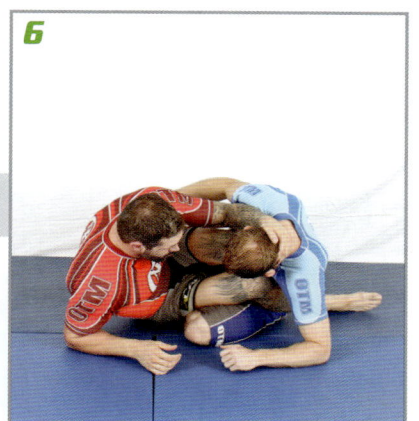

6

As Lance falls, I sit up onto my right elbow and grab the back of his head with my left hand, setting my left forearm to delay his forward movement.

7

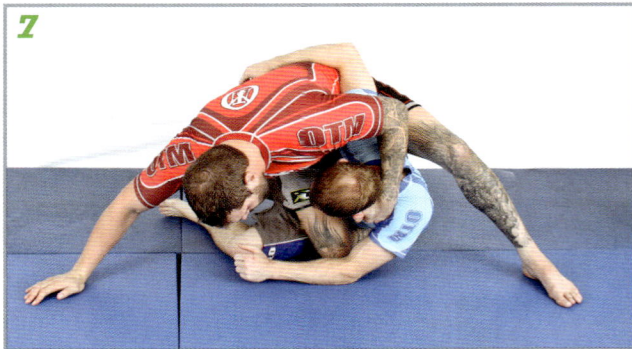

I throw my left leg around Lance's upper back, using the momentum to switch from posting on my right elbow to posting on my right hand.

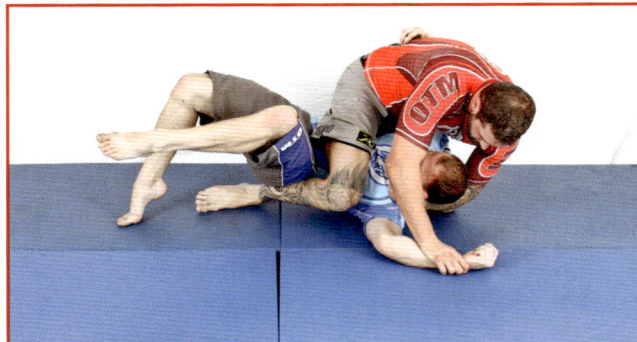

8

I kneel on my left knee, driving it forward to set my left thigh deep in Lance's right armpit. At the same time, my right hand pins his left wrist to the mat with an upward grip as I lift his head with my left hand.

9

I straighten my right leg, swinging it forward and clear it over Lance's left arm. I clear Lance's left arm by timing the release of his left wrist as my right leg swings over and around his shoulder. As I swing my right leg into place, I drop my butt on his sternum to eliminate space. Notice how I am curling my right heel to my left knee to tighten the triangle without yet locking my legs.

10

To figure-four my legs, I balance my weight on my right knee and head, allowing my left leg to maneuver quickly around my right ankle, locking the triangle.   pull Lance's head toward my right hamstring, squeeze my knees together and curl my heels to my butt to finish the choke.

COUNTERING THE SPRAWL FROM K-CONTROL

A savvy opponent will eventually deduce the mechanics of K-control. Even if he has never seen the position before, he will eventually realize that your leg hook is both wrecking his base and helping you to generate upward pressure with your knees. Your opponent will often attempt to smash his hips down and sprawl to defeat your K-control, kicking his legs out and dropping his chest. If he successfully sprawls, your K-control is done, but don't panic. He has beaten your K-control but given you the side scissor instead. I have found that when an opponent fights to escape K-control with a sprawl, he tends to land in an ideal position for the two birds–one stone triangle setup that you learned in the side scissor section. If that fails, use another side scissor technique to sweep or submit your opponent.

Lance is in my K-control.

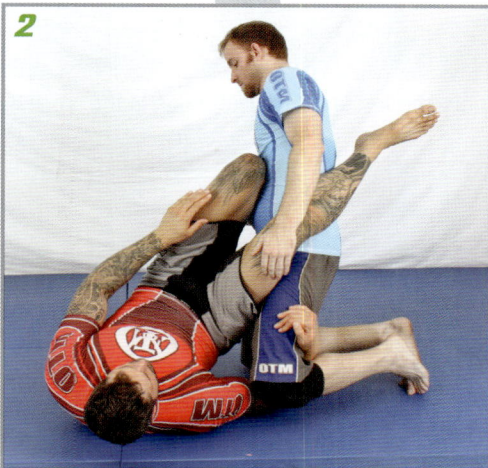

I use K-control to push Lance away.

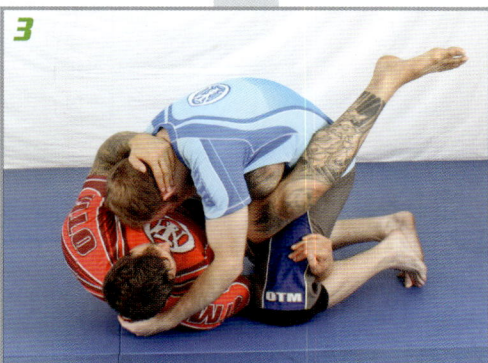

Lance counters by pushing my knee to his belt line and driving forward to smash into me. At this point, I control Lance's head to keep him stable, while I still have the leg hook.

4

I secure an overhook on Lance's right arm with my left arm.

5

I straighten my back and latch on to Lance's left wrist with my right hand.

6

I pass Lance's left wrist to my left hand to establish the two birds—one stone grip, pinning his left arm to my left thigh in the process.

7

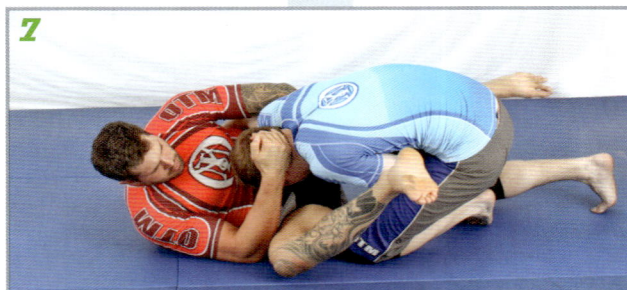

I control Lance's head with my right hand as I open my legs.

8

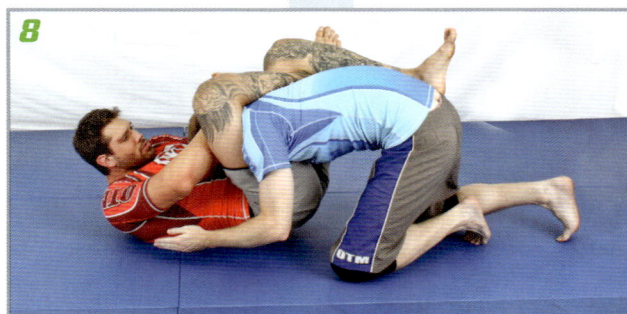

My left leg sets across the back of Lance's neck, and I lock my legs for the triangle.

CHAPTER SEVEN

HALF GUARD AND BUTTERFLY GUARD

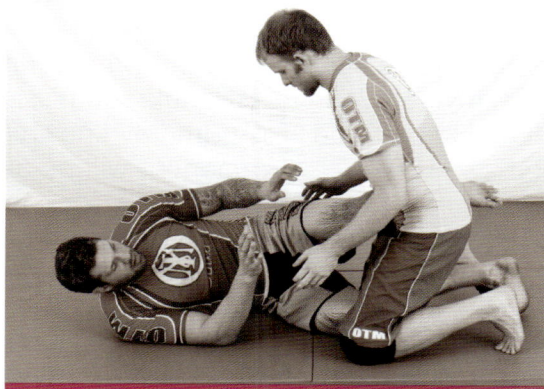

The grappling game is constantly changing. Grapplers adjust their game to adapt to the latest trends, and I'm no different. Being a coach at a gym like Xtreme Couture in Las Vegas, I get to see the latest and greatest techniques from grapplers that have traveled here from all over the world. As I try and stay up to date on these newest trends, I always remember that, while the grappling game is constantly evolving, it eventually all goes around in full circle. To prepare for the future it is important to study the past. A hundred years ago catch wrestlers were doing all the same leg locks that are just now being rediscovered in BJJ today. As much as I want this book to help bring back the popularity of full guard, I must recognize that the growing trend and popularity of the half guard and butterfly guard in submission grappling.

Half Guard

Over the last few years, the half guard position has evolved considerably. It used to be considered a backup position, something you cling to when your guard is almost passed. Now, many grapplers specialize in the half guard. They choose to pull half guard in a competition and have a whole system of sweeps and submissions that they work exclusively from the half guard. This makes them very dangerous, these athletes are winning grappling tournaments just on their half guard alone. No longer an "inferior" or transitional position, the half guard can no longer be overlooked.

I usually recommend for all grapplers to have a solid half guard sweep in their arsenal. Foundationally, the half guard is primarily a sweeping position and even though it can be used as a lethal submission platform, it's important not to lose sight of the sweep. Now, if you're a strict top game player you'll want to start looking for that sweep right away. But if you don't mind playing off your back, then use the position as a platform to launch both sweeps and submissions, utilizing them both in combination. The reason for this is that the wide array of sweeps available from half guard can be used to set up anything from leg locks, arm locks, and even to my favorite, triangles.

You're not going to have as many triangle set ups from half guard as you do from full guard, so that's not a benefit. However, what you do have going for you in this position is that you're off line and on your hip. This is something you can achieve from full guard, but if you have an opponent staying low and tight, committing himself to smothering your hips, the half guard might be one of the few options you have to getting off line and on your hip. I often switch from a full guard position to a half guard position because of an opponent that is either trying to smother me or simply will not engage with me. Even though you will see submission set ups from the basic half guard in this chapter, I usually prefer to work a side scissor half game. The reason for this is because I don't like to let my opponent in on my hips, unless I'm 100% committed to a particular sweep, submission, or a deep half position. Even though you want to attack, you still have to be mindful that your opponent probably wants to pass to side mount or mount. Making a mistake when your opponent is in on your hips will most likely end up with your guard being passed.

One advantage of the half guard over the full guard is the predictability of the underhook. When on top, in half guard, your opponent will most likely be looking for the far side underhook. If he doesn't, then he will give you an often overlooked opportunity, the transition to the back. It's something I hope you do not overlook. Most likely your opponent will fight for the far side underhook, giving you the gift of the whizzer. The only difference between an overhook and a whizzer is just pressure. A good whizzer should have some downward pressure. It can be used purely to get up or, as shown in this book, how to set up triangles. I use the whizzer from the side scissor half to stretch and control my opponent's body. This allows me to blend my trapping systems from my full guard game into my half guard game, giving me tight and hard to escape triangle set ups.

Butterfly Guard

One of the most common guard games that I see at tournaments today is the butterfly guard. I would say that it's growing more and more every year. Even in the world of MMA, fighters are using it to help themselves get off their back or just to create a scramble. Even though the butterfly guard is a great sweeping position, athletes like Marcelo Garcia are using it to set up a wide array of submission attacks. Now the butterfly game isn't really known for being a great guard game for setting up triangles, but that doesn't mean that triangle set ups aren't there. It all comes down to how you apply your technique.

The strategy for setting up triangles from the butterfly guard is the same as other strategies that you would use in other open guard systems like the side scissor or K-control. You utilize a sweep to establish an active threat, and use his reaction to that threat to set up a triangle. The keys to the butterfly guard are to use your legs and feet as elevating hooks, while your upper body fights for tie ups to control and manipulate your opponent for either a sweep or a submission. Stretching and off balancing your opponent will require him to post a limb for balance, giving you an opportunity to attack with a triangle submission. Since the butterfly guard is primarily known as a sweeping position, your opponent will be quick to react as soon as you attempt to rock him to one side or manipulate his body with your hooks. Your attempt to sweep him will not come as a surprise, but your triangle will.

As you have already seen in this book, there are many ways to set up unconventional triangle chokes. The butterfly guard is no different. One of my favorite triangle options from the butterfly guard is the sankaku. The sankaku is definitely an unorthodox choke from the butterfly guard position, but it is surprisingly easy to achieve. Once you learn the set up, you should be able to apply the technique very quickly into your live roll sessions. Once you learn it, I think you will make it one of your favorite triangle options from the butterfly guard, just like it is for me.

Something to always keep in mind about any open guard system like the butterfly guard is that sometimes your opponent might simply decide to back out and leave. We all tend to assume that when we are grappling that our opponent will stay actively engaged in the match—this is not always true. One problem for me that has never seemed to go away is that many people I roll with don't want anything to do with my guard game. They play it smart and stay away, leaving me to come up to a standing position and wrestle for control. This is a big reason why I prefer to use the closed guard over the butterfly guard. So keep this in mind, if you're going to play a game like the butterfly, your opponent might simply run and play away. It's frustrating as hell and can drive you crazy, but when you start to encounter opponents that won't go near your guard, it's really quite a compliment.

JACARE TRIANGLE SETUP

I saw Ronaldo "Jacare" Souza finish Dennis Hallman with this triangle at the 2005 ADCC grappling competition. He was side mounted on Hallman, going for knee-on-belly, when Hallman rolled. Jacare used his underhook off-line position from his opponent to his advantage, and simply slid his legs around his neck and locked in the choke. After that, I developed a way of landing this triangle from the half guard. While Jacare landed it using timing in a scramble, I've discovered the key to executing this choke from the bottom is to hip out and raise your hips up. This will force your opponent to keep his arm posted on the mat or risk being off-balanced. With your opponent frozen in place, you simply need to climb your legs up his back and corkscrew back into the triangle. Make sure to keep the head and arm locked up tight as you rotate back to the triangle to prevent your opponent from stacking into you and stuffing the attack.

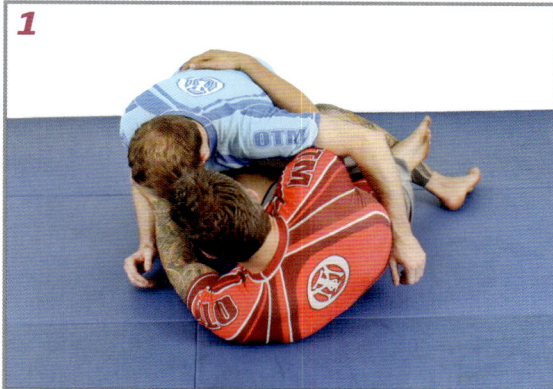

Lance's left leg is in my half guard. I have an underhook with my right arm under his left arm.

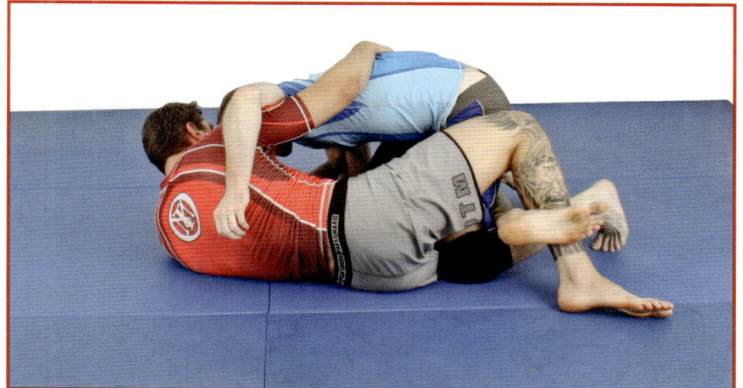

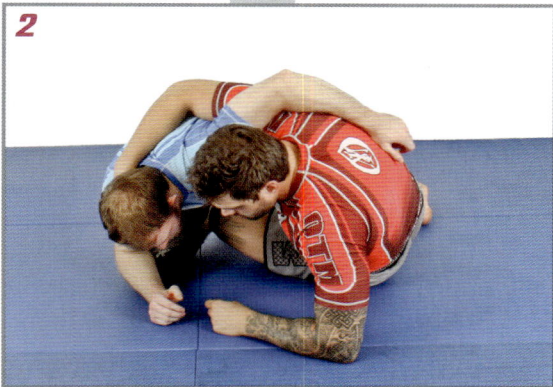

I use my right underhook to drive Lance to my left as I hip away and prop myself up on my left elbow. Simultaneously, my right hand cups his right shoulder.

I throw my right leg over Lance's back, shifting my weight onto his body. This forces him to carry his weight on his right arm.

4

I begin to fall forward, pressing him low in my guard with my right hand as I thread my left foot in front of his right biceps.

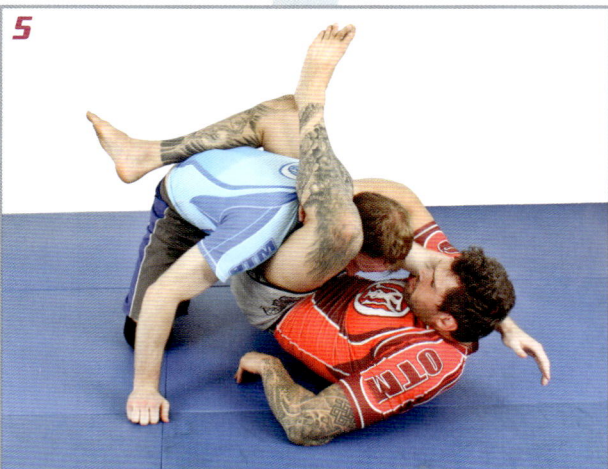

5

I rotate to the saucer back position, clearing Lance's arm by feeding my left leg under his body.

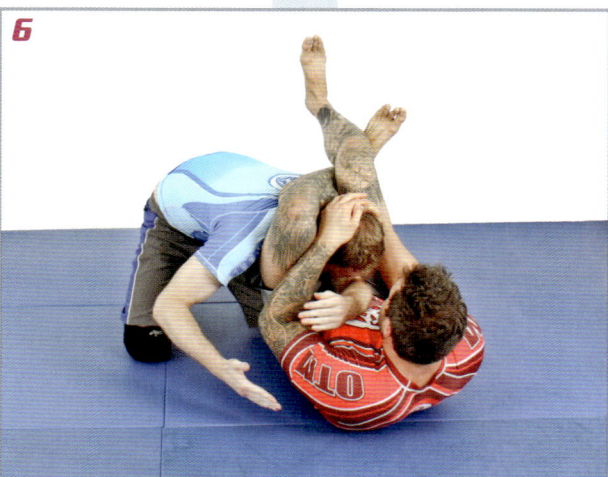

6

I adjust and finish the triangle.

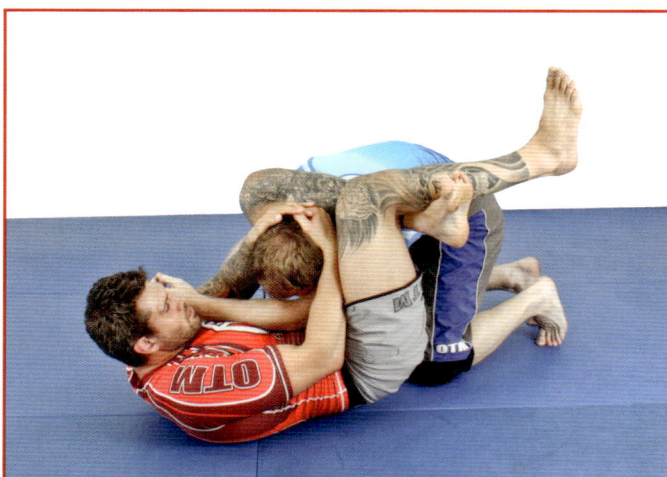

HALF GUARD KINGPIN

Although I prefer the Boston hand shake control, sometimes my opponent's pressure will deny me the grip. If my opponent drives his arm towards his hip as I secure the downward grip, the distance between my free hand and his wrist will be too great to get my preferred grip. In this scenario, I like to utilize the kingpin, hooking my foot in the crook of my opponent's elbow to isolate his arm. With my opponent's arm by his hip, I simply need to slide my foot across his lower back, lock up his arm, and slide my opposite leg out to lock in the choke. I actually prefer the kingpin from the half guard rather than the full guard, because I'm so far on my hip, it allows me to reach my leg further across my opponent's back and secure a solid control on his far arm.

1

I have the Irish collar secure on Lance.

2

I slide my left hand down Lance's right arm to begin forcing it away from his body.

3

I grab control of Lance's right wrist with my left hand and push his hand next to his right hip.

4

I keep my elbow straight to maintain the bend of Lance's right arm. My right foot shoots under it and hooks the crook of his right elbow.

5

I pull Lance's right hand toward my hip with my left hand, bending his right arm over my shin, locking it tight to his body.

6

I extend my right leg, driving Lance away and pushing him lower in my guard.

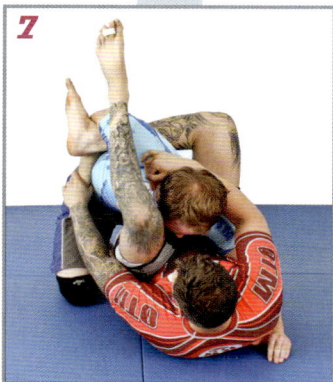

7

I flick my left foot out from between Lance's legs and kick it over his right shoulder without releasing the kingpin, head control, or the wrist control.

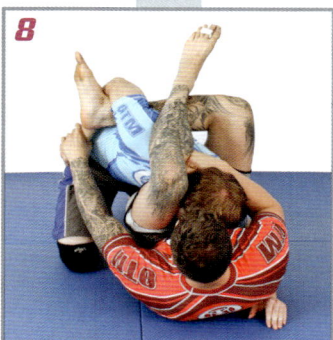

8

I curl my left heel into Lance's back to momentarily stabilize the position.

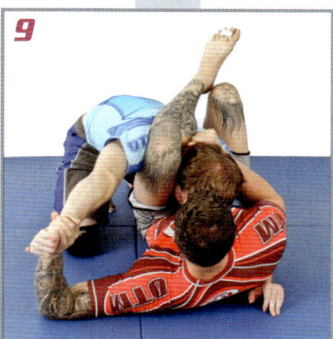

9

I pull Lance's right arm off my right instep, releasing the kingpin and then pull his right arm, extending it. Then, I post my right foot on his hip to set up my adjustment.

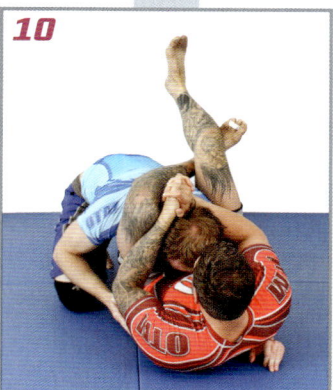

10

I finish the triangle with Lance's arm on the mat.

HALF GUARD DOUBLE WRISTLOCK TO SANKAKU OPTION 1

When fighting from half guard, controlling your opponent's wrist on the opposite side of your half guard is one of the keys to success. By controlling his free wrist, you give yourself many submission and sweep options. Here, I'm obtaining control over my opponent's free wrist, then sitting up to secure a double wristlock. Although I can attack with the double wristlock, in this situation my opponent defends by dropping his torso and grabbing his shorts. Rather than try to fight off his grip, I simply use my legs to create space on the far side of his body, keeping his near side arm trapped with my hands, and lock on a sankaku. This is a great submission to utilize when my opponent is low in my guard. If he were high and driving forward, he could counter my initial double wristlock attempt with a side choke. However, anytime my opponent is low, I can go over his shoulder, lock down his arm, and swing underneath his body to make an opening for the sankaku choke. For finishing options, refer to page 41.

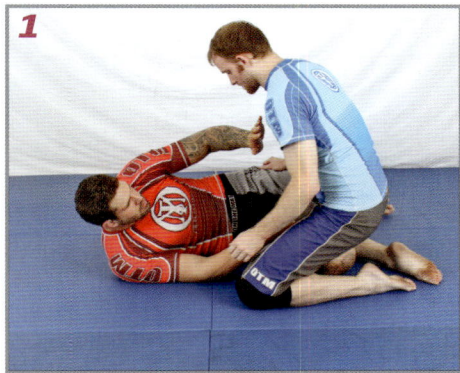

1

I'm in the closed half guard position with Lance's right leg trapped between my legs.

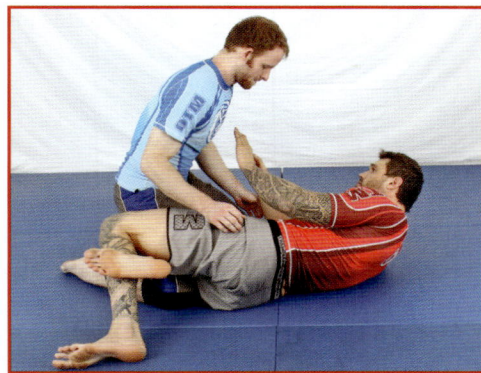

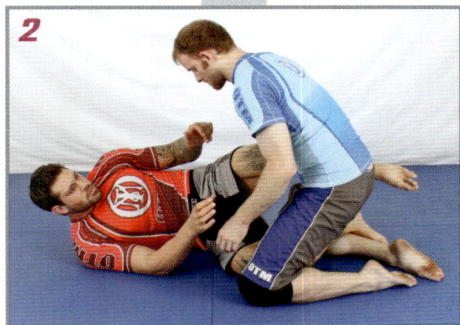

2

I unlock my leg and hook my right instep against Lance's right shin, while driving my left knee against his hip. This will force Lance to bend and hover should he try to move forward and pass.

3

My right hand latches on to Lance's left wrist.

4

I sit up, releasing my side scissor and shooting my left arm over Lance's left arm, lacing my left hand to my wrist to establish a figure-four. Notice that I relock my traditional half guard just in case I need to return to my starting position.

5

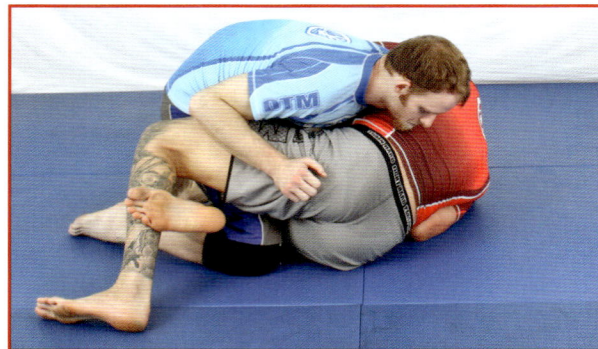

I lean onto my right shoulder and attempt to finish the double wristlock by cranking Lance's left hand behind his back and toward his head, but he resists by grabbing his hip. Rather than struggle to finish the shoulder lock, I use my figure-four grip to lock his hand to his hip, whether he wants it to stay there or not.

6

While maintaining the pin, I scoot my hips away from Lance, almost as though I am giving him side control. My head stays close to his right arm as I move my lower body back.

7

I throw my weight onto my right shoulder, allowing me to whip my leg out from under Lance's torso and over his head.

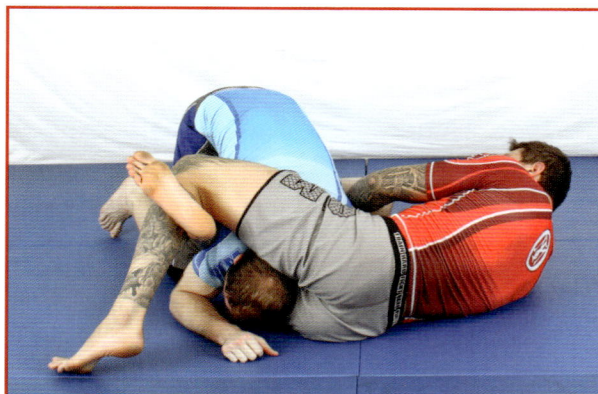

8

My right foot curls into Lance's armpit as I wrap my left leg over my right leg to secure the sankaku. I can now finish the choke or work a sankaku spine lock or sweep.

HALF GUARD DOUBLE WRISTLOCK TO SANKAKU OPTION 2

When most people fail on the double wristlock from half guard, they bail on the submission and attempt to secure position. The Sankaku Option 1 allows me to chain one more attack onto the end of a failed double wristlock attempt. However, it can be hard to apply pressure on the choke with the first sankaku option. If I still have control over my opponent's arm with a tight double wristlock, I can attempt option 2, which is a sort of granby roll under my opponent's body with his arm isolated. It appears to my opponent as if I'm turtling out of half guard. After my leg is clear from half guard, I roll under my opponent, while maintaining the double wristlock grip. This movement creates space and puts me into the correct position to pull my leg out and lock on a sankaku around his neck and free arm. As I'm spinning, his free arm will naturally fall in between my legs, allowing me to lock on a much tighter sankaku choke.

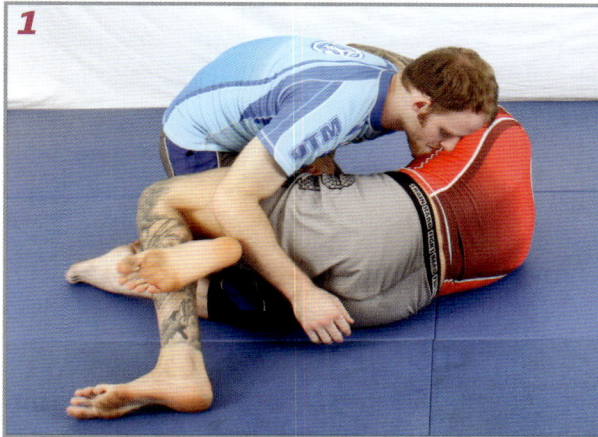

I have Lance's left arm locked in a double wristlock, and his right leg is in my figure-four half guard.

I push his left wrist to his left hip as I scoot my hips away and drive my left knee across his belt line, trying to touch my left foot to his left hip.

My right leg curls behind me, and I dig my right foot into the mat as I pull my leg under and out of the half guard.

4

Pushing off my right foot, I elevate my hips and roll over my right shoulder and neck, while still maintaining the figure-four.

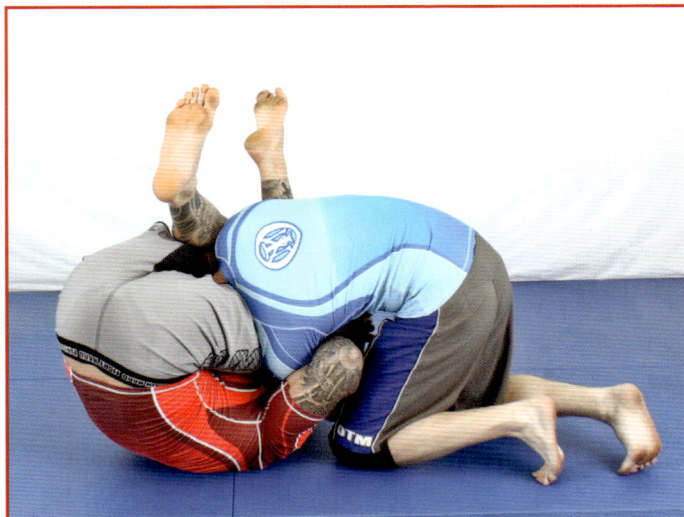

5

I swing my right thigh over Lance's neck and hook his right armpit with my left leg.

6

As my right hand cups Lance's triceps, I extend my right leg and curl my left ankle into the crook of my right knee. With the sankaku locked, I can either finish the choke or use one of the finishes from the first chapter.

SIDE SCISSOR HALF TO SHOULDER PIN TO MOUNTED TRIANGLE

I like to switch back and forth between open and closed side scissor half guard, depending upon the technique I'm trying to utilize the resistance my opponent offers. In this technique, I begin with a closed side scissor and seize control of my opponent's arm with a overhook as my opponent lowers his body. With this grip, I'm able to bring my leg high and lock in a shoulder pin on his overhooked arm. By rotating my body with the shoulder pin locked in tight, I'm able to create downward pressure on my opponent's arm, allowing me to roll him over his shoulder and into the mounted position. From there, I simply clear his arm, move my body perpendicular to my opponent's body, and curl my legs to lock in the choke. Because of the strong control and the ability to upset your opponent's balance, this technique is effective in either grappling or MMA context. One of my fighters, Ryan Couture, utilizes this technique from both side scissor half guard and full guard shoulder pin.

1

Lance is in my closed side scissor half guard. He is postured away.

2

Lance comes down to pass my half guard and gets an underhook with my right arm. I over-hook his right arm with my left and control his left biceps with my right hand.

3

I whizzer down slightly with my overhook and move my right hand to a crossface position over to Lance's right shoulder.

4

I drive my right forearm into Lance's shoulder, pressing him away, while simultaneously re-leasing my whizzer grip and quickly kicking my leg straight and raising it to my chest. At this point my left arm wraps around my left leg, with my left hand cupping Lance's right shoul-der. This secures the shoulder pin position.

5

I bring my right leg out from underneath of Lance, and I post the arch on my foot right above Lance's left knee.

6

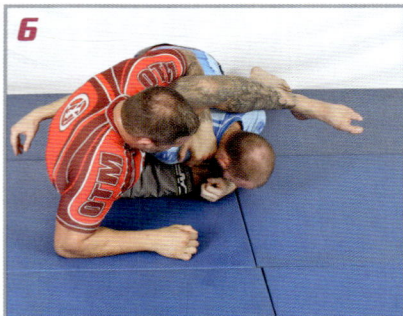

I straighten my right leg, while twisting my hips to my right as I come up onto my right elbow. The pressure from my hips driving down creates a shoulder pin whizzer effect, flattening out my opponent as I come up.

7

As I rotate my hips, I bump them forward, while simultaneously drawing my right knee towards my face. This pressure forces Lance to roll over towards his left shoulder.

8

As I land in a high mount, I release the shoulder pin with my left hand and seize control of Lance's head. During the rotation, my right leg has moved over Lance's left arm.

9

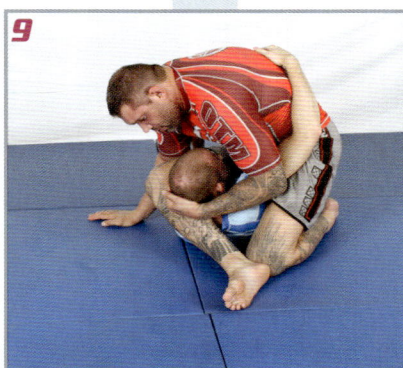

I pull up on Lance's head as I shift my weight onto my left knee and swing my right leg around Lance's neck.

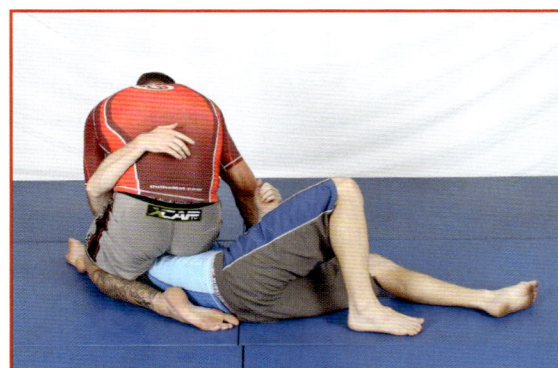

10

I lean to my right, posting my head on the mat, placing my body at a right angle to Lance's body. At this point, I figure-four my legs, curl my left heel to my butt and pull up on Lance's head. This applies pressure and finishes the choke.

HALF GUARD OVERHOOK TO TWO BIRDS—ONE STONE TRIANGLE

As I mentioned earlier, controlling the opposite side wrist from my half guard is key to success from the bottom half position. I like to use the position to sit up for a double wristlock and begin my series of attacks, but sometimes my opponent will drive down before I have a chance to secure his arm. My preferred way to utilize the half guard is the side scissor half guard. In this scenario, I use the side scissor combined with a whizzer to stretch my opponent out, which allows me to keep him locked in a hovering position. From there, I simply feed his free wrist to my overhook hand, trapping his arm and his wrist with my whizzering arm. This allows me to post on my free arm, sit up, and slap my legs through for the triangle. Precision is key with this technique. I used to practice the movement of this attack over and over with a rope while watching TV. The thousands of reps paid off, as I can slap on this choke lightning fast.

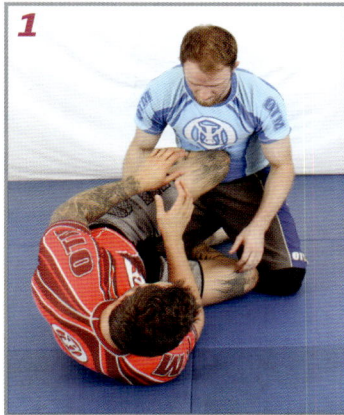

1

I am controlling Lance's right leg from the side scissor half guard

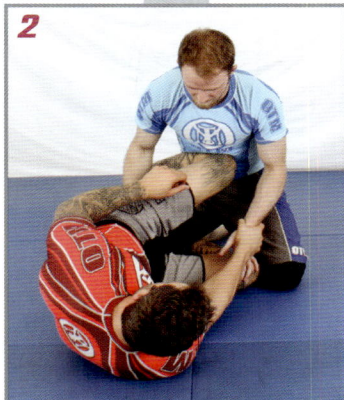

2

I grab his left wrist from my right hand, looking for the double wristlock.

3

As Lance lowers his elevation to pass, I secure a whizzer with my left arm and his right arm and post my right elbow on the mat.

4

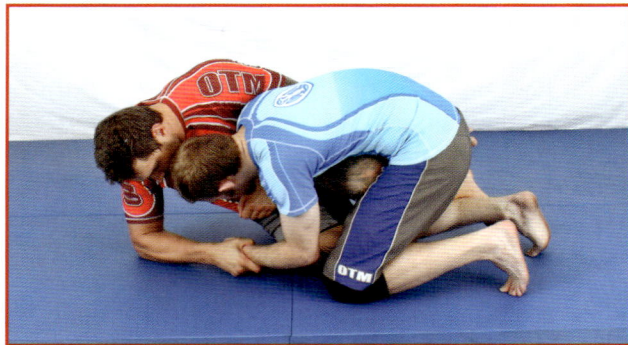

My left hand grabs Lance's left wrist. When my right hand releases his wrist, I do a triceps extension with my left hand to pin his wrist to my left thigh.

5

I fall back toward my right hip as I pull my right knee to my chest.

6

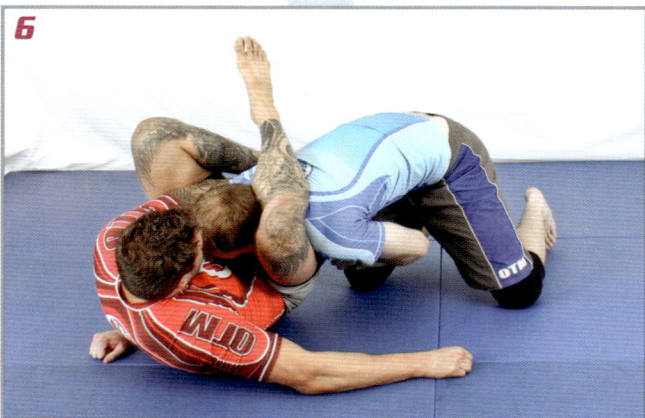

I straighten my left leg, causing Lance to fall forward into the triangle.

7

I finish the triangle with an arm on the mat finish.

HALF GUARD WHIZZER TRIANGLE

Here I utilize the side scissor half guard as well as a tight whizzer to begin a transition to my feet. In the transition, however, my opponent plants his hand on the mat as I stretch him out. This gives me the space needed to transition into a triangle choke. To get to your knees and threaten the get-up, you can't just turn your hips toward the mat, you have to first circle away from your opponent and force him to follow you. As you circle, his free hand will get farther and farther away, which spreads his base out, reducing the amount of weight that he has on top of you, while giving you more space to land the whizzer triangle. The key here is using the side scissor to drive my opponent's hips away, simultaneously applying downward pressure with the whizzer. My legs keep him from driving forward, and my whizzer keeps his hand pinned to the mat. Because of the downward pressure on his shoulder, if he removes his hand, he's simply going to face plant. There is some timing with this technique, but if you get him stretched you'll have plenty of time to free your leg and apply the choke.

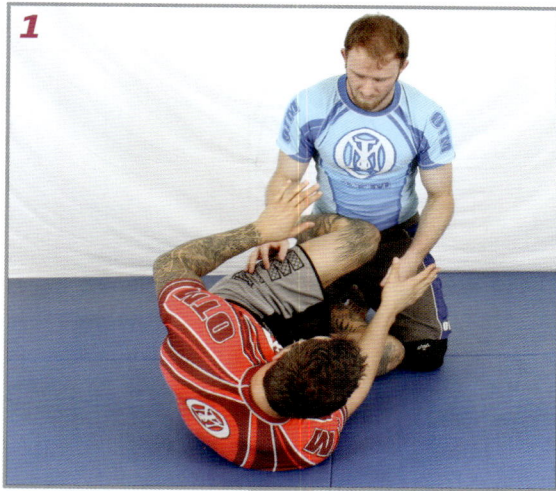

Lance is in my side scissor half guard.

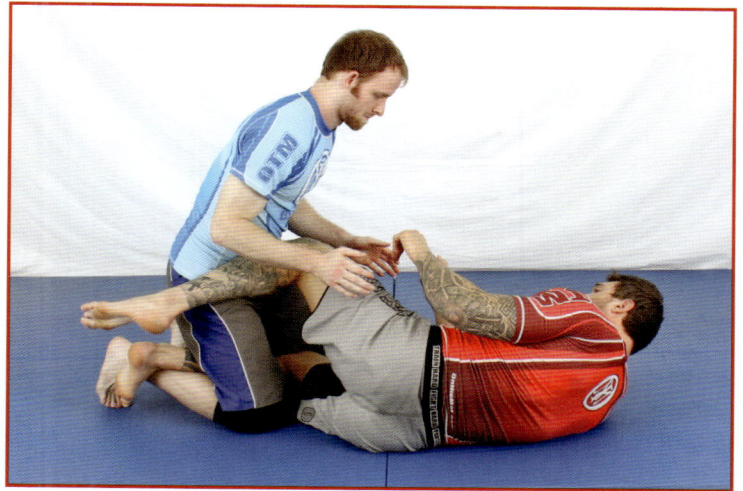

Lance drives forward and secures an underhook with his right arm. At the same time, I reach forward with my right hand and secure a grip on Lance's left wrist.

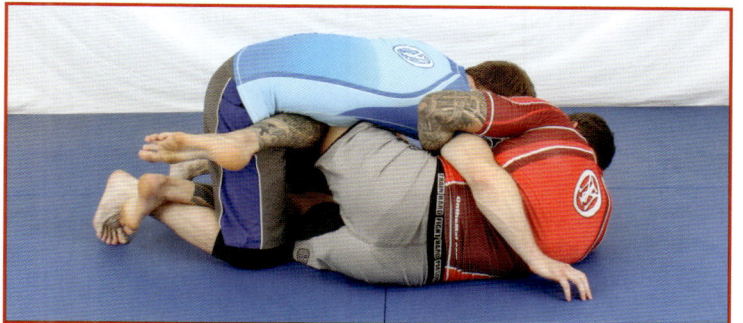

I whizzer down with my left overhook and belly out towards the mat.

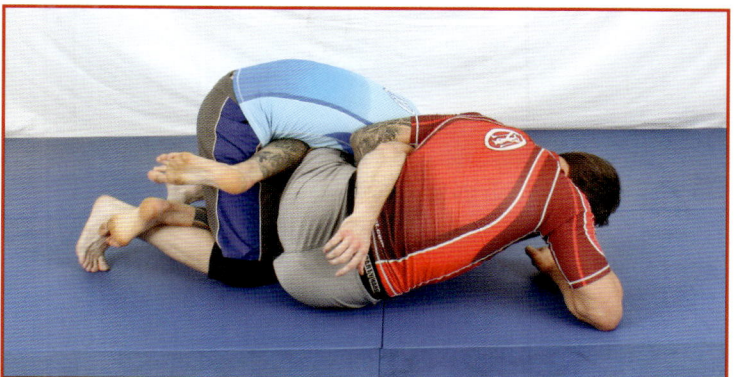

4

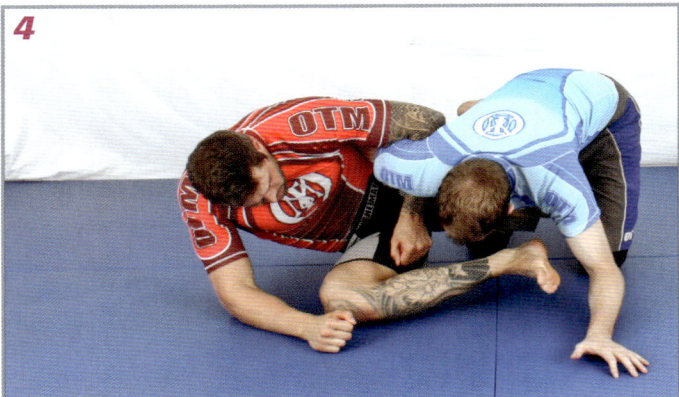

As I begin to move away, I slide my right leg out from underneath of Lance.

5

I swing my right foot in front of Lance's left arm and whip it over the back of his neck.

6

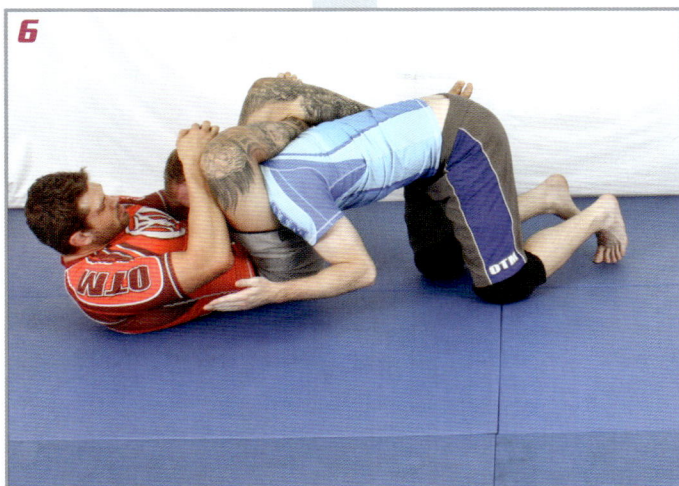

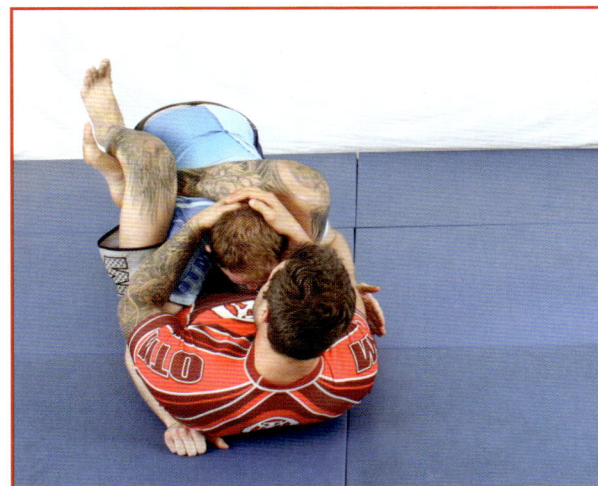

I lock my legs and finish the triangle.

FOOT SWITCH SANKAKU

Side scissor is a great position to off-balance your opponent and create openings for attacks. In this technique, my opponent recognizes the danger and postures up completely, evading all my attempts to control his upper body. In MMA this could be a risky position, as he can now throw head punches. To disrupt his balance and begin attacking, I start with a quick foot sweep to drive my opponent backward. As he counters and drives his weight forward, I slide my foot across his torso, switching my leg position. This allows me to attack the opposite side of his body, and lock on a sankaku. Although it's a tricky setup, as long as I secure the underhook as I switch my feet, I feel like I retain enough control to initiate a scramble event if I fail with the choke.

Lance is in my side scissor half guard, and I am using my legs to maintain distance between us.

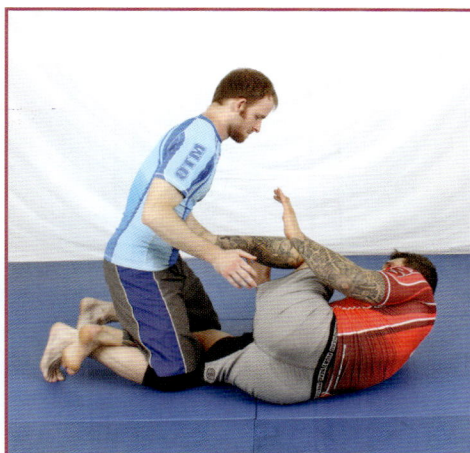

I put my left foot on Lance's stomach and pull my right foot towards my body, attempting the sweep.

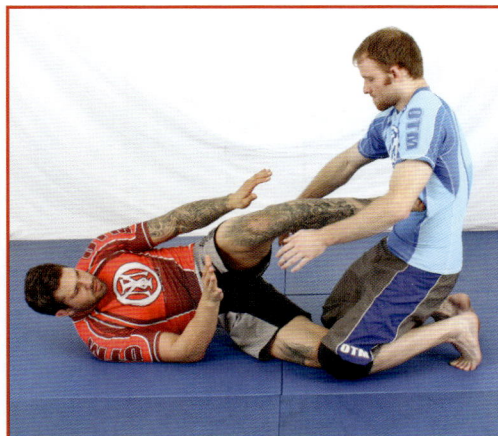

I press my left foot into Lance's stomach and pull my right foot towards my body, attempting the sweep.

Lance counters my sweep by throwing his weight forward to keep himself balanced. I quickly sit up and post on my right elbow as my left arm underhooks Lance's right arm and my left shin slides across his belt line. My right leg is still laced around his right leg.

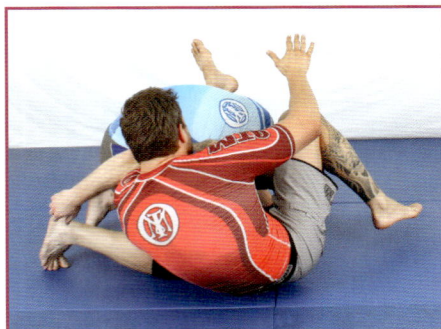

As I rock on my left hip (not my back), I whip my right leg out from underneath of Lance's body. Once it's clear I begin to lift my left leg upward.

I fold my right leg over my left ankle to lock the sankaku.

CLASSIC BUTTERFLY SWEEP TO LEGTHROUGH TRIANGLE

The butterfly guard is primarily a sweeping position. With your feet hooked under your opponent's thighs, you have a significant leverage advantage that allows you to manipulate his base. When you attempt even the most traditional butterfly sweep, as you do in this technique, your opponent will instinctively post to block the sweep and stay on top. As soon as he posts, you can pin his hand in place and throw up a leg-through triangle. The principle that makes this work is the same that drives the side scissor position: any-time you attempt a sweep your opponent is likely to try to post. If he posts, he is essentially pinning his own arm on the mat, giving you an opportunity to execute a leg-through triangle.

1

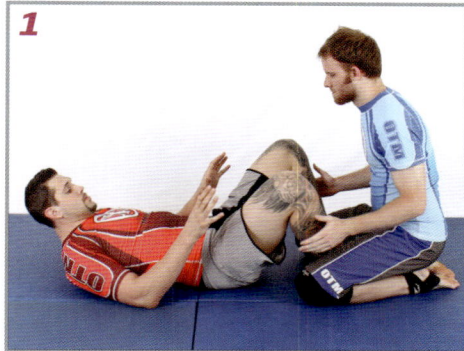

I hook inside of Lance's thighs with my feet, establishing my elevators, or butterfly hooks.

2

I use my butterfly hooks to pull myself to a seated position.

3

I position my chest in front of my hips and overhook Lance's right arm with my left and grip his left triceps with my right hand. Since I will be sweeping him to my right, I position my head in front of his left shoulder, next to his head.

4

I rock to my right and attempt to sweep Lance by lifting my left elevator. Lance posts his left hand on the mat to defend. I immediately slide my right hand down his arm and latch on to his left wrist as he posts.

5

Keeping the elevator pressure with my left butterfly hook, I whizzer Lance down towards the mat and towards his left post. This allows me to come onto my right hip. At this point I begin to hip out, creating space to feed my leg-through.

6

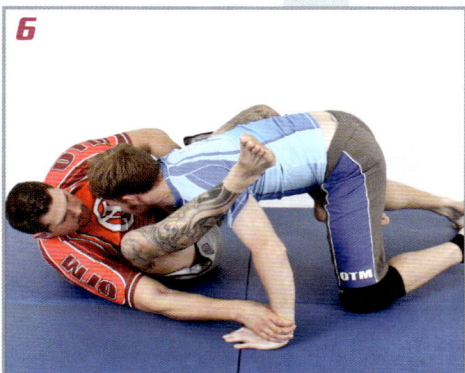
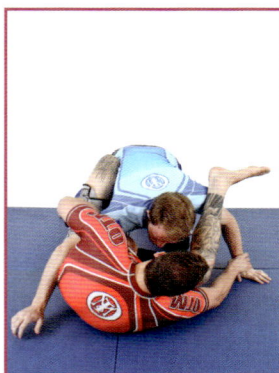

I sling my right foot under Lance's right arm and over his left shoulder.

7

Returning to the saucer back position, I curl my right leg over the back of Lance's neck.

8

I slip my left foot out from the butterfly position, figure-four my legs, and hook Lance's left leg with my right arm, locking in the choke.

BUTTERFLY WRIST PIN TRIANGLE

If my opponent manages to secure double underhooks, he's placed himself in a very good position to attempt to pass my butterfly guard. However, I can still can upset his base with my hooks and use the opportunity to attack with a triangle before he has a chance to pass. In this technique, my opponent initiates double underhooks, so I counter by grasping tight double overhooks. Then, to upset his base, I rock back and pump legs, stretching him out and compromise his balance. This gives me the opportunity to slide down to wrist control, pop out my legs, and slap on the triangle. The key to success with this technique is keeping the saucer back position as I drop back, and then quickly popping my legs out to stretch out my opponent. Although I wouldn't typically initiate this position while in butterfly guard, if my opponent forces the position I can take advantage of the opening, move quickly, and throw up a triangle choke.

I have Lance secured in my butterfly guard with double overhooks.

As I roll to my back, I use my overhooks to keep Lance's head against my left shoulder.

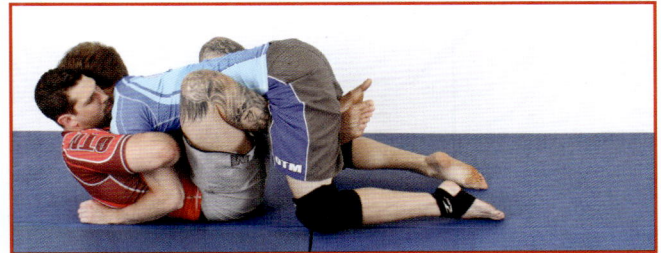

I extend my legs and extend them out wide. This attack's Lance's base, stretching him out. This motion helps me rock back up to a sitting position as well giving me space to sit out.

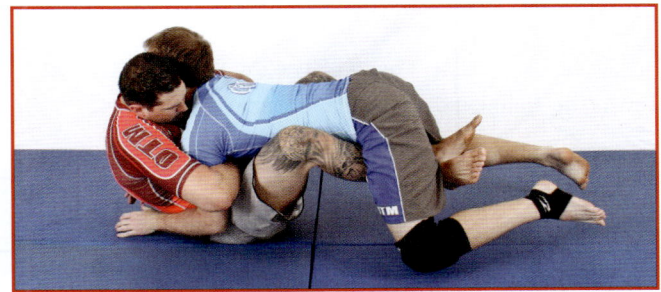

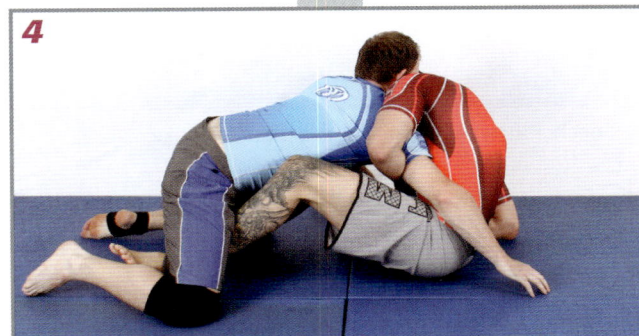

I sit forward, lean to my right, and latch on to a downward grip on Lance's left wrist with my right hand.

5

I snake my left foot out from under Lance and post it on his left hip.

6

To transition to the triangle, I extend my left leg to drive Lance away as I curl my right heel toward my butt and pin his left wrist to his chest.

7

I swing my right leg over Lance's left shoulder.

8

As I fall to my back, I angle my hips, setting my right leg across Lance's neck. I then set and finish the triangle choke.

FOOT SWITCH SANKAKU

In general, anytime you can threaten with a sweep from the guard, your submission success will be higher. With the butterfly guard in particular, the biggest threats are sweeps and leglocks. When you play a butterfly guard against your opponent, his mind will be focused on maintaining his balance and protecting his legs. In this technique, I seize control of my opponent's upper body, attempt a sweep, and then hit a quick foot switch and roll to a sankaku. When your opponent is backed out of your butterfly guard, you don't want to pummel with him. Ideally, you want to reach up, lock in your underhook shoulder pin, and jerk him towards the mat. Once you get the underhook shoulder pin, you can slow down your opponent's movements, but you should be ready to move quickly and attack with the sankaku right away. Out of all submissions, this is my favorite attack from the butterfly guard. Because my opponent is so concerned with the sweep, he'll leave his arm wide open, giving me ample room to lock in the choke and finish the match.

1

I am in the butterfly guard position with my insteps hooked against Lance's hamstrings.

2

My right arm shoots under Lance's left armpit as my left arm wraps around his head, and I lock my hands in the three-finger grip.

3

I squeeze Lance's upper body tight to mine, putting a great deal of pressure on his neck.

4

While maintaining outward pressure with my elevators, I roll my left forearm around Lance's head to the left side of his face without releasing the three-finger grip.

5

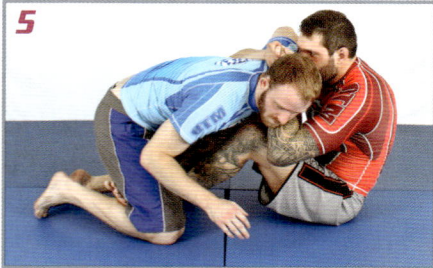

I drive my left forearm into Lance's neck to set the underhook shoulder pin.

6

To force Lance to post his right hand on the mat by elevating my right butterfly hook.

7

As I begin to rock toward my right hip, I slide my right foot across Lance's belt line, while keeping my left elevator locked tightly to Lance's right thigh.

8

I release my left elevator and crunch my left leg towards my chest. This brings my left knee against the left side of Lance's face.

9

I push my left knee against Lance's face as I rock to my right hip. This pops my left leg out and over Lance's head. My right leg follows this motion by curling up under Lance's right arm.

10

I figure-four my legs, locking the sankaku, then release the underhook and throw my left arm over his body. If I'm unable to finish Lance by squeezing my legs, I'll transition into a sankaku finish from the beginning of the book.

CHAPTER EIGHT
COUNTERING ESCAPES

Even though the majority of this book is comprised of triangle setups, the key to being a good triangle player is fighting through your opponent's last-second attempts to escape. Clearing an arm can be a challenge, but clinching and finishing the choke when your opponent is thrashing and trying to rip free is the true battle; it's also the battle that many grapplers lose. Some triangle escapes are technical, but many are violent and unpredictable, and the situation can be further complicated by fatigue and sweat. You need to program yourself to instantly identify and counter your opponent's attempts to escape so that you can properly set your finishing position. If you just lock your legs and squeeze, your success rate will be low. Your final adjustments need to be as methodical as your setups.

Elements of an Escape

When I was developing my triangle system, I knew that I needed a strategic approach to countering my opponent's escapes after I had cleared his arm. I had seen many grapplers fight to clear the arm only to lose the final battle of inches, and I didn't want that to happen to me.

I made it a point to analyze my techniques in every match to determine where I was making mistakes so that I could perfect my setups and finishes. What made the true difference, however, was analyzing what my opponents were doing right. If they escaped, I analyzed their movements to understand why they were able to slip that particular triangle, and I was sure to pay attention to the extremely talented guys to learn what escapes they tried first and considered reliable.

After countless hours of mat time and research, I distilled the basic elements that compose all triangle escapes. Some escapes use just one element, while others mix and match elements. I found that the two most common escapes were not technical at all. Most people will either stand or stack in to escape the triangle, and both of these options can be countered by a leg hook, so hooking your opponent's leg will almost always be the right choice, especially if you feel him start to move.

The next most common escape is the duck out, and there are a few technical ways to duck out of the triangle, but none of them are without risks. As I mentioned earlier, I look to apply an armbar triangle whenever my opponent's arm is extended in my triangle, and that comes into play when countering the duck out. Many fighters are so frantic to pull their head out of a triangle that they leave their arm trailing behind. Their backward movement extends their arm, giving you the triangle. If you are prepared for your opponent's attempt to execute this sort of movement, you can control the arm and lock the armbar before he breaks your triangle.

Many grapplers consider posturing to be the number one escape when caught in a triangle. Posturing can absolutely be effective, but it can depend greatly on the circumstances. If you began your triangle setup with a strong control of your opponent's head, he will find it very difficult to posture out and escape. If you have good head control, when your opponent attempts to posture he may help your triangle. By posturing, he will take just enough pressure off your hips to allow you to adjust your technique, giving you the perfect amount of space to finish.

Always keep in mind though that controlling the head when your opponent postures only delays his escape. The question is "will it delay him long enough to allow me to finish?" That again depends upon the circumstances. For me the most common denominator is whether or not my legs are actually figure-foured or are they simply crossed? In my experience, especially against high level grapplers, if I have my legs figure-foured I can almost always finish. So you're saying: "Of course, if I have my legs figure-foured then I have the choke locked up and complete."

That's not always true either. A lot of times you will have to open, adjust, and relock the triangle. Since it's hard to escape when my legs are figure-foured, I'm always in a hurry to get into that position. You probably already noticed in your triangle game that if you just have your legs crossed your opponent can fight through your head control easier and posture very strongly, creating the right circumstances to escape. Next time you're there, lock the figure-four up quickly even if it looks ugly and you know you can't finish the choke. This will still slow him down immensely and give you the opportunity to make another adjustment and finish the triangle successfully.

Damage Control

No technique works 100 percent of the time. If there was such a technique, submission grappling and MMA would simply be a race to see who can apply that one move first. In reality, your opponents will escape your triangle. If no one in your gym can, then you will eventually find someone in competition that can. Many factors can contribute to the success or failure of a technique, and some of these variables are out of your control. Your opponent could be sweaty, or strong, or just really skilled. If your setup is perfect, he could create half an inch of space and use that miniscule hole to leverage out of your triangle. If you lose the triangle and waste time lamenting the loss of your beautiful submission, your opponent will instantly get to work passing your guard and smashing you from a top position.

To be well-rounded, your triangle game needs to incorporate options for scrapping a submission or sweep out of a dire situation. The options that I provide in this chapter are effective, but I urge you to only use them if you are certain that you have lost the triangle. If you have the triangle position, you should do everything you can to finish from that position because your positioning is superior to your opponent's. Try again and again to set the choke or to use another attack from within the triangle to get the sweep or the submission. Leaving the triangle to pursue another attack is a waste of an opportunity, so only do it if your opponent has taken that opportunity from you.

COUNTER TO THE STACK ESCAPE

Many fighters use the stack to put pressure on the triangle to pop the legs open. By hooking your opponent's leg and controlling his head when he stacks, you can create an angle that nullifies the power of his forward motion, while setting the choke even deeper. I recommend looking for the leg hook as soon as you clear your opponent's arm. If you watch Ryan Couture's professional debut in Strikeforce, you can see just how effective this finish can be. Ryan slapped on the triangle in a scramble and immediately hooked his opponent's leg to make the adjustment, and the fight was over.

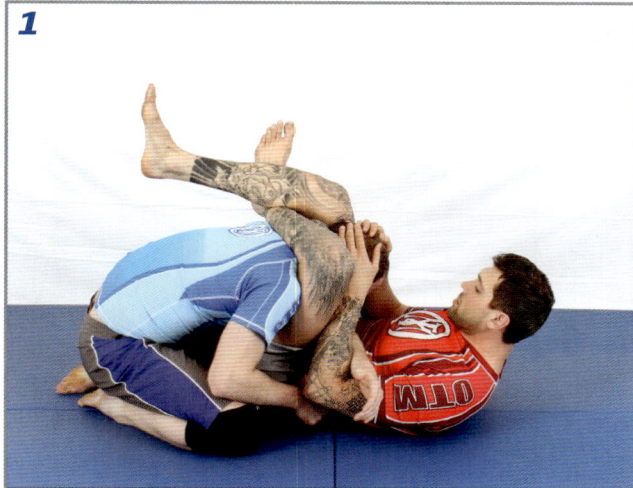

1

Lance's left arm and head are trapped between my legs and I am close to finishing the triangle.

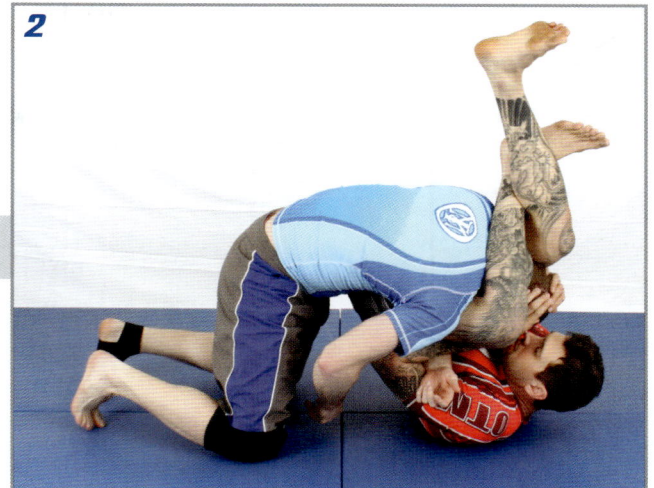

2

To escape the triangle, Lance begins to stack, driving my knees toward my face.

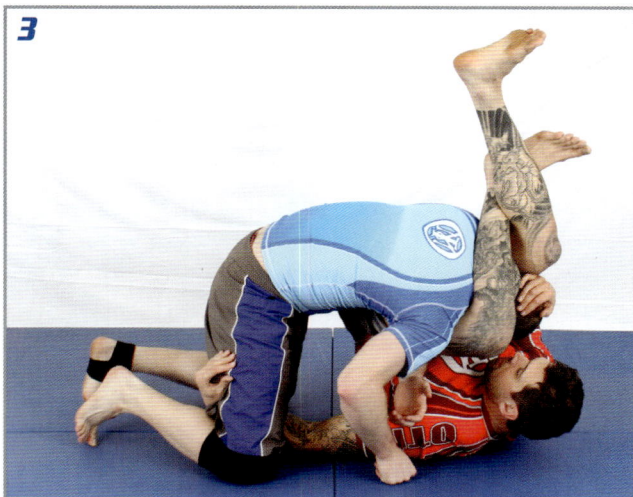

3

As soon as I feel Lance coming forward, I hook the leg closest to his free arm, which is his right leg in this case, and control his head with my right hand. By hooking this leg, I create an angle that relieves the pressure on my legs and tightens my choke.

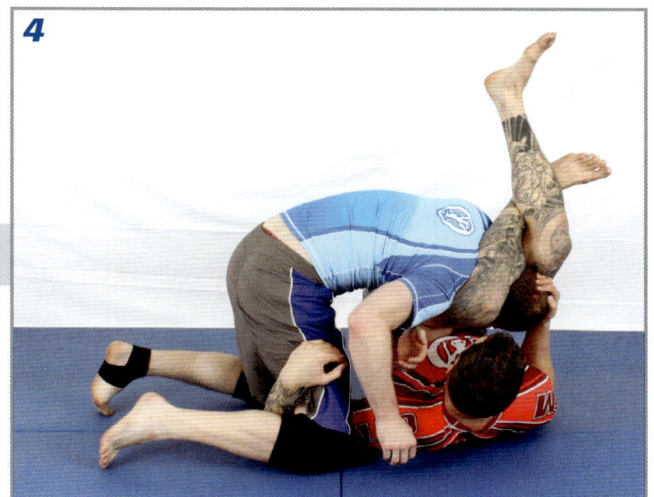

4

I pull my head to Lance's right knee to make the choke even tighter, while weakening his base.

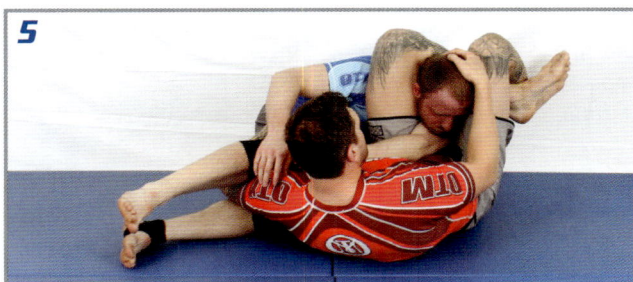

5

With a slight lift of my leg hook, Lance falls to his side. I do not attempt to mount because that would loosen my triangle. Instead, I saucer my back and finish the choke with him on his side.

COUNTERING THE STACK BY ROLLING MOUNT

Rolling to mount can be extremely advantageous, so long as your opponent gives the correct pressure to execute the transition correctly. The determining factor is the angle of his pressure. If he continues driving in the same direction once you have hooked your legs and angled yourself to the side, then you should drop him on his hip and finish without trying to mount, like you did in the first stack counter. If he stacks toward your skull even after you have hooked his leg and shifted, roll him to mount, but do not make the transition by dropping him on his side by lifting the leg hook. Counter his pressure by rolling back over your own shoulders as though you were doing a backward roll. By sweeping your opponent in this manner, you can keep your feet from ever touching the mat, which allows you to maintain a tighter triangle throughout the transition. When you practice this technique, pay close attention to your partner. He could pass out before the sweep is over.

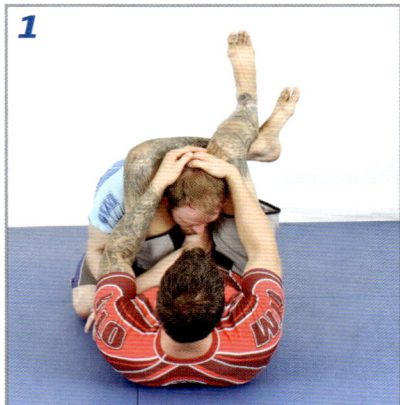

Lance is locked in my triangle.

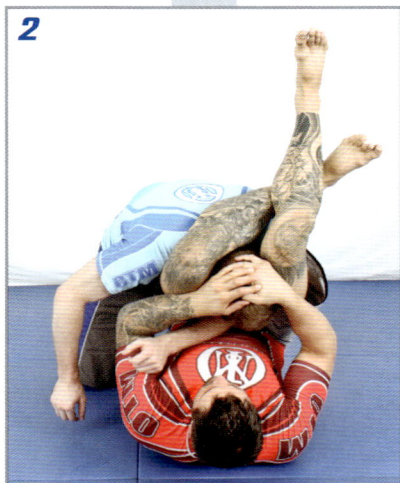

Lance begins to stack into my legs to counter my triangle.

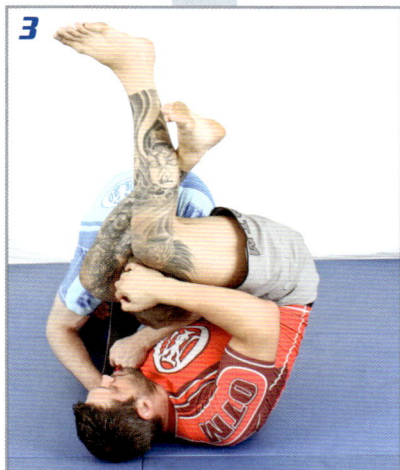

I hook Lance's right leg with my left arm and control his head with my right hand. He changes the angle of his stack and drives my legs toward my face, compacting my body to prevent me from dropping him on his side.

4

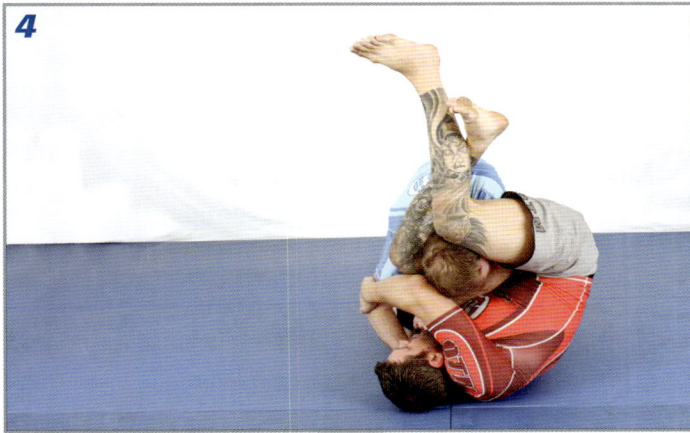

My right hand cups Lance's right elbow.

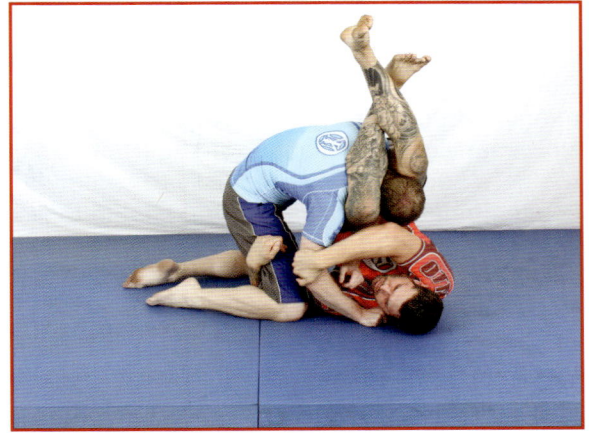

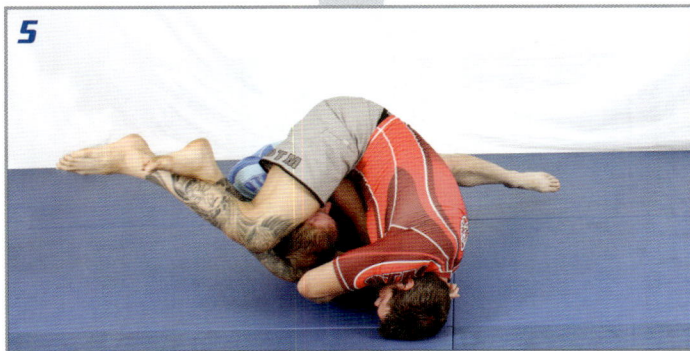

5

I pull Lance's right arm toward my chest with my right hand as I throw my legs over my left shoulder to begin the sweep.

6

I drive my knees to finish the roll, squeezing my legs tight throughout the sweep.

7

To finish the choke, I curl my heels toward my butt, pinch my knees, and pull up on Lance's head as I posture.

COUNTER TO STANDING ESCAPE

Quinton "Rampage" Jackson ruined the triangle choke for a lot of grapplers. When the video of him slamming Ricardo Arona hit the Internet, a new fear brewed within guard players, the fear of being "Rampaged." Now, many grapplers abandon the triangle as soon as a fighter stands, throwing away their chance to finish the fight because they are afraid to commit. If you are in a mixed martial arts environment, being slammed is a legitimate concern, but you should look to eliminate that possibility rather than running from it. The leg hook is the solution. The moment your opponent steps up on a foot to stand, you should be hooking his leg, which locks your shoulders to the mat and sets up a potential sweep. It should be instinctual. During training you should still hook the leg anytime your opponent stands so that you develop and maintain the habit. In this technique, I use the leg hook to drop my opponent to his hip to finish, but if my opponent stacks in, I will use one of the previous techniques.

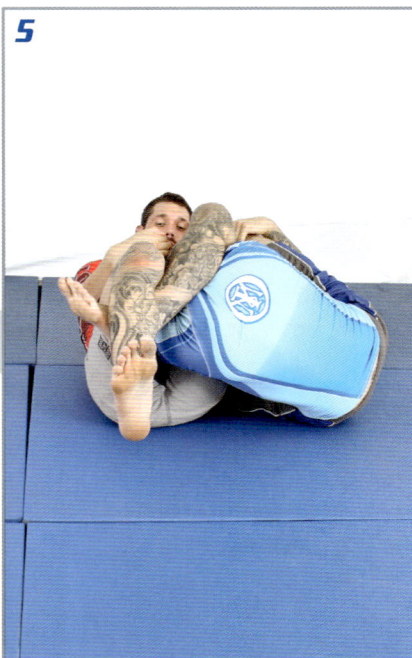

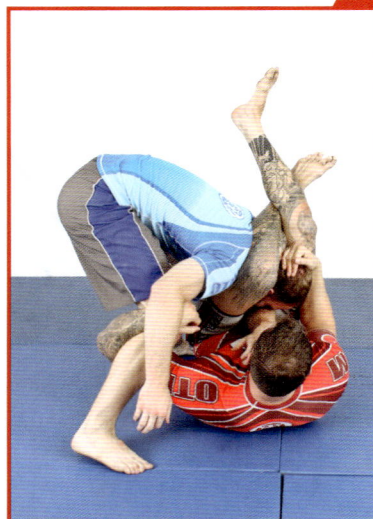

1) I have both hands on Lance's head and am close to tapping him with a triangle. 2) Lance steps up one foot at a time to stand. He is now in position to pick me up and slam me. 3) I immediately hook Lance's right leg with my left arm and cup his knee cap with my left hand, pulling my head toward his left foot. I continue controlling his head with my right hand. 4) The weight of my legs on Lance's back and my leg hook knocks him off balance and he falls to my right. 5) I trap Lance on his side by maintaining the leg hook and finish the choke by saucering my back and squeezing with my legs as I pull on his head.

COUNTER THE DUCK-OUT WITH AN ARMBAR

In his desperation, your opponent will try anything to escape. When his attempts to stack or stand fails, he will attempt to move in the last direction available to him, backwards. By the time an opponent decides that the duck-out is his best option, he is very close to tapping from the triangle choke. If he forgets about his arm when he pulls back as he's ducking out of the choke, applying the armbar is as easy as grabbing his wrist, turning your opponent's palm up, and bridging your hips. When you use this armbar, keep your triangle locked. Your opponent wants you to open your legs, and if you do, he will rip free. If you keep your legs locked during his attempted escape, you have more control, and can transition smoothly back into the choke if your armbar attempt motivates him to stack back in to protect his elbow.

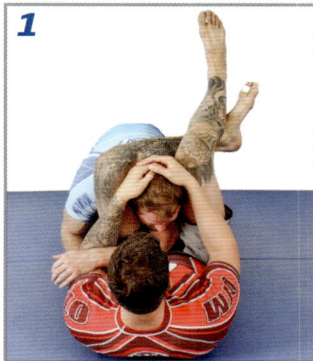

1

I am working to finish Lance with the triangle.

2

Lance hops to his feet to set up the duck-out.

3

When I feel Lance begin to throw his hips backward to escape the triangle, I latch on to his left arm with both hands.

4

I rotate Lance's palm up and finish the triangle armbar.

TRIANGLE TO ARMBAR

I will fight to finish the triangle at all costs, doing everything in my power to adjust, counter, and re-counter. If my triangle has been beat, however, it's been beat, and I need to recognize when that has happened, accept it, and transition to a new attack. In this technique, my opponent postures hard and my legs start to slip. I decide that I cannot recover the position and must transition to an armbar. I would never do this by choice. As long as my legs are locked, I will attempt every technique I know for setting and finishing the triangle over and over until one finally lands. I have had a lot of success with this approach, and I recommend that you adopt it as well. Transitioning from a triangle to another submission creates space and an opportunity for your opponent to escape. Use this technique only if you have to. It's a last-ditch attempt to win the fight before resetting your guard.

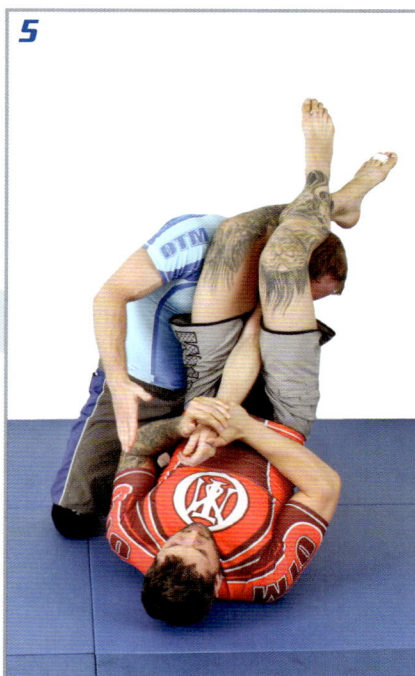

1) I have Lance in a triangle finish.

2) Lance explodes upward, breaking free of my double collar tie as he postures.

3) He continues to lift his head and chest, forcing my legs to slip apart.

4) Realizing that my triangle has been beat, I squeeze my knees together and latch on to his left arm with both hands.

5) I curl my left heel toward my butt to elevate my hips and slow Lance's posture as I swing my right leg over his face and cross it over my left. I then apply the armbar

COUNTERING POSTURE WITH WRISTLOCKS

When your opponent is in your triangle he can survive the choke if he can maintain a sliver of space between his carotid arteries and your legs. Your triangle looks and feels tight, but he is still fighting to get free. Against a really tough opponent, you may not feel comfortable opening your legs because you are afraid of him exploding out as soon as you loosen the figure-four. In this situation, you are in danger of exhausting your legs, which will cause you eventually to lose the triangle. If you release his head for an instant, you can count on him standing, in which case you would hook his leg and drop him on his side or roll him to mount, or he can posture. If he simply postures, keep your legs closed and attack his inside arm. Getting fancy is not necessary. A simple wristlock could be enough to force your opponent to make a mistake or tap, so get mean and start cranking his hands.

Option 1: Figure-Four Wristlock

Lance rips his head free of my grip. When he postures, I grab his left hand with my left hand and my left wrist with my right hand to obtain a figure-four grip. I then twist his left arm to my right as I smash his hand toward his left elbow. Because his left elbow is blocked by his hip, his arm is immobilized and my pressure applies the wristlock.

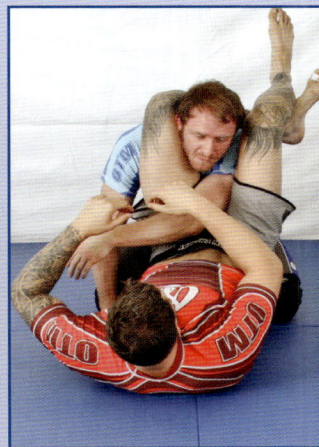

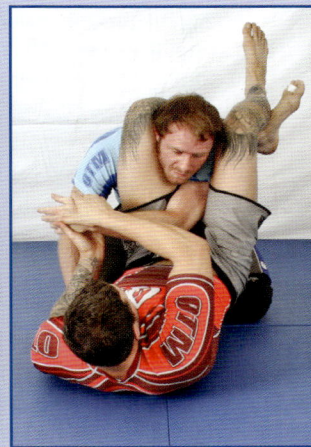

Option 2: Classic Wristlock

I could also grab Lance's left hand with both hands, digging my thumbs into his knuckles. I then twist his arm to my right and fold his hand back toward his wrist to finish the wristlock.

PUMMELING THE BLOCK

If your opponent creates a wedge by locking his hands together and rowing his elbow into your hip, his ability to posture can be extremely strong. In this scenario, I may not be comfortable opening my legs because I am afraid that my opponent will drive his head to the ceiling as soon as he feels my position loosen. By pummeling his inside arm to the mat, I can break his wedge and cinch an arm on the mat triangle. For many grapplers, this goes against conventional wisdom because most people want to finish the triangle with the arm across their body. When they are faced with a frame like the one in this technique, they remain fixated on dragging the arm across, even if their opponent is dead set on resisting it. Equipped with a slew of reliable finishes for the arm on the mat triangle that you learned in the first chapter, you should feel perfectly comfortable forcing his arm to the mat and finishing from there, especially if it means negating a potential escape.

Lance is in my triangle.

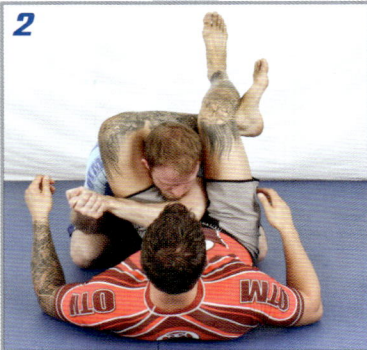

Before I can finish the choke, Lance locks his hands together.

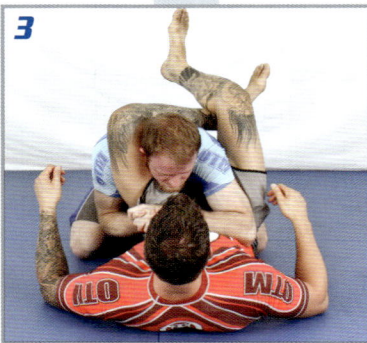

And he forces his left elbow back across my belt line, locking it against my right hip to relieve the pressure of my legs and create enough leverage to begin posturing.

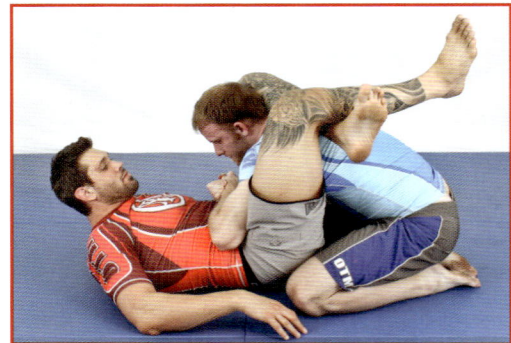

My left hand establishes a collar tie to delay Lance's upward movement as my right hand snakes under his left arm.

5 I pummel my right hand to the inside of Lance's left arm. If I have trouble digging my hand in, I can bounce my legs to wiggle my hand in little by little.

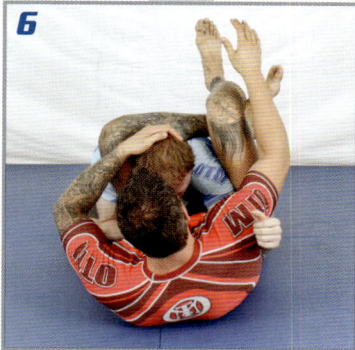

6 My right arm punches to the sky to force Lance's left arm to the outside and to the mat.

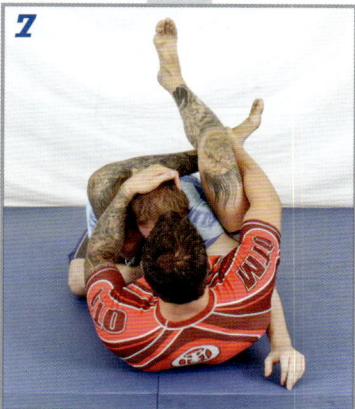

7 Without pausing, I grab my left ankle with my right hand.

8 I pull my left leg into the crook of my right knee to re-cinch my triangle.

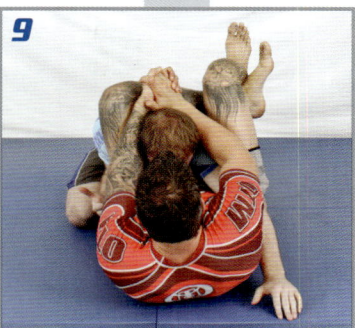

9 I squeeze my legs and pull on Lance's head to finish the arm on the mat triangle.

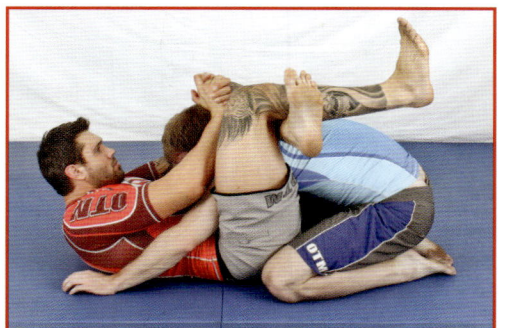

REVERSE TRIANGLE SHOULDER LOCK

When you swim your opponent's arm to the mat, he could transition immediately to overhooking your thigh, or overhooking your thigh could be his first choice for defending the triangle. With a strong overhook, he can begin to posture, and, given enough time, he could break your legs open and escape. Switching to the reverse triangle—relocking the figure-four on the opposite shoulder—is a relatively popular counter for this position, but my opinion of the reverse triangle differs from the norm. To me, the reverse triangle is not a reliable choke because my hamstring is not against his neck, and the position of my legs makes driving his shoulder into the other side of his neck difficult. If I get lucky, I can set my legs and squeeze hard enough to get the choke, but I do not like relying on luck. I prefer to pummel my opponent's arm out, apply an under-hook shoulder pin to hug his elbow to my chest, and rotate my shoulders to apply pressure to the shoulder lock. If his arm begins to slip the shoulder lock, you can transition to an inverted armbar. If he escapes that, he will have passed his arm back across your body, which allows you to switch back to a traditional triangle.

1

Lance's arm is on the mat, and I am working to finish the choke.

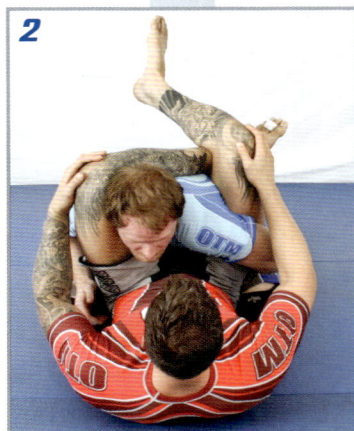

2

Lance overhooks my right thigh with his left arm and hugs it tight to defend the choke.

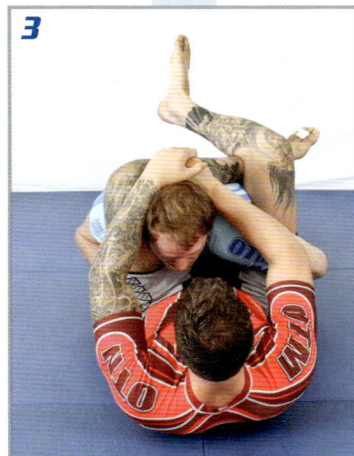

3

I pull Lance's head down.

4

Holding Lance's head down with my right hand, I unlock my legs and grab my right shin with my left hand, pulling it high up his back.

5

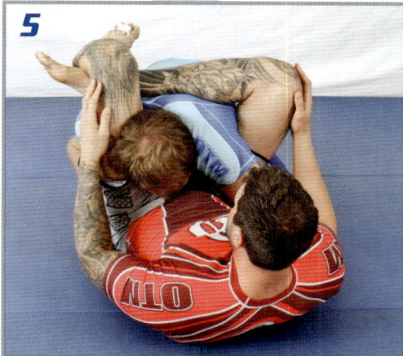

I figure-four my legs in the reverse triangle position.

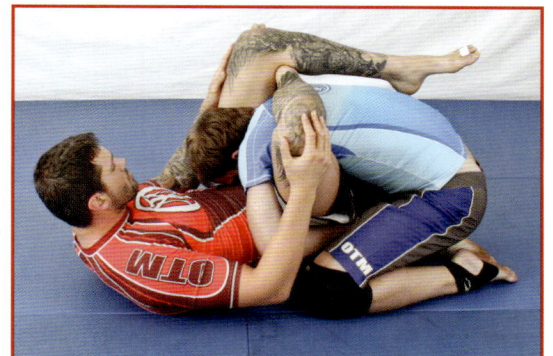

6

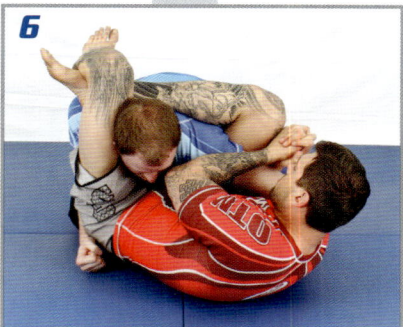

I pummel my right hand under Lance's left arm.

7

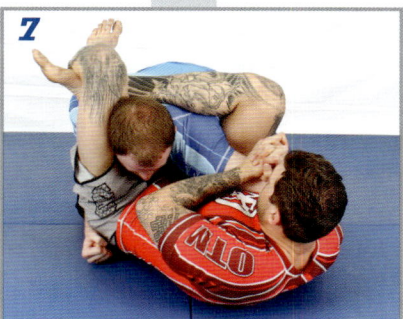

I lock a three-finger grip to establish an underhook shoulder pin. I hug Lance's shoulder and upper arm to my chest.

8

I first push Lance away with my hips then rotate my chest to the left to finish the shoulder submission.

Neil "The Ground Marshal" Melanson is one of the most sought after ground fighting coaches in the world, due to his intense and relentless grappling style and paramount fighting techniques. As a Hayastan Grappler, Neil trained under "Judo" Gene LeBell, Gokor Chivichyan, and received his black belt from Karo "The Heat" Parisyan.

At Hayastan, Neil learned this hybrid art of grappling that focuses on the use of neck and leg locks. Neil is well known as a master of the guard and has developed many different guard systems such as K-control, shoulder pin series, Irish collar, and others. Not only do guard players seek Neil out to learn and master the guard, but top game players do as well. Neil has made a name for himself as the man to see to learn how to beat the guard. He teaches an MMA style of grappling that focuses on protecting the head from strikes along with the practical application of the turtle in MMA.

Neil has trained champion fighters such as Randy Couture, Gray Maynard, Frank Trigg, Vitor Belfort, Michael Chandler, Chael Sonnen, and others, to become a legend in the world of Mixed Martial Arts.

Much of Neil's time is spent at Xtreme Couture MMA in Las Vegas, Nevada, but he also travels throughout the country to teach seminars.

Marshal D. Carper grew up in southwestern Pennsylvania running from bullies and playing video games. Now, much to the surprise of his family, his former bullies, and himself, he trains Brazilian jiu-jitsu under Pedro Sauer black belt Sonny Achille and writes about fighting. In addition to being the Editor-in-Chief of *Lockflow.com*, Marshal has been published in *Ultimate MMA Magazine, Fight! Magazine,* and the *Escapist.* He is also the author of *Cauliflower Chronicles: A Grappler's Tale of Self-Discovery and Island Living*, and coauthor of *Advanced Brazilian Jiu-Jitsu with Marcelo Garcia* and *Brazilian Jiu-Jitsu: The Open Guard with BJ Penn.*

Lance Freimuth is a writer, editor, and photographer who lives in Las Vegas, NV. He also teaches grappling at Xtreme Couture, one of the most highly respected MMA gyms in the world.